ACKNOWLEDGEMENTS

I need to start by thanking Nick Pugh of The Roundhouse for yet another striking cover design, and introducing me to the world's smallest pork pies. On the medical front, the doctors from Gloucester, Bill and Justine, provided helpful advice; as did Carol, who is doubly helpful because she's an ex-nurse and ex-policewoman. On the Swedish side, thanks go to Eva and Göran for finding the location that set off this story. And to Karin W G and Klas for showing us round Uppsala and doing extra research on Jacob Björnstahl. With the latter in mind, I'm indebted to staff at the National Library of Malta. Of course, Karin G provided her usual wide-ranging help on police and other matters over the odd bottle; it's not her fault that I may have strayed way beyond accepted Swedish police procedural practices. I must also mention Fraser and Paula for accommodation and tips on Swedish life. And to Linda for her support from the beginning and her promotion of *The Malmö Mysteries*. Last but certainly not least, thanks to Susan for her editing and painfully frank opinions that have helped improve the novel.

I would also like to thank family, friends and readers for their continued encouragement.

MENACE IN MALMÖ

Torquil MacLeod

McNIDDER & GRACE CRIME

Published by McNidder & Grace
Aswarby House
Aswarby
Lincolnshire NG34 8SE

www.mcnidderandgrace.co.uk

Original paperback first published in 2017
©Torquil MacLeod and Torquil MacLeod Books Ltd
www.torquilmacleodbooks.com

ISBN: 9780857161734

Designed by Obsidian Design

Printed and bound in the United Kingdom by
Short Run Press Ltd, Exeter, UK

ABOUT THE AUTHOR

Torquil MacLeod was born in Edinburgh. After working in
advertising agencies in Birmingham, Glasgow and Newcastle,
he's now settled in Cumbria with his wife, Susan, and her hens.
The idea for a Scandinavian crime series came from his frequent
trips to Malmö and southern Sweden to visit his elder son.
He now has four grandchildren, two of whom are Swedish.

Menace in Malmö is the fifth book in the series of best-
selling crime mysteries featuring Inspector Anita Sundtröm.

Also by Torquil MacLeod:
The Malmö Mysteries
Meet Me in Malmö ISBN 9780857161130
Murder in Malmö ISBN 9780857161147
Missing in Malmö ISBN 9780857161154
Midnight in Malmö ISBN 9780857161307
A Malmö Midwinter ISBN 9780857161741

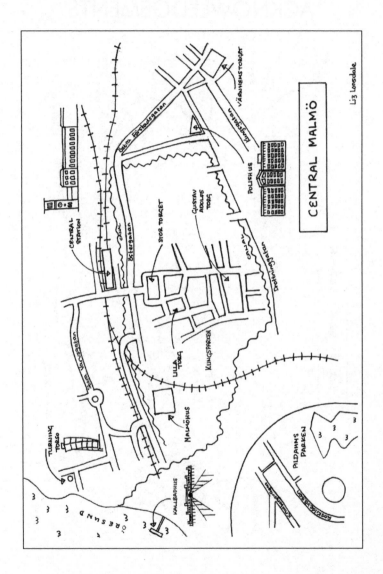

CENTRAL MALMÖ

Liz Lonsdale

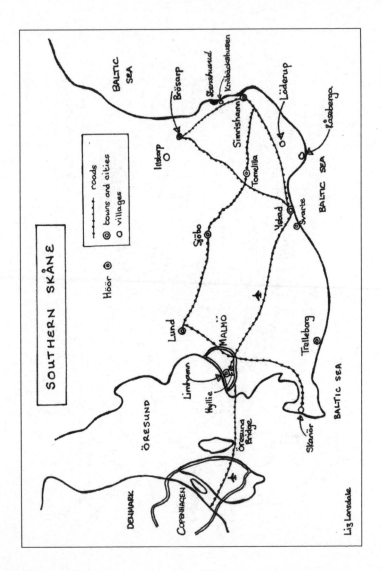

SOUTHERN SKÅNE

PROLOGUE

If he hadn't gone out that night, he wouldn't have seen what he did. And he wouldn't be having the nightmares that a ten-year-old should never have.

Kurt felt an illicit thrill as he twirled the cigarette in his young fingers. He thought it looked like a miniature magic wand. It was the first time he'd ever touched a cigarette. He knew they weren't allowed in the house. Mamma and his big sister wouldn't countenance them, yet he knew his dad sometimes sneaked outside and lit up at the end of the garden. Mamma must turn a blind eye to the garden visits, as it never came up in conversation, certainly not while he was around anyway. So to Kurt, cigarettes were the forbidden fruit which had to be tasted. He knew where dad kept his secret stash – at the back of the drawer in the garden shed. There was a cheap plastic lighter there too. He would have time to put the lighter back before his dad returned from his fishing trip with his friends; he always had a drink in Simrishamn before coming home.

He knew he should be in bed at this hour, but mamma was more lax during the school summer holidays. The beach, a local haunt, had been quite busy during the day, as it always was when the weather was sunny. Now it was a fine, warm evening; dusk beginning to hug the landscape. The beach was deserted except for a solitary man staring out to sea. Kurt recognized Linus, one of that rowdy group of young people that had spent most of the summer in the village. This was the second summer they'd come to Knäbäckshusen. Mamma wasn't keen on them. They made too much noise at unsocial hours – they stayed up too late and often didn't emerge until after midday. His mother couldn't abide the waste of summer days when, as she was always ready to point out, the winter would be on them soon enough. Mamma had a way at looking at the gloomy side of life. Dad called them "bohemians", though Kurt had no idea what that meant. But Kurt liked them. They were fun. And they would talk to him occasionally, which is more than his snooty sister did – she thought he was too young to be of any interest. And now she had a boyfriend in Hammenhög, she hadn't been around much these holidays. At least Kurt had been left more to his own devices during the long, hazy days. He'd played with his pals and got up to the usual mischief that boys do, but even he wouldn't tell his friends about the cigarette until he had tried it. If it worked, he would boast about it; if not, he would keep quiet. Anyway, he didn't trust John not to blab. The consequences of his mother finding out were too dreadful to contemplate.

Now he was safely in the cover of the trees above the beach. He couldn't be seen, even by someone taking a late stroll. He could hear the sea caressing the sand below. He was about to take the final exhilarating step and light the cigarette, clamped awkwardly between his trembling lips, when he noticed a light from the chapel's tiny window. The chapel was a converted fisherman's hut; a small stone building with a timber frontage and a thatched roof. Built into a high bank of sand, it perched snugly above the beach, next to a similar but smaller hut. It was only used for special occasions and visited by the odd tourist or seeker of a few moments' peace. Kurt checked himself. If he flicked on the lighter, anyone coming out of the chapel might see the flame. It was strange for anybody to be there at this hour. He retreated further back into the trees. He lit his cigarette and *sucked for all he was worth. For a moment, there was a tingle as something tickled the back of his throat. Then he started to splutter, and he found himself coughing violently. As he tried to suppress the noises he was making, his head began to swim. He felt nauseous. This was horrible. He flung the cigarette away and it hit a tree and fell to the ground, the end glowing leeringly at him from the shadows. He quickly realized that he must extinguish the ember, and he scuffed it with his sandal. All he wanted to do now was put his dad's lighter back in its drawer and forget about smoking forever.*

As he made his way back to the edge of the trees, he heard the creak of the chapel's wooden door, followed by someone padding quickly up the steep sandy path which led, past the bell tower at the top of the bank, to the village. Kurt gazed down at the chapel. It was then that he noticed a thin slit of quivering candlelight coming through the door, which had been left ajar. He didn't have the courage to investigate who was still inside. They would probably be praying or meditating. But the path past the chapel was the quickest and easiest way home, and now he wanted to get back as quickly as possible. He crept up to the door; he couldn't hear anything from inside. He scrambled up the path. At the top, where the building almost disappeared into the hillside, there was the small window he'd glimpsed before, which in the daytime illuminated a narrow brick altar. Kurt's curiosity got the better of him. It took a few moments for his eyes to adjust to the light as the candles flickered through the grimy pane. At first, he couldn't see much. The rough wooden benches against the side walls appeared unoccupied. He expected to see someone kneeling before the altar. Then, as he strained his eyes, he realized that a crumpled figure was lying on the floor. This was a funny way to pray. The person wasn't moving. He knew the chapel attracted all sorts of peculiar people, yet some sense was telling him that this wasn't right. Then he recognized the man. It was one of the "bohemians". By the long dark hair, he knew it to be the unfriendly one: Göran. Was he drunk? With his heart thumping against his chest, Kurt made his way back down the path and stood in front of the door. It wasn't like a church door at all – it was panelled like the one on his grandfather's barn. He peered through the slit. His mouth was dry. The door opened further with a loud creak as he swung it gently outwards. Göran was still there. He was curled up and was clutching his chest. Kurt tentatively took a couple of steps closer. He thought he detected a slight moan. This goaded him into action, and he approached the prone figure.

'Are you OK?'

There was no reply. Kurt now felt frightened. What was happening? He plucked up the nerve to go right up to Göran and he knelt down on one knee beside him. He saw the man's lips twitching. Was he attempting to say something? Kurt leant over as close as he dared and strained his ear. Then there came a muffled whisper. He wasn't sure if he heard the words correctly. It was at that moment that he noticed Göran's hands were all red, blood dripping through his fingers onto the brick floor.

Kurt staggered back. He thought he was going to be sick. He had to escape. He jumped to his feet and ran out of the chapel as fast as he could.

CHAPTER 1

He tried frantically to hold his breath. Though the wind was gusting through the wood and rustling the leaves loudly, his fear of detection was so great that he imagined the slightest sound he made would give him away. As he pressed his shaking body against the trunk of the tree, he tried to pick out signs of his pursuers. The pain in his ribs was compounded by the gut-wrenching running, and his left foot was sore and bleeding; his trainer had come off in the initial chase during his mad break for freedom. He wished Jack was with him, but *he* wasn't going anywhere now. Everything had changed that morning when the Boss had arrived out of the blue. Some innate instinct for survival had driven him to flee. He had done it alone and felt even more frightened. Now the battering his body had taken over the previous months was taking its toll, and he was wondering how much further he could go. He had no idea where he was. All he knew was that he had to get as far away from the camp as possible. He didn't even know where the camp was situated other than it was somewhere in this huge forest where he was now lost. Worse; he was in a strange country, and he didn't know the language, though he had heard some English spoken.

He edged round the tree to see if there was any sign of them. A twig cracked beneath his bloodied foot, and he started with fright. He was no longer sure he had the mental strength to go on. But he knew the consequences of giving himself up. That was enough to push him forward at a limping run. Soon he stumbled onto a rough pathway. It was tempting to follow it, for it must lead somewhere, but that would be what they would expect. Then he heard a shout. Then another. They were not far away. Swiftly looking in both directions and seeing that it was clear, he managed to dart across the pathway into a gap in the trees on the other side. Here, the undergrowth was thicker and the forest even denser. The shouts were getting nearer. He looked desperately about as he wiped the greasy sweat from his eyes. He must keep going.

He was about to launch himself away from the fringes of the path when he saw McNaught heading towards the section he had just crossed. There was no sign of sweat on him, despite all the running he had been doing. He was fit. And muscular. From his hiding place, he could see the Scottish bastard's rippling biceps almost erupting out of his tight, white T-shirt. He had been on the receiving end of many an assault from those arms. The combat trousers exacerbated the thuggish image, as did the bald bullet head and brutish face. The scar running down his left cheek was a mark of the toughness of which McNaught was ferociously proud. Camp rumours suggested he had either been in the paratroopers or the SAS. He stopped in the middle of the path and scoped his surroundings. The small, slightly squint, coal-black eyes took in everything. The eyes of a hunter; the eyes that had given him nightmares and brought fear to every waking hour; the eyes that had never left him, or Jack, or the others.

McNaught's gaze was interrupted by the arrival of the other two. They were out of breath.

'The little shit's not far from here. I can smell his fear.'

He almost stood up to reveal himself, such was the hold that McNaught exerted over him. But he fought the idiotic urge and tried to control his shaking limbs.

'Come on!' McNaught barked. 'He can't be far. Don't catch him, and you'll answer to the Boss.'

The threat galvanized the new arrivals and they sped off. It seemed like minutes before they were out of sight, though it must only have been seconds. He couldn't afford to wait a moment longer. His foot was in agony, and his body was racked with pain, but blind panic forced him to move from his temporary refuge. With a muted sigh, he pulled his weary frame up and without a backward glance he headed deeper into the forest.

CHAPTER 2

The train glided into Skurup station. Bengt Svefors was looking forward to the end of his shift. There were two more stops before Ystad – Rydsgård and Svarte. Though the 22.08 Skånetrafiken train was scheduled to go right through to Simrishamn, he would swap with the next driver in Ystad and then get a lift back on the 23.00 return to Malmö Central. That would arrive at 23.44, and he would get back home by 00.15. After a lifetime on the railways, Bengt Svefors was a man ruled by his working timetable, which inevitably spilled over into his domestic life. This obsessive timekeeping had proved too much for his wife of twenty years, and he had been single for the last ten. Now he and his ex-wife got on far better because they didn't have to live with each other but, of course, they still kept in close touch for the sake of the grandchildren.

A few people spilled onto the platform, and a couple climbed into the last carriage. At that time of night on a Monday, the train wasn't very busy. A few stragglers from Malmö making their way home from work or a shopping trip. With the new school year starting, there weren't the groups of kids he'd had last week. However, in early August, there were still holidaymakers using the line that ran from Sweden's third city across rural Skåne to the country's southern tip at Ystad and then on to the small fishing town of Simrishamn on the eastern coast. It was a pleasant journey at this time of year, before the leaves began to fall and the harvest golds and lush greens of the summer countryside transmogrified into the dreary, harsh browns and greys of autumn and winter. Now the sky was striated with orange streaks and pink candyfloss, and the last of the day was fading into dusk. Lights were appearing in the windows of the buildings close to the track. A couple of cars waiting at a level crossing had their headlights full on. Bengt Svefors effortlessly moved the train over the crossing and headed through the tangle of overhead power lines at the side of the track that would propel him and his passengers to Ystad.

He was already planning what he would do tomorrow. He'd worked the weekend, and he was due the next two days off. In a year's time he would be retiring, and then he would have some serious planning to do. He knew he would have to keep himself busy or he'd become bored. The job was his life, so once that had reached its terminus, he would have to work to a different timetable. That's why tomorrow, after breakfasting at 09.00 (this indulgence due to his late shift), he was going to his Spanish class at 11.00. One of the first things he'd promised himself when he hung up his driver's uniform was to go to Spain and travel on their Alta Velocidad Española (AVE), the high-speed train that some of his colleagues had spoken of with such awe. And he could combine the trip with some sun. What more could a northern European train buff ask for?

Then after lunch, he would pick up seven-year-old Lennart from school at 14.30. He'd take him to Folkets Park for a play on the swings and treat him to an ice cream. His daughter wasn't keen on the boy having too much sugar – the subsequent rush made him too boisterous, apparently. This modern dietary nonsense was beyond Bengt. Why couldn't the young fellow enjoy an ice cream? Anyway, it would be their secret. That in itself was fun. He just had to make sure that all the evidence was wiped away before Lennart was delivered home in time for his daughter's return from work at 16.00. He would stay for supper as per usual and be home for a spot of relaxation in front of the television by 19.00. The English detective series *Midsomer Murders* was on tomorrow night. A treat.

Rydsgård. 22.43. Exactly on time. Now another six minutes to Svarte, and then another seven minutes to Ystad and the end of his shift. Bengt Svefors gave a satisfied sigh. He worried when timings were out. He prided himself on getting his train to each station with punctuality. Of course, matters were often out of his control. The weather and the overhead power lines were par for the course, and, recently, the passport checks for illegal immigrants at Hyllie had proved an irritating disruption. All of these caused inconvenience for the passengers, but at least their anger was always directed at the guard and not at him, safely cocooned in his cab.

Now he was guiding the train towards Svarte. He liked this bit of the line as it began to run along the coast. It always gladdened his heart to see the Baltic suddenly expand before him, even when it was at its most leaden. But the last few runs had seen the water an aquamarine blue, a reflection of the good few days they had had. The forecast for tomorrow was a change in the weather. Typical. He suddenly realized how tired he felt. He blinked at the semi-darkness ahead. Maybe it *was* the right time to call it a day and spend more time with his grandchildren. He suppressed a yawn as the train approached a familiar bend in the line. After slipping round the corner and over the crossing, it was a straight run down the slope towards Svarte. He slowed the train down slightly, as he always did at this point, before starting to accelerate for the last stretch.

But something was wrong! As the train came out of the bend, Bengt could just make out a large object on the line at the crossing. It wasn't moving! Oh, my God! He braked desperately. But it was too late.

CHAPTER 3

She didn't stir. Anita Sundström leant over the edge of the cot and covered Leyla's legs. Anita half hoped that the little girl might wake and she would have the excuse to pick her up. She had arrived for babysitting duties after work, but Leyla was already down. Disappointingly, she might not be able to see her awake at all tonight. She gazed down at her granddaughter with a mixture of love and pride; the thick mop of dark hair and the slightly olive skin made her resemble her mother, Jazmin. That's what everybody said, but Anita liked to think that the chin and mouth came from her father, Lasse. Maybe it was wishful thinking, as though she was determined to find some family likeness. And she was a Leyla. When she had first been told the name, an hour after the baby was born, she immediately thought it was from the Eric Clapton song, *Layla*. But Lasse had explained the different spelling and that it was an Iraqi name meaning dark-haired beauty. Which is exactly what she was to Anita. Now she could hardly remember her granddaughter not being around. She had added something wonderful to her life. Someone had once told her that you love your children, but you adore your grandchildren. At the time, she had thought it was a silly remark, as she couldn't see past Lasse. But not now.

She returned quietly to the living room. The coffee she had made earlier was still by her chair. She had heard Leyla give off a little moan and had rushed next door to check her. The coffee was now cold, and she went into the poky kitchen to make herself a fresh cup. She hoped that Jazmin and Lasse were enjoying the cinema. They had hardly been out since the baby was born a year ago. They hadn't got the money. Anita had slipped two hundred krona notes into Lasse's hand as they had left the apartment. It was so they could buy themselves something better to eat than the street falafel her son had planned for their post-film dining. It wasn't just a philanthropic gesture; it also meant that they would be out longer, and she would have more time with Leyla. On the first occasion Jazmin had been persuaded to go out without her daughter, she had phoned in three times. Each time, Anita had reassured her that all was under control. Tonight she had only rung once. Things were improving. She had put her mobile phone on vibrate mode so that it wouldn't wake the child.

While she waited for the kettle to boil, she put on the radio so that it was just audible. She stared out of the kitchen window. It was hardly worth the effort, as all the blocks of apartments looked the same. A number of kids were playing in the street, even this late. There wasn't a white face among them. Malmö had changed a lot since she'd joined the Skåne County Police as a very inexperienced detective just over twenty years before. She was quite accepting of the influx of immigrants that now made up a significant percentage of the city's population. After all, her son was living with one and her granddaughter was half-Iraqi in terms of origin. Jazmin and her brother, Anita's police colleague Hakim Mirza, had both been born in Malmö and saw themselves as Swedish. Many of her fellow officers weren't so keen on the changing balance in their society and blamed the incomers for much of the city's crime.

The plastic kettle reached boiling point and subsided in a blast of steam. She spooned into a mug a couple of teaspoons of instant coffee. She reminded herself for the hundredth time that she must buy them some proper coffee for when she came round. Instant wasn't civilized – or strong enough. As she cupped her hands round her mug, she couldn't help smiling at the thought of Kevin Ash's experiences with Sweden's most essential beverage. Whenever he visited, she had to weaken the brew. And when she had visited him in Penrith last summer, she had taken her own coffee and made it herself. Her thoughts strayed further: she and Kevin seemed to have worked out their long-distance relationship fairly well. She was happy with it anyhow. They met up a few times and had fun, without thoughts of marriage or living together getting in the way. On the cusp of forty-eight, she had been single long enough not to want someone else sharing her life full-time. She suspected that Kevin wanted something more but was prepared to put up with the arrangement. For that she was grateful. She didn't want to live in England, and she knew that Sweden and its obsession with rules would drive him to distraction. And they both had police careers, though he got less satisfaction from his than she did from hers. Anyhow, now she had an extra reason to stay where she was. Leyla. When she had Skyped Kevin to show him her new grandchild, he had joked that she should go in for a Glamorous Granny competition. She remembered such things from the couple of years she had spent in Britain as a child. Even then she had thought the concept was odd. But so many things were odd about Britain. Maybe that's why she liked it so much and enjoyed her visits now. She also liked the self-deprecating British sense of humour; another thing that attracted her to Kevin. Even when they made love, he made her smile. Somehow it made the sex more joyous. Anyway, she was looking forward to seeing him in a fortnight's time when she was taking a week off to visit him; he'd promised to show her more of the Lake District and the Scottish borders.

The news came on the radio. There was something about a train crash, but she didn't catch it as she had heard a small cry coming from the bedroom.

The darkness of night may have given him cover, but it did little to quell his fear of being caught. He now knew what that would entail. During the hour or so he'd been tightly crouched in the hollow beneath a large tree, he'd had time to order his terrified thoughts. It began to dawn on him that what he'd seen couldn't be allowed to become public knowledge. He was a witness. Even if he promised the Boss and McNaught that he would never tell anyone, he knew he was a risk not worth them taking. There was too much for them to lose.

He was standing at the edge of the wood. He had been drawn to a distant light. He was sore all over, his foot throbbed constantly and he was very hungry. He could make out the shape of what he took to be a farmhouse and the outline of a barn. Yet he dared not approach. Being the nearest dwelling to the forest, it was an obvious place for McNaught to reconnoitre. Maybe he, or one of his men, was already sitting inside waiting for him to come. McNaught would have talked his way into the house somehow. If rough charm hadn't worked, he would have resorted to his default setting of intimidation. There was a field between the wood and the farmhouse. A gentle neighing alerted him to two horses grazing quietly. He didn't want to disturb them, for any noise might bring the farmer out. For one ludicrous second he even thought of trying to jump on the back of one and ride off. But he had never been on a horse in his life. And where would he ride to?

In weighing up his options, he wasn't sure if handing himself in to the police would be the answer either. He had no identification. Nothing to prove he was Danny Foster. He hardly knew who Danny Foster was any more. He had no idea how long he'd been in Sweden, as the days, weeks and months had melded into one another. He was now so fearful of what might happen to him that it might be best to avoid contact with anyone. For all he knew, everybody in this area might be in cahoots with McNaught. He realized he couldn't trust a single person. Except Jack. And look what had happened to him.

But he must eat. And drink. He was exceedingly thirsty. Then he noticed a bucket beside the field gate. He crept over towards it. He could just make out the shimmer of water half way down. He slumped to his knees, leant through the wire fencing, scooped up the horses' water from the bucket and lapped it up from his dirty fingers. It was no worse than the water at the camp. After a few handfuls, he retreated into the shelter of the forest verge. He would make a move towards the farm in search of food when the light in the house went out. Until then, he had time to contemplate how on earth he had got into this dangerous mess in the first place.

Anita reached her apartment in Roskildevägen just before midnight. Lasse and Jazmin had had a good night and were busy debating the film when she left – after one last peek at Leyla. Her son and his girlfriend had their ups and downs but, she thought, had enough in common to make their relationship work. They were equals. She and Björn had never been. He was always top dog. Maybe that's why he'd got bored and started to wander. And, of course, he was a man, and most of them thought with their dicks. But Lasse and Jazmin were part of the new multicultural Sweden. As was Jazmin's brother, her colleague Hakim, who was now dating Liv Fogelström, a constable on the force whom he'd met during the *tomten* murder investigation. Anita knew that Jazmin and Hakim's parents, though westernized before they fled Iraq, found the social transition difficult. She knew Jazmin faced pressure to marry, which she stubbornly resisted. And they were obviously disappointed with Hakim's choice. Anita wasn't sure how Uday and Amira explained their children's partners to the Iraqi community.

She was brushing her teeth when her mobile phone went off in the bedroom. With the toothbrush still in her mouth, she walked through and saw that it was Chief Inspector Moberg. What on earth did he want at this hour of the night? She picked up the mobile, her mouth still full of toothpaste.

'Anita, is that you?' Moberg sounded the worse for wear. She could tell he'd been drinking again. Now that he and his latest woman had separated – fortuitously, he hadn't married this one, unlike the previous three – he was back to boozing after work with Inspector Pontus Brodd. Brodd, who brought little to the work table in terms of effort, insight or intelligence, at least performed an expedient role in the local bar. And if it meant that other members of the team didn't have to escort Moberg on his binges, then Brodd was worth putting up with.

'Yes.'

'I forgot to tell you before you left.' He paused. Annoyingly, it sounded as though he was implying that she had left the polishus early. She hadn't. 'I need to see you first thing.'

'What about?'

'Make it nine. My office.'

'What about?' she asked more forcefully, managing to spray the mobile with bubbly toothpaste. But Chief Inspector Moberg had already hung up.

CHAPTER 4

As Anita drank her coffee and tucked into her Turkish yogurt at the kitchen table, the local news was full of the train crash outside Svarte. She knew the line well, and since her schooldays had often taken the train to and from Simrishamn. The accident sounded awful; the initial reports indicated that the Ystad-bound train had hit a van that had broken down on a crossing. The sixty-four-year-old driver had done his best to stop the train. His prompt action had saved the passengers in the first carriage, but the driver himself had died. A number of people had been taken to hospital in Ystad, but none had life-threatening injuries. As for the van, the three occupants, yet to be identified, were all dead. The line would be closed until further notice. It was a dreadful thing to happen, and Anita really felt sorry for the emergency services who would have had to sort out the mess. She also knew that it would throw Klara Wallen's commuting plans into chaos. Wallen, the other female member of Moberg's Criminal Investigation Squad, had moved with her partner to Ystad. They had become sick of the city, and she complained that she never seemed able to escape the job. Anita suspected that it was Wallen's partner, Rolf, who was behind the move, because Ystad was where he came from. As Anita had never liked Rolf – he was too full of bullshit as far as she was concerned – she was glad that the chances of running into him were now minimal. On the other hand, she had got closer to Wallen over the last year or so. They had more frequent chats in the ladies' toilets than in the past. Wallen had become more willing to discuss things with her – both professional and private. And she had emerged from her shell and was now more confident as a police officer. She no longer seemed cowed by Moberg and wasn't afraid to show her contempt for Brodd, whom she was often landed with as a working partner. Occasionally, Anita and Klara had a coffee or a glass of wine after work for a mutual bitch, often about Moberg or Brodd, though their cattiest remarks were usually reserved for Prosecutor Sonja Blom. Blom made all their lives difficult and was often loath to back them up unless a case was totally watertight. She was always covering her immaculately attired arse.

Anita reached her office just after eight. She made herself another strong coffee to try and stem the tiredness. The babysitting had made her bedtime a lot later than normal, and then she had started to worry about why Moberg wanted to see her. A summons like that usually spelt trouble. What had she done to warrant being hauled over the coals yet again? She'd managed to get on the wrong side of the chief inspector more than she would have liked during the course of their working relationship, but she'd been palpably towing the line over the last year or so. At the moment, she and Hakim were working on a fight that had taken place outside one of Malmö's popular clubs, but there was nothing to do with that that merited a visit to Moberg's office; they had made two arrests and were waiting for Blom to do her business in court. Anita took her glasses off and vigorously cleaned the lenses with a handkerchief – a sure sign that she was anxious. Hakim interrupted her fretting. There was a broad grin on his young face. He'd obviously been out the night before with Liv Fogelström. Whenever Anita saw them together, she couldn't help but be amused. Hakim was tall, thin and dark; Fogelström was squat, plump and blonde. They didn't seem to notice the incongruity, which was rather endearing.

'Morning. What have we got on today?'

'Not sure. Moberg wants to see me at nine. That's if he remembers. Called me after midnight.'

Hakim cocked his wrist and made a drinking motion with his hand. 'With Brodd again?'

'Yep.'

'Brodd won't be of use to anyone today then. Just seen him slumped over his desk. Hangover, probably.'

They spent the rest of the time before her meeting discussing the train crash. It would dominate the local news for the next few days.

'Come', Moberg grunted.

Anita entered. Moberg was tucking into what looked suspiciously like a burger in a bun. It seemed a bit early for such a delicacy. Maybe it was helping to soak up last night's beer.

'What do you want?' he snapped. There had been times in the last year when Anita thought the chief inspector had mellowed, and that their fractious relationship was becoming less spiky; he called her 'Anita' now and again, and he was more prone to give her some leeway in investigations and occasionally seek her opinion. He didn't have Henrik Nordlund to turn to any more, and Anita was now the most senior detective in the team. There was even the odd occasion when there was banter between them. But this wasn't one of them.

'I thought you wanted to see me. You rang last night.'

Moberg shifted his huge frame uneasily in a chair that was inadequate for his size. His lifestyle made an already-big man bigger. Wallen had even opened the betting on when Moberg would have his first heart attack. 'Ah, I did.' The last of the burger bun disappeared before he started. Then he indicated that Anita should sit.

'You may have heard that they've set up this Cold Case Group.'

'I heard a rumour. It makes us look as though we can't solve our cases. The papers are still raking over the Catrine da Costa business, and that took place in eighty-four.'

'I know,' Moberg agreed as he wiped his mouth with the sleeve of his jacket. 'But it's something Stockholm is keen on. Techniques are always improving, and evidence can be examined in a way that couldn't be done before.' Anita thought it would be a waste of time and only unearth old controversies. Hadn't the overstretched police enough to do without digging into the past? She decided not to vouchsafe her views to Moberg.

'Anyway, they're going to poke into some of our old cases. I think it's just an excuse to give some arse-licker a cushy number. But that's another matter.'

'But what's it to do with me?'

Moberg flipped open a thin blue file. 'I wasn't here at the time, but you were.' He took out a sheet of typed paper. '1995. A guy called Göran Gösta was murdered in the chapel at Knäbäckshusen. Do you remember it?'

Anita was quiet for a moment. Not because she was trying to recall the event, but because she remembered it only too visibly. 'Yes. It was the first big homicide case I worked on. With Henrik.'

'Says here that Henrik Nordlund headed up the case.'

'That's when I first worked for him. He always kept an eye on me from that day on until he...' There was no need to complete the sentence.

'If Henrik worked on the case, the investigation would have been carried out thoroughly.' They both missed Nordlund for different reasons.

'But why now? We know who did it. Linus Svärd. He was Göran Gösta's boyfriend. It's just that we couldn't prove it.'

Moberg arched his eyebrows. 'And the world knew it, too, as someone on the investigation blabbed to the press.'

Anita was crestfallen at the reminder. Her first case, and the whole team knew who was guilty, yet the perpetrator was going to walk away free. In a moment of unguarded madness, she had fed the information to a journalist contact, and the next day it was all over the front page. Nordlund had been furious, but had protected her from the flack from above. It wasn't her most glorious hour. The journalist thought that he had done her a favour, and suggested taking her to bed as a reward. He was to be disappointed.

'Apparently, they've unearthed some fresh evidence.'

'That's great if Svärd can be nailed now.'

Moberg put the sheet of paper back in the file and closed it. 'I don't know what they've got. However, they want you at the first briefing. You're the only serving officer left who was on the original case. Presumably, they want to pick your brains. I can't see your involvement being much more than that.'

'OK. If it means a result, even twenty-one years on, that's fine by me. And Henrik would be pleased that justice was done, eventually.'

'The briefing's at ten. Third floor.'

'Do you know who's running the cold case?'

Moberg reopened the file and glanced down. 'Oh, yes, someone called Zetterberg. Alice Zetterberg.'

'Shit!'

Danny Foster had spent much of the night curled up and shivering. The exertions of the previous day had left him in a state of complete exhaustion, yet he found it difficult to sleep.

He was still hungry, and his lower chest still hurt, but at first light he'd discovered a trickling stream that ran through a small gully in the trees. He started to construct a rudimentary shelter out of fallen branches and twigs. The night before, when the light had at last gone out in the farmhouse, he'd plucked up the courage to sneak across to the barn. There had been enough moonlight to enable him to see his way over, but it had been too dark inside the building to find any possible foodstuff. The only edible substance he laid his hands on was what he assumed to be horse cereal. It tasted like oats but was hardly satisfying. After his "meal", he'd retreated well back into the forest to try and sleep.

This morning he'd gone back to the edge of the wood, which was about ten minutes from his camp. He surveyed the landscape but couldn't see any other buildings. The farmhouse was indeed remote. He had seen the farmer; he looked as though he might be in his seventies. Yet he figured that the old man probably wasn't the only occupant of the house; horses indicated that someone must be around to ride them. Sure enough, ten minutes later, a younger woman with a hastily scraped-back ponytail appeared with a bucket of feed. Danny had also noticed that there was only one car parked in the yard. And he'd bumped into a tractor in the barn the night before. He waited for an hour in the hope that the farmer and the woman might leave in the car, or go off into the fields beyond, so he could go in search of food without being disturbed. When it was obvious that no one was going anywhere – the man was in the barn, and the woman had re-entered the house – he made his way back to his camp.

He sat by the stream and washed his foot. He winced at the pain as the water seeped into the deep lacerations. He must try and get hold of some shoes. Or at least a left shoe. He was still bewildered by what had happened, and he started at every unusual sound. He knew McNaught wouldn't stop looking for him. He hoped that the sadistic bastard would assume that he'd try and get as far away as possible. He gambled on the fact that McNaught wouldn't suspect that he'd stayed in the forest. He still hadn't formulated any sort of plan, other than staying put for the moment. Beyond the canopy of leaves above him, he glimpsed grey sky. Rain was on the way. Then suddenly, he heard a noise in the distance. He nervously scanned the perimeter of his small encampment. Nothing. Now the sound was more distinct. A tractor was starting up. The farmer was on the move.

Anita stormed back into her room and slammed the door. She hadn't realized that Hakim was still in there.

'Didn't go well, then?'

Anita slumped into her seat. She just sat there shaking her head.

'Have we done anything wrong?' he asked gently.

'No. It's nothing like that. It's just that I've got to go and see this new cold case lot.'

Hakim looked at her in alarm. 'You're not being transferred, are you?'

'Not a cat in hell's chance of that.' Hakim's relief was obvious. 'They're digging up the first murder investigation I was on. With Henrik Nordlund. Over twenty years ago.'

'So it wasn't solved?' Hakim said tentatively. He thought it might have been a sore point with Anita. It usually was with those who worked on cases that didn't have any conclusion. It was admitting defeat, and that didn't sit comfortably with any dedicated detective.

'No. It wasn't. We knew who'd done it, but we couldn't prove it.'

'Isn't it good then that it's being reopened?'

'Oh, yes, I suppose. That's not the problem. It's the person who's leading the investigation that's pissing me off.'

'Who's that?'

'Alice Zetterberg.' Anita virtually spat out the name. 'We have history.' She left it at that, as she wasn't prepared to give Hakim the back story of how she and Alice had originally been friends at the police academy and had then fallen out over Zetterberg's husband-to-be, Arne. Zetterberg had been convinced that Anita had slept with him, an impression he did nothing to dispel. Anita had liked him, but they had never gone to bed together. Zetterberg's dislike of Anita was later compounded by the fact that a couple of years after her wedding (to which Anita was not invited), Arne had gone off with another police officer from their year. As far as Anita was concerned, Zetterberg was a bitter old bitch. And when they'd come across one another two years ago, Zetterberg's professional behaviour had been nothing short of heinous, yet Anita wasn't at liberty to say anything to anyone about it. Only Kevin Ash knew, because he had been there at the time. Now the woman was yet again barging her way back into Anita's life. What made it worse was that Zetterberg's promotion to head of the Cold Case Group was obviously her payoff for services rendered to the Swedish state – services that had left Anita shaken to the core and questioning her loyalty to the country she served.

But what worried Anita most was that here was a heaven-sent opportunity for Alice Zetterberg to both humiliate her and smear Henrik Nordlund's reputation at the same time. And there was no way she could let that happen.

CHAPTER 5

There were six photographs on the wall. Anita recognized every one. They were so young. It might have been twenty-odd years since she'd interviewed them, but their faces brought back a whole host of jumbled emotions. She glanced down at the piece of paper they had all been given – the names of the six young people on the board.

At the time of the murder of Göran Gösta on Thursday, 27th July, 1995,
St. Nicolai Chapel, Knäbäckshusen:

Göran Gösta, aged 25, PhD student, Lund University
Ivar Hagblom, 24, PhD student, Lund University
Larissa Bjerstedt, 24, freelance researcher
Linus Svärd, 24, archaeologist
Lars-Gunnar Lerstorp, 27, unemployed
Carina Lindvall, 26, secretary, Malmö Commune

Alice Zetterberg had made the pretence of welcoming Anita and had introduced her to her small team. She already knew Bea Erlandsson. The slight detective with the pinched face and spiked brunette hair had been attached to Moberg's team a couple of times when they'd needed extra hands. Her semi-permanent expression of suppressed worry was occasionally wiped away by

21

an impish grin. Anita had liked her and wondered how someone that nice would survive working under a cynical and insensitive shrew like Zetterberg. The other member of the unit was a male officer in his thirties called Anders Szabo. He had swept-back, blond hair with a floppy fringe that he was constantly flipping with his hand. Anita knew that if she spent too long in his company, the habit would really start to irritate her. He looked to be the kind of man who wouldn't notice other people's vexation. She suspected that his best friend was a mirror.

Zetterberg herself hadn't changed much over the past two years. The slightly manly features of a square jaw, wide mouth, and the round, dark eyes that made her look as though she was staring all the time were the same. The only change, apart from carrying a little extra weight which her large-boned frame could take, was that the ponytail had gone and the hair had been bobbed. Maybe this was an attempt to make herself appear more efficient and professional. From Anita's jaundiced point of view, the attempt was a failure.

Zetterberg's introduction to the case hadn't endeared her either: 'Our job is to find the killer of Göran Gösta,' she said, pointing to the photograph of the young man in the middle of the board. 'He was murdered on Thursday, the twenty-seventh of July, 1995 at the chapel of St. Nicolai at Knäbäckshusen. The reason that Inspector Anita Sundström is here is that she was on the original investigating team, which was led by Inspector Henrik Nordlund. Our job is to succeed where that team failed.' Anita felt her blood boil, and she was about to say something when Zetterberg swiftly moved on. 'Not only do we need to achieve closure for Göran Gösta's family, we also need to reassure the public of Skåne that we never give up on a case. We never close a file; we are not afraid to admit our past mistakes.'

This was too much. 'We didn't make any mistakes. We *knew* who'd done it!'

'Sorry, Inspector Sundström, but I don't see anybody behind bars.' Anita noticed that Szabo smirked, while she could tell that Erlandsson was embarrassed. 'Unlike Inspector Sundström, I want you to approach this case with an open mind.' Anita found it hard not to get up and walk out, but she knew that if she did, Zetterberg would make damned sure she was reprimanded for not cooperating. She was painfully aware that Zetterberg now had friends in high places and wouldn't hesitate to use them.

Zetterberg returned to the photographs – two women and four men. 'First, I'll give you the background to the case, and I'm sure if I've misinterpreted any of the facts, Inspector Sundström will put me right.'

Anita listened to Zetterberg's summary with a mixture of annoyance at her superior tone of voice and frustration that the events being described hadn't provided Nordlund with the result his efforts deserved. Though he had never spoken openly about the Gösta case, she knew that it had plagued him for the rest of his career.

The people in the photographs were a group of students and ex-students from Lund University who were spending the summer at a cottage in Knäbäckshusen on the Skåne coast between Simrishamn and Kivik. The six were Ivar Hagblom, Larissa Bjerstedt, Linus Svärd, Lars-Gunnar Lerstorp, Carina Lindvall, and the victim, Göran Gösta. Four of them had left the university two years before, while Hagblom and Gösta had stayed on to do their Masters and were now doing PhDs. This was the second summer they had spent together at Knäbäckshusen, and all of them appeared to be genuine friends from their undergraduate days. In fact, at the time of the murder, they were three couples – Ivar Hagblom and Larissa Bjerstedt, Lars-Gunnar Lerstorp and Carina Lindvall, and Linus Svärd and Göran Gösta. But something changed on Thursday, 27th July, 1995.

On that day, they had had a barbecue on the beach, as they often did. It was holiday time, and a number of people saw them on that particular stretch of sand. There had been a row between the gay couple, Linus and Göran. Linus had stormed off, and the barbecue had carried on, though not in the same jolly vein as before. Then the five that were left gradually drifted away. At around ten that evening, a ten-year-old boy called Kurt Jeppsson went into a small stone chapel above the beach and discovered the body of Göran Gösta lying in front of the altar. He ran for help, and his mother, and father who had just returned from a fishing trip, went down to the chapel. The victim was certainly dead by the time they got there. Gösta had been stabbed with what the pathologist believed to be a kebab skewer, which had been thrust under his xiphisternum – the bottom of the breast bone – and into the left ventricle of the heart. And indeed, the investigating team had discovered that one of the kebab skewers used at the barbecue that afternoon was unaccounted for. It was never found. The missing skewer, one of a set, had a corkscrew shank like that of a gimlet, and a red, turned wooden handle. It was presumed it had been left on the beach. The pathologist had found traces in the fatal wound of the meat, tomato and mushroom that had been barbecued at the party. There were also minute traces of sand, further implicating the missing skewer; the others had all been washed. The team came to the conclusion that the murderer must have found the skewer lying on the beach and picked it up. Once the identity of the murder weapon was established, suspicion immediately turned to the other five friends. The team had ruled out other possible suspects after carrying out extensive interviews with local residents and the few holiday-makers who had used the beach that day.

When Zetterberg had finished, she turned to Anita and gave her a sickly smile. 'Is that how it was?'

'Yes,' Anita had to admit.

'So, why did you suspect Linus Svärd?'

Anita cleared her throat. Suddenly she felt on trial. Whatever she said now, Zetterberg and her colleagues would be weighing up whether she and the rest of Nordlund's team had done their job up to the expected standard. And Zetterberg was the judge who would pass sentence. What also unnerved Anita was that Zetterberg hadn't yet told her what new evidence they had. Anything she said might sound unprofessional in the light of fresh facts.

'Of the five, three didn't have an alibi. Ivar and Larissa alibied each other; making love, apparently. Carina was writing in her room, while her boyfriend, Lars-Gunnar, was smoking and drinking in the garden, which is where Carina claimed she saw him through the window. Linus said he was out for a walk. This was confirmed by young Kurt, who had spotted him on the beach on his way down to the chapel, which later transpired was shortly after the murder had taken place. We suspected Linus had been on the beach getting rid of the murder weapon. He claimed he was there trying to clear his head, as he was upset by the argument with his lover. It turns out that they had, in fact, broken up rather acrimoniously. To be precise, Göran had finished with him. He'd found someone else. After all our interviews and background searches on the five suspects, Linus was the only one with motive, means and ample opportunity – we know he was close to the scene of the crime. We believed that on his "walk", he may have been harbouring dangerous thoughts.'

'You thought it was a pre-meditated murder?'

'To an extent. We reckoned he hadn't formulated a plan as such but, fortuitously, he found the skewer on the beach, spotted Göran going into the chapel, and took his opportunity. Of course, he denied the whole thing; we didn't have the murder weapon, and we couldn't prove that he had been in the chapel that night. Footprints and fingerprints were of no use as all six had been in the building over the previous few days, along with a number of other visitors. Prosecutor Renmarker didn't think we had enough evidence to pin the murder on Linus, and he wouldn't even let us arrest him, despite pleas from Henrik Nordlund. We never got the chance to put pressure on him and break his story.' Anita shrugged helplessly. 'So, the investigation just fizzled out.' It seemed a rather feeble way to finish.

Zetterberg addressed her new colleagues: 'You two will be too young to remember, but despite Nordlund's lot failing to achieve a conviction, Linus Svärd was found guilty by the press, who received information that only Nordlund's team knew.' Zetterberg turned her gaze on Anita. The inference was clear. The two junior detectives appeared appalled. Anita blushed. She couldn't say anything to defend herself. She'd been stupid, but she'd been starting out on her career as an enthusiastic detective, and she was sickened that the person they knew to be the killer was getting away with the crime. The injustice of it all was too much. It was a hard lesson to learn.

'Which brings me to why this case has been reopened.' Zetterberg produced a clear polythene bag. Inside was a thin, twisted piece of pockmarked metal with a fragment of rotten wood tenaciously clinging to one end. Despite its ravaged appearance, it was still obvious what the object was – a kebab skewer. She held it up triumphantly: 'The murder weapon!'

'Where did that turn up?' Anita asked incredulously.

'In an orchard at the back of the village'

'What orchard?'

'It was an ordinary field twenty years ago. But the farmer turned it into an apple orchard a few years later. It was found when he was having a new irrigation system put in.'

Anita remembered how they had searched in vain for the skewer. Even local detectorists had been brought in, and divers searching the shallow waters off the beach. But she supposed a skewer would be an easy enough object to quickly shove deep into the yielding earth of the old field.

'This is *definitely* the murder weapon, as forensics have found Gösta's blood on it. It's amazing what they can do these days.'

'Fingerprints?' Szabo asked.

'Unfortunately, what's left of the handle has yielded nothing.'

'Is that all you've got?' Anita knew the murder weapon might not make a huge difference at this stage. They still wouldn't be able to place Linus at the scene of the crime, though if he were out and about that night, he would certainly have had time to bury the skewer, albeit not on the beach as they originally thought.

'No. We have new information, too.' Zetterberg picked up a photograph of a man of around thirty with light ginger hair and a serious expression. Anita thought there was something vaguely familiar about him, though she couldn't put her finger on it. 'This man was near the chapel on the night of the murder. His name is Kurt Jeppsson.'

Now Anita recognized him; the young boy who'd found Gösta. Obviously, after twenty-one years he looked different – the freckles had gone – but there were still traces of the boy she had talked to several times at the time of the murder. Nordlund had made her Kurt's contact; he reckoned that as she was the youngest member of the team and a woman and mother, she'd get more out of him than any of the others. They had become quite friendly.

'Kurt didn't reveal much – he had little to tell,' observed Anita, who could sense that that was about to change, and that Zetterberg would enjoy telling her what had been discovered.

'He's had second thoughts. He knew more than he let on at the time.'

'But why now?'

'Because he heard from his mother, who still lives in Knäbäckshusen, that the murder weapon had been unearthed and that the case was likely to be reopened.'

'So what's new?'

'Kurt was in the trees close to the chapel when the murder must have taken place because he heard someone coming out of the chapel and hurrying off to the village.'

'He never mentioned it at the time. Did he see the person?'

'Unfortunately not. However, that is not the most significant thing.' Zetterberg paused for effect. 'Gösta wasn't dead when Kurt entered the building.'

'He said that there was no movement.' Anita's mind swiftly went back to the days after the crime. They had been sure from the boy's description that Gösta had been dead when he'd found him.

'Well, now he wants to come clean. Gösta wasn't quite dead. In fact, he mumbled some last words. Kurt didn't catch what Gösta said first, and we can only speculate that that may have been the name of the killer. But what Kurt did hear, he's been carrying around in his head all these years and never told anyone about.'

'What last words?'

Zetterberg took a marker pen and wrote on the board in big red letters: BURNT IT.

Anita stared at the words. What did they mean? Nothing was immediately apparent.

'Can you shed any light on these words, Inspector?' Zetterberg asked.

Anita shook her head. 'But why didn't he tell us all this at the time?'

Zetterberg answered as though she were talking to a slow-witted child. 'You have to remember that Kurt Jeppsson had only just turned ten at the time of the murder. He was scared by all the attention. The reason he was there in the first place was that he had stolen a cigarette from his dad's secret supply – his mother strongly disapproved of smoking. The experiment was a disaster, but there was still the cigarette he'd tried to smoke lying in the small woodland above the beach. He was frightened he would get into serious trouble if it was found, so he didn't admit to being anywhere near the trees. He said he'd just walked down to the chapel. He couldn't mention the fact that, while trying his illicit experiment, he'd heard someone leaving the chapel, as he would have met that person on the path if the story he told you was true. And as for Gösta's last words – as I said, some of them he couldn't make out, and the ones he could he didn't think were worth mentioning, as he thought no one would believe him. His mother was always accusing him of making things up – a kid with an "overactive imagination" is how she described him. Fortunately for us, he's now decided to come forward with the truth.'

Anita sank back in her seat. If only they'd had access to that information back then, they might have had a better chance of pinning down their murderer.

'So, there we are,' Zetterberg said, still waving the red marker about in her hand like an accusatory finger. 'We've now got the murder weapon. And if we can decipher the meaning of those words, *this* time we might find the killer.'

CHAPTER 6

Danny Foster was still gasping for breath. He'd got safely back to his camp, but it had been a close thing. After hearing the tractor starting up, he had made his way to the edge of the forest. By the time he'd reached the trees, he could see the tractor disappearing towards some far fields. A couple of minutes later, the woman appeared from the house, got into the Volvo parked in the yard and headed off down the track. Danny had no idea where the track led to. A country road perhaps, then on to a village or town? This wasn't the time to speculate. He was too hungry for that. He would break into the house and steal some food.

Despite the coast being clear, it took Danny a great deal of nerve to actually start moving across the field. First he went into the barn. At the back, he saw an aging Volkswagen. So there were two cars. No food, of course, except for the horse oats. He fretfully made his way towards the farmhouse. There might still be somebody else inside that he hadn't accounted for. He stopped and took stock. Now he could get a better idea of the layout of the place. The house was tucked in behind and a few metres away from the barn. The barn itself was an ugly, dilapidated, corrugated iron building, but the house was in an even sadder state of repair. It was obviously old, and with some careful renovation could be beautiful. "Full of character", an estate agent would say. There were certainly plenty of original features. The low house was half-timbered, with a thatched roof pinned with wooden pegs along the ridge. But the window frames looked rotten, the once-whitewashed plaster was peeling and grey, the roof was now covered in moss, and huge clumps of nettles and brambles fought for space along the base of the walls, which looked damp and smelled of mould. If Danny hadn't seen the human and equine activity with his own eyes, he would have believed the place to be derelict. The strong breeze was drying up the rain that had fallen earlier. He reached the back door. To his surprise, it opened when he turned the handle. Why had it been left unlocked? Were people so trusting in Sweden? Maybe there *was* another person inside.

Abutting the wall on the other side of the door was a rack of shoes. Everything from boots and wellingtons to soft leather shoes, slippers, and a pair of trainers. Most were well worn. He picked up the trainers and tried the left one on. Too small. Must be the woman's. He chose a pair of light tan shoes. They weren't quite the right size, or ideal for skulking in the woods, but they didn't rub too abrasively against his swollen foot. Above the shoe rack was a line of coats hanging from pegs. He tried a few on. He decided on a grubby blue waterproof. The other jackets were too thick for this time of year, and he didn't want anything too cumbersome in case he was chased again. And he also thought the waterproof would blend in better. Still no sign of anyone else in the house; he began to breathe more easily.

The kitchen was off to the left. It was basic and rather a mess, with dirty dishes still in the sink. The only thing Danny was interested in was the fridge, out of which, from the bottom shelf, he yanked a carton of milk which he slurped back greedily. There was a left-over, yellowy rice concoction in a bowl, which he scooped out with his fingers. It was spicy. He returned to the milk for another gulp. He didn't want to hang around for too long, so he started filling his pockets with food – a lump of cheese, a packet of ham, and what looked like a sausage of salami. His frenetic attack on the fridge halted abruptly. Was that the sound of the tractor returning? He slammed the fridge door shut. On the work surface next to the fridge, he noticed a bread crock. Inside were a couple of stale buns. They would do. That was definitely the tractor. As he made for the door, he passed a large, earthenware fruit bowl on the rough wooden table in the middle of the kitchen. He grabbed a couple of apples and a blackening banana and added them to the foodstuffs already bulging in his coat pockets. One last thing caught his eye. A half bottle of some kind of schnapps. That went too as he dashed out of the room.

At the back door, he waited. The tractor was getting nearer. He slipped out into the yard. He could hear the tractor was now behind the barn. Would the farmer bring it round the corner or take it back into the barn? If it was the former, he would be in trouble. If the latter, he would have time to dash across the field and make the safety of the forest. He fought back a burp – he'd eaten and drunk too quickly. The tractor sounded more muted now; he felt a surge of relief. This was his moment, and he hobbled as fast as he could past one of the grazing horses. It lifted its head in surprise before lolloping over to pick up an apple that had fallen out of Danny's pocket.

'Right, let's get a bit of background on the victim and the suspects.' Zetterberg had had a short break while Bea Erlandsson was sent out to get some coffees. An embarrassed silence had followed. Szabo was engrossed with the laptop he had brought into the meeting. Zetterberg spent her time shuffling notes on the table in front of her, and both pointedly left Anita twiddling her thumbs. It had been a relief when Erlandsson returned. 'And this might be where Inspector Sundström could possibly prove useful, as we need to understand the dynamic of the group.'

Zetterberg took a sip of coffee before pointing towards the photo of Göran Gösta. The unsmiling face was pale; long dark locks drooped down to the shoulders. The eyes were determined and defiant as though throwing out a challenge to the photographer. 'He came from Umeå, up north. Humble background compared to the other five, who hailed from more affluent families. At Lund, he read Middle Eastern Studies with Ivar Hagblom. After the others left, he and Ivar stayed on to do a Masters and were into their PhDs at the time of the murder. There were high hopes that Göran would go on to a high-flying career, either in the academic world or maybe the diplomatic service in the Middle East. He was twenty-five when he died. The most pertinent point – certainly according to the original investigation – is that he was gay, and that Linus Svärd was his lover. Which brings us to Linus Svärd...'

This photo showed a smiling Linus on the beach at Knäbäckshusen. "Pretty boy" had been Nordlund's description of him. He was right. The cherubic features, the smooth, high cheekbones, the wide lips and wavy blond hair made him look like something out of a Rubens painting. It was a face that Anita had quickly grown to hate, and one she hadn't been able to totally erase from her mind over the years.

'Twenty-four at the time, Linus Svärd was a local boy from Lund. Bright and articulate, he studied archaeology. He joined the party late that summer, as he had been on a dig in Gotland. He and Göran had become lovers two years before. Apparently, he had been quite promiscuous prior to that but afterwards remained faithful. Hence his being so upset at Göran giving him the elbow.'

'Inspector Sundström, you mentioned that Göran had found someone else.' Szabo turned in his seat to face Anita. 'Do we know who this was?'

Anita nodded at the photo of Ivar Hagblom. Today the face would be described as televisual; which was appropriate because on the screen is where Anita had last seen it. Ivar had that slightly dishevelled appearance which takes hours of careful grooming to create: the permanent, unshaven stubble which never gets any thicker; the tousled ash-blond hair; and the slightly amused crease of the mouth, as though he was remembering some private joke that he was just about to let you in on. Undoubtedly handsome – and he knew it. There were unmistakable echoes of her ex, Björn. At the time, she had found that attractive. On seeing Ivar again, she realized that they were probably cut from the same arrogant academic cloth.

'But I thought he was hooked up with Larissa Bjerstedt?' asked Szabo in some disbelief. 'Did he swing both ways?'

'Not that I'm aware of. Göran's love for Ivar was unrequited.'

'Ivar Hagblom,' Zetterberg went on in that guttural drone that was perfect for delivering bad news, moaning, and finding the worst in any situation. 'Also twenty-four. Read Middle Eastern Studies with Göran. From a wealthy Stockholm family, so you can draw your own conclusions about him.' There was obedient laughter from Szabo. 'Made their fortune in newspapers and magazines – Hagblom Media – until they sold out about five years ago when Ivar's old man died. It was the Hagblom holiday home that the group were staying in that summer. It was the second summer they had all spent together. From the notes on the group left by Nordlund's team, it is clear that Ivar was the unofficial leader.' Zetterberg glanced over to Anita. 'Is that correct?'

'He certainly dominated the group. I think the others were in awe of him.' Anita didn't elaborate; she could see that Zetterberg just wanted to get onto the next person on the board.

'Ivar's girlfriend was Larissa Bjerstedt. Again, twenty-four; born and brought up in Malmö. Local girl who had done History at university.' Anita gazed at the classic Swedish blonde with long flowing hair and a glowing complexion, the result of a healthy outdoor summer on the beach. Anita remembered being aware of Larissa enjoying her role as the other half of someone like Ivar. They made the ideal young Scandinavian couple, stereotypical of hundreds of Swedish advertisements during the 1990s. 'They had been an item for over three years,' Zetterberg went on inexorably. 'As Inspector Sundström has mentioned, these two gave each other alibis. But alibis are there to be broken.' Zetterberg was starting to sound like Moberg.

'The last two are Lars-Gunnar Lerstorp and Carina Lindvall.' Anita remembered Lars-Gunnar as being tall and slender, and his photograph showed a face that was verging on the gaunt. Even then his wispy hair was starting to thin. She was sure he'd be bald by now. Carina had raven hair, with thick black lashes above penetrating eyes. To Anita, she was striking rather than pretty, but she had certainly turned a few heads. And she still did.

'Is that *the* Carina Lindvall?' exclaimed Erlandsson with some excitement.

'Yes. The crime writer,' Zetterberg added sniffily. 'Don't know her work; I spend enough time trying to solve real crimes without wasting energy on reading made-up twaddle.' Erlandsson was immediately quelled. 'Anyhow, Lars-Gunnar and Carina were an item at the time. He was the oldest of the group at twenty-seven, and his girlfriend was twenty-six. He did History with Larissa, and Carina was on an English course. Lars-Gunnar was from over in Borrby, while Carina was from here.' Zetterberg sat down and took another drink of her coffee. 'That is our cast of characters. I think we can safely assume that the murderer is one of those five. But which one?'

CHAPTER 7

'What we need to know, Inspector Sundström, is how the six individuals in the group related to each other. We know their actual relationships, but what was the mix like? What was the pecking order, and where was Göran Gösta's place within the set-up?'

Anita was taken back to that summer. She had been a similar age to the six and had felt a rapport with them. She was still living with Björn in Lund at the time, so knew the environment where the suspects had met and grown close. Carina had actually been one of Björn's English students. That had made Anita sympathetic to her. Björn had spoken highly of her at the time of the case; a student with a lively mind. Lasse was four, and they were starting to have fewer sleepless nights. Life seemed good. Handsome husband, a child she worshipped, and a job she loved and was really getting her teeth into, working on her first big murder case. Henrik Nordlund had kept an eye on her and guided her through the complexities of an investigation that was far from straightforward. But over time they had begun to home in on their chief suspect, only for him to wriggle off the hook because of vital evidence: they couldn't actually place him in the chapel. In his original statement, Kurt Jeppsson had told them that he'd seen Linus on the beach; he'd certainly been the nearest to the chapel and the first of the group to turn up after Kurt's parents had found the body, but he said he'd heard the commotion and had gone up to see what was going on. It seemed Kurt's new information shifted the timeline, putting Linus on the beach before the murder and not after. But did it make any difference?

'There were various connections before the six joined up,' Anita started tentatively, trying to marshal the information. She wished Moberg had told her about this meeting last night so she could have gone over her old case notes. She needed to reacquaint herself with the details, some of which she'd inevitably forgotten over time, squeezed out of her memory by the overriding conviction that Linus Svärd was guilty. 'Larissa and Carina both went to the same school here in Malmö. Though there was a two-year age difference, their parents knew each other, and it was only natural that they should hook up at university. Carina had taken time out and had travelled to "find herself". She ended up coming back at the same time Larissa started uni. Lars-Gunnar was a late starter and met Carina through Larissa, as they did History together. Ivar and Linus had met in their first year at Lund. On the face of it, they didn't have much in common, but got on really well. They'd spent their first summer vacation out in Egypt, where Linus was on an archaeological dig, and Ivar, who had private means, swanned around Cairo nightspots and environs soaking up the atmosphere, picking up girls and honing his Arabic. In his second year, he met Larissa at some party and they started going out; then he met her friends and in turn they got to know Linus.'

'So, Göran wasn't one of the original set?' observed Erlandsson. Zetterberg snorted her annoyance at the interruption.

'Quite right, Bea.' Anita gave the young detective an encouraging nod. 'He was an outsider in more ways than one. He came from way up north and apparently was rather looked down upon by many of his fellow students. He was also a bit of a loner. And being gay may have cut down his social outlets. But for some reason, Ivar took him under his wing. They were on the same course, Middle Eastern Studies, so they had that in common. And through Ivar, Göran met Linus, and the three couples were formed into one harmonious whole.'

'Obviously not that harmonious, as one of them killed him,' butted in Zetterberg.

'Obviously not. But before it all unravelled, they spent a lot of time together. They summered in Knäbäckshusen in 1994, a year after graduation. And they also spent a month together on Malta in the March of ninety-five. I don't know whether it was then or when they joined up again that summer that the cracks in the Linus/Göran relationship began to appear. Anyway, Linus was the last one to arrive at Knäbäckshusen that last summer. The group all claimed that everything was fine among them, except for the situation between Linus and Göran, which caused some tension. Basically, none of the others had an obvious motive.'

'You mean one that you could establish.' Zetterberg could make anything she said sound snide.

Zetterberg went over to a computer. She briefly fiddled with the keys. A map appeared on the whiteboard next to the photos of the victim and suspects. It showed the old part of the village of Knäbäckshusen, with the row of houses and their gardens. The house that the group had stayed in was marked with a neat red cross. It sat in a cul-de-sac off the main street. The garden at the back opened onto a large open area of scrubby grassland across which ran the path that led to the chapel bell tower, the chapel, and the beach beyond. Looking in the direction of the sea, the trees that Kurt had been hiding in were off to the left. The path and the chapel were both highlighted, as was the beach below. The orchard where the murder weapon was unearthed was also marked with a cross.

'Right, let's go back to the night of the murder. Three of the young people were at home. Ivar and Larissa doing things to each other. Carina was in another bedroom working.'

'What was she working on?' queried Szabo. 'Wasn't she meant to be on holiday?'

'What turned out to be her first novel,' answered Anita. She had followed Carina's career with interest and enjoyed her books.

Zetterberg pointed to the long garden area where there was an arrow next to the name "Lars-Gunnar". 'Lars-Gunnar was out here – this was confirmed by Carina, who spied him through a window. Over here,' she said, indicating the beach, 'we have the chief suspect, Linus. Of course, we now know that when Kurt Jeppsson saw him there, it wasn't after the murder as he originally claimed. He saw him from the trees *before* it took place. However, that still means Linus was geographically closest to the victim at around the time of his death.'

She moved closer to the map and used a biro as a pointer to indicate the movements of the characters involved. 'So, we have young Kurt going into the trees here to light his cigarette. As he does so, he spies Linus on the beach. Shortly after his smoking fiasco, he hears someone hurrying away from the chapel.'

'So, Inspector Nordlund's team assumed that Linus had gone to the beach after the murder,' reiterated Szabo slowly. 'But we now know he was there just prior to Göran's death. So, that begs the question as to whether Linus had enough time to get up from the beach and kill him.'

'Good point,' Zetterberg joyfully seized on the comment.

'That depends on how accurate Kurt Jeppsson's memory is,' put in Anita, who could see where this was going. 'The chapel is only a stone's throw from the beach, and it would take less than a minute for him to reach it.'

'He'd still have to be pretty quick,' Szabo persisted. 'And

how did he know Göran would be in the chapel anyway?'

'I think it was luck – or ill luck – that they were in the same place at the same time. Linus took his chance.' Anita was adamant in her own mind that that was what had happened, irrespective of the new information. She took a deep breath. 'Wouldn't it make sense if you all went down and took a look at the scene of the crime?'

'That's exactly what we're doing this afternoon,' Zetterberg said firmly. 'But I want *my* team to have full background knowledge before seeing the site.'

'Sorry to go on,' Szabo persisted. He glanced quickly towards Anita. 'but wouldn't Kurt have seen Linus with the skewer?'

'Not the easiest thing to see from that distance in that light,' suggested Erlandsson. Anita was relieved that she had someone in her corner.

Zetterberg jumped in: 'That's as may be. All we know is that Göran met someone at the chapel and ended up being stabbed. We don't know if the meeting was pre-arranged, or by chance, as Nordlund's team asserted. Whatever... the murderer was heard leaving by Kurt Jeppsson. Kurt then runs home and fetches his parents. Almost immediately after they find the body, Linus arrives. So, he was certainly in the vicinity. It's interesting that he never denied being out and about. If he'd committed the murder, one would think he'd try and distance himself from the scene of the crime.'

'Or do the opposite.' Anita wasn't going to let Zetterberg dismantle Henrik Nordlund's case just to prove a point and discredit the team that had worked so hard on the original investigation.

'Well, that's for us to find out.'

'And he did have blood on his T-shirt when he was first interviewed. Göran's blood.' Anita was still on the defensive.

'If I've read the original case notes correctly, Linus is

said to have rushed in when he recognized the body and immediately cradled his dead lover in a distraught manner. That would have produced the stains. The Jeppssons couldn't remember if he already had blood on his T-shirt when he first appeared, as they were in a state of horrified confusion. And the forensic people couldn't say whether the blood on the T-shirt was consistent with spatters one might expect from a stabbing by such a thin weapon because as Linus clutched the victim in his arms, they would be obscured by the blood seeping from the wound.' Anita kept quiet. She remembered that had been a point of much debate at the time. The evidence was inconclusive, as they couldn't get any corroboration from the Jeppssons. No other blood-stained garment was found, though the search for one didn't happen for some days because it had taken a while to establish who was most likely to have been involved in the murder.

'Our first job,' Zetterberg continued, 'is to track down the five members of the group and re-interview them.'

'Well, I know Carina Lindvall lives in Stockholm.' This was Erlandsson, who was obviously a Lindvall fan.

'And according to Wikipedia,' Szabo said, staring at his laptop screen, 'Ivar Hagblom is a professor at Uppsala University.'

'Of course he is,' Anita said impatiently. 'Don't you recognize him from the TV? He's the guy they always drag out to comment on the troubles in the Middle East. Every time Syria's mentioned, he's their go-to expert.'

'If you say so.' Obviously Zetterberg wasn't a regular television news watcher.

'I thought he looked familiar,' nodded Szabo. 'I can't find the other three, but they'll be easy enough to track down through our usual channels.'   'You might find it harder with Linus Svärd.'

'Why?' Zetterberg almost snapped at Anita.

Because Anita had kept an eye on Linus Svärd after the murder enquiry was wound down; she knew he'd spent a couple of years keeping a low profile in Malmö, and then had disappeared up to the far north after he was "outed" by a local newspaper. Residents had made it plain that they didn't want a suspected killer living among them. Anita had tracked him to Kiruna, but then he'd gone abroad on some archaeological dig in Syria – the authorities couldn't stop him. And then the trail went cold. What *was* clear was that he hadn't returned to Sweden, unless he'd used a false name and passport.

'He went abroad somewhere.'

'Well, let's find him.'

After Zetterberg had called an end to the meeting – 'I don't think we'll need to call on the assistance of Inspector Sundström again' – Szabo picked up his laptop, Erlandsson the original case files, and both left the room. Anita waited outside.

'Still here?' Zetterberg managed some mock surprise as she came out.

'I know you're trying to impress your new team and prove you're a tough cookie, but don't ever speak to me again like you did in there. Try and be more professional.'

'I was professional. It's not my fault that your shortcomings – and Nordlund's – are going to be exposed.'

'You're a conniving bitch, and I know how low you've stooped to get this job.'

'I know how to serve my country.'

'Stuff your country. And stuff you, too!'

Anita stalked off. She was furious that she was furious. She had sounded so pathetically petulant. She'd let Zetterberg wind her up, which would just encourage the woman to dish out more bile. She was in no mood to rationalize her thoughts, but the truth of it was that Zetterberg had sown the first seeds of doubt in over twenty years of righteous conviction.

CHAPTER 8

The meeting had consumed Anita's thoughts so much that after work she'd got into her car and driven across to Knäbäckshusen. The earlier rain had cleared, and it was an easy sixty-minute run as she cut across the middle of Skåne via Sjöbo and Tomelilla. She avoided the coast road, as it would be busier than usual with the train line out of action for the foreseeable future. She had already put up with Klara Wallen moaning about the situation – she'd had to take the emergency bus and, subsequently, been late for work. Anita noticed that Wallen had slipped off early to make sure she got back at a reasonable time to make Rolf's evening meal. She skirted Simrishamn and headed up the Kivik road. That in itself brought back bad, far more recent, memories. At Rörum, she found the turning to Knäbäckshusen. The road curved through fields and orchards before straightening out as it entered the village. She knew that Zetterberg's little gang would have been and gone by now so there was no likelihood of running into them; that would have been difficult to explain. Zetterberg had made it perfectly plain that she was no longer needed in their reopened investigation. So why was she here? It wasn't a question she could answer coherently. She ruminated as she parked her relatively new second-hand Skoda in a gap by the kerb. Was it the thought that the new investigation was totally out of her control? Other people trampling over the evidence that she and Nordlund and the rest of the team had spent months accumulating and dissecting? Was she afraid, deep down, that Zetterberg might find something they had missed?

Anita locked the car and walked along the street, which doglegged through the old part of Knäbäckshusen. The village consisted of attractive traditional fishermen's cottages, picturesque with roses and hollyhocks. Except it wasn't all that it seemed. These houses had only arrived here in the mid-1950s. The buildings were genuinely old, but their location wasn't. They came from the village of Knäbäck, which lay twenty kilometres to the north. When the Swedish military decided that their Ravlunda artillery range needed extending, they wanted to raze Knäbäck because it was in the way. Despite widespread protests, the military got their wish. But the houses survived the demolition squad: a building contractor called Carl Liljedahl moved them to a new site. Now the village is made up of both full-time residential property and holiday homes, one of which had belonged to Ivar Hagblom's parents – Stockholmers seeking the sun, sand and serenity of Österlen.

Anita passed a few stragglers coming back from the beach. At the end of the street, on the right, was a grassy square, on the far side of which was the house where the friends had spent the summer of 1995. The house itself was single storey, half-timbered with whitewashed walls and the typical widely spaced stonework so prevalent in Skåne. It had a deeply pitched thatched roof secured at the apex in the traditional way by a row of wooden pegs. A wide chimney breast of stone and stucco dominated the middle of the front section of the roof, and a quaint arched dormer window nestled in its shadow. Anita walked to the open ground at the end of the street, known to the locals as Lilla Heden – the Little Moor – across which ran the path to the bell tower and down the slope to the chapel below. Except she noticed that this wasn't the route that today's visitors were taking. A new path with wooden steps ran along at the edge of the trees that Kurt Jeppsson had once hidden in. But Anita continued along the old route. The bell tower was a basic structure – two wooden posts supporting a little pitched roof from which dangled three bells of differing sizes. As she stood in its shadow, Anita gazed down the rough path to the chapel. It was up this bank that Göran Gösta's killer had scrambled after piercing his victim's chest with the skewer. Now she knew Kurt Jeppsson had heard someone, it might change things. If only he'd told them the truth twenty-one years ago. The killer must have passed the bells, cut across the corner of Lilla Heden and into the trees which separated the Moor from the field beyond where he had hidden the murder weapon. She could imagine him pushing his way through the undergrowth which even now was struggling ceaselessly to reclaim the path. Down the short, steep slope, she came to the entrance of the chapel, which, in 1958, had been converted from a fishing hut by the Reverend Albert J. Lindberg for his summer confirmation students. He would have been appalled at how it had been desecrated forty years later. Anita glanced up at the wooden cross that was attached in finial position at the top of the front gable. Twenty years ago she hadn't recognized how striking it was in its simplicity. She opened the wooden door and entered. The Reverend Lindberg's confirmation groups must have been pretty small, as you could hardly swing a cat around inside. The low brick altar with its white cloth draped along the top supported two unfussy candle holders bookending a jar of fresh, wild flowers, which had been placed immediately below a crucifix. Anita could see how this was a place of peace and mediation, but for her it would always be the crime scene of a brutal murder. Was it standing here, all those years ago, that she began to realize what a tough, uncompromising world she was working in? A world where people did really bad things? Was it an indictment of her and the job she did that she was no longer shocked by what she saw? The killing of Göran Gösta had been the start of that erosion process.

Anita left the chapel and took the narrow path down to a flight of wooden steps that led directly onto the sand. The scene had changed since she was last here; the rocks that had edged the top of the beach on the left had gone. Now it was nothing but sand, which appeared to stretch as far as the promontory of Stenshuvud, where Linus had gone on his walkabout. In the other direction, she could see the villages of Vik and, further round the bay, Baskemölla. The strip of sand between the tree-lined banks and the sea was narrow. Twenty-one years ago not many people had used it. That had made their interviewing job easier. In recent years, the beach at Knäbäckshusen had been "discovered", and tourists and locals alike flocked to the shore, their cars bunging up the small, compact village, much to the annoyance of the residents.

Anita noticed a mother rounding up some children, and an elderly man in bulky shorts strolling along the shoreline where the rocks had once been. Otherwise, this section of the beach was hers. She wandered towards the rippling sea and stood looking out at the great expanse of blue stretching to the horizon. A couple of tankers could be seen in the distance, apparently almost sinking under the weight of their cargoes of oil. There was a fluttering sail closer in. At weekends this coastline was littered with such sails, like a flight of cabbage white butterflies hovering over the water. Anita half-twisted round and screwed up her eyes as she scanned the trees to the right of the chapel. She reckoned that must have been about the spot from where the young Kurt Jeppsson had seen Linus Svärd – standing just here, where she was now. He said Linus was gazing out to sea. Now she knew that it was *before* the murder and not after. It did make a difference. During the original investigation, they assumed, thanks to Kurt, that the deed had already been done and that Linus was on the beach disposing of the murder weapon. It fitted. It also explained why he was the first of the group to reach the chapel. He'd have noticed Kurt's parents arrive at the scene and would have heard the ensuing hullabaloo. Fru Jeppsson had screamed, and her husband had been shouting. So, now Anita had to reconsider the timings. While Kurt disappeared into the trees to light up his cigarette, Linus must have made straight for the chapel. He'd found the skewer lying on the beach where it had been left or dropped. Then he must have seen Göran go into the chapel. From where she was standing, she couldn't see the entrance, but she knew it had been possible to do so twenty years before because she had made a note of it at the time. The surrounding bushes had grown up since then. She checked her watch and then strode across the beach towards the steps, which she quickly scaled, and then up the path to the chapel. She was slightly out of breath when she got to the door. She flung it open and stepped inside. Forty-seven seconds. Quick argument; Linus stabs Göran and then leaves. He made his escape up the path, as heard by Kurt. Anita did the same and walked as swiftly as possible without running. She skirted the bell tower and then cut across to the new track. It only took another minute and thirty-three seconds to reach the field. This landscape, too, was completely different now. At the time of the murder, the field was open to the road which ran along the back of the houses. Now, it was heavily fenced off, and the brown ploughed soil of twenty-one years ago had been replaced by neat rows of apple trees burgeoning with fruit, and a carpet of lush green grass. Linus couldn't have hidden the skewer so easily now.

Kurt had been hiding in the wood behind her. Linus must have made his escape before the boy had emerged from the trees nearer the beach. Then Linus must have hung about, maybe in the same clump of trees that Kurt had just vacated, because he hadn't returned to the house. Anita glanced around.

The crime was still doable, only the timings were different. There was no reason to question Nordlund's conclusion that the murderer was Linus Svärd.

Hakim pushed his plate away. He was full. He smiled across at Liv Fogelström, who was still finishing her pizza. He'd had too much of the free salad beforehand. He never learned. Every time they visited this city-centre pizzeria, he made the same mistake. His eyes were too big for his stomach.

'Where do you put it all?' Liv laughed. 'And you're still so skinny. It's just not fair. It just goes straight to my hips.' It was true, but Hakim was too gallant and too in love to confirm her self-assessment. She was on the chubby side. He didn't care. And, to him, she was just so pretty with her blonde hair, bright eyes and bubbly laugh.

'Anyway, have you thought where you'd like to fly to?' he asked as he patted his tummy.

Liv held her knife and fork in mid-air. 'Your sister recommended Tenerife. It'll be hot.' That was a definite attraction as far as Hakim was concerned. This had been a reasonable summer compared with all the rain they had had last year, but a bit of pre-Christmas sunshine would be ideal.

'You're getting quite friendly with Jazmin these days.' The arrangement pleased Hakim, as it diffused the somewhat stressful relationship that he'd had with his sister over the years. They hadn't got on, and his being in the police had just widened the divide. But now that Jazmin was a mother and living with the son of his detective partner, she had mellowed. And Jazmin had taken to Liv. Who wouldn't? She was a popular figure at the polishus. He would now go as far as to say that he and Jazmin were on good terms. For this, his parents were relieved and delighted, though he knew their children's choice of Caucasian partners still caused tension. They would never totally come to terms with the situation.

'Yeah, I like your sister,' Liv beamed. 'I like the way she takes the piss out of you.'

'Oh, thank you,' he gasped, pretending to be hurt.

'You know she's asked me to be the non-religious godmother to Leyla at the naming ceremony?' Heavens! That was quite a step. He knew that Lasse and Jazmin were going to have the ceremony in Pildammsparken to coincide with Anita's birthday at the end of the month. There was going to be a barbecue in the park afterwards. He knew that Anita and his father would end up paying for it, as Leyla's parents hadn't any spare cash. He had offered to help out as well.

'That's quite an honour. But I suppose you're virtually family.'

Liv squinted at him in amusement. 'Am I?'

He shifted uneasily in his seat. Not because the thought was appalling; more that it was appealing. He'd been wondering when to ask Liv to marry him. He didn't want a Jazmin-Lasse situation where they just cohabited. Though he would never say it because the notion would be ridiculed, he didn't really approve of Jazmin starting a family while still unwed. He was more conventional than he would care to admit. He and Liv didn't live together, and he didn't want to until they were at least engaged. And a noisy pizzeria wasn't the place to pop the question.

'Of course you are.'

'I don't think your parents think so.'

And there was the stumbling block. Before he proposed, he would have to talk them round. 'I'll sort things out.'

Liv couldn't finish her pizza. 'I give up.' She took her glass and supped the beer. Silence followed. Liv filled the gap. 'Oh, I passed Anita Sundström coming of out the building tonight. Didn't look very happy.'

'She's been in a mood since that meeting with the new cold case bunch.'

'She's not moving there, surely?'

'No chance,' Hakim grimaced. 'It's the head of the new unit. She's called Alice Zetterberg. They have a "history".'

Liv leaned across the table, her face agog with anticipation. 'Go on, tell all. Like a bit of gossip.'

Hakim shook his head. 'She wouldn't say. All I know is that they were at the Police Academy together.'

'Bet it's a man.'

Hakim returned a sceptical glance. 'Surely not.'

'Trust me; there'll be a man behind it.' Hakim held up his hands in a gesture of surrender. When it came to relationships, romantic or otherwise, Liv definitely had the edge on him. 'You've got to find out the full story.'

'How am I going to do that?'

'You're the detective!' she giggled.

Out on the street, they headed towards the bus stop from where Liv could get a direct bus to her apartment. Hand in hand, they wandered along, taking in the evening crowd. The restaurants and bars were filling up. On reaching the stop, they could see from the electronic board that Liv's bus was due in four minutes.

'I've got the weekend off. Do you fancy going to Ystad on Sunday?' Liv asked expectantly. 'We can go to the beach at Nybrostrand. Or you could treat me to something special at the spa hotel if you want to push the boat out.'

'I'm free, but the train still might not be running after the accident. It'll take ages to clear that up.'

'You're right. Funnily enough, I heard a rumour that there's something strange about the crash.'

'Sounded straightforward enough. An old van had broken down on the crossing. That's what it said on the news earlier.'

'It was about the van. Or the bodies inside. They've released the name of the driver, but not the passengers.'

'I suspect they're so mangled that it would be difficult to identify anyone in that wreckage. Wouldn't like to be working on that job.'

Liv glanced past him. 'It's coming.' A long, green bus snaked into view.

'Found him?'

'No.'

There was silence at the other end of the line.

'What a fucking mess! Right,' the voice was emphatic. 'I want the operation moved. Like now!' it growled.

'Already underway. They'll be over the border within forty-eight hours.'

'Good.' He could hear the relief in the word. 'Are you still there then?'

'Aye. It's better that I operate alone.'

'You understand that not a word of it must come out – ever. You get my drift?'

'Aye, message received.'

'Afterwards, get your arse out fucking quick.' That was a given. 'One last thing: I was never there!'

CHAPTER 9

Danny waited at the edge of the wood. The Volvo hadn't returned. Maybe the younger woman was an occasional visitor. The horses might be hers and the farmer may live on his own. Yet the trainers had been too small. They had to belong to her. All was quiet except for some whinnying. He hadn't heard the tractor this morning, but he could see the barn door was open. He'd been so hungry that he'd wolfed down all the food he'd stolen the day before. In fact, he'd eaten more than he had on any one day in the last few months. Though the work had been hard and physical, they hadn't been given sufficient food to give them the energy to do it. He had never been so thin. His dad wouldn't recognize him now. He realized how skinny he had become when he'd seen his reflection in the window of the van they'd used for their jobs.

He wasn't sure how long he'd waited before he ran over to the barn. The tractor was standing steadfastly in its place, but there was no sign of the Volkswagen. If the farmhouse door wasn't locked, he would have the kitchen to himself. It wasn't, and he let himself in. This time he found a plastic bag, which he proceeded to fill up with food, though making sure he didn't clean the farmer out. Though tempted, he didn't take a half-full bottle of whisky that he'd spotted on the dresser. The schnapps he'd pinched the day before had been a godsend, as he'd been able to bathe his swollen left foot in it. It had stung, and he'd taken a swig to counter the pain. The mouthful of liquor had nearly choked him as it burnt his throat. After his plundering, he sat down on a wooden chair and took in his surroundings. The kitchen was basic but homely; the furniture solid and dependable. Few modern appliances as far as he could see, just a small electric cooker and the fridge. The sink was stone with just one tap, and a hot water geyser was balanced precariously on a bracket above it. There was an ancient stove in one corner, which still had some glowing embers in its grate. There was something comforting about the smell of old wood and the aromas of natural produce and recently cooked meals. It reminded him of his school friend who was a farmer's son: he used to go to play with him, and they'd end up in the farm kitchen where his mother would always have fresh baking on the go. It was a welcoming place, unlike his own home. After his mother's premature death, that had been a battleground, with volleys of abuse fired at him by his dad – and returned in good measure. The bitter skirmishes of his teenage years that no one had won had widened the gap between him and his father that no peacekeeper – in this case his older sister – could resolve. The nine months he'd spent in prison hadn't helped. He sighed at the irony of his last contact with his dad – the brief phone call to say he'd got a good job with prospects of making plenty of money. It had made him feel great – it was his way of shoving all those "get-off-your-arse-and-get-a-proper-fucking-job" jibes down his old man's throat. But if his father could see him now, he'd be the one laughing. That's if he even cared.

Danny had a sudden twinge in his stomach and realized that he needed the toilet. He'd eaten too quickly the day before and his system was unused to so much food. He got up and went in search of the bathroom. The creaking floorboards made him edgy until he reassured himself there was no one in the house. The bathroom emulated the kitchen, with no sign of fripperies. There was a shower in one corner, the grimy plastic head hanging from the wall by a hook; there was no curtain. It was tempting to wash himself properly, but nature was calling urgently.

It was as he was finishing that he heard the car. He frantically pulled up his trousers and went to the window. There was no fancy frosted glass or blind to shield him. The Volvo was coming along the rough track. He pulled back and sneaked another look. The car pulled up in the yard just beyond the bathroom window and out stepped the woman he'd seen the day before. She struck him as older than he'd first thought, probably in her forties. Again he shied away from the window so he couldn't be seen. He didn't dare flush the toilet as any sound would alert her. She disappeared from sight and he heard her coming in the house.

'*Papa!*' she called out. 'Är du hemma?' He could hear her footsteps ringing out on the stone floor of the kitchen. He tiptoed across to the door and flattened himself behind it. What if she came in here? What would he do? Then it happened: the clomping of boots heading towards his hiding place. '*Papa!*' He held his breath as the sound came nearer. She stood for a minute without moving and Danny thought his lungs might burst. There was a heavy sigh just the other side of the door and then the footsteps retreated. Soon there was the sound of the back door loudly swinging shut. He gingerly made his way back to the window. He caught sight of her disappearing towards the barn. He waited, still unable to flush the toilet in case she returned.

He must have been there about fifteen or twenty minutes when he was alerted by the heavy clopping of a horse's hooves on the cobbled yard. He stood up and saw the farmer's daughter on the grey. A couple of light kicks to the animal's flanks, and off it trotted. He flushed the toilet.

Alice Zetterberg sat staring at the suspect board while she waited for her team to arrive for the prearranged morning meeting. She wasn't sure what to make of the case. She knew that this was a perfect opportunity to get one over on Anita Sundström. Coming across her two years earlier had been an unpleasant surprise, yet she had been able to manipulate that situation and reactivate a career that she had hoped would achieve so much, yet at the time seemed to have reached an impasse. The upshot was her present role and a solid stepping stone to more senior advancement. "They" owed her that. She knew things about the fate of Albin Rylander that no government would ever want revealed. As long as they looked after her, she was happy. It seemed a lifetime ago that she and Anita had been friends at the Police Academy. Looking through the bitter prism of time, she had to admit that she had never really liked Anita from the outset. If she were honest, she had befriended her because she was one of the most attractive young women on the course and, as such, was popular with the men. Anita gave her a social outlet and through her she had met and fallen in love with Arne. And then the blonde girl with the fancy arse that seemed to obsess all the guys had jumped into bed with him! When she'd confronted Arne, he'd just shrugged, as though sleeping with Anita was a totally natural thing to do – a rite of passage – and it was ridiculous to blame him. Of course, Anita had denied it. The slut and the shit! Despite it all, Alice had married Arne because she couldn't face living without him. And then a couple of years into their posting in Norrköping, he'd buggered off with Juni, who just happened to be another friend of Anita's from the Academy. It wouldn't have surprised her if Anita hadn't engineered the whole situation. Alice had gone off the rails for a while, had slept around – lashing out at Arne, she reckoned – and her career stalled. Now her new unit's first case was a chance for further revenge. Prove that Anita and her team had been wrong, and then the inadequacies of the original investigation would be publicly aired in court.

The fact that Linus Svärd had been thrown to the wolves of the press would be a further humiliation for Sundström. The only worry was that Linus Svärd could still be guilty, and she might end up exonerating her rival and confirming the findings of Nordlund's team. That was one bridge she would have to cross if and when she came to it. Whatever the outcome, she was sure there would be some spin she could put on it which would show Anita in a poor light. Another consideration, and one that even Zetterberg had to admit was just as, if not more, important than scoring over Sundström, was that she had been given six months to prove that the unit was worth investing in. Success with this case would lead to the promise of more resources, more manpower and, ultimately, more influence.

Szabo and Erlandsson came in armed with laptops and took their places. Szabo had thoughtfully brought Alice a coffee as well. He would go far if he played his cards right and did as he was told. Once they had settled, Zetterberg opened proceedings.

'OK. We've had a good recce of the murder scene and the village. So you can both picture the location and where the various participants were – or weren't – according to the first investigation. At the moment, I've got an open mind as to the identity of the killer because the evidence we have now creates a slightly different timeline for Linus's movements. Did he have time to come up from the beach and kill Göran between being seen by Kurt and Kurt hearing the killer leaving the chapel? Now, if we take Linus's original statement at face value, it's unlikely that they had a prearranged meeting, so was it just coincidence that Göran just happened to go into the chapel? And Linus being the first of the group to turn up at the murder scene – is that significant? If he *was* the killer, he would have had to go all the way up to the field to get rid of the murder weapon. So why did he come back so quickly? His prompt arrival on the scene made him appear suspicious because the original team thought he'd come up from the beach, having got rid of the murder weapon there. But now we know that wasn't the case. With this new scenario, wouldn't it have made more sense to make himself scarce? Or certainly have a better alibi?'

'Maybe he just didn't have time,' suggested Erlandsson. 'Spur of the moment.' Zetterberg frowned. She could see that Erlandsson's previous affiliation with Anita might mean that she would be biased towards proving her colleague had been right.

'Everything is open to question at this stage,' she said sharply. 'But it's no use speculating too much. What we need to do is re-interview the five living members of the group. Have we tracked them all down?'

'We've got Ivar Hagblom living up in Uppsala.' Szabo spoke very deliberately, making the information clear and concise. 'He's a university professor now and appears a lot on the TV talking about the Middle East. Needless to say, he's been on frequently over the last year or so. Whenever Syria's mentioned, or the immigrant crisis, out he comes. Domestically, he's been married twice. Two kids by his first wife. They live with their mother, but he sees them regularly.'

'So, he and Larissa Bjerstedt must have split up at some point after the murder,' interjected Zetterberg.

'I don't know when exactly. But he first married in 1999. At that point, he'd got his doctorate and was lecturing in Lund. Moved to Uppsala a couple of years later. So, they couldn't have lasted too much longer after the murder if he was married within four years.'

'We'll ask Larissa. Where's she then?'

Szabo continued: 'Larissa Bjerstedt. She's still here in Malmö. As far as we can see, she's never married. Of course, she may be living with someone. She worked as a researcher for a documentary company here in Malmö for a few years and then in various libraries, including a short spell up in Uppsala which will have coincided with Ivar moving there with his new wife. Right now she's based at the Malmö University Library. Been there since 2010. No criminal record. Pays taxes on time. Clean driving licence. Sounds pretty dull to me considering her ex-partner is now a high-profile figure.'

'And what about our other well-known personality?' Zetterberg's eyes bored into Erlandsson. 'Your precious crime writer.'

Erlandsson spoke confidently. She wasn't going to let her new boss intimidate her. 'Carina Lindvall lives in Norra Langö, Stockholm County. She's been a full-time writer for several years with a series of novels about Stockholm detective, Erik Dahlberg, and, according to her website, a TV company is interested in turning them into a new cop show. The books have been translated into twenty-one languages, and she often travels abroad on book tours and to attend crime-writing festivals. She's not married at the moment, though she's managed to get through two husbands. No kids. No criminal record as such, but has had a couple of run-ins with paparazzi; she broke a photographer's camera outside a nightclub in Gothenburg. Owns an apartment on Malta. Often goes there for winter sun and a quiet place to write, apparently.'

Zetterberg pointed to the photo of Lars-Gunnar Lerstorp. 'What about Carina's ex-boyfriend?'

'He's more interesting,' continued Erlandsson, 'because he does have a criminal record. He was into drugs in a big way, particularly after the murder. Really went into freefall. Went from user to supplier and was arrested three times for theft in between. Had a period in prison 1997/1998. Then he seems to have got himself sorted out on a rehabilitation programme and is now married with two children and lives in Veberöd. He's a postman working out of Ystad. Hasn't been in any trouble since. Seems to have turned into a model citizen and even goes to groups to try and help other addicts.'

Zetterberg mustered a half-grin. 'Presumably he was into drugs at the time of the murder, so maybe he was high that night. I expect they all indulged. Those types do,' she added disapprovingly. 'He's got no alibi. Off his head – does something drastic. Interesting that he went downhill after the murder. Ah well, that gives us something to go on.' Zetterberg planted a finger on the photo of Linus Svärd with some force. 'And the chief suspect?'

Szabo came in this time. 'Drawn a blank as to his whereabouts. Inspector Sundström was correct about his being in Malmö and then Kiruna before going off to Syria. We've tracked him to various university excavations round the Mediterranean, and he turned up in Egypt at one stage and then in Sicily. But nothing since 2010.'

'Keep digging in the digs.' Szabo realized this was his boss's idea of wit, so smirked appreciatively. 'Maybe when we talk to the others, one of them may know where he is.'

'What if Linus is already dead?' Szabo asked.

'It won't stop us finding out the truth,' Zetterberg said fiercely. There was no way she was going to let her first case with her new team turn into a non-event. 'We can still prove he did it or didn't do it, as the case may be. It'll just be harder. But hopefully, he's alive and we find him. And anyway, it's better to speak to the others first and eliminate them before we tackle Linus.' She stood in front of them and put her fists resolutely on her hips as though looking for an argument. 'What we need to establish is whether any of these five gained by Göran's death. Maybe something that wasn't obvious at the time has become apparent since. I don't know... something like Göran had the original idea for Carina's crime novels. That's not a good example, but you know what I mean. Maybe the motive is not emotional, sexual... whatever. What I propose is that we divide up the initial interviews. You two can take Larissa and Lars-Gunnar down here, and I'll head up to Stockholm and Uppsala and speak to Carina and Ivar. Can you arrange that, Szabo?'

Szabo nodded. 'No problem.' Erlandsson's immediate suspicion was that Zetterberg wanted to meet the more glamorous suspects while they got the less interesting ones. She had been hoping to meet Carina Lindvall herself.

'Right,' Zetterberg said brusquely, 'let's find our murderer.

CHAPTER 10

'I knew he'd come to a bad end!'

Moberg's delight was obvious. He had bounced into Anita's office in the middle of her showing Hakim the latest photos of Leyla on her phone. Hakim wasn't disappointed at the interruption and wondered if he would ever end up cooing over kids. He was sure that Liv would.

'Who?' asked Anita, who was slightly annoyed, as she hadn't reached the photo that she was particularly keen to show off.

'Egon Fuentes!' Anita and Hakim glanced at each other uncomprehendingly. It was clear that neither had the faintest idea who the chief inspector was referring to. 'He's a bastard with a past. And luckily, no future.'

'Fuentes isn't a very Swedish name,' observed Anita.

'Grandfather was a Spanish sailor who berthed in Malmö and never left. More's the pity.'

'I gather he's dead.'

'You bet. He was one of the three guys who were hit by the train the other night. He's the only one that they've managed to name so far because he was the only one with identification on him.' Moberg had his hands shoved in his trouser pockets and was rocking back and forth on his feet. He was like a swaying mountain. Anita felt she would be safer if he sat down, but he seemed too excited to do that.

'I assume he has a record?'

'Oh, yes. As long as the fucking Öresund Bridge.'

'And what was he doing at the level crossing?' asked Hakim, who felt that the chief inspector wanted some prompting.

'Good question, Mirza. What was he doing? Up to no fucking good, that's what he was doing.'

'Specifically?' questioned Anita.

'I have no idea. Yet.'

'So, what's Fuentes' background?'

The gleam in Moberg's eyes flitted away. 'He's a conman. Was a conman. He could talk anybody into buying anything. Especially the vulnerable. The old in particular. He started in petty crime. Thieving mainly. Did a couple of short stretches before moving on to bigger stuff. He used his charm. He got into lots of scams. Fake time-share holiday homes in Spain, an internet dating site for mature people, flogging dud gems, investing in sustainable forests in Costa Rica – you name it, Fuentes has done it. Where I came across him was insurance fraud. His big mistake was swindling my old mamma out of her life savings.'

'Personal,' observed Anita dryly.

'Damn right. I hunted the shit down. The money was gone, but he did time. Not enough for the harm and distress he caused to so many innocent folk. He must have kept a low profile since getting out, as his path hasn't crossed mine until this morning.'

'Maybe he was going straight.'

Moberg's bark of laughter dismissed Anita's suggestion.

'People like Egon Fuentes don't know how to go straight. It's not in their DNA. I want to know what the fucker was up to. So, Anita, would you like to accompany me to visit his widow and pay our last respects?'

Danny Foster was sitting by the stream washing his face. He'd taken his top off and was splashing the cold water under his armpits and round the back of his neck. He hadn't had a shower or bath for months and was contemplating sneaking back into the farmhouse to have a proper wash. Though that in itself might be dangerous. After his two foraging visits, the farmer must be aware that his food was disappearing. Mind you, he looked old, so his memory might not be brilliant.

The water was bracing as he rubbed it over his now-wiry frame. He had been chunkier before he had started all the graft laying drives and patios for people who probably didn't want them. They weren't going to quibble when McNaught was around. The thought of the Scot made him shiver, even though it was warm that morning. Where was the bastard? Then he heard the crack of a twig behind him and swung round. Was it him?

Standing next to the tree nearest him was a man brandishing a shotgun. Danny was paralyzed by fear. He couldn't move from his crouched position. It was the farmer. The rough-hewn face was of a man who spent his life in the elements. He wore an old baseball cap which shielded his eyes, so Danny couldn't register his reactions. Over the last few months he had got used to studying eyes; the fear and confusion in those of the people he had worked with – and the hardness and cruelty in those of whom they had worked for. The farmer had a day's growth of grey stubble around his chin. He was dressed for work in a faded, light-blue shirt with rolled-up sleeves, and a pair of brown trousers equally well worn. The boots were newer. Danny reckoned he'd been right on his first sighting; he was probably in his seventies.

'*Vad gör du här?*' he asked in Swedish. Danny didn't comprehend.

When no answer came, the farmer waved the shotgun at him. '*Vem är du? Vad gör du på min mark?*'

Danny raised his arms as though in surrender to show

that he had no aggressive intent. He twigged that the farmer wanted to know what he was doing in his wood. 'I'm Danny. My name is Danny.' He spoke slowly so that the farmer could understand him. 'I am English.'

'English?' the farmer repeated. He didn't move, as though weighing up this young intruder on his land. He crooked the shotgun under his right arm and peered forward, revealing his bushy eyebrows. He could see the red wheals across the flesh and purple patterns of multiple bruises all over the young man's torso. With his free hand he waved for Danny to follow him.

Danny picked up his T-shirt and, cautiously, followed the farmer, who had lowered his shotgun. For a split second he thought he should run for it. Would the farmer turn him in to the police? With no passport or form of identification, he could be in serious trouble. Would they dig up his previous police record in England? And what would he tell them? What he had seen? They wouldn't believe him. Worse still, he might even be returned to the camp if that weaselly Swede with the silver tongue managed to talk them into handing him over. Then his life would be finished. McNaught and the others knew what he had seen. But the gun banished all thoughts of escape. The farmer looked like someone who knew how to use it. And Danny was tired and frightened.

The farmer didn't say another word until they'd reached his back door. Danny was already familiar with what was inside.

'Come,' said the farmer, indicating that he should go in.

Once in the kitchen, he indicated that Danny should sit down at the table. He left him there for a few moments before returning without the shotgun.

'Coffee?' the farmer said in English.

So no police. Not yet anyway. 'Yes. Yes, please.'

The farmer busied himself with getting the coffee out and soon had it bubbling away.

'Me, Leif,' he said pointing to himself. 'You Danny?'

'That's right. I'm Danny.' It wasn't much, but it was a long time since someone had talked to him in an unthreatening way. No more was said until the coffee was poured and a steaming mug was placed in front of Danny. It was black, but Danny thought it would seem ungrateful if he asked for some milk. Besides, he'd already drunk most of that.

The farmer sat down opposite and cast an eye over the nervous young man who was cradling his mug of coffee. He could sense the fear and desperation. He knew it must have been this fellow who had taken food from the fridge. And his shoes. He was wearing them. He hadn't told his daughter about the missing items, as she would think that he was just imagining things. She was already darkly muttering words like "dementia" and "Alzheimer's", and that maybe it was time to give up the farm. Where would her horses be stabled? She would find somewhere. What he would do without the farm and its reassuring seasonal routines, he had no idea. She certainly hadn't offered to let him move in with her and her husband in Malmö. That would be far too inconvenient. It would interfere with their hectic social lives. Her only suggestion was an old folk's home in Hörby. Well, bugger that! They would have to carry him off the farm, boots first. So, what was he to do with this Englishman who had been badly mistreated? Shouldn't the police know?

'Polis?'

There was instant alarm in Danny's croaked 'No!' He put down his coffee. 'Please. No police.' Danny's pleading unnerved Leif. What awful things had happened here in Sweden that had had such an effect on this poor youngster?

'OK.' Leif waggled his index finger at Danny. 'Your body. Who did?'

Danny grimaced. 'Bad men. They beat me. And the others. They make us work so hard.' Leif couldn't figure out who these people could be. He had heard of gangs from Russia and Eastern Europe operating in Sweden. But why was an English boy here in such a state? This didn't fit into his idea of Britain: so cultured, so civilized, so important in this world with such a famous royal family. This Danny needed help.

'Food?' Leif suggested. Danny nodded gratefully. 'We eat. Eating is good, no?'

Helga Fuentes' apartment block was at the top of a grassy bank above Hyllievångsvägen. She lived on the fifth floor with a yapping dog. Not that Anita and Moberg saw the dog because they never got beyond the threshold. Helga was about fifty, but looked older. She might have been quite attractive before she let herself go. But now, seemingly oblivious to how undignified she looked, she was wearing a tight, red top and skirt that only highlighted the bulges. Her lipstick matched her clothes; it was badly applied and there was far too much of it. Her blue eyeshadow was equally gaudy and had the effect of making her look like a bad drag artist. Moberg had explained to Anita in the car that Helga Fuentes was German and Egon had picked her up in Spain during his time-share days. Whatever he had promised to get her to move to Sweden and marry him had not matched the brochure, and now she was trapped in a country she quite obviously disliked.

'You've got a fucking nerve coming round here.' Her German accent was already fighting with the Swedish vowels, and now had the slurs generated by her morning tipple to contend with. 'You put him away, and I was left in the shit in this arsehole of a place.' Anita was surprised that Moberg let her continue her rant – which was punctuated with the occasional backward glance and yelling at the dog to shut up – without getting annoyed or shouting back. When she had finished, he spoke:

'Do you know what Egon's been up to lately?'

'Of course I fucking don't.'

'Are you sure?'

'I kicked that good-for-nothing shyster out of here two years ago. What could he offer me other than even more grief?'

'You lived very nicely off his endless scams.'

'And it was you who put an end to that!' she said fiercely. 'So you can piss off with your tart here and if you see that wanker of a husband of mine, tell him to go screw himself.'

As they made their way back to the car, Anita said. 'Shouldn't you have told her that her husband's dead?'

'She'll find out soon enough when it gets into the papers. Loathing Egon is probably the only thing that keeps her going. I didn't want to spoil it for her.'

'I'm sure she'll quickly replace loathing him with loathing you and the rest of Sweden.'

'True.'

Danny let the water cascade over his weary body. It was a wonderful sensation even if it wasn't the hottest or strongest of showers. In fact, it was very basic. Yet as he rubbed the soap suds over his chest, he wasn't totally at ease. He wasn't sure if he could trust Leif. He had seemed sympathetic. But he *had* mentioned the police, and Danny didn't want to stay in the shower too long in case the old farmer was ringing for help while he was in the bathroom. Despite Leif's limited English, they had been able to communicate. And the old man had been thoughtful and cooked him the best meal he had had in months – and he'd given him a beer from his larder. Could have been colder, but Danny could hardly complain. As he'd tucked into his chicken, he had been overcome with guilt that he had been robbing this man who was showing such kindness toward him.

He gathered from Leif that his daughter came up a couple of times a week to ride her horses. Other than that, he had few visitors. That was reassuring from Danny's point of view. He still had no idea what his next move was to be. He couldn't stay here forever. And he certainly wasn't going to stay in the farmhouse, as Leif had suggested. It was too much like waiting in a trap, to be sprung at any moment by McNaught or the police. He would remain in his makeshift camp. There he could hear any approach, though he chided himself that he hadn't heard Leif with his shotgun; that was sloppy. But he wouldn't be caught off his guard again. He had reached the point of distrusting everyone – and that included Leif. He knew he would have to make a decision on his next move before Sunday because Leif's daughter would be back to see to her horses. How would *she* react to some stranger hanging around her dad's isolated farm? She would definitely be on to the authorities.

He turned off the shower and swept the water from his hair, which was getting quite long. He took the towel that Leif had produced. It must have survived years of washing. It felt coarse against his back and thighs. What would he give for a fluffy towel and soft sheets to sleep in? In between the hard physical graft and the constant fear, it had been thoughts of home comforts that he had taken for granted when he was younger that he yearned for. What a silly shite he'd been!

'Well, Helga was a waste of time. I'd heard she'd chucked him out, but Egon's the type to go crawling back if he's in a spot of bother.' Moberg's head was almost touching the car roof, and he had to hunch slightly over the wheel in order to see through the windscreen. 'Which means that he *was* up to something if he hadn't gone back.'

'She could have been lying,' Anita suggested. She would have felt happier if she had been doing the driving, as Moberg tended to try and talk at her instead of keeping his eye on the road.

'I had plenty of dealings with Helga in the past. She was careful not to get too involved with Egon's activities, so when we came calling, we had nothing on her, though she knew exactly what had been going on. I don't think she'd let herself get involved with him again.'

'You know we shouldn't be doing any of this. It isn't our case. Presumably Ystad are looking into it.'

'It'll come our way. The vehicle is Malmö registered, and the only identifiable victim is from here. And if I can find out what he was up to, they'll have to give us the investigation. If necessary, I'll bully the commissioner.' This really was personal. Not that Anita had time to dwell on the fact, as Moberg then tried to light a cigarette while negotiating the traffic. After a couple of curses, he succeeded, but not before he was honked at by an irate driver who had had to take quick, evasive action. Moberg yelled back, totally unjustifiably in Anita's eyes. She hadn't been this nervous in a car since she'd taken Lasse out for a spin when he was learning to drive. It had only happened once. A bottle of red wine had been opened early that night.

'Where are we going?' she asked anxiously as she realized that the chief inspector was not heading back to headquarters.

'Limhamn.'

'Bit posh for this sort of investigation,' Anita observed dryly.

'The miscreant I'm after doesn't *live* there. Could never afford it. Well, certainly not after I got his number.' His spluttered laugh almost propelled his cigarette out of his mouth. His fat lips managed to hang on to it. 'He works there, stacking shelves at ICA on Linnégatan.'

As they turned off Lorensborgsgatan onto Rudbecksgatan, with its neat rows of bungalows and their well-tended gardens set back from the street, Moberg asked her how she had got on with Inspector Zetterberg.

'Have you come across her?' He shook his head, his bull neck quivering slightly. 'She seems hell bent on proving that

Henrik Nordlund and the team were going after the wrong man.'

'Has something changed?'

Anita gazed out of the window, her eye catching a tall, thin flagpole in the garden they were passing. The blue and yellow Swedish flag hung limply in the sunshine. 'They've found the murder weapon. And a witness has come forward. Actually, it was someone who we spoke to at the time. A ten-year-old boy. Now he remembers events differently.'

Moberg blew a cloud of smoke out of his mouth. Now that she didn't touch cigarettes, or even snus, Anita was beginning to find the smell intrusive and unpleasant. She feared she was turning into a smoking fascist. 'Does it make any difference to Henrik's conclusion?'

'Not as far as I'm concerned. It's still Linus Svärd. It always was.'

He glanced across at her. 'I hope for your sake you're right. I've not met this woman, but I've heard things around the polishus. She sounds like a political manoeuvrer who'll make the most of the situation if she finds Svärd wasn't responsible; even more so if she discovers who was. Then, knowing him, the commissioner will want to be seen to instigate an enquiry into the first investigation, and Henrik's name – and yours – will be dragged through the mud.'

'It's not as though it'll turn out to be a miscarriage of justice. No one was ever arrested for the killing.'

'All the same, be warned!' He took another puff. 'And don't get involved because you'll only make it personal. And that always clouds your judgement.'

Cheeky sod! Anita couldn't believe it. 'What's all this with Egon Fuentes then if it's not personal?' she protested.

Without batting an eyelid, he said: 'That's different.'

Adolf Frid was a man in his fifties. He had a greying beard

and thinning hair. Anita would have described his eyes and demeanour in general as shifty, but that may have had something to do with the hulking presence of Chief Inspector Moberg. Frid wore a red ICA top and black trousers. Anita hoped that he wasn't touching unpackaged food, as his hands could have been cleaner. They had wandered through the store before being shown to the back, where Frid was found moving boxes. Anita sensed that Frid's first instinct on seeing Moberg was to run. But he thought better of it, and they all retired to the car park behind the store and stood in the sunshine near the covered walkway. About half the parking spaces were filled; this wasn't their busiest time. Moberg offered Frid a cigarette, which was refused. Moberg lit up.

'Inspector Sundström, may I introduce you to my lowlife friend, Adolf Frid?'

Frid fidgeted nervously. 'I hope this won't take long, Chief Inspector. People here don't know—'

'—that you're a lying, good-for-nothing loser. But you're *my* lying, good-for- nothing loser.'

'You shouldn't come to my work.'

'Well, I'm not going to go to that shithole you call an apartment. Inspector Sundström has got sensibilities. Besides,' he said, waving an arm up in the air. 'It's a beautiful day. You should try and get out more; you look like a ghost.'

'What do you want?' Frid pressed his hands together.

'What's the hurry?' Moberg was enjoying Frid's discomfort. 'Let me acquaint you with my relationship to Adolf Frid, Inspector Sundström. I came across my friend here nearly thirty years ago. He was one of the first people I nicked. Petty thief. Our paths crossed fairly frequently after that, but he did little to strike fear into the citizens of Malmö until he fell in with one Egon Fuentes. Egon had big plans and even bigger scams, and Adolf here was a willing accomplice. But then Adolf had a sudden epiphany – with the help of a bit of persuasion – and did the dirty on Egon in exchange for a lighter sentence. Since then he has occasionally produced the odd bit of information that has proved useful to the Skåne County Police. That's about right, isn't it Adolf?'

Frid mumbled something unintelligible. He was clearly cowed by Moberg, and Anita could well imagine what sort of "persuasion" Frid had been subjected to all those years ago.

'Actually, the aforesaid Egon Fuentes is the reason I'm here.'

'Haven't seen him for ages.' Frid's answer came too quickly. But Anita assumed that it might be true if Frid had fingered Fuentes. Moberg quickly disillusioned her.

'That seems odd because, you see,' Moberg said in an aside to Anita, 'Adolf's squealing didn't come out in court. We made sure of that so he would be useful to us in the future. No crook likes a grass, so Adolf has been under my protection.' He put a far-from-friendly hand on Frid's shoulder. Frid twitched. 'I want to know what Egon has been up to.'

'Ask him yourself.' At least Frid was capable of some resistance.

Moberg's resting fingers suddenly squeezed Frid's shoulder and he gave a little yelp. Anita's natural inclination was to intervene, but she knew that would only make Moberg more aggressive. The chief inspector withdrew his hand. 'I'm sorry, Adolf. Old habits. Policing is not so hands-on these days; I can see Inspector Sundström doesn't approve.' The comment was laced with sarcasm. He returned to his cigarette before he spoke again. 'You see, Adolf, I've got a problem. I can't ask Egon directly because he's dead.'

'He's dead!' parroted Frid as though he couldn't actually believe what he was saying.

''Fraid so.'

'Who killed him?'

'That's interesting,' said Moberg as he pushed his face

close to Frid's. 'Why do you assume he was killed? He could have died of a heart attack in the street. Or drowned saving someone's pet cat. Your reaction says a lot about the company that Egon kept. But he actually died in a traffic accident. The van he was driving was hit by a train.'

'That accident over at Svarte?'

'The very same.'

'Poor bugger.' Anita could tell he was shocked. And also a trifle relieved?

'But what we want to know is what he was doing in the van in the first place. What was he up to?'

'How would I know?' Frid's eyes were cast firmly on the tarmac beneath his feet.

'You know what's going on, Adolf. That's how you supplement your wages from this place. And you wouldn't want me to have a word with the manager and tell him about some of the stuff you've been up to over the years, would you?'

'The management know I've been inside.'

Moberg grinned. 'I'm sure you got a good reference from your probation officer, but I could fill in some of the gaps. I'm sure you're not above a bit of pilfering in there.' Moberg inclined his head towards the store.

'OK, OK. I saw Egon a few weeks ago. I just bumped into him, totally out of the blue.'

'I believe you.' Moberg obviously didn't.

'Said he was sort of going straight.'

'What the hell does "sort of going straight" mean?'

'It was bordering on illegal, I suppose.'

'Any idea what *it* was?'

'Not entirely sure, but it was something to do with building.'

'Not another housing scam?'

Frid shook his head firmly. 'Not like that. But they were certainly getting stuff from a dodgy building supplier.' He held up a hand as though he thought Moberg was going to strike him. 'And before you ask, I don't know who the supplier was.'

'You said "they"?'

'He was with some kind of gang.'

'Local?'

'No. No. Abroad.'

'Russian? Croatian? Iraqi?'

'From Britain. Or Ireland. Yes, something to do with Ireland.'

Moberg flicked away his cigarette. 'I can't see Egon getting his hands dirty on a building site. Not his style.' Frid didn't have an explanation, or one that he was willing to share.

'And that's all you know?' Moberg flashed a sceptical squint.

'Honest, Chief Inspector. That's all I know. But he was making good money. He paid for my *fika*.'

CHAPTER 11

Alice Zetterberg relaxed in her seat in wagon 4 of the Malmö to Stockholm train. She was relieved to escape the south for a while and a city she no longer had much love for. Its pretence of cosmopolitanism would never match the sophistication of Stockholm. She strove, however, to keep her resentment in check; she reminded herself that the Cold Case Group was a stepping stone to better things. Her goal was a senior position with the National Police based in Stockholm. That was where everything of any consequence took place. Besides, such elevation, if it were ever realized, would cock a snook at her snooty sister. Linnea had always been the high achiever in the family. She was now working as an advisor to the Ministry of Foreign Affairs and was involved in high-level decision-making policy. As a mere police inspector, Alice couldn't compete, yet she knew secrets that even officials at her sister's level would never be party to. That was gratifying up to a point. Telling Linnea what she knew would be even more satisfying, though she understood she would never be able to. On the other hand, that knowledge could well propel her to the top, and she would be able to look her sister in the eye as an equal. The truth was that she didn't really like Linnea. She had always been jealous of her younger sibling. Her elder brother, Morgan, had been useless and no competition at all. They had never got on, and she was relieved more than anything else that they hadn't communicated for at least five years. He was wasting his life in some crappy school in Karlstad. Alice was only staying with her sister on this trip because it was convenient, and Linnea lived in a nice house in a good area of the city with her husband, Christer, and their two children, Linda and Louise. Having both the girls' names beginning with an L was so twee; Linnea's idea, of course. However, it was Christer who was the real attraction of the weekend. He, too, was a government employee, but was more approachable than Linnea. He had always shown an interest in Alice's police career and would be impressed that she was playing an integral part in solving a twenty-one-year-old mystery involving some interesting suspects. After her own unsuccessful marriage and a string of broken relationships, Alice had set her sights on Christer. She would love to steal him away from her sister, but she knew he was too fond of the children to put his marriage in jeopardy. That didn't mean that she hadn't stopped trying, and she had come close to seducing him on a couple of drunken occasions. She'd even managed to get her hand down his pants, and it had produced a reaction that she had played over in her mind many times since. He'd tried to laugh it off, but she knew she was getting closer to her objective. It would be another secret that she could keep that would make her feel superior to her sister.

The train moved quickly beyond Lund and the rich farmland of Skåne. After Hassleholm, it was sucked into the Sweden of endless pine forests, shimmering lakes, orderly towns and impossibly neat villages. It was the Sweden she was comfortable in. This was going to be a good few days. She hoped the train wouldn't be late; just a couple of months before, the Stockholm to Malmö train had been stuck for six hours. Such delays were becoming more frequent these days – one aspect of modern Sweden even she couldn't blame Anita, immigrants or her ex-husband for.

Szabo and Erlandsson approached Larissa Bjerstedt, who was working behind a computer screen in the university library.

As Larissa glanced up enquiringly, she took off her large-framed glasses and let them dangle from a cord round her neck. Erlandsson noticed that she had lost a lot of her youthful beauty. Gone was the perfect skin and flowing tresses from the photograph on their board; the hair was now cropped short and there were crow's feet around the eyes. The features were harder. But the smile was still bright as she asked: 'Can I help you?'

Szabo whipped out his warrant card. 'Inspector Anders Szabo and Inspector Bea Erlandsson,' nodding in his colleague's direction.

'Police?' Larissa said in some alarm.

'Nothing to worry about. We just need to have a little chat.'

'Has there been trouble with the students?'

'No. We're from the Cold Case Group. It's about Göran Gösta.'

The colour seemed to drain from Larissa's face. 'My God, not that again. After all these years.'

'Yes.' Szabo looked around. Though the library was fairly empty at this time of year because of the summer vacation, he decided there might be a more conducive location for such a potentially upsetting conversation.

Larissa seemed to read his thoughts. 'Let's go to the café.'

Five minutes later, they were settled down in a quiet area with a huge picture window offering unrestricted views over the old quayside and the lighthouse. Away to the right stretched the docks.

To the left, high, modern buildings now blocked the view of the Turning Torso. Erlandsson reflected that this part of town was turning into a mini Manhattan. It was Larissa who opened proceedings.

'So, why now? It's been over twenty years.'

'New evidence has come to light,' explained Erlandsson.

'What new evidence?'

'I'm afraid we can't reveal that at the moment,' cut in Szabo, 'but it's enough to re-examine the case. That's why we need to talk to all of you who were staying in the house in Knäbäckshusen in the summer of 1995.'

'All of us?'

'Yeah.'

Larissa shifted in her seat, her hands clasped on her lap. 'OK.'

Szabo kicked off with: 'Can you describe the events of the day of the murder?'

'Well, I won't forget it in a hurry. It was a nice day, so we agreed to have another barbecue on the beach. They were always fun. Usually we had too much booze, and the food would get burnt, but we didn't care. We were young. Lars-Gunnar would bring his guitar and sing a bit. We'd join in. Badly, in Linus's case.' She grinned to herself at the memory.

'But Linus probably wasn't singing that day,' prompted Erlandsson.

'No,' Larissa replied thoughtfully. 'Not that day.'

'So, what went wrong at the barbecue?' asked Szabo with some vehemence. 'In the original file there were reports from other witnesses on the beach of an argument.'

'Linus and Göran had a falling out big time. Mind you, looking back, it had been a long time coming. Linus was nuts about Göran, but Göran had started to lose interest.'

'We heard that his affections had been transferred to your boyfriend at the time, Ivar Hagblom.'

Larissa smirked. 'He couldn't have picked on a more heterosexual guy. It was never going to go anywhere.'

'Did it cause Ivar any problems?' asked Erlandsson.

'You're joking. Obviously you haven't met Ivar. He takes people worshipping him for granted. They just got on as normal.'

'Back to that day...' Szabo was showing a hint of impatience.

'Well, the tension that had been brewing between Linus and Göran boiled over. Of course, it was some silly remark someone made that kicked it all off. Can't remember who said what, but the result was Linus taking a hissy fit and charging off down the beach. I didn't see him again until the rumpus of finding Göran's body. Needless to say, the argument killed our party on the beach and we all drifted away. Sorry, no pun intended.'

'Right. Now you said in your original statement that your alibi for the time of the murder was that you and Ivar were together in your bedroom.' Szabo flicked his mop of hair back. 'Do you still stick by that?'

'You mean were we fucking? I may be getting older and not have as clear a memory as I once had, but you don't forget being screwed by Ivar.'

'That's very candid.' Szabo wasn't sure if he was embarrassed or slightly excited.

'I can't put it any other way.'

'So, what was the first you knew of the murder?'

'When Carina came into our room. I found out afterwards that it must have been about half an hour after the body was discovered.'

'And had you seen Linus between the time he left the barbecue and the period after the murder?'

'No. He told us that he had gone up the hill at Stenshuvud and sat up there deciding what to do with his life. He then came back to the beach later on. He heard the commotion at the chapel. That young kid had found Göran and alerted his parents. Can't remember his name.'

'Kurt,' Erlandsson added helpfully.

'Anyway, Linus said he'd stayed with the body until the cops showed up.'

'And how did Linus react to Göran's death?' Szabo

watched Larissa intently as he knew it was a vital question.

Larissa spread her hands. 'He seemed beside himself with grief. We couldn't get him to calm down afterwards.' She seemed to have nothing more to add.

Szabo peered at the notebook he was holding. 'Can we go back to when you think things started to go wrong with their relationship?'

Larissa stared out of the window as though seeking inspiration, or maybe she was just gathering her thoughts together. 'Probably Malta.' She nodded confirmation. 'Malta. We spent a month there earlier that year. There was nothing specific, but I got the feeling that maybe not all was well between them.'

'And the group as a whole?' This was Erlandsson.

'What do you mean?'

'I was just wondering... as there was growing tension between Linus and Göran, and Göran's attentions were turning to your boyfriend, it might have affected the group dynamic.'

Larissa waved away the suggestion. 'No. There was nothing like that. We just got on as per usual. It was just that Göran was tetchy with Linus, that's all. All relationships go through periods like that.'

'Why did you all go to Malta?' Szabo queried.

'Winter sun, basically. We'd all met up in Lund for New Year. After plenty of booze and moaning about Swedish winters, Ivar announced that he fancied going to Malta. So everybody else drunkenly agreed. We had a good time.'

'Carina Lindvall has an apartment there,' Erlandsson said.

'Does she?' Larissa seemed genuinely surprised.

'You didn't know?'

Larissa shook her head.

'Are you still in touch with any of the others?' Szabo asked.

She almost winced when replying. 'No, not really. I did

bump into Lars-Gunnar a few years ago in Triangeln. He had a little child in tow.'

'He's got two now.'

'Lucky him.'

'Got over his drug problems, too.'

'Yes, I could see that. I was pleased for him. We did the usual thing of promising to meet up for a proper chat. But it never happened. You know how things drift.'

'Carina?'

'Carina Lindvall, Queen of Crime,' she said mockingly. 'She's done all right for herself. I've not seen her since the Christmas after the murder. She split up with Lars-Gunnar shortly after that and disappeared up her own arse; or to Stockholm anyway. When I was working in public libraries, I used to have all these old dears coming up and asking if Carina's latest gruesome crime book was out yet.'

Szabo and Erlandsson exchanged a quick glance. Carina and Larissa must have fallen out.

'And Ivar Hagblom? When did that finish?' Szabo was intrigued as to how this would come out.

Larissa smiled sweetly. 'The following year. After the murder, I mean. I think it affected us all in different ways. Things could never be the same again. In my case with Ivar, it just came to a natural end. We wanted different things out of life. He had his sights set on stardom and has achieved it. He's the darling of the press at the moment. They hang on his every word about all things Middle Eastern.'

'Did you feel left behind?'

'Why? The rarefied academic world he inhabits is not one I'd be comfortable in.' Larissa gestured round the huge room. 'This is more my style. A relatively new university without the pretensions of Lund and Uppsala.'

'But didn't you move to Uppsala University at the time Ivar was up there?'

She shrugged. 'It was just for a job. It didn't work out, and I came back south. This is my town.'

'And did you come across Ivar when you were up in Uppsala?'

'A couple of times. But, as I've said, we'd moved on.'

'Any contact since then?'

'Is that relevant?'

'Depends.'

'Look, he was married by then and starting a family. That wasn't anything I was interested in. Still not. His wives would hardly have been ecstatic to have an ex-girlfriend sending Christmas cards or emails or whatever. I had a great time with Ivar, but it was never going to last. And I'm pleased he's done well because he deserves it. He's a good guy.'

'And Linus? Did you come across him after the murder?'

'Yeah, we kept in touch. I felt sorry for him. I thought Göran was a shit the way he treated him. If you want me to be blunt, I never really liked Göran, but I put up with him because he was Ivar's friend. But I found him manipulative. I always felt he was using Ivar. And I only think he hooked up with Linus so he could become part of Ivar's gang.'

Szabo scribbled furiously in his notebook. Erlandsson took over. 'So, you kept in touch with Linus while he was here in Malmö?'

'That's right.' She started to toy with the cord that secured her glasses. 'For a while, anyway. I was probably the only one. Even Ivar dropped him after the press came out with all the stuff from the police investigation.'

'We heard about that,' Erlandsson confirmed.

'Then a couple of years later, he skipped town when one of the papers revealed where he lived. It was horrid. We lost contact.'

'So, you don't know where he is now?'

'Haven't a clue.'

Szabo flicked his notebook shut. 'Oh, one last thing. Göran's last intelligible words were "burnt it". Do they mean anything to you?'

Larissa was surprised. 'Who did he speak to? We heard he was dead when he was found by that kid.'

'That kid, Kurt Jeppsson, has now changed his story. Does "burnt it" ring any bells?' It came out more forcefully than Szabo had intended.

'No. Sorry. I can't think what it refers to.'

Szabo didn't bother hiding his disappointment. 'Do you think Linus killed Göran?'

'Ah.' Larissa paused for quite some moments before speaking. 'Time gives you a different perspective on the past. When it all happened, and during the aftermath, I couldn't believe that one of the group could have done it. But now? Well... because I'm sure it wasn't any of us other four, I think it must have been Linus.'

Larissa watched the two detectives leave. After they'd gone, she wandered over to the window and gazed across the still water towards the imposing Post Office building and the Central Station tucked in behind. The road was busy; the noise and frenzy in stark contrast to the quiet inside. She surveyed the room briefly before slipping her glasses back on and taking out her mobile phone. She flicked through the numbers in her phonebook and selected one.

For a while her thumb was poised above the keypad, and then she pressed decisively and put the mobile to her ear. It rang a few times before it was answered.

'Larissa here. We've got to talk.'

CHAPTER 12

Zetterberg snapped off a row of Marabou fruit and nut chocolate. She had bought a big bar at the Co-op store at the Central Station before boarding the train. She knew she shouldn't because she was always conscious of her weight, but this was a treat. It went nicely with the coffee she'd bought from the refreshment car in the next wagon. As she savoured the indulgence, trying not to get slivers of chocolate on her immaculately pressed trouser suit, she noticed the royal crest and the words "Purveyor to the Royal Court of Sweden" on the wrapper. They had good taste. Unlike a number of her contemporaries, she was a royalist. That had been the source of a number of early arguments at the Police Academy with Anita Sundström, the lefty republican. Ignorant slut! As far as Zetterberg was concerned, there was no place for officers with Sundström's views in the force. She'd even heard that Sundström's son was living with an immigrant. That just shows what could happen when subversive views were given free rein. This was a Sweden that had to be protected from unacceptable outside influences. That's why she had been quite happy to help in the cover up of Albin Rylander's death. She felt a wave of anger well up inside her as she thought about Sundström. Only another two rows of chocolate managed to restore her equilibrium.

Zetterberg became aware that her phone was ringing. She'd

dozed off somewhere after Nässjo. The call was from Szabo. He was reporting in after his interview with Larissa Bjerstedt. She knew that he and Erlandsson weren't happy that she had used the other suspects as an excuse for a weekend away in the capital. Well, they would have to live with that because, quite frankly, she didn't care one jot what they thought. The sooner they realized that, the sooner they'd do things her way.

The call itself wasn't promising. Larissa Bjerstedt had stuck to the story she'd told twenty-one years ago. She had appeared to be on reasonable terms with Ivar Hagblom despite their split, which had been entirely amicable. She could check that out when she talked to Ivar on Monday. Larissa hadn't been in touch with any of the others for a number of years, though she had once bumped into Lars-Gunnar Lerstorp. And she seemed to have been the only one to remain friendly with Linus Svärd after the murder, but hadn't seen or heard from him after he'd left Malmö for good a couple of years later. She certainly didn't know where he was now. The only remark of any real interest was that she indicated that she now believes that Linus *was* Göran's killer.

Zetterberg wasn't sure what she had hoped for, but it wasn't this. She so needed Sundström to be wrong! The train glided into Norrköping, and her bitterness almost overwhelmed her. The surroundings were all too familiar. This was where she had wasted herself on her brief marriage to Arne, and then been stuck in a city that had seen her career and love life stall simultaneously. And she had spent all those useless, fruitless, listless years building up the case in her mind against Anita Sundström, whose selfish action had been the cause of her misfortune. But they say revenge is best served cold, and she was not going to miss this chance of dishing hers out.

After the last few months Danny wasn't afraid of hard graft. Bending down wasn't difficult, especially as he knew he wouldn't be beaten up afterwards if he hadn't put in enough effort or had upset McNaught and his nutcase pals. And by picking the small field of potatoes, he was doing something to repay Leif's kindness. With the sun on his back, he felt good, even if his body still ached from its recent ravages. The bruises still hadn't faded, and at some angles he still had the occasional twinge that caught his breath, especially the ache in his chest. But physically he felt better than he had for a long time. Yet he couldn't help stopping regularly and glancing around to see if anybody was about. He couldn't strip the fear away and think clearly about what he should do. He mentally measured how far the edge of the wood was from his position in the field just in case he had to make a dash for cover.

He tossed the plant heads to one side after scraping off as much earth from the potatoes as possible before lobbing them into a large box. He wiped the sweat off his brow. Leif had been touched that he'd wanted to give a hand. He indicated that his grandson used to come and help, but he'd turned into a lazy so-and-so. In their fleeting time together, Danny had grown fond of the old man. They had sat outside the previous evening watching the sun going down and had gone through the whisky that Danny had left after his kitchen raid. Leif had produced some old photographs of his family when he was younger. His wife had been sturdy rather than pretty, but he could see the old man's eyes moisten when he looked at the pictures of her round the farm and with his daughter in her arms. He kept lapsing into Swedish and then would suddenly apologize, though it wasn't needed. Danny felt a connection he had never had with his own father. And he knew it was going to be hard to leave because this was the sort of place he could rebuild his life, albeit temporarily. But he also knew he had to make his move before Sunday and the arrival of Leif's daughter. The problem was that he wasn't sure where in Sweden he actually was. He couldn't find any maps or an atlas in the house. He had asked Leif in a vague kind of way so as not to alert him, and the farmer had mentioned some names of places close by. They meant nothing to Danny. He hadn't strayed too far from the farm or the protective covering of the forest, so he wasn't sure where the nearest main road was, or whether there were any buses. And, of course, he had no money. Jack had had the little they'd gathered together for their escape, and McNaught had found that. He could try and hitch a lift, but that might be dangerous. And where would he ask to go? He guiltily thought about Leif's battered Volkswagen in the barn. He knew where the keys were kept. That would get him out of here. Then he could just dump it for someone to pick up and return. Leave a note in it with Leif's name on. But after all that the old man had done for him, it would be such a betrayal. Was there any other way? As he bent down to continue the row, he realized that it was his only option. But when?

CHAPTER 13

Hakim was nervous. Today was the first time that his parents had invited Liv to come and have a meal with them at their home in Sofielund. They'd met Liv before for a tense *fika* in Möllevångstorget but since then, he'd kept her away from them and their disapproval. And then a sudden invitation. He wondered if his sister Jazmin was behind the offer; Lasse had now been grudgingly accepted after they had produced a beautiful granddaughter. Though Hakim's natural inclination had been to refuse, Liv's enthusiasm won over his scepticism. She said she was up to meeting his parents again, and he prayed that her natural ebullience would sway them. He really wanted them to see what he loved about her.

But he had somewhere to go first. Earlier that morning over a late breakfast, he'd had a call from Reza. Reza was an old school friend from his Rosengård days who had ended up on the other side of the tracks. Officially, he ran a second-hand store beyond Värnhem, but Hakim knew that it was really a front for all sorts of other activities, mainly illegal. In short, Reza was a cheery, low-level fence. His brushes with the law were minor, and Hakim had occasionally turned a blind eye in return for information. Reza kept his ear to the ground and had been useful in the past. And Hakim liked him. And Reza liked Jazmin and had been very disappointed when she had ended up with Lasse.

Reza's shop was packed: dilapidated furniture, electricals

that had seen better days, mismatched crockery, a couple of racks of motley clothing, tasteless knick-knacks, stacks of moth-eaten books and magazines, and rows of DVDs and CDs. There was no way he could make an honest living out of all this junk. But he had a sleek car sitting out on the road, and he was well dressed in expensive jeans and an open-necked, short-sleeved white shirt. His dark hair was slicked back and his demeanour relaxed when Hakim found him sitting in an armchair with a smartphone clamped to his ear. A huge grin crossed his face as he saw his friend walk through the door. There were no other customers. Reza jumped out of his seat and waved Hakim in as he finished his conversation.

'Just business,' he explained with a smile as he flipped the phone into his shirt pocket. He was shorter than the tall Hakim and he looked up to him as they shook hands.

'And how is business?' Hakim said with a smirk as he glanced round the shop.

'Busy.' The surroundings suggested anything but. 'Coffee?'

'No thanks. Going to my parents. Taking Liv round.'

Reza's mouth twisted in a grimace. 'Is this the white girl I heard you were knocking around with?'

'Yes. Liv's a colleague.'

'Muslim?'

'Of course not.'

Again Reza's face contorted. 'Tricky. Mind you, that lovely sister of yours has pulled it off with that lanky fellow. Kid as well. Oh, of course, it's Uncle Hakim now! Suits you,' he said, giving Hakim a playful slap on his shoulder.

'I'm afraid I haven't got long, Reza.'

'Right.' Despite the fact that the shop was empty, he lowered his voice. 'I've heard that there's a guy trying to get hold of a shooter.'

'And that's news?' There were so many illegal guns floating around Malmö that someone trying to get hold of one more wouldn't make much difference.

'This guy's not the usual sort.'

'Reza, you're not selling are you?'

Reza held up his hands in shock. 'How could you think such a thing? Not everything I do is legit, I admit, but nothing that heavy.'

'OK.' Hakim wasn't totally convinced that Reza's protestations were genuine. 'So, what's different about this man?'

'As I said, he's not the usual sort. Gang stuff and all that. It sounds like... from what I heard on the grapevine...' he added quickly, 'he's from the UK. Really hard-looking fella. Scar on his cheek. Not someone to be messed with. Again, that's what I've been told.'

This was intriguing. 'And what sort of gun did he want? Sawn-off shot gun? Automatic weapon?'

'Hand gun. Untraceable. Money no problem.'

'And did whoever passed on the news to you know whether he's succeeded in buying one?'

'I swear he didn't get it from here, but I heard he got what he wanted.'

Liv had made a real effort. She'd eschewed her usual plait and let her blonde hair cascade naturally. She'd put on a pink, summery dress, making sure it wasn't too short. She knew she hadn't really got the legs for it, but it made a change from the trousers she usually hid them in. Her service uniform was a great cover for her fuller figure. After the awkward *fika*, she was hoping for an easier ride this time. Maybe the Mirzas had come round to the idea that Hakim was dating someone from outside their community. However, from the moment she entered the apartment, the conversation had been stilted. Liv had tried her best to be her natural vivacious self, but it had been hard work with the three of them – Uday, Amira, and a surprisingly uncommunicative Hakim. She had complimented Amira on the wonderful meal and the Middle Eastern décor of the apartment; she had told Uday how much his son was respected in the force, all of which seemed to briefly please the parents. Though not asked, she had resorted to telling them about her family, and her brother who lived in Helsingborg with her two nephews; about her upbringing and schooling in Halmstad, and her joining the police after her father, a serving officer, had died of cancer at a relatively young age. Her mother had died when she was ten. This had brought sympathetic sighs from Amira. Though Hakim's parents seemed like nice people, Liv was struggling and was hoping the lunch would end soon.

Out of the blue, Uday turned to his son. 'And are you intending to marry this young lady?'

Hakim was as stunned as Liv. For a few moments he was speechless.

'Father, that's not something you should be asking.'

'And why not?'

Liv could see that Hakim was now seething. However, she felt it wasn't her place to intervene.

'What we decide will be up to us, and no one else.' Hakim was trying to control his temper. 'Is it because Liv is white? Or not a Muslim? It's all right for Jazmin but not for me; is that what you're saying?'

'No, no,' Amira interceded. Whether or not she had been aware that Uday was going to spring such a question on Hakim, she could see that it had gone horribly wrong. 'Your father is concerned, that's all.'

'Concerned that I might not marry into the faith?' Hakim stared furiously at his father.

'We don't want you to make the same mistake as your sister,' Uday replied calmly. Liv didn't know where to put herself.

'Mistake!' Hakim exploded. 'What mistake? She's living

with someone she loves. Someone Swedish like she is. They've given you a grandchild and even given her an Iraqi name. Shouldn't you be grateful?'

'We are, we are,' Amira said, desperately trying to smooth things over.

'I'm Swedish. I'm Muslim. I'm proud to be both. And thank goodness I live in a country that allows me to make my own choices. And if we decide to get married, then no one, especially you, father, is going to stop us.' Hakim stood up abruptly. 'Come on Liv, we've been here long enough.'

Hakim made for the door.

'Please, please don't go, Hakim,' Amira pleaded. But Hakim was no longer interested in listening.

A deeply confused and embarrassed Liv followed him. She turned before she reached the front door, which Hakim had already opened. 'Thank you for a lovely meal.'

This was Granny time. Anita was spending the afternoon with Leyla while her parents did some shopping and treated themselves to a film. The latter seemed a waste to Anita in this nice weather. But it was their way of unwinding, she supposed. She'd taken Leyla across to Pildammsparken, and they'd had a little picnic near the lake. They'd started off by feeding the geese that waddled around the water's edge. Leyla hadn't been fazed by the size of the birds and had giggled every time Anita had thrown breadcrumbs in their direction causing a cacophony of flapping and squawking. Afterwards, down the bank from the lake, Anita had laid out a blanket, and they'd settled down to their picnic. Leyla had drunk all her milk, and they'd played games. A particular favourite was for Granny to build a tower of plastic cups which Leyla would knock down again.

The little girl was tottering around quite successfully now and would be walking confidently very soon. Anita remembered that Lasse had been almost eighteen months before he'd eventually learned to walk. She smiled at Leyla's determination, as each time she stumbled, she'd pick herself up and unsteadily meander off again. In Anita's somewhat biased opinion, she was so beautiful. She had large, dark eyes that lit up at the slightest thing. Her giggle was infectious, and she rarely cried, though Anita knew that she was still keeping her parents up at night. Granny was enjoying this time of bonding and knew she would miss her granddaughter when she headed off for a week's holiday with Kevin the following weekend. Not that she wasn't looking forward to seeing her "Brit boyfriend", as her ex-husband Björn had sarcastically referred to him; Kevin was an antidote to the Swedish men in her private and professional life. And he'd promised her a nice relaxing break – lots of scenery and tearooms, and not too much history (a passion of his that could become boring after a while; though everything was always leavened with humour, which ensured that he didn't get too serious for too long on the subject he was enthusing about). And, of course, there would be the sex. She missed that in the months they were apart. What had surprised her was that during her enforced periods of celibacy, she didn't find herself needing the occasional substitute to tide her over. Was this an age thing? Or maybe she was growing up after too many unsuccessful and unsatisfactory sexual encounters since Björn had left her. Björn! He was back in her life, of course; besotted with his new granddaughter, which had surprised both Anita and Lasse, who'd assumed Björn would be too vain to admit that he was old enough to be a grandfather. Anita was pleased that he cared so much about Leyla, though she was also happy that she would be jumping on a plane at Kastrup next Saturday when Björn was due to come down from Uppsala for the weekend. She was letting him stay at her apartment – Lasse and Jazmin's was too small – while she was away, with the one proviso that he didn't bring his latest floozy with him. He'd promised that the only woman he wanted to spend the weekend with was Leyla.

Anita reflected that this was the perfect time to take a break as there was no big case on, and she could happily leave Moberg to his daft pursuit of Egon Fuentes' nefarious activities. She was sure that wouldn't lead to anything anyway, particularly now that Fuentes was dead.

Leyla came wobbling back onto the rug and plonked herself down. She began to play with the plastic cups, which were adorned with letters and patterns. Anita's phone buzzed. She hoped it wasn't Lasse, as she wanted as much time with Leyla as possible. It was Hakim. He sounded grumpy.

'What's up?' Anita was also slightly irritated that her afternoon was being interrupted.

'I've just had a disastrous lunch with my parents. Liv was there.'

'Oh dear.'

'It was so embarrassing. Liv was being so nice to them, and then my father blurts out whether I was going to marry "this lady". And then it emerged that he didn't want me to make the same mistake Jazmin made.'

'Ah, that's not good.' Anita was just thankful that Jazmin hadn't been there or else they would have had to call in UN peacekeepers. 'I'm sure it'll blow over. Is Liv OK?'

'She's a bit shaken. I don't think she's ever seen me lose my temper like that. She hated the fact that I was falling out with my parents. She regards parents as special, as she lost hers when she was young.'

Leyla was still playing contentedly. 'Buy her a stiff drink.'

She could hear a resigned sigh at the other end. 'I'm just so...'

'Well, are you going to marry her?'

'Not you as well!' He had the grace to laugh. 'I'm sorry. That's not why I was ringing. I had a call from my old friend Reza this morning.'

Anita had never met Reza, but she knew all about him from Hakim and had seen his name crop up in various files.

'Someone approached a "contact" of his – though I suspect it might have been him – looking for a hand gun. Unlicensed. Untraceable.'

Anita kept an eye on Leyla. It was worrying that her gorgeous granddaughter was being brought up in a country with an increasing gun culture. Maybe she should whisk the little girl and her family away to Britain.

'And has he found one?'

'Reza reckons so.'

'It wasn't Reza who supplied him?'

'He's not that stupid. He's into all sorts of dodgy stuff, but guns aren't his scene. Or certainly never used to be. I was thinking this one might be for a specific job. A contract killing perhaps?'

'Why a contract killing?'

'Because this guy isn't local. Reza thinks he's British.'

'British?' That did sound odd.

'Could have been sent over to do a number on someone, pick up a local weapon then disappear out of the country without trace.'

This was ominous. 'Have you a description?'

'Not really. All Reza would say was that he was "hard". I read that as meaning intimidating. Oh, he did mention he had a scar on his face.'

'See if you can press Reza for more.'

As she finished her call, Leyla glanced up and gave Anita a wide-mouthed smile. Anita's heart jumped with the usual delight, even though her mind was wondering who this British gunman might be. And, more importantly, who was the target?

Something was wrong. As Danny approached his camp, he had a feeling of uneasiness. All that day he had been tense.

He'd helped Leif out in the morning shifting hay bales for the horses, as his daughter was due the next day. As the day had progressed, he had felt increasingly guilty in the knowledge that he was going to nick the Volkswagen. He still wasn't sure what he was going to do for money. He would have to steal some elsewhere; he couldn't bring himself to pinch cash off the farmer. It was a dilemma that he'd been battling with over the last couple of hours while venturing round the edge of the forest to try and give himself an idea of the lie of the land and where the road might lead to. He'd found the tarmacked road at the end of the farm track and had walked along it without getting any sense of where he actually was. It would be pot luck – he would have to go one way or the other. He'd decided that he would take the car that night while Leif was asleep.

As he tentatively approached the camp, his heart missed a beat. His rudimentary dwelling had been smashed up. It would only have taken a couple of well-aimed kicks to do the damage, but who was responsible? That all-enveloping fear that had been steadily building up over recent months suddenly overwhelmed him, and he found himself shaking. He was paralyzed; his brain seemed to freeze. His breathing became erratic and he thought for a moment that he was going to black out. The feeling slowly passed.

There was no sign of anyone around. But they could still be in the vicinity. There was only one thing he could do: go to the farmhouse – Leif was expecting him for an evening meal. Maybe the old man could tell him if he'd seen anyone around. It might be kids larking about in the woods. Then again...

He made his way cautiously to the edge of the forest. There was no other car around, so Leif hadn't got a visitor. He was still on edge when he crossed over the horses' field to the barn and round to the house. He couldn't hear Leif, though he was probably in the kitchen making something for their supper. He wasn't sure how he'd handle the situation, knowing what he'd got planned. Could he even look him in the face? The kitchen was empty.

'Leif?' Danny called out.

He made his way along the corridor. All was quiet. Maybe the farmer was still out in a far field, though that was unlikely. As he entered the living room, he came to an abrupt halt. There was Leif sitting on a chair. Then Danny saw, to his horror, that the old man was strapped to it. His eyes were closed and his face was badly bruised. There was blood on his clothes and on the floor. Suddenly, he slumped forward, and Danny gasped. The back of his head had been blown off.

CHAPTER 14

Danny had never felt so sick before without being able to vomit. What in God's name had happened? Though rooted to the spot, his shredded wits began to slowly reform into some coherent thought process. This was the second dead body he had seen in the last few days, and both the deaths seemed terrifyingly similar. It began to dawn on him that whoever had trashed his camp had also done this. An image of McNaught flashed into his mind. The bastard always used his fists before asking questions. But the gun? Danny couldn't bring himself to look at the back of Leif's head. He'd never noticed McNaught carrying a gun, though he was sure that this was his work. McNaught, the hunter, had found his hideaway. But Leif? Why kill a nice old farmer who hadn't done anyone any harm? Then the ghastly thought occurred to him – Leif might have been trying to protect him. Refusing to give him away – and he'd paid for his silence with his life. The poor, tortured body only meant one thing to Danny: McNaught had been interrogating him. There had been whispered talk in the working camp that McNaught had been in Iraq. There, beating up prisoners for information had been common, according to the papers back in Britain.

What the hell was he to do? He knew he couldn't hang around here. McNaught must be somewhere close. Did he drive here? Or was he on foot? There was no sign of a car. He might still be roaming around the forest searching for him. He had to think quickly. There was no way he could report the death. As soon as the police found out who he was and why he'd gone to prison, they would think it was him. He glanced around anxiously. The daughter was due tomorrow to exercise the horses. That meant the body wouldn't be discovered for nearly twenty-four hours. He had to put his original plan into operation earlier. He knew the farmer kept his keys, including the car keys, on a hook near the back door. But he'd need money.

In a totally panic-stricken, random way, Danny ransacked the living room without success. Then, in a chest of drawers in Leif's bedroom, he found a wad of notes. He didn't stop to count how much he'd stolen; there wasn't time. He hurried back through the farmhouse and into the kitchen; he'd need food. He stuffed a few things into a plastic Lidl bag and headed out of the house. Everything he did was swept along on a sea of adrenaline and instinct. He was still in a state of shock at the brutality he'd seen, and the realization that he was almost definitely the cause of a good man's murder.

Danny crossed the deserted farmyard at a quick trot and made for the safety of the barn. There, he managed to coax the Volkswagen into life and he eased it through the barn doors. It was difficult grappling with the controls, as he'd never driven a left hand drive car before. The Volkswagen bounced down the rutted track away from the farmhouse and its gruesome contents. Danny knew it was only a matter of time before the police would begin to work out that someone else had been there other than Leif's daughter over the past few days. His fingerprints would be everywhere. He hoped that he had enough time to get out of the country before they got round to liaising with the British police and discover who he was. That's if McNaught didn't get to him first.

At the end of the track, the road stretched out in both

directions. Which way? After a moment's indecision, he turned right.

Alice Zetterberg flashed her Stockholm Access travel card at the barrier and made her way through to the Monday morning commuter train that would take her to Gamla Stan, where she was meeting Carina Lindvall. The weekend had not been all that she had hoped for. Her sister was as annoying and as arrogant as usual. Her brother-in-law, Christer – and the real reason for the visit – had been there on the Friday night. When he suggested that they take the two girls into the city centre the next day to visit the History Museum – Linda was doing a school project on the Vikings – Linnea had excused herself on the grounds she had a number of important domestic chores to do. Zetterberg had jumped at the chance of spending the day with Christer without her sister around and had volunteered to go. When Christer was unexpectedly called into work the next morning, Zetterberg found herself having to accompany her two nieces, neither of whom she was particularly fond of, round a museum she found utterly tedious. The Sunday barbecue in Linnea and Christer's garden had plenty of drink flowing, but the presence of some of their dreadful friends had afforded her no opportunity for any sly flirtations with the man she had set her sights on. He and Linnea had then disappeared to bed early that night with work beckoning the next day. Zetterberg had been left feeling frustrated and bitter. Linnea had it all, including the right man. She didn't deserve it.

Zetterberg stepped onto the train and sat down. She began to flick through a copy of the free Metro newspaper. It was full of the usual rubbish, though there was an article on oral sex, which seemed an odd feature to have in at that time in the morning. It only made her more annoyed at her lack of weekend activity. Then one small column caught her eye: a farmer had been found murdered near Höör in Skåne yesterday. Zetterberg sighed. It only went to show what a load of hicks they were down south. The sooner she earned promotion to Stockholm, the better.

Danny sat in the car and looked out to sea. This was the second night he'd spent in the vehicle. The first had been on an overgrown, seemingly disused track off a side road somewhere. He hadn't driven too far, as he'd had difficulty adjusting to driving on the right. On one deserted road, he'd instinctively strayed onto the wrong side until a large tractor had come barrelling along in the other direction and he'd had to swerve to avoid it. It had given him a fright, and he hadn't driven too much further – he feared his lack of confidence might become noticeable. The strange names on the road signs hadn't helped either, with all their weird double dots and circles – like the sign for Sjöbo. The next day – he knew it must be Sunday as that was the day Leif's daughter was due to go to the farm and would discover the body – he'd decided to go as far away as possible. He'd avoided Sjöbo, which he assumed might have a police station, and ended up, after an hour's slightly more confident driving, at the coast. It was near a place called Skillinge. He had gone through it and had nearly had a heart attack when a police car passed him going in the opposite direction. Skillinge appeared to be a fishing village. There were boats bobbing about in the harbour. His knowledge of the sea was virtually non-existent, having spent most of his life in rural Herefordshire. He'd braved a shop to buy some cold pop, making sure he didn't speak and just shoving a note over the till and holding his hand out for the change.

After leaving the village, he'd found the spot he spent the night in. It was while musing over what he should do next that he happened to open up the glove compartment and discovered an old road map of southern Sweden. Though it looked very out of date, the places couldn't have changed that much. He found Skillinge and realized he had gone in the wrong direction. He could see that he must make for Malmö. Though the old map didn't show it, he remembered that the van they'd been transported from England in had crossed over a long bridge in the middle of the night. Though half asleep, he'd noticed a lot of lights in the distance. They'd skirted any big town that might have been there, and then he'd fallen asleep again before waking from his slumber at the camp – and the nightmare had begun.

Now it was morning, he finished the last of the food he'd taken from Leif's kitchen. He knew what he was going to do. He would make for Malmö and then dump the car, which, he guessed, the police would soon be looking for. Once in Malmö, he could plan an escape from this dreadful country that had become his prison. He wasn't sure how yet, but he had to do it before McNaught or the police caught up with him.

Zetterberg made her way through the crowd of people who had poured off the train at Gamla Stan Tunnelbana station. She jostled through the commuters, and the tourists and day-trippers who were drawn to Stockholm's atmospheric old town on the island of Stadsholmen, with its narrow, cobbled medieval streets and colourfully rendered merchants' houses. Attractions like the Royal Palace, the cathedral and the Nobel Museum are a must-see, and an expensive meal in one of the many trendy or traditional eateries that are tucked in alongside the craft shops and the tourist tat emporiums is all part of the experience. But this was not the Stockholm that Zetterberg longed for, though she recognized that her capital city had something for everyone. It was the cool, powerful, modern Stockholm that was calling someone with her ambitions.

She cut through a side alley from Munkbrogatan onto Lilla Nygat. The hotel was near the top end of the street opposite the Post Museum. She marvelled at how Stockholm had the ability to create a museum out of even the most mundane things. She stood on the other side of the street and gazed at the hotel entrance opposite. For some reason she felt nervous. Was it because she was meeting someone famous? Or was it because she was desperate for something to emerge from the conversation that would throw light on a suspect other than Linus Svärd? She glanced at her watch – 9.29. Perfect timing.

Carina Lindvall was late. Coming out of the glass lift, she breezed into the hotel lobby. Her black, shoulder-length locks partly curtained the dark glasses. If the shades were being worn to make herself inconspicuous, the ruse hadn't worked, as a couple of the guests checking out immediately recognized her. So did Zetterberg; she'd scrutinized her numerous photographs on the internet before heading north. Carina's black jacket and short, black skirt made her appear more like a business executive than a writer. The white blouse did little to hide the impressive breasts, and the sleek dark shoes looked stunningly expensive. Zetterberg had already made up her mind that she wasn't going to like Carina Lindvall, and nothing about her appearance did anything to change that. Carina came over to the standing Zetterberg and offered a perfunctory handshake. Zetterberg could smell cigarette smoke on her.

'Inspector Alice Zetterberg. Thank you for coming,' Zetterberg began, and then wondered why she was thanking a potential murder suspect for turning up to be interviewed. Is that the effect famous people have?

'I'm here to help,' muttered Carina as she eased herself into her chair and crossed her legs, showing an ample portion of thigh as she did so. Zetterberg noticed one of the male guests trying to get an eyeful. 'But I'm amazed that all this has come to the surface again after so long.' The voice had the throaty timbre of a lifelong smoker.

'I've ordered coffee.'

Carina waved a manicured hand in horror. 'Oh, no! So bad for you! Green tea. Must have green tea.' Zetterberg got up and went over to reception to change the order. Ridiculous that someone who smoked as much as Carina obviously did should pretend to be so health-conscious. She disliked the novelist even more.

They sank into commodious, tan-leather seats. 'I love this place,' explained Carina as she glanced about, taking in the clutter surrounding her. Ships' figureheads bent imperiously over the sofa backs, marble busts of naval personages gazed sightlessly from their plinths, model sailing ships of all sizes encased in glass adorned the wide window sills, and the walls were crammed with seascapes and marine memorabilia. 'There are ships everywhere throughout the hotel – in cases, in bottles, in paintings. It's fabulous. Even the bedrooms are named after seafarers. Mine's Kapten Lundh. Old photos of him, his ship and his wife in the room. It's my little getaway in town when I can't be bothered to go back home to Norra Lagnö. I was at a little soirée last night, and it was easier to put my head down here.'

Just then a handsome young man in his mid-twenties with a clipped hipster beard and smart casual jacket and drainpipe trousers emerged from the lift. A broad smile crossed his face as he spotted Carina. He came over and bent down and offered an air kiss to each cheek.

'Thank you for last night,' he grinned.

'Thank you, darling.' Then she gave him a dismissive wave. 'Ciao.'

After he left, Carina sank back into her chair. 'Fun but exhausting. Trouble is I can't remember his name. That's another advantage of coming here – I can spend a bit of quality time with people I don't want anywhere near my home. Don't want the neighbours to get the wrong impression.' I bet she doesn't, thought Zetterberg, who reflected once more on how badly she had done in that direction this weekend with an uncooperative Christer.

Carina took off her sunglasses, blinking at the light coming through the window from the street outside, and secured them in her hair like a pair of headlamps. She had weathered well, thought Zetterberg. But then again, she could afford to. There had been rumours of Botox and possibly even more drastic action, but despite peering closely at her, Zetterberg couldn't detect any signs of artificial rejuvenation, more's the pity. She waited until they were served before starting the interview.

'Let's go through what you remember about the day Göran Gösta was killed.'

Carina took a sip of her green tea and wrinkled up her nose at the same time. 'Some days it's a distant memory, and then others it's like it all happened yesterday. I suppose it was like most days that summer. I did a bit of writing in the morning. I'd got a job in Malmö working for the commune. Secretarial sort of thing. Very dull. But I was writing on the side. That's what I'd always wanted to do, and I was encouraged by my tutor.' She suddenly put her tea cup down on her saucer with a flourish. 'That's right. There was a young detective on the case who was married to my tutor, Björn Sundström.' Zetterberg was about to interrupt, as this was drifting away from the point. But she was glad she didn't as Carina half-smiled to herself. 'It was a bit awkward actually. I'd bonked her hubby a few times after tutorials.' Zetterberg suppressed a grin. This was a nugget of gold which she would enjoy using at an opportune moment.

'Can we get back to that day?'

'Of course. In the afternoon, we had a barbecue, which went spectacularly wrong. Linus and Göran had this nasty bust-up. Mind you, it had been coming for some time.'

'Larissa Bjerstedt told my officers that she thought things

had begun to go wrong between them when you were all on Malta.'

'Probably right,' she waved a hand airily. 'After the fracas on the beach, things were so flat that we just drifted back to the house.'

'And at the time of the murder you were writing again?'

'Yeah. I'd had a bit to drink, but sometimes intoxication produces a creative flow, and I just had to go with it.'

'Which means you didn't really have an alibi?'

Carina pulled a face. 'You sound like my detective, Erik Dahlberg. He's always saying that.' She leant across the coffee table and said in a confidential whisper: 'And he could be saying it on TV soon. That's why I'm looking all business-like today. I'm meeting a producer and TV executive in a couple of hours. Hush-hush, but I think a deal's in the bag. It'll do wonders for sales.' Zetterberg thought it couldn't be that hush-hush if Erlandsson had read about it on Lindvall's website. 'By the way, have you read any of my books?'

'Yes,' Zetterberg lied instinctively. 'Very... erm... very realistic.' Carina seemed extremely pleased.

'If I'd known, I'd have brought along a signed copy of my latest.'

'Anyhow, your boyfriend at the time, Lars-Gunnar, couldn't vouch for you; isn't that right?'

Carina snorted. 'You're kidding. Darling Lars-Gunnar. He was probably out of his head at the time. I saw him through my window at some stage that evening zonked out in the garden.'

'Drugs?'

'Yeah. He was getting worse then. In fact, that's one of the reasons we split, because I couldn't cope with his habit. I couldn't afford it!' Zetterberg looked at her askance. 'I was working and he wasn't, so I was footing the bill. It hadn't been too serious at first. Basically, we were all smoking something or other. Of course, it was Göran's fault, and that's why I was never that keen on him.'

Zetterberg sensed this was an important moment and seized upon it. 'You're saying that it was Göran's fault that Lars-Gunnar was so into drugs?'

'Yes. I suppose it didn't come out at the time. We were all pretty tight-lipped. Göran was Lars-Gunnar's supplier.'

Zetterberg sat upright. 'So, Lars-Gunnar might have been out of his head that night. He could have done anything without even knowing what he was doing?'

Carina's mouth twitched. 'I suppose.'

'Do you think Lars-Gunnar and Göran could have fallen out over the drugs? If he didn't want to ask you for more money – maybe he felt guilty about it – then it might have pushed your ex-boyfriend over the edge. Or Göran was asking too much, which Lars-Gunnar couldn't afford?' This could certainly put Lars-Gunnar in the frame.

Carina looked pained. 'Doubt it. He was too far gone that night.'

'But presumably you didn't see him all the time you were working?' Carina's silence did nothing to quell Zetterberg's budding suspicions. She would let those thoughts marinate. 'Why didn't the drugs link come out in the original investigation?'

Carina uncrossed and re-crossed her legs. There was still too much thigh on display. 'I suppose we closed ranks. We were young and didn't want these things to ruin potential careers. Ivar didn't want Göran's name dragged through the mud.'

'Ivar? You mean he didn't want to be associated with that sort of thing?'

'You're probably right. The Hagblom family were furious that their holiday home was being mentioned in the investigation. Throw in drugs, and the publicity would have damaged their name even more. The murder certainly didn't get much coverage in the family's newspapers.' She paused before putting on a theatrical frown. 'Of course, it was one of the Hagblom rags that broke the story about Linus being the killer, but I suppose they needed a scapegoat so that dear Ivar wasn't tainted.'

Zetterberg changed tack. 'You know that Göran said something before he died?'

'Did he? First I've heard of it.'

'He mumbled something and then was heard saying: "burnt it".'

Carina registered puzzlement. 'What does that mean?'

'I was hoping you might know.'

'Search me! Maybe Göran was referring to burning the meat on the barbecue,' she joked. 'He was crap at that. And he certainly had a weird sense of humour.'

'I'm sure he wasn't trying to be funny as he was staring death in the face,' Zetterberg said severely. Carina was unabashed by the barb. 'Let's move on to Ivar,' Zetterberg suggested as Carina took a more thoughtful sip of green tea. 'He and Larissa Bjerstedt were in their room making love at the time of the murder.'

'Yeah. They were always at it. Larissa was a bit of a screamer. Mind you, Ivar was always a bit of an athlete in that department.' What made Zetterberg think that Carina had been on the receiving end of that athleticism? 'He's had as many marriages as I have, though I think he's still with his second one. She's very glam. But he was always tactical in his choices.'

'What do you mean?' Someone this indiscreet was every detective's dream.

'Well, when he dumped poor old Larissa, he hitched up with the daughter of the head of his faculty at Lund. Did his prospects no end of good. And then, when she'd produced the family heir and spare, and he was on the television every five minutes, he found someone younger and more photogenic. Looks good to have someone like that on your arm at trendy dos: film galas, concerts, big academic shindigs and the like. We run into one another occasionally. We went to each other's last book launches. Have to admit that I hadn't read his. Some hefty tome about discontented Arabs. Of course, it's been lauded to the skies, but his books haven't been translated into as many languages as mine,' she chortled throatily.

Zetterberg drained her coffee. 'OK. The investigation at the time concluded that it was Linus who was the murderer, which is what the press got hold of. But I hadn't realized that there was the Hagblom connection. The papers at the time took the lovers' quarrel angle.'

'Rubbish!'

'Why do you say that?'

Carina rearranged her sunglasses ever so slightly as to make no difference. 'Because Linus isn't the murdering sort. He's a nice guy. He couldn't harm anyone. He might have been promiscuous – and I'm sure he still is – but that doesn't make you a killer. His misfortune was that the one man he really did fall in love with turned out to be a complete twat. He was better off without him.'

Zetterberg sighed. 'We'd love to ask him for his version of events, but we've no idea where he is.'

Carina gave a guttural laugh. 'I have. He lives in my apartment on Malta.'

CHAPTER 15

'Anyhow, my mother rang me yesterday and apologized on behalf of my father. I'm sure he wasn't aware that she was phoning me. She'd probably waited until he'd gone out.' Hakim had run over the eventful meal with his parents and Liv once again while Anita listened patiently.

'How did Liv take it?'

Hakim shrugged. 'Upset, naturally. Thinks my parents – or my father anyway – will never accept her.' He shook his head sadly. 'And I think she may be right.'

'She'll win them over,' Anita said brightly. 'She's a lovely girl.' Her enthusiasm wasn't matched by what she really thought. She knew that Uday hadn't been happy about Jazmin and Lasse. He'd come to terms with it grudgingly when they'd produced a granddaughter. But Hakim was his golden boy, despite a career in the police. Though he'd been westernized long before fleeing from Saddam Hussein's Iraq to the safety of Sweden, Uday's faith had remained strong, and some traditions were hard to break. He was also incredibly stubborn. It was a trait that his son had inherited, and Anita was sure there wouldn't be a happy rapprochement any time soon.

'Maybe you're right. Anyhow, it's not your worry. You've got your holiday to look forward to. Packed yet?'

Anita grunted, 'You're kidding. Always last minute.'

'What time's the flight?'

'Early. Can't remember the time.'

Hakim grinned. 'So you'll be gone before Björn turns up?'

Anita grimaced. 'Ah, you've heard about that.'

'Jazmin.'

'Moment of weakness. I'm letting him have the apartment while he's visiting Leyla. And if he leaves it in more of a mess than I leave it in, then he's in big trouble.'

Just then Klara Wallen popped her head round the door.

'Moberg wants us.'

'What for?' asked Anita.

'Don't know, but he's got Eva Thulin with him so there's likely to be a dead body involved.'

Anita, Hakim, Klara Wallen and Pontus Brodd were all sitting in the meeting room when Moberg entered, with Eva Thulin trailing in his wake. Brief speculation beforehand was that it was something to do with the murder of a farmer near Höör that had been on the television that morning. Wallen had assured them that Kristianstad were handling that since the reorganization.

'Morning,' Moberg said curtly as Thulin and Anita exchanged smiles. Anita regarded Eva Thulin as the best forensic technician she'd worked with. She also liked her and often wished that they had mixed socially. It had never happened, and Anita knew that Thulin was happily married and probably didn't want to spend her spare time with people connected with her often-gruesome job.

Moberg stood at the end of the table. 'I knew that Egon Fuentes was up to no good. Now we have confirmation. Eva has some interesting information for us.'

The blonde Thulin was about to produce some photos from a bag and then thought better of it. 'The Svarte crash a week ago resulted in four deaths: the driver of the train, and three people in the van that had stalled on the track. As you can imagine, the three inside were smashed up pretty badly. You can see the pictures after if you're interested. The first one we were able to name was Egon Fuentes because he had identification on him. He was sitting in the passenger seat. We still don't know who the other two are.'

'So why are we here?' This came from a lounging Brodd.

'Just listen, will you,' Moberg roared impatiently. Brodd appeared chastened. He sat up straight.

'However,' Thulin carried on, 'we do know that the man in the driver's seat was around his mid-thirties. He had nothing on him other than the clothes he was wearing, which were from a British store called BHS. The label on his shirt gave it away,' she added with a self-deprecating smirk. 'The third body is the interesting one, because he was already a body before the crash.'

'Already dead?' asked Wallen.

'Yes. He was the youngest of the three, in his early twenties possibly, and must have been lying in the back of the van. He had been badly beaten. Marks of trauma all over the head and upper torso. Obviously, it was difficult to find these initially given the state all the bodies were in after the accident. This young man had been beaten to death. Whether the other two were the perpetrators is up to you to decide. What does appear to have happened is that the two in the front of the van were driving the dead victim from one location to another, presumably away from where the murder took place.'

'Do you know how long he'd been dead before the crash?'

'I'm afraid that's difficult, Anita. But my guess is it was some hours.'

'Right,' said Moberg, rubbing his gargantuan paws together gleefully, 'we've got a murder on our hands. And it's all tied up with my old pal Egon Fuentes.'

Szabo and Erlandsson waited outside the Ystad post office

building at the Lagmansgatan entrance. Vans came in and out of the low-slung, red-brick depot to collect fresh batches of mail. The supervisor had told them that Lars-Gunnar Lerstorp was due back just after twelve from his morning run. The officious little man had been worried when approached by the police, but Szabo had explained that it was merely a routine enquiry. As soon as the supervisor realized that the matter had nothing to do with the postal service, he was fine and left. The sun was out and the day was pleasant, so it was no hardship hanging around. Across the Kyrkogårdsgatan thoroughfare they could hear children playing in the pretty Norra Promenaden park. Szabo lit a cigarette and blew out the first satisfying lungful of smoke.

'So, what do you make of the boss?' he asked casually.

Erlandsson was immediately on her guard. Was this a trick question? She knew Zetterberg had taken to Szabo, though she'd shown nothing but indifference to her.

'Focussed,' she offered tentatively.

Szabo grinned as he swept back his hair with the fingers gripping his cigarette; a dangerous manoeuvre, Erlandsson thought. 'You could say that. I'd say obsessed.' She flashed him a look of surprise. 'She seems intent on finding someone guilty of this murder as long as it's not Linus Svärd. She's particularly interested in Lars-Gunnar after her chat with Carina Lindvall this morning. With Göran as his supplier, there might be a new angle there which wasn't investigated before. Basically, we're here to prove Inspector Sundström wrong.'

'Seems that way. I thought the boss was very disrespectful,' Erlandsson ventured.

'You know her, don't you? You've worked with Sundström?'

'Yes.'

'What's she like?'

'Good. A good cop, though she's been in a few scrapes over the years from what I've heard in the polishus.'

Szabo took another long puff of his cigarette. Through the

113

exhaled smoke, he said: 'They must have some sort of history, Zetterberg and Sundström. That behaviour's not normal, even among warring cops. Can you shed any light on that, Inspector Erlandsson?' There was a twinkle in his eye.

'I'll ask around.'

Szabo's attention was diverted, and he flicked his half-smoked cigarette away. 'I think it's him.' A yellow postal van drove up, and a man in the distinctive blue postman's uniform eased himself out of the driver's seat.

Szabo sauntered over to the postman. 'You Lars-Gunnar Lerstorp?'

The tall, angular man with a bald head crowning a thin, drawn face with sunken eyes surveyed Szabo with suspicion. He nodded.

'I'm Detective Anders Szabo and this is Detective Bea Erlandsson. We want to speak to you about the murder of Göran Gösta.'

Lars-Gunnar's glance darted between the two detectives and the sanctuary of the sorting office. 'That's ancient history.'

'It's unsolved ancient history.'

'It's nothing to do with me. That was in a different life,' he mumbled as he made a move back towards the van.

'Hey!' Szabo shouted. 'Where do you think you're going?'

'Work.'

'We want to talk to you.'

Szabo and Erlandsson watched in disbelief as Lars-Gunnar slipped quickly back into his van and drove off at speed.

Moberg had distributed the photos of the three dead men after Thulin had gone. Anita was having second thoughts about the coleslaw she had planned to have at lunchtime. They were hardly recognizable as human beings, more mangled flesh and bone. Once again, she marvelled at how much people like Eva Thulin could deduce from so little.

'Right, I've been onto the commissioner this morning, and we've got this case because of the Malmö connection.' Anita could tell that he was relishing the prospect of heading this investigation. It was a long time since she'd seen so much enthusiasm from her boss, who had become decidedly jaded over the years. Egon Fuentes had really bugged him. 'Egon Fuentes was a long-term conman who had spent time inside. I put him there,' he added proudly. 'What we do know is that he was involved with some new gang, possibly English or Irish. We don't know anything about this outfit other than that it has something to do with the building trade, according to one of my informants. Fuentes was dealing with some bent building supplier. We need to find out who this was; it may give us an idea what he was up to. So I want you, Wallen, to follow that up. Talk to all the suppliers in and around Malmö. Thulin said there were half a dozen paving stones found in the van, so start with people who do that sort of thing. Drives, patios, tarmacking, whatever.'

Moberg was warming to his subject. 'Brodd, I want you to find out where the Fiat transit van came from and who bought it. Or if it was rented. It was in a bit of a state even before the crash, so unlikely to have come from a reputable dealer. And I want you,' he said, turning to Anita, 'and Mirza to get down to the train crash site.'

'But that wasn't the crime scene,' Anita pointed out.

'No. We have no idea where that is at the moment. But Fuentes and his companion were taking the body from point A to point B. A is the most important, but that's not going to be easy to find. The potential area is huge; it could be anywhere in Skåne north of the railway. Given how close to the sea they got, B can't be that far from the crash site. Find it and it might give us some clue as to where they came from, or the location might have some connection with the gang that Adolf Frid mentioned.'

'The sea itself?' Hakim suggested.

'They would need a boat for that to make sure the body didn't reappear. But that is a possibility. They were heading southward towards Svarte. See what's around. It doesn't seem likely that they were just going to bury the body as they could have done that anywhere around that area; plenty of woodland about. They didn't want this body found. Generally, we need to find out if there were any sightings of the van that day or previously. OK, anything else?'

Anita pointed to the photo of the mangled mess that was the young man. 'From what you've told me about Egon Fuentes, this doesn't seem his style.'

Moberg ran a meaty hand across his jowly jaw. 'Good point, Anita. Ever since I got the news of the murder from Thulin, that's been puzzling me. As you say, it's not Egon's modus operandi. He'd sell his grandmother to the Arabs without a qualm, but murder?' He shook his head doubtfully. 'Makes me think he got in with a ruthless bunch and found himself out of his depth.'

CHAPTER 16

After leaving the built-up suburbs and industrial estates of northern Stockholm, the train to Uppsala glided through fertile country. This had once been a seabed, and retreating waters had left a flat and fruitful land that farmers could exploit. It had been many years since Alice Zetterberg had been to the university town with its pink castle perched on a hill, dramatic twin spires of the medieval cathedral, and its famous Linnaeus connections. Not that Zetterberg was overly interested in the passing countryside as she busily surfed on her phone. As she did so, she was interrupted by a call. It was from Szabo. She caused her fellow passengers to look up when she started to lose her temper and blast Szabo for failing to interview Lars-Gunnar Lerstorp.

'Go to his home and sit on his bloody doorstep until midnight if you have to. Get him interviewed. Embarrass him in front of his family – I don't care what you do. If he doesn't cooperate, drag him into headquarters. He's turning into a possible suspect.' She should have carried out all the interviews herself. Why was she plagued with such useless subordinates?

It wasn't until the train had arrived at the new, utilitarian Uppsala station – the attractive old building had been converted into a restaurant – that she had calmed down enough to ring Szabo back. As Göran had been Lars-Gunnar's supplier, it was this angle that they had to push him hard on. 'No pussy-footing, even if it upsets your little friend Erlandsson.'

As she finished the call, she gazed over towards a whole line of fussy, modern apartment blocks and a low, curvaceous Radisson Blu and wondered where on earth they had appeared from. This wasn't the Uppsala she remembered.

There was very little evidence of the crash at the level crossing up the slope from Svarte. The clearance operation had been extremely efficient, and the line had been restored. No bits of wreckage or bent overhead cables, and the only clue that four people had met their deaths here a week ago were deep ruts in the adjacent field. The lack of damage showed how quick the reactions of the train driver had been. It had cost him his life, though he'd saved many more. Down the line, in the distance past the rolling fields, was a church spire modestly peeking above the tree line at Svarte; beyond that, the Baltic. The sea was that sparkling azure that Anita knew would have Kevin rushing down to the beach for a swim. She suddenly found herself hoping that this investigation wasn't going to stop her going on her holiday. The sooner they solved it, the less likely Moberg would want her to stay around. Anyhow, this was his case.

'The van came from that direction,' said Hakim, pointing inland. A few metres further back was a red-brick house behind a neat hedge. On the other side of the road, a field. 'But where were they heading?' In the opposite direction, the road navigated its way between fields until it curved away up a slight incline into some trees and out of sight.

'Moberg didn't think it was the sea, and I have to agree,' opined Anita. 'They'd need a boat, and then they might get spotted. And they must have had plenty of opportunities to bury the body somewhere else.'

There was no traffic around, and Hakim stood in the middle of the road, his gaze fixed on the westerly aspect.

'Why were they even moving the body? Presumably either to make sure it was never found or because, if it was, there would be no link to the location it came from.'

Anita blinked into the sun. She'd set off without her sunspecs. 'Could be either. But does it matter?'

'What do you mean?'

'Well, the murderers of our nameless young victim are probably the guys who were killed in the crash. We may never know who the victim was, or who his killers were, other than Egon Fuentes.'

'But as you said to the chief inspector, killing isn't Fuentes' style. There might be others involved. That guy you met at the supermarket talked about a gang.' He smirked at her. 'You're mentally on holiday already.'

'No, I'm not,' she replied indignantly. But she knew he was right. Her heart wasn't in it. She could see this being a fruitless case. The only case that she was preoccupied with was the one she wasn't involved in. She had run into Bea Erlandsson "accidentally" that morning, and the petite inspector had filled her in on what had happened so far: the chat with Larissa, which had yielded nothing significant, and their proposed visit to Lars-Gunnar. Meanwhile, Alice Zetterberg was interviewing Carina that morning before going on to Uppsala to meet Ivar. Erlandsson had promised to discreetly keep Anita in the loop.

Hakim pulled out his smartphone and began fiddling with it. Anita wandered over to her parked car and opened the driver's-side door. She reached in for a bottle of water and took a swig.

'I suppose we'd better trace a possible route – that way,' Anita called over, pointing to the other side of the level crossing. 'Not that we're likely to be able to work out where the van had come from. But we might spot somewhere with CCTV.'

Hakim was still fiddling with his phone. 'The lot in Ystad didn't come up with anything. Obviously, they talked to people in that house back there and others on the route, but found nothing, and there's no CCTV in the immediate area anyway.'

'Ystad are probably happy to hand this one over to us.'

Hakim wasn't listening. He suddenly held up his phone. 'I think I know where they might have been going.'

'Really?'

He walked across to her as she lolled back against the warm car, her arms folded.

'Look,' Hakim said, holding the phone in front of her. She squinted at the Google map on the screen. 'Turn right just a bit further along there, over that bump,' he said, nodding in the westerly direction. His long finger traced the road in question on the screen. 'That runs alongside this.' He brought the image up and then turned the map into an aerial photograph. 'A disused quarry. It's filled with water now. What a good place to get rid of a body – permanently.'

Zetterberg made her way down to the station underpass, where she had the unpleasant sensation of being hemmed in by concrete with a draft thrown in. She was all for modern, but this was soulless in a town famed for its character. Her faith, however, was quickly restored when she set eyes on the Tripolis building, which was literally five minutes' walk from the station. It was far larger than its neighbours on Väderkvarnsgatan, yet it was a thing of beauty and delicacy – five storeys of yellow, art nouveau finesse. Built in the run-up to the First World War, it was desirable not so much for the size of the apartments, which didn't have the state-of-the-art facilities found elsewhere, but more because it was like owning a piece of architectural history. Many an Uppsala resident cast an envious eye on Tripolis. Zetterberg found the entrance with the names of Ivar and Jenny

Hagblom among those of the residents listed next to the heavy wooden door. She pressed the buzzer.

Ivar Hagblom was everything Zetterberg had expected. She knew he was handsome, but she hadn't expected the animal magnetism that he exuded. It took only moments for her to be captivated as he welcomed her into his apartment: the warm handshake, the hints of manly musk and the clear blue eyes that made her momentarily wobbly as they gazed into her own. He was attentive and polite. Ivar hid the vanity that Carina had alluded to well.

'Lucky you've caught me. We only got back from the family summer house on Runmarö this morning. If was good enough for Strindberg, then it's good enough for us.' Zetterberg got the reference and the implication that the Hagbloms could afford a place on one of the islands in the Stockholm Archipelago.

While she waited in the living room, he disappeared into the small kitchen they had passed to make some fresh coffee. The room was dominated by a boudoir grand piano. It wasn't a huge space to accommodate an instrument of that size, yet because of the high ceiling, it didn't distort the feeling of relaxed sophistication. The score on the music rack was Scott Joplin, and the few pictures on the walls were abstract and looked original. The furniture was expensive and stylish and, despite being modern, didn't look out of place; the only item that seemed inapt was a large flat-screen TV affixed to the wall – no doubt an essential piece of equipment for the gorgeous couple to snuggle up in front of to watch the charismatic Ivar on yet another boring news programme. Strangely, the room was devoid of books, except for the one carefully placed in the middle of the coffee table – *The Middle East in Meltdown* by Professor Ivar Hagblom. It was a thick, daunting volume; no wonder Carina hadn't waded through it.

Ivar came back in and introduced Zetterberg to his wife, Jenny; a slim, elegant woman with beautifully manicured hands and a ready smile. She was just the sort of younger eye candy that Ivar was happy to parade at his various functions, both private and public. She apologized that she had her piano teacher coming in to give her a lesson – darling Ivar had forgotten of course, but he was such a scatterbrain – and that she hoped the noise wouldn't disturb them. Ivar suggested that, as it was warm, they go outside into the courtyard and have their meeting there.

They sat at a wooden table in an arbour covered in a late-flowering purple clematis, and a rampant kerria japonica. The courtyard ran the full length of the interior of the Tripolis complex. The yellow stuccoed walls towered above them, with myriad windows opening onto the garden area, which included further seating alcoves, a children's sandpit and benches for the residents. At this time in the afternoon, there was only a young couple sitting at one of the other tables; one reading, the other glued to her computer. Ivar laid down a silver tray with coffee cups and a thermos. There was also a plate of thin cinnamon biscuits.

'Hope you don't mind coming out here, but it's my wife's latest passion. We bought the piano a couple of months ago, so the sounds she produces are a bit hit and miss.' He flashed a confidential wink. 'She is getting better, though. I'd thought about teaching her myself but busy, busy...'

Zetterberg had already spoken to Ivar on the phone so he knew exactly what the meeting was about, yet there wasn't a whiff of concern on either his or his wife's part. He was totally relaxed, and Zetterberg realized that she would have to fight against being lulled into acquiescence by his easy charm.

'You mentioned on the phone that you have new evidence, Inspector. Sorry, that sounds so formal. What is your first name?'

'Alice,' Zetterberg found herself saying.

'Alice, are you in a position to tell me what the evidence is?'

She had to cough to compose herself. His approach to the interview was disarming. And she didn't like to let men get the better of her. 'I'm afraid I'm not at liberty to tell you that at the moment.'

He held his hands up, palms facing Zetterberg. 'Fair enough. Anyway, how can I help? I'll dredge my memory banks, but to be honest, Alice, it's a period of my life that I've tried hard to forget.'

'We haven't forgotten it. A murderer wasn't brought to justice. A murderer who we believe was one of your friends.'

He ran his hand across the impeccable stubble on his chin as though he had a hard decision to make. 'I know. Linus. It was quite a shock when the story came out.'

'In one of your father's newspapers as it happens.'

'Could have been,' he said absently. 'But in the cold light of day, one can see where they were coming from. It was particularly difficult for me. Linus was a very good friend. I'd introduced him to Göran, who was a pal as well. It was bad enough them splitting up and the awkwardness that that caused. But murder...' Ivar let his voice trail off to denote how awful it must have been for him.

'Of course, it must have been terrible. But do you think you could take me through the events of that day?'

'I'm sure my statement at the time will be more accurate than anything I can tell you now.'

'Viewing things in retrospect may throw up things that didn't occur to you at the time.'

They could hear the piano faintly through the open kitchen window. There was a sudden discordant thump on the keys followed by a tinkle of embarrassed laughter. Ivar raised an amused eyebrow. 'The lesson's going well.'

He began to tell Zetterberg how things had unfolded on the day of the murder. What he had to say tallied with both what Larissa had said to Szabo and Erlandsson, and her own conversation with Carina. All were sticking to the same stories they'd told twenty-one years previously. However, though nothing was obviously visible from Ivar's lucid description – he didn't go into any intimate details of his sexual activities with Larissa on the night in question – she instinctively felt that the slightest of cracks was appearing. She had been furious with Szabo for letting Lars-Gunnar escape. They had to get him to talk.

'What I'm really interested in is when the relationship between Linus and Göran began to break down. Larissa Bjerstedt told my officers that she thought it started to go wrong on Malta. This was confirmed to me by Carina Lindvall this morning.'

'Ah, so you've spoken to the lovely Carina. She came to the launch of my new book. Said she loved it. Bollocks, of course. I don't think she'd even opened it. Yes, sorry, I digress. Malta? Yes, Carina's probably right. The odd argument. Not that I paid much attention. I was just having such a good time. A break from my studies, a bit of sun on my bones. It's a great place. Stacks of interesting history, which is why I wanted to go there. What's not to like? I mean, just take the Great Siege of Malta. If the Knights of St. John hadn't held out against impossible odds, and the Turks had captured the islands, the Ottoman Empire would have had a base to attack Sicily, Italy and France. That could have led to a Muslim takeover of Western Europe. They already had the Eastern Mediterranean sewn up.' Zetterberg hadn't the faintest idea what Ivar was talking about, but found it hard not to be caught up by his enthusiasm. '1565 was such a pivotal year. La Valette, the Grand Master, said at the time that "it is the great battle between the Cross and the Quran which is now to be fought. A formidable army of infidels are on the point of invading... ". And doesn't it strike you that we're now facing a similar pivotal moment in our own time?' Zetterberg struggled to put a more animated response into her blank stare. 'I'm sure you can see the way that Islam is being etched into the very fabric of western life, which is no bad thing, but malignant forces like ISIS are just as intent on conquest as Sulieman the Magnificent.'

She didn't. 'I suppose so.' She was finding it so easy to agree with him. She could understand why few women had said "no" to him. But she had to get back to the case. 'From talking to one of the members of the original investigating team, it appears that Göran had transferred his affections from Linus to you.'

The suggestion didn't seem to faze Ivar. 'There is some truth in that, but nothing was ever going to happen. He drunkenly tried to kiss me one night after a few drinks outside a bar in Valletta. I made it clear that I wasn't interested. Next morning, it was fine. He apologized. Never mentioned it again.'

Even in Zetterberg's spellbound state, the nagging seed of suspicion that is embedded in the minds of all detectives began to germinate. Was that too simple an explanation? Was Göran the type of person to just meekly submit?

'What was Göran like? I know he appears to have been a bit of an outsider. I'm not sure that the girls were fond of him.'

Ivar arched his fingers like a church steeple in front of his mouth. 'He was an outsider in many ways. He could be prickly; defensive about his background. To get into somewhere like Lund was a huge achievement for the son of a factory worker; a family without any academic aspirations.' The fingers remained in their thoughtful pose. 'Being gay was no big deal in Lund, but he kept it from his parents. So there was guilt there. From my point of view, we shared a course and a love for the Middle East. Passion, really. In that respect he was interesting, often stimulating. And when he let his hair down, he could be fun. He certainly made Linus happy for a time until... ' He broke off and let his hands flop onto the table top.

'So, do you think Linus killed Göran?'

Ivar gave her a fixed stare. 'Put it this way, Alice, I haven't seen or spoken to Linus since that summer. Does that answer your question?'

'It's interesting that Carina doesn't think it was Linus, and that he's actually staying at her apartment in Valletta.'

He nodded his head slowly. 'She told me about the Malta arrangement. That's up to her.'

While Zetterberg had been waiting for Ivar in the living room, she had noticed the family photos. Ivar with smiling kids, Ivar and Jenny grinning at a camera at some party, Ivar at some university event wearing an academic gown and shaking hands with another robed dignitary; and a stern figure in a fashionable sixties suit whom she took to be his father, the prosperous newspaper proprietor. Now she wondered how much *he* had influenced Ivar's decision to cut Linus out of his life. There had been no pictures of any of his old friends.

'Did you know that Göran managed to speak before he died?'

She could see Ivar's mask of affability slip for a moment before quickly being repositioned. 'No. No one said anything about that at the time. I assume he didn't name his killer, or else you wouldn't be here.'

'He mumbled the words "burnt it". Strange, don't you think? Unless you can shed some light on it?'

'Burnt it,' he repeated quietly. 'No. Sorry. It means absolutely nothing. For a moment I wondered if there might be some Arabic connection, but there's none that I can think of.'

'Never mind. Right, I know you're in touch with Carina,

but what about Larissa and Lars-Gunnar?'

'Ah, Larissa. She was fun, but we went our separate ways.'

'Carina didn't think it was that straightforward. She used the word "dumped".'

His face fashioned a hurt expression. 'That's a bit harsh. Our relationship was a student fling; it was never really serious on my part.'

'From our records, we see that Larissa got a job at the university library here at about the time you came up with your family. Was that coincidence?'

'Alice, is that really relevant?'

'Indulge me, please, Professor.'

'It got slightly bizarre. I have to admit the split wasn't entirely amicable. I'd met the girl who was to be my first wife then, and I was ready to move on. Horrible cliché, but true. I'm afraid Larissa couldn't accept the situation, even when I got married. When we moved up here, it was quite a shock when I ran into her in the Carolina Rediviva. She wanted to carry on as though nothing had happened. Of course, I had a new wife and a new university position. Alice, I'm afraid I had to be brutally honest with Larissa.' He spread his arms wide in a "what-can-a-man-do?" shrug. 'I felt awful, but eventually she took the hint and left. I assume she's in Skåne somewhere now.'

'Malmö. The university library.'

'Good for her.'

He may have meant well, but to Zetterberg it sounded bloody patronizing. Was the comment starting to break the spell Ivar had cast over her from the moment she'd entered the apartment? It certainly made her more business-like.

'And Lars-Gunnar? Are you in touch with him?'

'Lars-Gunnar!' he exclaimed. 'Poor fellow. He fell foul of drugs. Have no idea what he's doing these days, or even if he's alive for that matter. Isn't that awful?' An apologetic grimace followed. Zetterberg was beginning to realize that Ivar Hagblom could switch on an appropriate tone of voice and matching expression at will.

'He's alive and being uncooperative, according to my team who tried to speak to him this morning.'

'Is he still hooked?' Ivar asked with apposite concern.

'No, he's clean. He has a family now.'

'I'm pleased. I know his habit got too much for Carina.'

'Wasn't that Göran's fault? I believe he was supplying Lars-Gunnar?'

'That was the unpleasant side of Göran's character. I have to say I wasn't really aware of that until that last summer. Or certainly the extent to which it was going on. I only really understood the problem when Carina had it out with Göran a couple of days before his death. Blazing row.'

Zetterberg was quick to respond. 'You're saying Carina fell out with Göran over supplying her boyfriend with drugs?'

'I hope I haven't talked out of turn.'

Zetterberg bit her bottom lip. Those cracks were definitely appearing.

CHAPTER 17

He could see the cityscape ahead. He realized that he must be approaching Malmö. Now Danny had a clearer idea of what he was going to do. He knew that it was Monday and that he had to act quickly. He reckoned that Leif's body would have been found by his daughter yesterday when she went to the farm to ride. The police would have been called. It would take a while before they matched his fingerprints to his record back in England, so he had time. However, she would also have noticed that the old farmer's car had gone. A description of the vehicle was sure to be posted, so he had decided that he would have to ditch it.

He now had a better idea of where he was and the geography of this part of Sweden, though he still couldn't work out where the working camp had been based. He'd taken the risk of talking to a stranger down by the harbour at Skillinge. He pretended to be a tourist, and the young man he spoke to had excellent English, unlike the older people that he'd done paths, paving and patios for over the previous months. The young man had said that the easiest way to get to Denmark was to cross over the Öresund Bridge. Danny had cursed himself for not driving there straight away, though at the time, he hadn't known where he was and how to get there. Now it was too late. If a description of the car was out, he was bound to be stopped at the bridge. Besides, he didn't know if he would have to show a passport to get into Denmark.

The two-lane road was now getting busier as the suburbs of the city appeared on either side. Though he was now more confident driving on the right, he became nervous when the traffic increased around him and the car behind was almost touching his bumper. What he was looking for was a big public car park. There, he figured it would be easier to lose the Volkswagen for a few days than on a lonely street where neighbours might be suspicious of an unfamiliar vehicle. The road he was on was very straight and seemed to be taking him towards the centre of the city. He didn't want to get too close to the heart of Malmö as he wasn't sure of the roads and might get horribly lost. There would also be CCTV cameras in the centre, and he wanted to make it as difficult as possible to be spotted.

He was trying to register any landmarks that might be useful. Coming up on his left was a twenty-four-hour McDonald's. Further on were buildings that must once have been factories and had now been turned into shops. The parking areas were too small and too open. Then there was a sign to Mobilia. Among the plethora of alien logos, he did recognize Burger King and Specsavers, which suggested Mobilia must be a shopping centre. He eased off to the left, and about three hundred metres up on the right, he saw what he was after – a multi-storey car park. He took a ticket from the machine at the entrance and then drove up the ramp to the second level. He was relieved to see that the bays were nearly full. He got out and locked the car. The first thing he was going to do was buy himself a massive burger with lashings of chips. No, that was the second thing he'd do; the first was get rid of the car keys. After all, they were of no use to Leif now.

Lars-Gunnar Lerstorp's face dropped when he opened the door and saw Szabo and Erlandsson standing in front of him.

'Now you've finished work, we really want to talk to you.' Szabo was curt.

'I've nothing to say.' Lars-Gunnar tried to shut the door, but Szabo's foot prevented him completing the manoeuvre.

'No, you don't! It's either here in front of your family, or we can march you down to headquarters in Malmö.'

'Who's that?' a female voice called from somewhere within the house.

For a moment, Lars-Gunnar looked panic stricken. 'Can we do it in the garden?' he hissed.

Szabo nodded.

'Just some people,' Lars-Gunnar shouted back. 'We'll just be in the garden.' He seemed grateful that they weren't going to burst into his home and cause embarrassment in front of his wife and kids. Zetterberg had been right.

They walked into the large garden at the back of the house. The lawn was neatly cut, and what flower beds there were seemed to be work in progress. Near an open French window, there was a large sandpit with an assortment of plastic toys strewn around. The high wall at the back topped with a wooden fence served as a screen from the main road. Some trees and bushes at street level made an attempt to block the noise of the traffic but only partly succeeded. The well-maintained Dutch bungalow was like most of the others on this pleasant but anonymous estate. It didn't sit easily with what they knew about the old Lars-Gunnar. Maybe the man had reformed and wanted to hide away from his past. He couldn't have chosen a better place than Veberöd.

'Why did you do a runner this morning?' Szabo asked aggressively.

'You freaked me out,' Lars-Gunnar said nervously. 'Suddenly turning up like that.'

'Is that all?' Erlandsson's tone was gentler, more probing.

Lars-Gunnar scratched his neck. 'It's all that Göran business. Brought back bad memories.'

'A murder would.'

'No, no, not that. It was a bad time in my life. I was starting to lose control.'

'The drugs?'

'I can't deny it. They were getting in the way of my friends... my girlfriend.'

'Carina Lindvall?'

He scratched distractedly again. 'Yeah. She tried to help me, but I didn't want to be helped. I didn't like myself a lot in those days.'

Szabo wasn't having any of this self-pity. 'We heard that Göran was supplying you.'

'Who told you that?' His surprise was evident. Perhaps because of his height, Lars-Gunnar stooped, and he now planted his hands firmly in his trouser pockets as though he didn't know what to do with them. The stance made him appear disconcertingly unbalanced, as though he might tip over any second.

'I know it didn't come out at the time, but your old friends are being more forthcoming than they were twenty years ago.'

Lars-Gunnar grimaced. 'Yes.' The admission was reluctant. 'He was. The daft thing is that he didn't do drugs himself. The only one of our group who didn't. But he used it to pay his way through university. He was good at exploiting other people's weaknesses.'

'So on the night of the murder, you were allegedly in the garden drinking and smoking on your own.' Szabo managed to inject enough incredulity into his voice to startle Lars-Gunnar.

'I was. Carina said so to the police. She saw me flaked out on a recliner. She was working inside.'

'Can you remember?'

Lars-Gunnar gave Szabo an anxious glance. 'I think so. I'd had quite a lot to drink at the barbecue we'd had on the beach. When we got back, I had a couple of spliffs with Carina and

Ivar, I think. Then I can't remember much more. God knows what I took after that. I know that there was some commotion later on, and then there were police about. All a bit of a haze.'

'That's convenient.' Szabo still sounded unconvinced.

'What do you mean?'

'You were in such a state, you could have wandered down to the chapel and killed Göran yourself.'

'Of course I didn't!' Lars-Gunnar protested. 'Why would I?'

'Göran was your supplier. Maybe he wouldn't give you any more.'

'Why wouldn't he?'

'Because your loving girlfriend had an argument with him a couple of days before about him supplying you. She was trying to protect you.'

Lars-Gunnar was now stupefied. 'I didn't know she— '

'Which also puts her in the frame,' Erlandsson suggested.

'Come on, that's a ridiculous suggestion. Carina could get angry, but she wouldn't kill anyone.'

'If she loved you enough...' Erlandsson left the suggestion hanging.

Lars-Gunnar twisted away from them and stared towards the high wall at the end of the garden. A couple of invisible cars passed along the main road above. Erlandsson glimpsed a worried-looking woman at one of the windows of the house. She was holding a youngster in her arms. When she saw Erlandsson looking, she quickly drew back.

'So, both you and Carina Lindvall have potential motives.' Szabo felt they were really getting somewhere. Lars-Gunnar turned back to face them, his head shaking.

'It was nothing like that,' he objected. 'OK, we weren't that keen on Göran. He was Ivar's friend. And, of course, he and Linus were an item. I liked Linus.' It was almost thrown in as an afterthought.

'As you were too out of it to tell us much about the day of the murder, you can tell us about Göran and his relationships with everyone.'

Lars-Gunnar flicked away a small clump of stray grass with his foot. 'Göran was very driven. Everything he did was calculated. Carina reckoned he got friendly with Ivar because he thought Ivar would be useful. And then he started up with Linus to be part of Ivar's group. I don't know if it was true. He wasn't that easy to like.'

'Except when he kept your habit going.' Szabo couldn't help the cynicism. Lars-Gunnar ignored it.

'I think the girls thought he was a bit creepy. He didn't strike me like that, but maybe it's because I'm a man. At first he was ingratiating, until he became more confident. Then his competitive streak came out. Especially with Ivar.'

'In what way?' Erlandsson asked.

'Just the odd thing. Mucking about playing football on the beach. That sort of thing. Then it was more like contradicting Ivar on subjects that they were studying. Ivar was always spouting on about Arabic countries and that sort of stuff, and then Göran would jump in and disagree. He would try and shoot down Ivar's ideas. Not exactly putting him down, but definite points scoring. I think their whole PhD thing was turning into a competition to see who would come up with the most lauded research. They were interested in the same things so, at some stage, they would have been going for the same jobs after university. The whole thing gave the group a bad vibe.'

'So it wasn't all sweetness and light?' Szabo mocked.

'We were friends and we stuck together. For a while, anyway.'

'It all fell apart after the murder?'

He swayed in front of them. 'Not straight away. But once the investigation seemed to be going nowhere, we all split up.'

'Are you in touch with any of them now?' Erlandsson asked.

'Nah. Carina lives in a different stratosphere now. So does Ivar. I did bump into Larissa a bit ago. In Malmö. But I haven't been in contact since. And I've no idea where Linus is. They were all part of a different life, one that I don't want to be reminded of.' His hands emerged from their hidey holes. He gestured towards the house. 'That's my life now.'

Szabo's only response was a raised eyebrow.

'Do the words "burnt it" mean anything to you?' Erlandsson asked. 'It was the last thing Göran said.'

Lars-Gunnar shook his head. 'Odd thing to say.'

'All right,' Szabo said finally. 'That's all for now.'

Lars-Gunnar looked anxious again. 'You'll be back?'

'Oh, yes. This is just the beginning.'

Szabo nodded to Erlandsson and they began to walk away. Then Szabo turned. 'Who do you think killed Göran Gösta?'

Lars-Gunnar's wide-eyed stare was accentuated by his gaunt features. 'It was Linus, wasn't it?'

Back in the car, Szabo and Erlandsson didn't exchange thoughts until they'd cleared Veberöd.

'What did you make of that?' Szabo asked.

'He wasn't very happy to revisit the past,' Erlandsson replied from the driving seat.

'And with good reason. He certainly could have done it, whether he knew what he was doing or not. Just blanked everything out. Too bloody handy in my book.'

'He was shaken to hear that Carina had had it out with Göran.'

'He was, wasn't he? She's definitely now in the mix. That'll please the boss. I got the impression she wasn't very keen on your crime writer.'

Erlandsson slowed the car down at a junction. She

completed the left turn before speaking again. 'I thought the Ivar/Göran thing was interesting. I wonder if Zetterberg got the same impression when she spoke to Ivar?'

'I suspect it's just a guys' thing. We're all competitive.' He pulled out his mobile phone. 'Anyway, I'd better get onto the boss and report in. Show we've been good little cops.'

Zetterberg put her phone away, lost in thought. She was standing in Uppsala waiting for a train to take her back to Stockholm. It was a warm evening. She'd already had a drink – two actually – before deciding on her next move. Now she knew what that would be after what Szabo had just told her. She could feel her pulse racing. The case was just starting to open up. There were definite signs of porosity in some of the stories, and some new nuggets of information were being squeezed out. The most significant was Göran's role as Lars-Gunnar's pusher. That had been divisive. In fact, Göran was the source of a lot of discontent and tension. While he was fracturing relationships, was it Ivar that had kept them together? She reckoned that Lars-Gunnar could well have had a motive. And now Carina had one too. That was pleasing. Ivar had mentioned her argument with Göran, though it seemed to be news to the dope-addled Lars-Gunnar. For all Carina's "luvviness", Zetterberg was sure that there was a rod of steel running through her that had driven her to the success she had achieved. Could she have killed to protect the fast-sinking Lars-Gunnar? After all, she'd admitted that she blamed Göran for his drug problem. So that was a definite "yes" as far as Zetterberg was concerned. Which is why she was planning to go knocking on the crime writer's door nice and early tomorrow morning. One thing she did find frustrating was that none of the four seemed to know what Göran's last utterance meant. No, that wasn't quite right – there was something in Ivar's momentary change of demeanour that made her wonder if "burnt it" had some significance for him. Further speculation was curtailed by the approaching train.

The Stockholm-bound train came to a halt, and Zetterberg stepped from the platform and boarded. She took a window seat, got her phone out and started scrolling through it, which is the normal default action of someone addicted to the technology. The last semi-date she'd been on had ended with the man getting up and leaving the coffee shop because she'd spent more time glancing through her phone than looking at him. She forced herself to look away from the screen as another thought about what Szabo had extracted from Lars-Gunnar occurred to her. As the leader of the group, Ivar probably wasn't used to being challenged. He'd already rebuffed Göran's unwanted advances. Despite his own denials that they were good pals, this didn't exactly fit with Lars-Gunnar's description of their competitive natures. She was fairly sure that Ivar hadn't committed the crime, but what if one of his acolytes had done the deed to rid Ivar of his upstart tormentor? Larissa? She was his loyal girlfriend. From Ivar's description, obsessively so. Carina? Possibly. Zetterberg had a sneaking suspicion that Carina and Ivar had more in common than they were letting on. And Linus? He was Ivar's oldest university friend. Maybe it wasn't jealousy at being overthrown by his lover; perhaps he wanted to defend his friend? The thought that Linus was very much back in the frame instigated a brooding frown. It was a thought she would banish when she got to Stockholm and had found a bar. This first cold case investigation was shaping up. She deserved another drink to celebrate the fact that she had got so much further than Sundström had twenty-one years ago.

CHAPTER 18

It was typical of Carina Lindvall to live so far out of Stockholm. Norra Lagnö was a picturesque peninsula in the Värmdö Municipality, at least a couple of Swedish miles east of the city centre. It meant that Alice Zetterberg had had to make an early start from her sister's place in Spånga, which was situated in the opposite direction. Alighting from the early commuter train, she took a taxi from the Central Station. She knew it would cost 400 kronor one way. That irked her, and she would make sure she got it back on expenses. As it was such a fine morning, she had flirted with the idea of taking the ferry, but that took nearly two hours, and she wanted to catch Carina off guard. The taxi ride took about half an hour through the suburbs of Nacka and Boo. On reaching Norra Lagnö, Zetterberg could see the attraction. It was very leafy and surrounded by water, through which the regular Baltic ferries sailed on their way to Mariehamn on Åland, Riga and St. Petersburg.

The taxi drew up in front of a large wooden house painted a subtle shade of willow green. As the driver was obviously from some Balkan backwater, she only gave him a meagre tip. Unsurprisingly, a glum expression was all the thanks she got. She wasn't going to pay him to hang around until she'd finished with Carina. She would make other arrangements.

The house was on a small bank and looked to have been built in the latter part of the 19th century. With its red roof, dormer windows framed in white and air of permanence, it presided over this particularly pretty corner of the peninsula. Zetterberg strode up the gravel driveway and up a short flight of steps bordered by a white balustrade. Carina wasn't looking so glamorous when she opened the door. She was wearing a white T-shirt and grey jogging bottoms, and her hair hadn't yet been brushed. She blinked at Zetterberg, who was feeling almost as bad as Carina looked. Her one drink back in Stockholm had turned into several, and her mouth was still dry, despite getting through a bottle of water on the journey.

'God, what time is it?' Carina groaned.

'Five past nine.'

'I don't receive visitors before twelve.' But she reluctantly let Zetterberg in. Carina led the way into the living room, whose décor was in sharp contrast to the exterior of the house. Two sink-into sofas with high armrests and enormous cushions sat on opposite sides of an expensive cream shag pile rug, upon which stood a sturdy, oblong, light-oak coffee table. A modern cylindrical cast-iron stove graced one corner of the room, and other small items of contemporary furniture with the typically unostentatious contours of Scandinavian design filled alcoves and niches. A large flat-screen television dominated the main wall and a couple of what looked like genuine Carl Larssons paid deference to it. The space was light, and the sun was streaming through the high, elegant windows. Carina opened a silver box and took out a cigarette, which she proceeded to light. 'Can't even think without one,' she drawled, before shooing an overweight ginger cat off a chair and plonking herself down. The protesting cat scuttled off into the next room. Carina didn't offer Zetterberg a seat, but she sat down all the same.

'Your visit isn't entirely unexpected. Ivar was on the phone last night. He was worried that he might have dropped me in it.' Wonderful! That will have given her time to dream up a logical explanation for the argument with Göran. Zetterberg had hoped to catch the writer on the hop.

'Well?' Zetterberg asked pointedly.

'You want to know about the disagreement I had with that fink, Göran?' She took a drag of her cigarette and then let a whoosh of smoke out of her wide mouth. This was not the image that her adoring public saw. 'As I said before, Göran was encouraging Lars-Gunnar's habit. It was pissing me off and I had it out with him a couple of days before the murder.'

'How did he react?'

Carina looked around for an ashtray. She leant over to a coffee table and retrieved a small one made of cut glass, which she then balanced on her lap.

'He couldn't give a toss. He had the nerve to tell me that it was Lars-Gunnar's business. I told him it was mine, too, as I was footing the bloody bill. He said more fool me. I slapped him on the face and told him no one wanted him around.' She returned to her cigarette.

'And how did he respond to you hitting him?'

'Laughed, actually. I didn't hit him hard enough, unfortunately.'

'And to the fact that no one wanted him around?'

Carina stubbed the half-smoked cigarette out in the ashtray, which she removed from her lap and put back on the coffee table. 'That was a bit odd. At first he ranted about what supercilious shits we all were and that we'd always looked down on him and that sort of thing. Then he said that our precious Ivar would suffer the most.' She held up a hand with yet-to-be-painted fingernails. 'And before you ask, I haven't the foggiest idea what he was on about. And I never found out because he was dead before he carried out his mysterious threat.' Even though Zetterberg was still feeling slightly hung over, she could see that this was a potentially interesting new avenue.

'Of course, you realize that you had a motive? You could have killed Göran to protect your boyfriend.'

'Oh, please! I may bump off tons of people in my books, but I'd be useless at doing it in reality. My readers love all the gratuitous mutilations and graphic serial slayings, but I can't stand the sight of blood. Lars-Gunnar was a lovely guy who I was very fond of for a while, but to kill someone on his behalf...' She shook her tousled hair in disbelief.

Zetterberg wasn't so sure. She pressed on with her next question. 'We've heard that Ivar and Göran were very competitive.'

'Did you hear that from Ivar?' Carina queried.

'No.'

'Yes, they were. You wouldn't think Ivar was like that when you first met him. I'm sure you found him delightful.' Zetterberg shifted in her seat. 'I can tell you did. Charm the pants off any woman. And he often did, literally.'

'Did he charm the pants off you?'

'That's a bit personal,' Carina barked sharply before giving way to a husky laugh. 'I'm not going to confirm or deny the accusation. Anyway, I thought you wanted to know about the boys' battles.'

'I do.'

'It was funny at first, until it started to seep into their university work. It was like, who was going to be the most lionized? Academics are nightmares when it comes to one-upmanship.' She put on a childish voice: *'I get more articles and books published than you.* Bloody juvenile behaviour, if you ask me. And most of what these people write about is a total waste of time, and the money could be better spent on proper research. Saving people from hideous diseases, not "how many children did Lady MacBeth have?". Honestly! Anyhow, Ivar and Göran were getting on each other's nerves. Göran was always criticizing anything Ivar said. It became unpleasant. Spoiled the family atmosphere.'

'Ivar said they got on well. Said he found Göran "stimulating". That they shared the same passion for the Middle East.'

'They did. Until Malta. Something changed there.'

'Göran tried to get off with Ivar. Well, that's Ivar's version of events.'

Again the deep chuckle. 'That might have had a bit to do with it. I don't know what it was, but Ivar left Malta on a high. He was cock-a-hoop about something.'

'Personal thing?'

'Don't think so. Nothing changed from that angle afterwards. He was still with Larissa.'

'My team got the impression that Larissa didn't like you.' Zetterberg couldn't help herself. In fact, she rather enjoyed bringing it up.

Carina arched an eyebrow. 'Envy, darling. We were friends back in our Malmö days. And Lund, of course. I find one tends to grow out of one's old friends. And I'm sure she's jealous of all this.' Carina indicated the elegant surroundings. 'She's probably stuck in a hole somewhere. A beautiful-looking girl who didn't make the most of her assets. She couldn't cling onto Ivar for starters, and look where he is now.' Zetterberg really did think that Carina Lindvall was unpleasant. 'Anyway, getting back to Malta. Whatever had got Ivar all excited can't have had anything to do with Göran's death. But shouldn't you ask him?'

'I will.'

Danny had slept late. He couldn't remember the last time he'd woken up in a proper bed. He lay still as he heard the voices of people passing in the street below. He'd had to open the window during the night as it had been warm and humid. After the last few nights, it felt odd to be sleeping within four walls.

He turned over and wondered what the time was. He would

have to buy a cheap watch. But he knew this was a Tuesday; two days after Leif's body would have been discovered. Through bleary eyes, he surveyed his Spartan accommodation. It was functional, and that was all he needed. It had taken him some time to find the hostel, which was near a big theatre with a glass frontage.

After dumping Leif's car, he'd had a huge helping of burgers and chips, which had almost made him sick, as his stomach wasn't used to having so much food shoved into it. He knew that the shopping centre he was in was called Mobilia, but he had no idea where it was in relation to the centre of the city. He'd tried to catch a bus. To his surprise, he'd been turned away because he hadn't got something called a *Jo Jo* card; the driver pronounced it *Yo Yo*. Did people in Sweden not use money anymore? He had no option but to walk into the centre. After one false start which landed him on the edge of a big park, he'd doubled back and managed to follow a wide street which passed a large square with a colourful market. Further on, he found himself on a long, pedestrianized thoroughfare full of shops, most of whose names meant nothing to him. He crossed a wide canal and then found himself wandering through an older part of the town, which was even more crowded. Eventually, he reached another canal – or was it the same one? – and what appeared to be the main railway station. Here he had found out about trains out of the country – and been sent to the tourist information office across the road. On the Malmö city map they gave him, the helpful staff there had shown him where the hostel was located. They had offered to ring ahead and book him in. He hastily declined the offer, as he didn't want to give his name. He'd found the hostel on the corner of a side street. He'd booked in for four nights, though he had no intention of staying that long. It had been a good move, as he hadn't been able to produce a passport when asked – he explained that he must have left it at the tourist information office and would collect it later. As he was staying for a while, the receptionist said to pop it in whenever.

He eased himself onto the edge of the bed and stretched. He leant over and took a handful of crisps from a large packet he'd bought yesterday. There was a small supermarket below, and he'd stocked up. He didn't intend to go out except for essential trips. The first of these was to buy some new clothes and a watch. It would help him get his bearings. Then he would discover the best way to get out of Sweden. It still preyed on his mind that he hadn't got a passport.

He also knew that time wasn't on his side. The police would soon match up his fingerprints with his criminal record back in England and come up with his identity. They might find the car at any moment, which would place him in Malmö. And then there was McNaught. Despite the warmth of the room, he shivered at the thought. He knew it was that bastard who had killed poor old Leif. A brutal action like that showed that he'd stop at nothing to find him and silence him for ever.

Ivar Hagblom was mounting the steps outside the university library when his phone started buzzing. He nearly didn't answer it, as he was late for a meeting with a couple of his PhD students. He liked to be punctual. And he certainly liked his students to be punctual, as his time was precious, especially with the new term only a fortnight away. But it might be a TV station wanting him to make an appearance, or a newspaper eager for a quote. When he took his phone out, the incoming number didn't ring any bells.

'Ivar Hagblom.' He put on a cheery voice because the caller might be important – or useful. The pleasant smile he'd combined with the voice disappeared when Detective Alice Zetterberg announced her name. He had hoped that he'd seen the last of this rather unattractive and unappealing woman. 'How can I help, Alice?'

'You weren't exactly straight with me, Professor.'

'I don't know what you mean.' He glanced up and acknowledged a colleague who was coming out of the building. He threw in an exasperated expression, to which the colleague grimaced sympathetically.

'It turns out that you and Göran were becoming quite bitter rivals. By the sound of things, he was poisoning the group and was getting very argumentative with you in particular.'

'Honestly, Alice, it was just the usual academic thing. Each one of us wanted to do better than the other. After all, our PhDs could open up amazing possibilities, and we were operating in the same field, so to speak. It was only natural that there was rivalry. It was nothing personal.' He protests too much, thought Zetterberg.

'OK. I get the picture.'

'Look, Alice, sorry to rush you but I'm late for an appointment.'

'Just one thing, Professor,' Zetterberg put in quickly. 'When you were all on Malta, Carina Lindvall says that you were "cock-a-hoop" about something. What were you so happy about?'

'Goodness me, Alice; it was over twenty years ago!'

'It made an impression on Carina – she still remembers it.'

He glanced distractedly at his watch. 'It was probably something to do with the Great Siege. I was interested in the changing balance of East and West. I learned so much on that trip.' Why did Zetterberg feel he was being evasive? 'I can't remember anything specific. It was just a wonderful experience.' Almost with irritation creeping into his voice: 'Is it really important what I was feeling?' Then he added with a harder edge: 'Or are you just fishing, Inspector?'

CHAPTER 19

Moberg was still in a disarmingly upbeat mood as they gathered in the meeting room. It wasn't matched by the others, who just wanted an excuse to get out of the polishus and take advantage of the sunshine. Moberg was more than content to avoid the heat, and was one of the few Swedes who didn't love the summer. He smacked his hands together for attention and plunged straight into the meeting without any preamble.

'Latest news we have from forensics is that they've managed to get fingerprints off the murder victim and the driver. They don't match anything we've got on the national database. That doesn't necessarily mean that they're not Swedish, but I've asked for the search to be widened anyway. We're checking the prints with British and Irish police to see if they can come up with anything. My little pal, Adolf Frid, reckoned that Egon Fuentes was working with a British or Irish gang. Hopefully, it'll throw up something. OK, where are we at? Brodd, any luck with the van?'

Brodd beamed back. 'Oh, yes.' The others were amazed that Brodd had got off his arse long enough to find something out. 'I tracked down the garage where it was last sold from over in Fosie. Bit of a dump. Not sure how roadworthy some of the vehicles are. The van was fifteen years old. Probably explains why it stalled.'

'And?' said Moberg, clicking his fingers impatiently.

'It was definitely Fuentes who bought the van. The guy

recognized his photo. Paid cash; no questions asked. The garage guy did say that he peeled off the notes from a big wad. You don't see that sort of thing these days.'

'You can bet it wasn't Fuentes' money,' commented Moberg. 'Egon never used his own dosh. So someone must have bankrolled him. Next? Wallen?'

'Up against a brick wall,' said Wallen. 'Which seems appropriate. I've been around a number of building suppliers. Most of them seem above board. None of them recognized Fuentes. Or if they did, they're not saying. I've still some more to visit today.'

'Well, you'd better get moving as soon as we've finished here.'

He nodded at Anita and Hakim. 'Get anything useful from the scene of the accident?'

'Not really,' replied Anita, 'though Hakim worked out where they were probably heading.' She let Hakim take over.

'I think they may have been going in the direction of an old, disused quarry. We went there, and now there's a lake in the bottom. Doesn't really help. The quarry's long gone and the company that owned it has gone too. It's a pretty desolate spot and a good location to lose a body. If that *was* where they were aiming for, then they were keen that it should never be found.'

'It also suggests that they wanted to take the body away from the scene of the crime,' Moberg mused. 'Why?' All Hakim could do was shrug in reply to the rhetorical question. 'Did you get anything useful from Ystad about where the van might have come from?'

'They've interviewed householders and farmers in the area, but nothing that we can pinpoint,' Hakim continued.

'Any CCTV?'

'There's virtually nothing around there. We'll have to keep working further north.'

'Isn't there a good chance that the murder was committed

by the two other men in the van?' Anita was only articulating what the others were thinking. It was met with a fierce response from Moberg.

'You're fucking kidding! There's a lot more to this. I'm convinced that Egon Fuentes didn't kill that young man. His passenger might have, but there's a bigger picture here. There's a lot of money involved; Fuentes told Adolf Frid that. Your garage owner, Brodd, mentioned a wad of readies. For starters, there was no cash found at the scene of the accident. It's not just three people falling out. If Egon was involved, you can bet your life there was a huge scam going on. That means there were victims. We need to find them, too.' There was no mistaking the evangelical passion. 'So, we carry on. No stone unturned and all that. Do you understand?'

All the detectives sat in silence. Anita wished she'd kept her mouth shut. The sooner she was on holiday, the better.

'Right. I'm going to pay Adolf Frid another visit and shake his tree and see if anything falls out. Brodd, I want you to get our press lot to get Fuentes' photo out to all the newspapers and media outlets in the whole of Skåne. I want to see his smarmy face on TV tonight. See if it jogs any memories. The rest of you, carry on doing what you're doing. Just find me something!'

'Yes, Boss.' Brodd was such a crawler, thought Anita. Wallen's and Hakim's expressions confirmed her view.

Moberg's tone changed abruptly: 'By the way, when you're out and about, there's a car that Kristianstad are trying to track down. They think the killer of the farmer up at Höör is using it. Could be anywhere, but keep your eyes peeled. Details are on an email that's being sent round.' Then he was back to normal, and he wafted his hand dismissively. 'Right, bugger off and keep digging. Find anything of interest, and I want to hear from you immediately!'

Hakim managed to grab a bite to eat with Liv Fogelström at

a café they frequented near Värnhemstorget. It was close to the polishus, yet rarely patronized by staff from headquarters. They both had a salad and cold drinks.

'Honestly, don't worry about the other day.' She hoped the sympathetic smile would calm Hakim. His anger had started to rise up the scale like the heat outside. It seemed to work.

'He's just so rigid,' he mumbled.

'Have you spoken to him since?'

'You're joking! I'm waiting for an apology. Actually, you should be getting the apology. He wasn't courteous. That's unforgiveable for a host.'

Liv put down her fork and placed a hand over his and gave it a squeeze. 'I'm sure he'll come round in the end.'

'I hope so. He has to understand that you'll be part of the family.' He suddenly pulled his hand away when he realized the implication of what he'd just blurted out. So did Liv. She glanced away. An awkward silence followed.

It was Liv who broke the spell. 'What are you doing this afternoon? Exciting that you've got another murder case.'

'The chief inspector thinks so. I've never seen him this motivated before. He's treating it as a crusade. That's why we're off to all points north of the accident to try and find somewhere with CCTV in an attempt to find where the van in the crash was coming from.'

With a mouthful of coleslaw out of the way, Liv asked: 'What does Anita Sundström think?'

Hakim snorted. 'She thinks the killers are already dead. But her mind is miles away. She's winding down for her holiday. Too busy thinking about her boyfriend.'

'And what's wrong with that?' Liv made big moon eyes at him.

'You know what I mean,' he scolded. 'She's only going through the motions. If you ask me, she's more interested in the cold case. It's like an itch she can't stop scratching.'

'Ah, now, did you find out what was behind why she dislikes Zetterberg so much?'

'I forgot,' came his bashful reply.

'Hakim Mirza, you are totally useless sometimes,' she giggled. 'When I ask you to find out gossip, that's not a request; it's an order!'

Hakim had the opportunity to follow Liv's "order" when he and Anita were returning from a fruitless afternoon drive around the Scanian countryside. The nearest they'd got to a nibble was a roadside garage, which did have CCTV but, after some initial excitement, they couldn't find anything in the hours leading up to the crash. Egon Fuentes had deliberately kept to the back roads and had only really emerged to cross the railway line, which was an obstacle they couldn't avoid if they had been making for the disused quarry.

'So, do you know how the cold case is going?' he asked tentatively as he kept his eyes on the road.

'Don't know much,' Anita said offhandedly as though she wasn't remotely interested.

'Really?' He feigned surprise.

Anita puffed out her cheeks. 'Well, I do know they're re-interviewing the old suspects. Except, of course, the one who actually did it. They can't find him, apparently. They won't get anything new out of the others. Despite that, *she's* gone up to Stockholm and Uppsala.'

'You mean, Inspector Zetterberg?'

'Yes,' she huffed.

'Why all the friction with her?'

Anita shot him a sideways glance. 'I just don't like her.'

'It sounds personal.' Hakim was fearful of getting too deeply into the matter, but he wanted to come away with something to tell Liv. He felt he needed to make it up to her after the weekend and his slip of the tongue at lunchtime. He cursed himself for that because it betrayed how he was feeling about her. But did she feel the same about him?

'Goes back a long way. Police Academy. It was to do with one of our fellow cadets. A misunderstanding.'

'A man?' Hakim knew he was pushing it.

'It might have been,' said Anita cagily.

'Yesss!'

'I beg your pardon?' Anita retorted in amazement.

'Sorry. Sorry, it's nothing,' he hurriedly apologized. 'It was... it was nothing. Well, no, that's not quite true.' He kept his eyes firmly fixed on the road so he didn't have to look round and face Anita. 'Liv was wondering about the antagonism between you and Inspector Zetterberg. She said that there was bound to be a man behind it.'

'Did she now?'

'She meant nothing by it, honestly.' He knew he'd put his foot in it. 'Blame it on me.'

'Well, you can tell Constable Fogelström that it wasn't what she thinks it was.' To his relief he heard Anita laugh. 'Cheeky cow. But she's got the instincts of a good cop.'

The new-look Danny turned into Malmö's Central Station, trying hard to fit in with the other commuters. The clothes felt good. A check shirt, blue jeans, tan loafers and a thin summer jacket. Even the underpants were new. They felt the best of all. He'd waited until the rush hour so that the station would be packed and he wouldn't stand out. The shops and the food concessions were doing a roaring trade on the main concourse.

He bought himself a coffee so that he blended in. On the departures board he could see that there were regular trains to Copenhagen every twenty minutes. This was his way out of Sweden. Could he risk trying to get on board a Denmark-bound train without a passport? What would be waiting on the Danish side? He had never been abroad before and was unsure of the protocol. He hadn't even had a passport until he'd met Mr Cassidy; he'd fixed it all up for him. He'd never even looked at it properly, as when he left England in the transit van with Jack and the others, it had been promptly taken off him by Paddy, or whatever the Irish guy was called. Cut from the same cloth as McNaught; turned out to be just as brutal.

He was finishing his coffee with the intention of heading off and buying himself a falafel, a fast food which seemed to be available everywhere. He was casting around for a bin when the hairs on the back of his neck stiffened. Among the moving mass of passengers coming up the escalator from the lower-level platforms was an unmistakable bald head; and then the telltale scar. The man turned towards Danny. Fighting back throat-wrenching nausea, Danny sank to his haunches as though he was picking something up off the tiled floor. His head was turned away as McNaught approached. He kept his eyes shut as he heard people trundle past. He was gasping for air and he thought he might actually collapse. He was waiting for that frighteningly familiar Scots voice to bark some order at him. Surely he couldn't kill him in such a public place? He'd hustle him out to some quiet spot and finish him off there. But the voice never came, and after what seemed like hours, he furtively raised his head. McNaught wasn't there. Danny stood up. McNaught was gone. But he *was* in Malmö, and Danny knew it was only a matter of time before he found him.

CHAPTER 20

It was half past eight, and Bea Erlandsson wondered if it was going to be typical of her new boss to call a meeting this late. She and Szabo had been left hanging around all day without instructions from Zetterberg, awaiting her return from her jaunt to Stockholm. Erlandsson had already cancelled what would have been a second date with Maria, the Brazilian student she'd met a few nights before at her favourite bar in town. Maybe that's why Zetterberg was so down on her, because she'd heard she was a lesbian.

Zetterberg had already outlined her various conversations with Carina Lindvall and Ivar Hagblom. Even Erlandsson was impressed with the new information Zetterberg had managed to extract from the two. Szabo had then again gone over the notes that they'd compiled from their chat with Lars-Gunnar in his garden. They'd also done some further background checks on Lars-Gunnar and Larissa in the hopes that something incriminating might emerge. Now Zetterberg stood in front of the photographs of their five suspects.

'Right, I think what we've managed in only a few days is to unearth far more than the original investigation managed in several months.' The self-satisfaction was naked. 'Having interviewed four of the five suspects, we have already come up with potential motives for three of them. Let's start with Lars-Gunnar Lerstorp. He was into drugs. Göran was his supplier, though he doesn't appear to have been a user himself. Could they have fallen out over drugs? Carina Lindvall had angrily warned Göran off only a few days before.'

'He denies knowing about that incident.' Erlandsson had believed Lars-Gunnar.

'He would,' Zetterberg said dismissively. 'On the other hand, if Göran had heeded the warning, where did that leave Lars-Gunnar? Without a regular supply? Did he try and persuade Göran to carry on? When he wouldn't, did he kill him? His alibi is pretty tenuous. Carina said she saw him spaced out in the garden. Or was she covering for him? Even if she wasn't and was working as she claimed, she wouldn't be staring out of the window every five seconds, so he could have disappeared for long enough to commit the crime. For all we know, Lars-Gunnar might have been so far gone that he didn't even realize that he had killed Göran. So, there is a big question mark hanging over him.'

'He certainly wasn't keen to talk to us,' Szabo said with a glance at Erlandsson.

'He's in the mix. As is the far-from-delightful Carina,' continued Zetterberg with a nod in the direction of the crime writer's photograph. 'She had it out with Göran. Maybe Göran paid no attention to her warning. Did she kill him to protect Lars-Gunnar, who was self-destructing? She's a confident, strong-minded woman who's used to getting her own way. Did Göran get in her way because he was destroying the man she loved at the time?' Zetterberg put her hands on her hips as she swivelled back round to the board. 'And I'm also intrigued by her relationship with Ivar Hagblom. I suspect they're more than just friends. But were they that close back then?'

'Does it really matter what their relationship was back at Knäbäckshusen?' queried Erlandsson.

Zetterberg swung round and flashed her a filthy look. 'We don't know. The point is that it might be significant. After all, she also gave Ivar and Larissa an alibi: said they were at it in the next room.'

'And they also alibied each other,' pointed out Szabo.

'True. But as I've said before, alibis are there to be broken. The more we hear about Göran, the more we gather that he and Ivar weren't the best of friends, as Ivar had initially indicated. As you've said, Lars-Gunnar pointed out how competitive they had become. It almost sounds like Göran was belittling Ivar. That would be hard for him to take considering he was the self-appointed leader of their little set. And Ivar's relationship with Larissa wasn't as hunky dory as she made out. Basically, he passed Larissa over when he found someone better – or of more use to his career. All that stuff about her going to work in Uppsala sounds a bit weird. I want you two to talk to her again. There's something not right there.'

'Will do,' nodded Szabo.

Zetterberg tapped the photograph of Ivar Hagblom. 'It's also apparent that the Hagblom family downplayed the murder. Very little coverage in their newspapers at the time. And later on, it was one of their papers that "outed" Linus Svärd, thanks to the blabbing Inspector Sundström, and then eventually drove him out of Malmö a couple of years later. It's plain where they were laying the blame.'

'You mean that they were finding a scapegoat?' suggested Szabo.

'Possibly,' Zetterberg agreed. 'They were certainly distancing Ivar from the murder, which is understandable. It did involve their holiday home. There *is* such a thing as bad publicity. Or unwanted publicity.' Zetterberg paused and picked up her paper coffee cup. She took a sip and pulled a face. It had gone cold. 'We've gathered from our interviews that Göran wasn't popular. No one professed to like him except Ivar. They tolerated him for Ivar's sake. Yet it all seems to have started to unravel during their stay on Malta. Carina reckoned that Ivar was excited about something while on the island. She had no idea what it was, and when I asked Ivar about it, he claimed he couldn't remember what she was referring to. Whatever it was, even he admitted it must have been something historical; something to do with his research. So, when you speak to Larissa, ask if she can shed any light on it. Maybe nothing, but I don't want to overlook any detail, however insignificant it might seem.'

'It's a pity we can't find Linus Svärd,' mused Szabo. 'We've drawn a blank there.'

Zetterberg's faced creased into a Cheshire-cat grin. This was one piece of information she'd deliberately kept back. 'I've found him.' She drank in the amazement on her subordinates' faces. 'He's on Malta. Currently, he's shacked up in Carina's holiday apartment.'

'Bloody hell!' Szabo exclaimed. 'So one of them *is* still in touch.'

'Yes; the only person who protests his innocence.'

CHAPTER 21

Anita was in early on the Wednesday morning. She wanted to get odds and ends sorted out before her holiday. She knew that she could see to administrative tasks while the rest of the team worked on the murder of the young man in the van. She was surprised when there was a knock on her door and Liv Fogelström entered.

'Sorry to disturb you, Inspector Sundström...'

'Not at all. Come in Liv.'

The constable hovered nervously in front of Anita's desk. She obviously wanted to say something, though she was finding it hard to come out with it. Anita tried to put her at her ease.

'Can I get you a coffee?'

'No. No thank you. That's very kind.'

Anita pointed towards the spare chair opposite. 'Why don't you sit down and tell me...' Fogelström self-consciously plonked herself onto the chair. This wasn't the usual cheery, popular-throughout-the-polishus Fogelström that Anita had become accustomed to since she'd become Hakim's girlfriend. 'Is there a work problem?'

Fogelström plucked up her courage. 'It's about Hakim.'

'Ah.'

'It's your advice I'm after.' Her voice was almost entreating.

'I'm not sure I'm the right person to be talking to.'

'Oh, but you are.' She took a deep breath. 'I think Hakim

is going to ask me to marry him.' Silence followed. Anita wasn't sure how she was meant to respond. It wasn't exactly a surprise. 'I don't know if you heard about the meal we had round at his parents' on Saturday.'

'Hakim told me. Can't have been pleasant for you.'

'It wasn't very nice for anybody. Hakim was so angry. You see, I'm a problem as far as his parents are concerned. I'm not a Muslim. I've not got the right background.'

'Well, they seem to have coped with Jazmin cohabiting with my Lasse. It hasn't always been easy.'

'That's why I've come to you. You've seen all this at first hand.'

'It's Lasse you should be speaking with.'

Fogelström gulped. 'Herr Mirza said that he didn't want Hakim making the same mistake as Jazmin.'

Anita screwed up her face. She knew that Uday wasn't delighted with his daughter's choice, though she now wondered if she had underestimated the strength of his feelings. He was an intelligent, often charming, cultured, westernized Iraqi. She had never personally had any problems with him, though she was aware that Lasse had. As someone without any particular faith, she didn't find it easy to comprehend those who had an unbending creed, though she had no difficulty in accepting such doctrines. In the course of her work, she had come across many people, both criminals and victims, who had been driven by their theism and guided by their beliefs; often clashing with those who held conflicting philosophies. Malmö was a melting pot. Over forty percent of the city's population were from foreign backgrounds – twenty percent of the residents were Muslim.

'I don't know what advice I can offer you, Liv.'

The normally confident, ebullient girl clasped her podgy hands nervously on her lap. 'What should I say to Hakim when he asks me?'

'Do you love him?'

'Of course I do. What I'm really asking is: is it going to cause on-going resentment? Will parental pressure break us? Break him?'

Anita sighed helplessly. 'I can't answer that. Only Hakim can.'

Just then the office phone rang to save her. 'Excuse me.' Anita picked it up. 'Anita Sundström.' She listened for a few moments. 'I'll come right along.' She put the receiver back. 'Sorry, Liv, I've got to see the chief inspector urgently.'

Fogelström quickly stood up. 'Thanks for listening to me.'

As Anita followed the young constable out of the room, it dawned on her that she would make a rather useless agony aunt.

By the time Anita returned to her office, she was fuming. She kicked the spare chair in annoyance. It hurt her foot, which only stoked her fury further. Her brief meeting with Chief Inspector Moberg had started ominously with his opening words: 'Do you want the bad news or the bad news?'

'Neither.'

'Hard luck. Bad news number one; you're going to have to cancel your holiday.' There wasn't a shred of sympathy in his tone. It just came out as a bald statement.

This had led to her first explosion before he'd even given her a reason. When he had a chance to justify himself, he explained that it was because the murder case they were investigating had a possible British or Irish dimension and he needed someone on hand with excellent English and British connections. Anita hardly thought that was a good reason to keep her there. She knew it was more to do with Moberg's obsession with Egon Fuentes that was behind the decision, and he wanted the full team working on the case.

Then came the double whammy. 'However, we are

sending you somewhere sunny first. The Skåne County Police are paying for you to go to Malta.'

'Malta?' Anita had no idea what he was on about. What had that to do with Egon Fuentes?

'The possible downside of this trip is that you'll be accompanying Inspector Zetterberg to interview a suspect in the case that she is currently working on.'

'You can't be serious!'

'This has come from on high,' he said, pointing to the heavens. 'Commissioner Dahlbeck, no less.'

'What the hell for?' Anita was incredulous. Losing her holiday was bad enough, but this Malta business was too horrendous for words.

'Again, your linguistic skills. Apparently, Zetterberg's English isn't deemed good enough to deal with the local police or authorities. And she certainly doesn't speak Malti. Who the hell does? As this is a potentially sensitive case in terms of dealing with another country, the commissioner wants to play it safe.'

'I bet Zetterberg doesn't want me there.' Anita spoke through gritted teeth.

'It'll give you two a chance to reminisce,' Moberg chuckled. He was enjoying her exasperation.

'And who are we supposed to be interviewing?'

'Don't know. She'll brief you later on this morning.'

Anita's head was swirling with vexatious thoughts. At this moment she couldn't decide whom she hated most: Moberg, Egon Fuentes, Zetterberg or Commissioner Dahlbeck.

'But what about our murder case?' Anita protested. 'I thought you wanted me here.' There must be a get out.

'I can spare you for a couple of days. So, you'd better go and pack your bag. Your flight is first thing tomorrow morning.'

Anita could hear the bitter disappointment in his voice. That touched her. She realized how much Kevin had been looking forward to her visit.

'Look, I'm sure we can rearrange. I really want to see you.' Her initial anger and frustration was spent, though it had re-emerged briefly when she'd explained to Kevin why she wouldn't be on the plane to Manchester on Saturday morning. He had tried to be understanding.

'Yeah, yeah of course.' He didn't sound positive. 'It's just I'd arranged the trips you wanted. To Dove Cottage, and Edinburgh. And I'd booked a meal at the Sharrow Bay, though it was going to cost a month's pay.'

'I'm sorry.'

'And I've bought a new bed. I wanted you here to christen it.'

'I'll make it up to you.' She cooed seductively: 'I promise your new bed won't go unchristened.'

Kevin perked up. 'I'll hold you to that. Well, I'll hold something.'

'I'll let you.' Her thoughts briefly turned to what they might get up to. But they quickly returned to matters in hand. 'Oh, and I'm off to Malta tomorrow.'

There was a momentary silence at the other end. 'So, you're buggering off to the middle of the Mediterranean while you leave me in a wet and miserable Cumbria.'

'Don't worry. It's not going to be fun.'

'Am I meant to be reassured? Leanne went to Malta, and I know she had a lot of fun there!' He sounded bitter.

'It's work. And you'll never guess who I have to go with.'

'As long as he's an ugly dwarf with no sex drive, I'll be happy.'

'That would be preferable, believe me. No, it's Alice Zetterberg.'

She heard Kevin's low whistle at the other end. 'How on earth has she popped up again?' Kevin had known at first-hand what Zetterberg was like. Memories of her involvement in the Rylander case still plagued his dreams and troubled his waking thoughts.

'She's heading up a cold case. My first ever murder investigation, in fact. We knew who'd done it, but we hadn't enough evidence to convict him. Now the witch is trying to prove we were wrong. Prove me wrong!'

'I can see her enjoying that.' Then he added brightly: 'But as I'm sure you were right in the first place, maybe Malta's your chance to show her that you were.'

Anita gave an involuntary grunt. 'I think Malta's going to be a bloody nightmare.'

CHAPTER 22

You could hardly call it a meeting. Zetterberg showed her displeasure in having to travel to Malta with Anita in no uncertain terms.

'You're coming with me under sufferance because I've got no choice. I don't want you there. So, the way it's going to work is that you turn up, you talk to the local police, and you keep your trap shut when I'm interviewing the potential suspect. You don't interfere, you don't make observations, and you don't make any suggestions. Then we fly back. End of story. End of your involvement. You made a mess last time, now I'm doing what you should have done then.'

Anita bit her lip. She managed to control herself, though she would have quite happily lashed out at this overbearing, malicious and manipulative woman.

'And who is it that *you* are interviewing?'

A hint of a smile seeped across Zetterberg's face. 'Linus Svärd.'

So, they had tracked him down to Malta. Anita was intrigued as to what he was doing there.

'Be at Kastrup at half seven.'

There was nothing left to say, and Anita left. Maybe Kevin had been right. This was a chance to prove at last that Linus Svärd was the killer and vindicate Henrik Nordlund and the team.

In the corridor, she came across Bea Erlandsson.

'I hear you're accompanying my boss to Malta. Lucky you.' The face that Erlandsson pulled showed that Anita had the young detective's sympathy.

'It's not a happy prospect, though I'm impressed that you've managed to find Linus Svärd. I lost track of him.'

'Turns out he's living in Carina Lindvall's holiday home on the island.'

That was interesting, too. 'The trouble is that your boss won't give me any information on how the case is going. I don't know what you've dug up.'

Erlandsson eyes flitted along the corridor in case someone emerged from behind the door with *Cold Case Grupp* emblazoned on it. 'I can fill you in, but not here.'

Anita understood. 'Tell you what, Bea. Why don't I treat you to a drink after work? I'll meet you in the Pickwick. It's not the sort of bar that Inspector Zetterberg is likely to frequent.'

Bea nodded conspiratorially and scuttled off along the corridor.

Danny hadn't ventured out of his room since he'd fled back from the station the day before. The sight of McNaught in Malmö had totally rattled him. McNaught was slowly tracking him down. And Danny knew he had a gun – he might not even bother taking him to some quiet spot to finish him off; he might just shoot him the street. He had to get away. But how? Having no passport was a huge stumbling block.

It was anxious hunger that drove him out of his room at midday and down to the supermarket below. He grabbed a few things off the shelves without really taking in what he was buying. He just wanted to get back to the safety of his room. He hurriedly paid for his items and didn't even wait for his change.

Five minutes later there was a knock on his door. Oh, God! Had McNaught found him already? At first he was just frozen to his bed. Beads of sweat ran down his tingling spine.

Was this it? The final moment?

The knock came again. 'Hey, buddy, are you in there?' The voice was unmistakably American.

Danny got up slowly and carefully opened the door a slit. The man standing in the corridor was young and black-haired and had a thick beard. He wore a collarless white shirt, baggy khaki shorts and flip-flops. He held a plastic bag of groceries in his left hand.

'Christ, are you OK?'

'Fine,' mumbled Danny

The American held out his right hand; there were some coins in the palm. 'These are yours. You didn't pick up your change in the supermarket. I was behind you in the line. Seen you around the hostel. English, right?'

Danny reached out and took the money. 'Thanks.'

'Is anything the matter?'

Danny wanted to shut the door, yet he found it difficult. Here was a friendly face.

'If you want a drink later, just let me know. I'm two doors down.'

Danny nodded. 'Maybe.'

The American gave him a wide, gleaming, white-toothed smile. 'I'm Brad, by the way.'

Brad retreated towards his room.

'Brad?'

He turned. The beaming smile again. 'Yeah?'

'Do you know anything about passports?'

Brad ambled back up the corridor. 'What do you mean?'

'I had mine nicked. Getting it sorted out, but I wanted to visit Denmark while I'm here.'

Brad scratched his beard thoughtfully. 'Well, you've no problem going out. There's no check on the train to Copenhagen. In fact, you can go back to England without having your passport checked. Until you hit your British Channel.'

'English,' Danny couldn't help correcting.

'Whatever. Coming back, though... with all the immigrant stuff, they're checking passports at Kastrup.' Danny looked blankly at him. 'That's the airport for Copenhagen. And they also check everybody at Hyllie. That's the first stop on the train in Sweden.'

'Thanks, mate.'

Once the door was closed, Danny's face creased into relief. He could escape Sweden without a passport, and there was no way on God's earth that he was going to come back in! He could get to a Channel port then try and catch a ferry. That might be problematic, but he'd find a way. By then he would be safely away from Sweden and, more importantly, McNaught.

Klara Wallen was pleased that Moberg was pleased. She had made a breakthrough of sorts. She had found the building supply merchant that Egon Fuentes had been dealing with. It had been a lucky fluke as it turned out, but successful investigations often turned on such moments. She had been to a company run by a Bo Joneberg, a couple of kilometres outside Husie. Joneberg was an unpleasant bull of a man who had been aggressively unhelpful. He denied knowing Fuentes or dealing with any British or Irish customers. It was on leaving the yard that Wallen had engaged in conversation with a young man who was smoking outside the gates. He was having a break. On the off chance, Wallen had produced Egon Fuentes' photo. He immediately recognized him.

'Yeah, he comes in a few times.'

'By himself?' Wallen asked.

'No. One or two quite rough types. There was one guy who was completely bald. Scar on his face. The boss is frightening enough, but that guy! Wouldn't like to meet him on a dark night.'

'Did they speak English?'

'Yeah, they did actually.'

'And what were they taking away?'

He flicked his cigarette onto the dusty track outside the gates. 'Paving materials mostly, for patios, drives... paving slabs and bricks, aggregates, stones, that sort of thing. Tons of cement, of course. To be honest, it was all bottom range. Cheap. I was amazed that the boss managed to palm off some of the stuff he was selling them because a lot of it was virtually unusable. But when I helped load it, they seemed quite happy with it.'

Moberg sat at his desk thoughtfully. 'Good work, Klara. Good work.' She wasn't sure which delighted her most: his congratulations or the fact he'd used her first name – both were so rare.

'So, it's beginning to look as though Egon was the middle man. He's the local who deals with the supplier. This gang are buying inferior materials for their jobs. As a consummate bullshitter, he probably persuaded people to have their patios and drives redone from scratch.'

'So where's the con?' From Wallen's point of view it could be a legitimate business; just that they were using poor quality materials.

'I've heard of this sort of thing before. Not just here, but around Europe, particularly in Norway. You get these gangs turning up, offering to improve your drive, say. Increase the value of your property and all that. They take money up front, usually way above the real market price, and then do a bad job using shite materials, and disappear before the punters have time to complain. Or sometimes the householders are too intimidated to object. Many of these gangs are nothing more than thugs. And Egon would have been the front man; the man with the Swedish. And knowing his record, he'll have picked out the most vulnerable targets. I bet most of them are old. He'll have promised them that it would be a good investment. And when the whole thing turns out to be a mess, they would be too frightened to do anything about it.'

Moberg roused himself from his seat like a whale emerging from the ocean. 'Get Hakim to go through our records, or those of the commune building inspectors, and see if there've been any reported cases of complaints about shoddy work in the last few months. Might throw up a lead as to who the other two were in the van. From the description of the bald hard man, he obviously wasn't one of them, as they both had full heads of hair. We need to speak to someone who's come across this lot. And I want you to go back and see this Joneberg fella and get him to spill the beans on Egon.' He saw the doubt in her eyes. She had described him as intimidating. 'Take Brodd with you. If Joneberg's being uncooperative, drop into the conversation that he might be an accessory to murder. That should concentrate his mind.'

Moberg shrugged on his jacket. It could have made a useful-sized tent. 'Give yourself a pat on the back, Klara. Now, I'm going to enjoy a well-deserved lunch.'

Anita was relieved that there wasn't a large early-evening crowd in the Pickwick. The British-style pub had become a favourite haunt in the last couple of years. It reminded her of Kevin, imagining him in similar surroundings over in Cumbria. Besides, she liked most things British. She ordered a pint of Bombardier for herself and a glass of white wine for Bea Erlandsson. The girl behind the bar gave her a friendly nod of recognition. Anita didn't regard herself as one of the regulars as she didn't patronize the place enough for that, but it was a comforting spot to come to escape work and domestic problems. Faces were becoming familiar, and she no longer felt awkward if she came in on her own. Lasse even thought it was cool his mamma had a "local".

She returned to the table by the window, under the

hanging model of a Spitfire and close to the fireplace. No one was near enough to overhear them. 'Here's to Malta!' said Anita, raising her glass. 'I may never come back after I've murdered Alice Zetterberg. But it'll be worth going to prison for.'

Erlandsson appeared slightly horrified, not knowing how serious or jokey Anita was being.

'Don't worry. I'll make it look like an accident. I've got a lovely granddaughter to come back to. Not even Zetterberg's going to get in the way of that.'

Erlandsson took a sip of her wine. She was beginning to wonder if this was a good idea. Should she really be telling someone else about the case when she knew her boss would go berserk if she ever found out? Anita read her mind.

'Look, Bea, I know this isn't correct procedure as such, but I've been asked by Commissioner Dahlbeck to go with Zetterberg to Malta to interview Linus Svärd. Zetterberg is deliberately keeping me out of the picture, yet I'm a serving detective who should at least be apprised of the facts even if I can't act on them. After all, it was she who asked for my input at the beginning of your investigation.'

Erlandsson put her glass down decisively. 'You're right. You should know.' And she proceeded to fill Anita in on what they had discovered about Lars-Gunnar and his drug connection, Carina's argument with Göran before the killing, and the general attitude of the group towards the murder victim. She told Anita about the conflicting versions of the Larissa/Ivar break-up, and the "something" that Ivar was so excited about during their month on Malta.

'So, Lars-Gunnar and Carina have motives,' Anita mused.

'And less-than-solid alibis,' added Erlandsson.

'None of this emerged in the original investigation,' Anita said bitterly. 'Were we that shoddy?'

'I think time has played its part. Back then, they all stuck together; told the same story. It was difficult for your team to break that down. The cracks have only shown up now.'

Anita knew Erlandsson was trying to be kind. 'All the same, were we thorough enough?' She stared at her virtually untouched pint. 'Who do you think was the killer?'

Erlandsson didn't answer straight away, as though weighing up exactly what she was going to say. 'Despite the new findings, there's nothing to suggest that Linus Svärd didn't do it. All of the others think he committed the murder – except Carina.'

'And now she's provided him with a refuge.' She raised her glass again. 'Maybe it will all become clear on Malta.' And then she took a deep, unladylike swig of beer.

CHAPTER 23

Anita felt better when the seat belt signs flashed off and the aircraft was now cruising and the cabin crew was stirring. She was never quite sure whether the plane would actually get into the air after the mad dash down the runway. Another relief was that because of the last minute booking, she didn't have a seat next to Zetterberg. They had met up at security and had silently gone through the bag check. To Anita's amusement, Zetterberg had been body- searched. Afterwards, they headed in different directions – Zetterberg to get some food at one of the overpriced Kastrup food kiosks; Anita, who wasn't much of a breakfast person, to find a seat in the corridor leading to their gate, where she took out her book. As she eased herself into a slightly more comfortable position, she could see the back of Zetterberg's head a few rows up. It was bent, presumably poring over her phone, which she seemed permanently attached to. What on earth did she look at that kept her attention for hours? Surely no one could possibly want to communicate with her – or the other way round? But if it kept her out of Anita's hair, all well and good. The hotel might not be so easy. Yet she had to admit that she was getting increasingly excited at the prospect of facing Linus Svärd, even as an unwanted observer. This would be the chance to catch him at last. Had Zetterberg got the ability to do it – or the motivation? She wasn't a terrible detective. Anita could tell the difference between a bad person and a bad cop. Westermark had taught her that much.

As she thumbed through the in-flight magazine, she also thought about the Egon Fuentes case. She had hoped to sidestep that one. Now that wasn't happening, she was going to have to give it her all. She'd spoken to Hakim on the phone after she'd got back from the pub. After Wallen's initial visit to the building supplier, he had managed to dig up a complaint that had come in from a householder in Genarp. He was going to check it out in the morning. Wallen and Brodd's second trip to the building supply yard had been successful. The threat of a full police and forensic search of the premises looking for evidence regarding a murder had worked. Good for Wallen, thought Anita. She wouldn't have done that in the Westermark days. Bo Joneberg had suddenly backtracked and admitted that he had dealt regularly with Egon Fuentes over the previous months. It was always cash in hand and didn't go through the books. He had no idea who the others involved were, though one constant was a bald-headed Brit with a scar, who organized the collection of the materials. Even the hulking Joneberg sounded wary of him. He was usually accompanied by a couple of young men who didn't speak. It wasn't always the same young men. Hakim reported that the chief inspector was getting increasingly animated, as a picture was beginning to emerge of what the gang might have been up to. But why was the young man in the van murdered? That was still a mystery.

Anita had asked how Liv was. Hakim had given an evasive answer. She gathered that Liv hadn't mentioned their conversation of earlier in the day. It turned out that Hakim hadn't seen much of her, as she had been called out with her patrol partner to the multi-storey car park in Mobilia. The car that had been reported missing from the scene of the farmer's murder by the Kristianstad police had turned up in Malmö. She'd organized its transport to forensics, who would go over it for fingerprints. Anita hoped that Liv and Hakim would sit down and talk through any potential parental problems. Liv was good for Hakim, and she hated the thought that Uday might drive her away.

'Would you like any refreshments, madam?' Anita gazed at the full trolley and the perma-tanned flight attendants. This wasn't the flight she had imagined she would be taking this week. And this wasn't going to be any sort of holiday, but she still bought herself a plastic bottle of red wine, even though it was only ten o'clock in the morning.

Herr and fru Gradin lived in a verdant part of Genarp, a mainly residential area in the south of the Lund Municipality. Their single-storey, yellow-brick house was one of many ordered homes in a quiet neighbourhood. The house and garden were neat in all aspects except for the cracks in the paved driveway. There, there were gaps where the pebble-grey block paving was meant to join. It was as though a mosaic had been attempted by a drunken Roman artisan. A number of the two-hundred-millimetre by one-hundred-millimetre blocks were split. Though the front garden was flat, there were clear bumps and undulations in the level of the drive. It was a mess and, as a still angry herr Gradin described to Hakim what had happened, fru Gradin slowly wept into a clutched handkerchief. As the story unfolded, Hakim, too, became angry that this elderly couple should have been ripped off so badly.

Two months before, Egon Fuentes (herr Gradin recognized straight away the conman in the photo that Hakim showed him) had knocked on their door. He was charming, polite and persuasive. He could see that the drive needed sprucing up and assured them that his firm would do an excellent job at a very "favourable price". He said they were a British-backed company called *Pave the Way*, which had a huge reputation in the UK and were now bringing their skills and expertise to Scandinavia. Fuentes had used an iPad to show them examples of work carried out by the firm and a number of enthusiastic endorsements from satisfied customers throughout Skåne. Hakim assumed these had been dummied up for the presentation. After choosing the materials for their drive from those displayed on the iPad, Fuentes costed up the job. Though slightly steeper than expected, the Gradins agreed, as they thought it would look good (Fuentes had used the expression "increased curb appeal") and would enhance the value of the property. They shook hands on it, and Fuentes promised to return in a couple of days to collect the money up front as, he explained, they could get the best quality paving of the type that they'd requested at an advantageous price if he moved quickly. He'd described it as a "small window of opportunity", but they would eventually get the best possible job for less than from local paving companies. He'd even done a price comparison on his iPad, which had particularly impressed herr Gradin. Hakim assumed that had been fabricated, too.

Fuentes did return, and they paid him. He said he was very pleased with himself as he'd managed to get hold of even more expensive, even better quality blocks for the original quoted price, and he was sure they would be delighted with the end result. Work would commence a week later and take two days to complete. It did.

'You can see the result,' Gradin said bitterly. It was too much for his wife, who retreated into the shelter of the house.

'Didn't you complain?'

The laugh was bitter too. 'I tried to. But the man in charge was very aggressive. And I didn't understand him clearly. He spoke English with a very strong accent. My English is not good. So, after they left and I rang Fuentes – he'd given me his mobile number and said I was to ring him any time – he apologized if there had been any problems and he would call by in the next couple of days. Of course, he never turned up. And when I tried to ring him again, the number was unobtainable. And now we're left with this...' He waved a hand disconsolately at his patchwork driveway.

'The man in charge. What did he look like?'

'Nasty. He was bald. Totally. Chilling, dark eyes.'

'Did he have a scar on his cheek?'

'Yes. Yes, he did. I have to admit I was a bit frightened of him. So were the two lads who were doing the work. Young fellows. They worked hard, but I don't think they really knew what they were doing. Well, obviously not.'

'And the young men?'

'They were OK. Didn't speak. Well, one did. In English. It was when their boss was away for an hour. Usually, he just sat in the van listening to the radio playing loudly. But, as I say, he disappeared for a bit, and my wife offered to make the young lads a sandwich. She thought they needed feeding up. Didn't look in great shape. He was polite. But just as they were about to eat, the boss returned, and they went straight back to work without eating their food. That's what I mean by frightened. He was angry because he suspected they had been talking to us. It was all so unpleasant. I don't know how we got into all this trouble.' Hakim knew exactly. The chief inspector had been spot on about Egon Fuentes' persuasive skills.

'Could you describe the young men?'

'The polite one had really curly black hair; you know a bit like those perms footballers used to have in the eighties. He was medium height, I suppose. The other was light brown. Hair that is, not his colour. And a bit taller.' It wasn't much to go on. 'Funny thing was that it was nice and hot the first day they arrived. But they didn't take their shirts off despite the heat. They were sweating away. My wife noticed that when one of them was shovelling away and his T-shirt rode up, there was a big bruise on his lower back. Thought he must have been in a fight. I didn't see it, but she mentioned it. She's observant like that.'

Anita was hit by the wall of heat the moment she stepped out of the plane and onto the top of the airstairs. With the possible exception of Moberg, this is what Swedes spend their winters dreaming about. She was thankful that she had abandoned her default fashion setting of jeans and T-shirt and was wearing a thin, brown cotton skirt and white sleeveless top – smart enough for meeting the local police yet practical enough to cope with the high temperatures that she knew Malta would throw at her. She was glad her legs were just passably brown enough. She'd also tied her hair back. It was still shoulder length – Kevin liked it that way, so she'd decided to keep it. She was joined by Zetterberg on the bus to the terminal. Not that Alice paid her much attention, as she continued to be fixated by her phone.

An hour later, they were being taxied to the centre of Valletta. Zetterberg made sure that Anita sat alongside the chatty driver, who turned out to be English. His sailor father had married a Maltese girl when the islands were part of the Empire and an important naval base for the British Mediterranean fleet. He had returned to the land of his mother to escape British winters. After a fifteen-minute drive, they were whisked through the ornamental arched gate, Porta des Bombes, and along the wide boulevard of Triq Sant' Anna with its elegant facades and palm trees running down the central reservation. The taxi turned off to the left and a few side streets later, they were dropped off at the Malta police headquarters in Floriana, the district bordering Valletta. The neoclassical, stone building, with its balustraded parapet and its high antenna tower, had formerly been the Central Hospital until the 1950s. Zetterberg let Anita handle the administrative process needed to make sure their visit matched the appropriate international protocols. Anita assured the helpful Maltese police official that they merely wanted to speak to a Swedish national currently residing on the island. If they felt that further action needed to be taken, they would, of course, consult with the Maltese police first.

Another short taxi ride (they could have walked as it turned out) brought them to their hotel, which overlooked the Grand Harbour. This is when Zetterberg lost her cool when she discovered that she and Anita had both been booked into the same twin room. She demanded another room, but was told politely that at the height of the season, they were lucky to get the one they had at such short notice. Anita wasn't exactly thrilled either. Though Anita was dying for a coffee, Zetterberg only allowed time for them to park their bags, and off they set to try and find Linus Svärd.

Linus's apartment was only a few minutes' walk from the hotel, near the top end of Triq San Pawl. The narrow street had terraced villas on either side and dipped steeply to a central point before rising gracefully towards a distant speck of Mediterranean ultramarine. The houses were an attractive shambles of well-to-do dwellings and crumbling edifices in a state of complete dereliction. Valletta had originally been built in the mid-16th century on a rectilinear system, and the baroque style of its buildings reminded Anita of a holiday in Venice she had had with Björn when they were both still wrapt in love's young dream. The jumble of oriel windows, supported by elaborately carved corbels, sometimes protruding up to a height of five storeys, lent wings to the imagination as to the centuries of secrets they concealed. However, no secrets were concealed in Linus's apartment, as he wasn't there. Having raised a sleepy-sounding neighbour from an afternoon siesta, Anita established that Linus was down on the waterfront taking passengers from cruise ships on walking tours of the old city.

'Do you want to come back later?' Anita asked Zetterberg after the neighbour had grumpily turned off the intercom. Her stomach was starting to gurgle and she wanted to find somewhere to grab a bite to eat.

'No. We're here to talk to Linus Svärd, and that's exactly what we're going to do.'

Hakim reached Moberg's office to report back just as Brodd was leaving. Brodd decided to hang around to see what he had to say. Hakim filled them in on his conversation with the Gradins.

'That's Egon, all right,' Moberg confirmed with a shake of the head. 'Smarmy shit. So, one of the workers was a young man with curly black hair. He could well be our murder victim.'

'That's what I thought.'

'Now we know exactly how they operated. Talk to our media people. Tell them we want something put out that we're looking for people who have been scammed by this lot. Gradin reckoned they were British-backed? Pity Anita's not here to contact the UK and find out if the police over there know anything about this mob. What's your English like?'

'Passable,' Hakim admitted reluctantly.

'Get onto whoever and see if anything comes up. And the boss man? Could we get Gradin and his missus to help put together an identikit?'

'I'm sure they will. Well, herr Gradin will. His wife was terribly upset.'

'Well, this bald bugger's not the driver in the van, so he must still be around somewhere. They may still be operating.'

'Without Fuentes?' Hakim wondered.

'Good point,' Moberg mused.

'They've probably moved somewhere to regroup,' observed Brodd, who wanted to be part of the conversation.

'Yes. They've lost their front man and possibly two of their workforce. What I can't understand is why kill the young guy? It's not as though it's an industrial accident. Someone beat the hell out of him.'

'Sounds like it could be this bald fellow,' said Hakim. 'Both Joneberg and Gradin mentioned how intimidating he was.'

'And Joneberg's a big man,' confirmed Brodd. 'It takes something special to make him cautious.'

'OK, let's keep digging. But fast. Baldy may have already disappeared, but here's hoping. Oh, by the way, I need to let you know that we've had word from the Kristianstad station that they've got a match on the fingerprints at the murder scene up at the farm near Höör.' Moberg scanned a piece of paper on his desk. 'They turned nothing up over here but when they went international, they found him. He's called Daniel Foster, aged twenty-two, from somewhere called Hereford in the UK. He was part of a gang that stole slates off roofs. Got a suspended sentence that time, as it was a first offence. Then he did nine months of a year's sentence in prison for GBH. So, he's got a record of violence, and, apparently, the farmer was beaten up first before being shot. They've sent a photo through, which they've already distributed to the media. An officer is coming over from Kristianstad this afternoon to check on forensics' findings on the car that was left at Mobilia.'

'The British are causing trouble everywhere,' Brodd joked.

'Anyway, the whole force needs to be on the alert. There's probably a dangerous gunman running around the streets of Malmö.'

CHAPTER 24

Anita and Zetterberg walked along together but apart, each one wishing she was somewhere else. The trendy, redeveloped Waterfront was thick with cafés and bars. Anita was feeling the heat and looked enviously at the tourists and young Maltese enjoying their cool beers – and eating. Her stomach was starting to rebel. And the sweat on her face would soon cause her glasses to irritate her nose. At the end of the promenade, a short flight of wide steps led to the quay where the cruise ships berthed. One giant craft, which looked more like several apartment blocks inelegantly welded together, had a stream of passengers reboarding. Their next Mediterranean destination would be just another short-lived visit, and the memories would quickly fade until they were renewed by photos and films.

It was Anita who spotted Linus Svärd first. He was shaking hands with a middle-aged couple who were both as large as each other. Linus wore that rictus grin that he must keep going until the last of his tour party had passed. The relief on his face was palpable when the couple waddled off in the direction of their ship. The prettiness Anita remembered had long faded. The cheek bones and wide girlish lips were immediately familiar, though the wavy blond hair was now cut short. All the old feelings of anger and frustration came flooding back. Life appeared to have taken its toll on Linus; Anita hoped it had. He wore a white linen jacket, a cotton shirt, beige slacks and white sneakers. Dressed for his clients.

He didn't notice their approach as he was counting his tips. He must have done well; satisfaction was writ large upon his face. That was soon wiped away when Zetterberg strode up to him. 'Linus Svärd?'

'Yes,' he said guardedly in English.

She spoke in Swedish. 'I'm Detective Alice Zetterberg, Skåne County Cold Case Group. This is—'

'I know who this is,' he said bitterly. He was staring hard at Anita. 'You were the one who...' He left the sentence incomplete.

'Inspector Sundström is here at the wish of the police commissioner.' The inference was clear.

'I knew you'd come eventually. Carina warned me. But I didn't expect *her*.'

'I'm afraid she's part of the package. You'll find that I have an open mind, so it would benefit you to speak to me. Us,' she added after a meaningful pause.

Linus was still holding his tips. He shoved them into his pocket.

'We need to ask you some questions. You're entitled not to answer them, but we've talked to the Maltese police and I'm sure that, through them, we can make life unpleasant for you here.' Anita was quietly seething at Zetterberg's high-handed threat. She knew the only way they could finally prove that Linus was the murderer was to get him to open up.

'Do the Swedish police specialize in bitches?'

'Only when suspects don't cooperate.'

Linus's eyes darted from Zetterberg to Anita and back to Zetterberg. 'I'll talk to you. I've nothing to hide. But she,' he said raising a finger at Anita, 'is not to be there. I don't trust her.'

'The commissioner wants another officer to be present so we won't be accused of fitting you up. We'll record everything,' Zetterberg took out a small, hand-held recorder before glancing towards Anita, 'so nothing can be twisted or misinterpreted.'

'How do I know what I say won't end up all over the newspapers?' This was accompanied by a glare at Anita.

'I'm glad to say we're more responsible these days.'

Linus wavered. 'All right.'

'Shall we start now? Here is as good as anywhere.'

'Can't. I've got another group in fifteen minutes. Come to my apartment at ten tomorrow. It's—'

'I know. We've been there.'

'At ten then,' said Anita, speaking for the first time. 'I can't wait.'

'She's made contact with Linus,' Szabo said, putting down his mobile. 'She and Sundström are seeing him tomorrow morning. We should know a lot more after that.'

'Did you tell her about Larissa?' asked Erlandsson, hanging her bag over the back of her office chair.

'Mmm... not too pleased.'

'It's hardly our fault that she's in Oslo on some librarians' conference.'

'Our new boss isn't exactly the world's most patient person. And I bet she's making your friend Sundström's life as awkward as possible.'

Erlandsson sat down. Should she tell Szabo that she had confided in Anita about aspects of the case? She thought better of it. She didn't know her new colleague well enough yet, and she couldn't trust him not to go straight to Zetterberg and land her in it.

'We're not exactly stretched here. Do you fancy a drink after work?'

'Sorry. Got a previous engagement.' After some difficulty, she'd managed to rearrange her second date with Maria.

There was no one on the hostel desk as he sneaked out. He was relieved at this because he was afraid they would ask if he'd picked up his passport. And he was leaving without paying. Not that he had any luggage with him that would give him away, other than the small knapsack he'd bought to put the rest of his newly bought clothes in. It just looked like he was going out for a wander round the city. He'd already been to the nearest station, which was the cavernous underground one at Triangeln, and had failed to work out the complicated ticket machine. He'd have to go to the Central Station to buy his ticket to Copenhagen. Once there, he would decide how to progress further. Probably a train to Germany and beyond, depending what was available.

The good weather of the last few days had broken, and drizzly rain spat down from leaden skies. It might be a precursor to heavier showers, and he hurried on over the bridge by Kungsparken and along Slottsgatan. He constantly glanced over his shoulder, on guard in case McNaught was around. He tried to reassure himself that the Scottish bastard had moved on and was looking elsewhere.

By the time he'd recrossed the canal that circumferenced the old part of Malmö, the rain was more persistent. At the station, he made for a ticket desk and bought a single to Copenhagen. There was a train in ten minutes. The woman behind the desk directed him to the platforms below the main concourse. As he went down the escalator, he realized that this was the very one that McNaught had been travelling up the day before last. The thought nearly made him lose his nerve. Then it was superseded by a more practical one. What was the Danish currency? He still had some Swedish money left, but didn't know how far it would go. Could he change it? He had never done anything like this before.

The Copenhagen train was due in five minutes. He counted his money again. He still hadn't worked out how much it was worth because he was forever trying to mentally convert it to sterling. He slipped the notes back into his pocket. It was then that he noticed an elderly woman in front of him reading a newspaper. He almost threw up. There was a photo of himself on the inside page. It was an old one taken at the time of his arrest and imprisonment. He had no idea what the headline read, but there was no escaping the fact that they had discovered who he was and they were looking for him. Now the scraggy beard that he'd grown since his escape from the camp made him appear slightly different. And he was thinner. It might be enough to stop people immediately recognizing him. He readjusted his new baseball cap, pulling it further over his eyes, and sidled away from the woman, keeping his head down until the train pulled up alongside the platform.

He was still nervous as he took a window seat. He scanned his fellow passengers, and none were reading newspapers. Most were engrossed in their phones or chatting quietly. He knew there was a stop at Triangeln and then one more, called Hyllie, before crossing the bridge into Denmark. He couldn't relax yet, as he knew that at Hyllie there would be police and security personnel checking the incoming trains. Brad had reassured him that outgoing trains were fine. If he just kept his head down, he would be all right.

After travelling for a few minutes underground, the train eased into the cathedral-sized Triangeln station. The doors swished open, and a flood of new passengers embarked. Many had large suitcases and were making their way to the airport that Brad had mentioned. Some had to stand in the aisle, as there were no seats left. Danny felt himself relax for the first time since he had left the hostel.

After another few minutes, the train emerged into the open. The window soon became streaked with rain. One last stop and he'd be free. It was then that he heard the voice: ''Scuse me.' The language was English, but the accent was unmistakeably Scottish. Danny slumped down as best he could and eased down his cap to try and cover his face. He shut his eyes, pretending to be asleep. He heard the voice again, only closer this time. McNaught was pushing his way through the train and was now in this carriage, steps away from his prey. Danny tensed, desperately trying to stop himself quivering. The beatings and the humiliations came flooding back. He could almost smell the brutal strength of the man who was only an outstretched arm away. Then he was past. Danny squinted up and saw the bald head moving slowly down the carriage. He must know that I'm on the train, Danny thought wildly. He must have seen me get on at the Central Station. He knew he couldn't stay. He'd have to jump off at the next station; the last stop before Denmark. He sensed that some of the passengers were stirring, getting ready to alight. He would follow them, in the opposite direction to McNaught.

Danny managed to squeeze past the stacked cases and squashed travellers and move towards the door. About half a dozen people were waiting there. The door opened and he slipped out. The station was built of cold concrete and was partly covered by the road and massive shopping complex above. There was a wide stairway leading up from the platform, and that's what the passengers were heading for. He tried to lose himself in their slipstream, though there weren't enough of them to completely block him from any eyes watching from the stationary train. He was on the third step, his gaze fixed, zombie-like, straight ahead of him when he heard a couple of people shouting in annoyance. He glanced behind and saw McNaught pushing his way off the train and onto the platform. He'd seen Danny.

It was sheer fear that propelled Danny upwards, pushing his way through the startled people in front of him. At the top, he hesitated. There were huge modern buildings all around. A backward glance, and he saw McNaught mounting the steps two at a time like an over-muscled gazelle. Danny found himself running along the road that spanned the station below. There was no hiding in the massive glass-fronted building opposite. And to reach it, he would have to cross a wide open carriageway, which would give McNaught a clear shot. But the road that he was on was as straight as an arrow. He had to get off it! Ahead, an enormous car park beckoned, enticing him with momentary cover, if only he could reach it. The first shot scuppered that idea as he felt a fierce jolt in his right shoulder. It nearly took him off his feet, but he had the presence of mind to veer off down the only gap available: the steps descending to the other platform. A second shot whizzed past his head as the first step took him a fraction below McNaught's line of fire. Realizing he'd been shot, he scrambled down, waiting for the pain to hit him. Near the bottom, he tried to jump the final six steps in one go. He landed awkwardly and fell, his left hand instinctively wrapping itself round the blasted shoulder. He lay in a crumpled heap, his nemesis halfway down the stairs. McNaught stopped, legs slightly spread, and in a measured fashion, raised his gun, cupped in both hands, for the final kill; Danny unable to crawl away.

But the shot he heard didn't come from McNaught's gun. Stupefied, Danny watched him turn and flee up the steps, a policeman wielding a pistol following him. He watched in disbelief, too shocked by events to feel relief. Then the pain kicked in.

CHAPTER 25

The Upper Barrakka Gardens were ablaze with reds and pinks and oranges, laid out in the Victorian tradition of formal bedding; another hangover from the British, thought Anita. But unlike the parks in England she was used to, these beds were shaded by palm and banyan trees.

In the centre was a fountain, the tinkling of which cooled the senses in the stifling heat. Beyond the fountain was a large, bronze statue. 'Lord Strickland,' Anita read aloud. Kevin would have been able to tell her all about him. Once again, she missed his enthusiasm for history, his incessant chatter and light-hearted banter.

Anita walked through one of the tall archways behind the statue and looked over the parapet. A battery of eight cannon, one of which is fired every day at noon, guarded the old port. The view beyond was breathtaking. The sunlight on the limestone of Fort St. Angelo and Point Vedette across the Grand Harbour gleamed with a soft, yellow radiance, and the startling blues of sea and sky seared the scene like the confident daubs of an artist's brush. Anita sat in the sun for a few minutes, letting its warmth saturate her bones, before retreating to a seat under the spreading fronds of one of the palms in the garden beside the fountain so she could cool off. She closed her eyes and felt relaxed for the first time on the trip. Then she became aware of someone standing in front of her. She opened her eyes slowly and automatically raised her hand to shade them. It was Linus Svärd.

'I'm innocent.'

Anita felt uncomfortable. He shouldn't be here talking to her without Zetterberg being present. And she didn't want to speak to him in an informal setting. This had to be played by the book.

'This is not the place to—'

'Why did you blab to the press? Why?' It came out as a distorted mixture of anger and pleading.

Anita found she couldn't answer. She didn't know how to justify her actions now she was faced with the man she'd thrown to the wolves. But why should she?

'Because you got away with murder.'

Anita felt at a disadvantage with Linus towering over her. She was mentally pinned to her bench.

'You really believe that?'

'Yes.'

He slowly shook his head. 'You are so wrong.' He slumped down on the bench beside her. She had to get away. This was unnerving. 'I couldn't have harmed Göran. I loved him.' He raised his eyes and gazed at her. 'Do you know what love is like?' She didn't answer.

Linus stood up again. 'You and your boss were so convinced that it was me. You didn't bother looking elsewhere.'

Anita found her voice at last. It sounded hoarse. 'Should we have?'

Despite the park being full of tourists busily snapping the Grand Harbour in the early evening light, the only sound Anita could hear was the fountain playing behind Linus's back.

'Yes.'

'Well, tell me.'

There was a hint of a smile. 'I can't talk without your colleague being present. I'll see you at ten tomorrow.'

'Klara's just got back from that shooting at Hyllie station,' said a wide-eyed Brodd who had burst into Hakim's office as he was busy at his computer.

'Any fatalities?'

'No. A young guy was chased by some loony with a gun according to early reports. He was shot in the shoulder but he should be OK.'

'It'll be some gang vendetta,' Hakim proclaimed confidently. They were common in Malmö these days.

'He'd probably have been killed, but with all the cops and security people checking the incoming trains for immigrants, they were on the spot and reacted quickly. He's been taken off to hospital.'

Hakim returned to his computer. Brodd shrugged as he realized he had no more useful information to impart. Then he had a thought. 'Oh, by the way, an Inspector Blentarps from Kristianstad is in with the boss right now.'

'And?' Hakim's interest was piqued again.

'He's been over to forensics, and the car they found at Mobilia did have Daniel Foster's prints on it. So after the murder, he took the car and abandoned it here, so may well still be around town.'

'His photo is out there now. If he's here, we'll find him. Being British, he might not know Malmö too well, so it'll be harder for him to go undetected.'

Brodd still seemed reluctant to leave. Hakim wished he'd just shove off. He was frustratingly drawing a blank with his researches, and he was still unsure how he was going to sort out his parental problem with Liv.

'Any joy?' said Brodd peering over Hakim's shoulder.

'No. I can't find any reference to this *Pave the Way* outfit anywhere; and certainly not in Britain or Ireland, where they supposedly operate. I think we're going to have real problems tracking these people down.'

Anita treated herself to a pint of Cisk in The Pub. It was a rather unimaginative name for a pub. It was small and intimate. One side of the room was decorated in naval memorabilia, mainly the cap bands of several Royal Navy ships. This must have been a regular watering hole for thirsty sailors for generations, though most had made straight for the infamous Gut, a long narrow street once heaving with bars, brothels and dance halls. Since the closure of the British naval base in 1979, Strait Street had gone straight and shed its notorious reputation. On the opposite wall were plastered pictures and articles about the British film star Oliver Reed, who had had his final, fatal drinking session in The Pub. It was a shrine to an actor who had an insatiable appetite for life, even if it ended up killing him.

She took her pint outside and sat at one of the tables on the street. Tourists and locals drifted languidly past. It was pleasantly warm still, and the beer went down well. She was still dwelling on what Linus had said to her earlier. Of course, he was bound to say he was innocent. But he wasn't. She even began to think about the practicalities of taking him back to Sweden. She assumed, as Malta was a fellow member of the EU, that there would be no trouble extraditing him.

A couple of raucous British holidaymakers, with bright shirts and long shorts, staggered past her table and disappeared into the pub. Kevin was always complaining about his fellow countrymen when abroad in hot climates and with easy access to gallons of cold booze. She smiled to herself, got out her phone and gave him a call.

'I'm sitting outside a bar on a warm evening with a pint of cool beer. Malta is heaven,' she teased.

'It's been pissing down here all day,' Kevin replied dryly. 'I suppose you're just enjoying winding me up?'

'Of course. But I have to say that what I've seen of Malta so far is amazing. And that's given me an idea.'

'You're going to transfer to the Maltese police.'

'Ah, that's an even better idea. Maybe I could half-transfer – do the summers in Malmö and winters on Malta. No, actually, it's somewhere teeming with history. And I thought this is exactly the sort of place you would love, and you could discover plenty of facts to bore me with at the end of each day. So, why don't we have a holiday here next year?'

She could almost hear the smile at the other end. 'I've always fancied Malta. Great Siege. Knights of St. John. Second World War, of course.' He stopped himself. 'And you, too. Being with you would be the most important thing.'

'Glad to hear it.'

'So, how's it going? Has the witch driven you to drink?'

'Zetterberg's as cold as this beer. She's hardly said a word to me the whole trip. But we have met the suspect. Actually, I've seen him twice.'

'And?'

'He's still guilty. We've got a proper interview with him tomorrow at his apartment. I'm going to have to keep my mouth shut whatever happens. I just hope she's got the guts to really put the pressure on. I'm sure I'll find it impossible not to jump in when I think things aren't going right.'

'Stay calm, darling. She'll use it against you if she thinks you're overstepping the mark.' She could tell he was warning her more out of hope than expectation.

'I will, Kevin. Just for you. But first I've got to sleep in the same room as her. Someone's idea of a joke back at headquarters, I suspect. And before you get any erotic ideas about two women in the same bedroom, I bet she snores.'

'And you don't?' he laughed.

'You cheeky thing; you can't talk. Anyhow, I'd better go and get something to eat. There are some nice-looking restaurants around here. What are you having tonight?'

'Beans on toast.'

CHAPTER 26

The entrance to the building which accommodated Linus Svärd's apartment consisted of an intricately carved wide double door sporting two substantial brass knobs, above which perpetually leapt a couple of supple fish-shaped metal knockers. Zetterberg pressed the intercom buzzer and, almost immediately, it was answered by Linus. The door clicked, and in they stepped off the hot street.

The hallway was cool, with thick, cream-painted stone walls, and was full of antiques – oak chests, leather-upholstered chairs, ceramic vases, brass urns, earthenware amphorae, lanterns, cannon balls piled in pyramids, and pictures of ancient knights and coats of arms. Beyond was a high atrium filled with foliage; ferns and palms and ivies cascading from unseen balconies. A raised pool full of magnificent carp nestled in one corner, and the sound of running water gave the whole an air of serenity and tranquillity like an Arabian palace. Anita looked up and could just make out a small rectangle of deep azure sky. A wide staircase led from the atrium; the steps worn in the middle from centuries of use. The conversion of the house into apartments had been tastefully and carefully done, and none of the former grandeur of the central living space had been sacrificed.

When Linus let them in, the apartment was small but perfectly serviceable, though it didn't exude the affluence of the communal area outside. The gallery window of the living room Anita and Zetterberg were shown into looked out onto the street and did nothing to muffle the noises of everyday Maltese life. Anita was thankful for the fan in the middle of the ceiling, which gave welcome relief from the energy-sapping heat. A lot of the furniture was large, dark and heavy, and there were richly patterned rugs on the floor, but the décor was light and the pictures were modern.

Linus appeared nervous. He didn't bother offering them coffee. Instead, he lit up a cigarette, which he puffed at with a vehemence that couldn't be doing his lungs any good. Zetterberg took the most comfortable armchair. Anita had to sit down on the small sofa. She felt at an immediate disadvantage, as the other two were higher than she was.

'Right, let's get started,' Zetterberg said in her best business-like manner. She produced the promised recorder. 'You'll have to put up with Inspector Sundström's presence.'

He blew out some long-held smoke. 'That's OK. I spoke to Inspector Sundström last evening on the way back from the waterfront.'

'Did you?' Zetterberg glared at Anita. 'That is most irregular. Why didn't you tell me?'

'There was nothing to tell.' Anita felt awkward, like a child who's been caught out lying.

'I didn't reveal any details. I just told her I was innocent.'

'That's for us to decide.' Zetterberg was clearly irked. What capital would she make out of it when they returned to Malmö? She clicked on the hand-held recorder. 'I want you to go through the day of the murder as you remember it.'

Linus flicked ash into the saucer he was using as an ashtray. 'I'll not forget that day in a hurry. It didn't start well, as Göran was in a shitty mood. In fact, he'd been like that almost from the moment I arrived from Gotland.'

'You'd been on a dig there,' Zetterberg confirmed.

'Yeah. Viking site near Visby.' Despite the recorder, Anita

was making additional notes. Zetterberg should have been doing that, as it was her case, but Anita hadn't objected because it gave her an excuse to get more involved. After a sleepless night listening to Zetterberg snoring, she had been plagued by pinpricks of doubt that Linus might not have been their killer of twenty-one years ago. Today, she was determined to find out once and for all. 'It hadn't been right for a while. I wasn't sure why. We still had sex...' His mind wandered for a moment. Zetterberg shifted uneasily in her seat. '...but the love had gone. On his part.' Linus twizzled the saucer, which disturbed and flaked the fresh ash. 'It was a hot day so we decided to have a barbecue. Well, Ivar decided, and when he wanted something, it usually happened. I wasn't in the mood, and Göran certainly wasn't.' He frowned. 'Actually, Ivar was a bit wound up about something, too. Not his usual self.'

'None of the others mentioned that,' queried Zetterberg.

'If they didn't, then maybe it was nothing. Anyhow, it didn't take long for Göran to pick a fight. I could see the others were getting uptight with him around, and I couldn't stand it anymore, so I lost my rag, probably yelled a bit and then flounced off. I realized that I had to reassess my life.'

'Which you did up Stenshuvud?' Anita was annoyed at Zetterberg's interruption. It was as though she wanted to get through the interview as quickly as possible.

'Yes. It's beautiful up there, and you can find a quiet spot if you keep off the main paths. I had a lot to think about. I could tell there was no future with Göran. He'd changed. He'd been loving at first. I wasn't sure if it was something I'd said or done. He was sensitive about certain things, and I may have upset him somehow. I just don't know,' he said hopelessly as though the thought still bothered him.

'He'd transferred his affections to Ivar.'

Linus suddenly guffawed, which sounded odd coming out of those feminine lips. 'All that was ridiculous. Ivar's as straight as they come. No, I think it was more that Göran was in awe of Ivar. We all were. But when I came back from Gotland, I could see that there was a change in Göran's relationship with Ivar. Something wasn't right.'

'We'll get back to that later. I want to know more about the day of the murder.' Zetterberg's impatience was increasingly evident. Maybe it was her own presence that was putting her off, thought Anita.

Linus flicked more ash before continuing. 'It was late by the time I returned along the beach. I was down by the shore when I heard shouting up at the chapel. I rushed up. I can't remember much, but I realized as soon I saw the body on the floor that it was Göran. I don't even remember who was in there at the time. I just lost it. I grabbed him, which I shouldn't have done because you're not meant to touch a body. But I was so emotional. Whatever I'd been thinking about on Stenshuvud disappeared in a flash.' His voice quavered. 'The love of my life was lying there, dead.' The image that he seemed to be recreating in his mind halted his flow completely. 'Even now...' he started again but stopped.

'What happened after that?'

He took his time before he continued. 'The rest was a blur. I think the others appeared, or some of them. Larissa took me back to the house. I remember that. She cleaned me up. My T-shirt was covered in Göran's blood from when I'd held him. Then the police came to talk to us. It was some detective called Nor-something.'

'Nordlund,' said Anita.

'Him. He took away the T-shirt. After a couple of weeks, it became obvious that the police were concentrating on me. Weren't you?' The accusation was aimed at Anita.

'What was it like around the house in the following weeks?' Zetterberg asked.

'What do you think?' he said angrily, stubbing out his

cigarette. 'Crap. No one could believe it had happened at first. Everybody stuck to their stories, and no one accused anybody else. It slowly dawned on me that some of my friends began to believe that I was responsible, though none of them were really upset by Göran's death, except me.'

'And later?'

'When we were allowed to leave the cottage, we all split up. I went to Malmö for a while. I tried to get my life together again. But it was impossible to get an academic position in Sweden because of the publicity the case had stirred up, especially when *she* went public.' Anita kept scribbling, which helped her avoid his fierce gaze.

'How did the others react to you?'

'Ironically, it was the girls who stayed connected. Larissa was in Malmö and was supportive. So was Carina until she moved up north and started her brilliant career. She's the only one who's stayed in touch.'

'And Ivar and Lars-Gunnar?'

Anita could detect genuine sadness in his eyes. 'After we left the cottage, Ivar never spoke to me again. We'd been very close since the first weeks at uni. But not a word. Lars-Gunnar was the same after he split from Carina. But I don't blame him as much; his brain was addled by drugs by then. He had no idea what he was up to. No wonder Carina felt she'd had enough and left him.'

By now Anita was getting thirsty and wished she'd brought a bottle of water. She would have asked for some, but she didn't want to break the flow of the interview.

'You mentioned earlier that something wasn't right with Göran and Ivar.' Zetterberg spoke as though measuring her words. 'When did this start to surface? You must be the one most likely to know as you were a good friend of one and the other's lover.'

'Here, I suppose. Malta. That ill-fated trip, as it turns out.'

'The others seemed to think it was fun.'

Linus crossed his arms thoughtfully. 'They probably did. But not for me. Göran began to act strangely. It was only meant to be a break. Bit of sun, plenty of drinks, some laughs. An escape. Except for Ivar, it wasn't. He was keen to find out as much as possible about the Siege of Malta and spent a lot of time in Valletta. I don't think Larissa was too pleased. She just wanted to relax like the rest. But Ivar was really into the Knights of St. John and the whole Christian-Muslim, East-West thing. He spent a lot of time in the National Library here, and at the Grand Master's Palace, and in book shops. He liked to drag me along because I was interested and he could bounce ideas off me. In fact, it was in an old bookshop in Archbishop Street that he came across Björnstahl. The shop's derelict these days.'

'You say Björnstahl? Was he another student?' Zetterberg queried sharply.

'He was a Swedish orientalist, linguist and traveller.' This was Anita's first contribution.

'What was he doing here?' demanded Zetterberg, who was annoyed that Anita knew of someone she didn't.

'I don't know if he was ever here as he died in the 1770s. Istanbul I think.'

'Well done,' Linus said with some admiration. 'He spent three years in Constantinople as it was then, but he actually died in Salonika in 1779. I don't think many people have heard of him these days, even in Sweden.'

'I remember my ex-husband talking about him. An academic.'

Linus clicked his fingers. 'That's right. I'd forgotten that one of the cops on the case had a Lund University connection.'

'Just tell us about this bloody Björnstahl!' Zetterberg snapped. 'If it's at all relevant.'

'I'm not sure if it is, but it caused problems between Göran and myself.' Linus left them waiting while he lit up again. 'We were in this dusty, old second-hand bookshop when Ivar came across *A Tour Through Sicily and Malta* by Patrick Brydone. It was in the form of letters to William Beckford. Ivar was fascinated because, though worn, it was a first edition. He was really excited.' Anita noticed Zetterberg's eyes glaze over. 'After he bought it, we went off to a bar so he could have a look through it. Obviously, the bits he was interested in concerned Malta. But then, as we were about to leave and head back up to Mellieha, where we were staying, Ivar discovered some musty leaves of paper stuffed in the back of the book. It was four pages of a letter. They were old and written in Swedish. The first part was obviously missing, so Ivar couldn't work out who it was to. But it was signed by Jacob Björnstahl. It was quite a find.'

'So this was new material that no one had seen before?' asked Anita, who, after her years with Björn, could appreciate that such a discovery could have been highly significant for an academic.

'Precisely. It was part of a discourse on the Malti language. He'd written about the origins of Malti briefly in one his own books of travels which came out in—'

'This is all very interesting,' Zetterberg cut in, 'but can we get to the bit where this find caused a problem between you and Göran?'

Linus shrugged. 'Ivar swore me to secrecy about the Björnstahl letter. Göran sensed there was something he was missing out on because Ivar was so pleased with his discovery. Göran was seriously hacked off with me, as he realized I must know what Ivar was up to and I wouldn't tell him. It was difficult for me, but Ivar was my best friend at the time. I think it was at that time that Göran tried it on with Ivar. As you know, he didn't get anywhere, and Göran didn't take rejection well. I sometimes wonder if he only tried to get close to Ivar sexually as a way of finding out what Ivar was up to academically. They had become serious rivals.'

'That's what I want to talk about next,' said Zetterberg, who was keen to step onto safer ground. 'This rivalry between Ivar and Göran. Lars-Gunnar and Carina both mentioned it. Did it destabilize the group?'

'I suppose it did eventually. I think it really only developed after they both started doing their doctorates. I hadn't seen much of either of them after I got my degree, as I was away on digs for weeks or months on end. Obviously, I was in regular contact with Göran, but I didn't fully realize what was happening until I saw them together that time on Malta. Not an edifying sight when they were both arguing. It was all about points scoring.'

'I get the picture,' Zetterberg sighed. 'What about you and Göran? Did you know he was supplying Lars-Gunnar with drugs?'

Linus blew out a shaft of smoke which he then batted away with his free hand. 'Yes. But not at first,' he added quickly. 'He supplied us all. Just for recreational use. Nothing heavy. He just seemed to know where to get hold of stuff easily. We didn't ask any questions. I don't think any of us realized that Lars-Gunnar was getting in deeper and deeper.'

'Except Carina.'

'I assume she must have known before the rest of us. Things had got really bad between Malta and meeting up in Knäbäckshusen that summer. I hadn't seen Lars-Gunnar in the meantime. By the time I got to Skåne, it was obvious he was heading in a bad direction.'

'How did you feel about Göran fucking up your friend?'

'I didn't believe it at first. Until Carina came and begged me to get Göran to stop supplying him. I became angry and confronted Göran. He just laughed and said it was Lars-Gunnar's life; if he wanted to destroy it, that was his problem.'

'Angry enough to kill him to protect a friend? Or murder

him because he jilted you?' Zetterberg asked accusingly.

'No! No.' Linus waved his hand emphatically, causing the ash from his cigarette to scatter and flutter towards the floor. 'I didn't kill Göran. I know it looks as though I had reasons...' He stopped. His eyes began to moisten. 'Despite everything...' His voice grew hoarse. 'Despite everything he did, I still loved him.' Anita had to strain hard to hear his next words: 'I still do.'

'But you know that Carina had a row with Göran shortly before he died?'

Linus found his voice again. 'We all did, except Lars-Gunnar. The rest of us were in the garden of the cottage, and Carina had cornered Göran in the kitchen. The window was open. She ended up slapping him and saying some pretty nasty things to him. I was mortified to hear this in front of the others. It was true, of course. By then, the rest of them had had enough of Göran.'

'Why didn't he just leave?'

Linus shook his head dolefully. 'He was going to, but I persuaded him to stay. I still thought we could build bridges. If I hadn't, he might be alive today.'

'And what about the threat he made to Carina?'

'What threat?'

'About your precious Ivar suffering the most?'

'That was nothing. He was just grandstanding. Lashing out against Ivar because he knew we all loved him. Anyhow, even if there had been some sort of threat, he certainly never had the chance to carry it out.'

'Do you know that Göran was still alive when he was found?' Zetterberg expected this news to shock Linus.

It did, and Linus's mouth dropped open. His voice was almost inaudible. 'But he was... you know... when I found him with...'

'We now know that he was still alive when the young boy,

Kurt Jeppsson, found him. Not only that, he said something.'
Anita could tell that Zetterberg was deliberately testing
Linus. If he had killed Göran, then could the dying man have
implicated him?

'What did he say?' A bead of sweat appeared on his temple.

'"Burnt it." That's what he said.' Was that relief or
puzzlement on his face? Anita wasn't sure. 'Mean anything?'

As Linus shook his head, Anita could tell he was now miles
away. Was he back in that chapel? Zetterberg stared hard at
the man whose life had changed irrevocably that night.

Anita couldn't help finding out what he had been up to
since his disappearance from Sweden. 'How come you ended
up back here in Valletta?' Zetterberg flashed her one of her
trademark looks of annoyance. She was merely there to take
notes and keep quiet.

Linus pulled himself together. 'I was taken with the place
on that first visit. And after I left Sweden, I worked on a
number of digs around the Mediterranean. Egypt and Syria
mainly. God, what a mess Syria's in now. What they've done
in Palmyra is unforgiveable.' There was more than a hint of
rage. 'Sicily as well. It's just over the water. So Malta seemed
an ideal place to use as a base.'

'So why are you a tourist guide for wealthy Americans?'

'They tip well,' he said flippantly.

'The real reason?'

'Ah, the truth.' He squinted at the whirring fan above
his head. 'Disgraced myself on a dig in Egypt five years ago.
Pretty Arab boy. Didn't go down well, and now I'm persona
non grata in that line of work. That's why I'm in here,' he said
indicating the apartment. 'Down on my luck. My only friend,
Carina, came to the rescue. And when she comes over to
write, I vanish and stay with a friend over in Sliema. They're
not crazy about gays here, but we're tolerated, in case you
were wondering.'

'As far as I can judge, Carina's the only one who thinks you're innocent.' Zetterberg was taking over again. 'Now, she's either doing that because she really thinks you are or she's trying to make up for the fact that she killed Göran and ruined your life. What do you think?'

'I don't think. I merely exist.'

'That's not an answer,' Zetterberg spat back fiercely.

'All I know is that I didn't kill Göran.'

'You've had years to mull it over. If it wasn't you, which one of your supposed friends do you think did?'

'I have no idea.'

Once they were out in the street, Zetterberg turned to Anita. There was a look of triumph in her eyes. 'I think you got it wrong all those years ago. He didn't do it.'

CHAPTER 27

Everything about Malta has a maritime ambience. Wherever you are, the sea is never very far away, and the entire history and culture of the island are inextricably linked with its pervasion. The main thoroughfare in Valletta had seemed eerily quiet the previous night after her meal and late night stroll to avoid having to go back to the hotel and Zetterberg – all signs of life hidden behind grills and shutters – but today, it was teeming with humanity: little shops opening in unexpected niches, café tables springing up on the pavements like mushrooms, and golf cart lookalikes for ferrying tourists around negotiating their way through the crowds like dodgems.

Anita sat down in the shade of a parasol in Republic Square under the watchful eye of a statue of Queen Victoria. Behind her stood the flamboyant frontage of the Bibliotheca, the National Library of Malta. She needed a *fika*, so ordered a black coffee and a local delicacy called *kannoli*, which the waiter explained was a crunchy, cigar-shaped biscuit filled with ricotta cheese and candied fruit. She reckoned she deserved it after having to stay virtually silent throughout an interview with the man who for over twenty years she had been convinced was a murderer. She had found it so hard not to intervene; there were things she wanted to ask Linus Svärd. Though it wasn't a comfortable thought, the experience had begun to undermine her long-held convictions about the case. Linus had sounded plausible in a way that he hadn't all those years before. He was more mature now.

Gone was the gauche young man she'd encountered. His life had gone from bad to worse, and now he was eking out a living showing disinterested travellers around historical sites that would be forgotten the moment they reached their next port of call. And he was living off the charity of the one old friend that didn't believe him to be guilty, according to Zetterberg anyway. And she had to admit that Zetterberg had made an interesting point about the crime novelist – did she really believe that Linus was innocent or did she *know* he wasn't guilty because *she* was the killer? At the time of the murder, they had known that Lars-Gunnar took drugs and was probably wasted on the night it happened, but they hadn't discovered the drug connection with Göran, nor had they known about Carina's efforts to get Göran to lay off Lars-Gunnar. So many things were now emerging that weren't obvious at the time. Was the original investigation so flawed? It wasn't a happy thought. Yet circumstances had changed, and the united front that Nordlund's team had faced had disintegrated over the years, and the fractures that had appeared were revealing new information that they hadn't been privy to. And if the suspects *had* been more forthcoming, would Prosecutor Renmarker have allowed them to take action?

The smiling waiter arrived with her *fika*. She took a long swig of coffee. It helped to subdue the craving that had been growing throughout the interview. If Zetterberg had been more relaxed about the whole thing, she might have persuaded Linus to serve up something to drink. She then took a massive chunk out of her biscuit. Delicious! Around her, all the tables were occupied by a mixture of holidaymakers and older locals passing the time of day. The only hurrying was being done by the waiters and waitresses who brought the customers their orders from the Caffe Cordina across the street. Anita was also being sucked in by the relaxed atmosphere after escaping the constant irritation of being in Zetterberg's presence. After Alice's declaration that Anita had been wrong about Linus, she had dismissed her with a

'You can do what you like for the rest of the day. There's nothing else to be done here and I've got to report back to my team on my case.' What had irked Anita was not so much the possibility of being mistaken about Linus, but that the investigation was beginning to develop, and she was totally excluded. Life would be intolerable if Zetterberg cracked a case she had failed to.

She went through each suspect again with what she'd gathered from the Linus interview, what little Zetterberg had revealed, and her useful chat with Bea Erlandsson. Lars-Gunnar now had motive and opportunity if he wasn't as totally wasted as people thought. Carina was now definitely in the frame. But the two lovers, Ivar and Larissa? Was their alibi unbreakable? Carina had said at the time that she heard them at it that night, so probably it was. Yet Anita had been intrigued by Ivar's discovery of the Björnstahl letter. Zetterberg had quickly dismissed it. But her own acquaintance with academe, through her marriage to Björn, had given her an insight into the in-fighting that could go on and the constant battle for prestige and acceptance. Ivar and Göran were rivals in the same field. Ivar wasn't going to share his discovery with Göran, which had only caused further friction between Linus and his boyfriend. Throw in Göran trying to seduce Ivar, and it was a toxic mix. But enough to lead to murder? What she had to do first was to see if she could find out the significance of this Björnstahl discovery and how Ivar used it. She polished off her biscuit and drank the last of her coffee. The Bibliotheca was just behind her. Maybe she could find the answer inside.

Anita went through the impressive portico of the Bibliotheca and pushed open the large wooden door. The library was the last great building erected by the Knights of St. John in Valletta before Napoleon threw them off the islands on his way to invading Egypt. It was blessedly cool inside, and Anita enquired at the reception desk as to whether they had any references to Jacob Jonas Björnstahl. The pleasant, bespectacled man picked up a phone and talked to someone elsewhere in the library. 'They will look and see if they can find anything for you. If you don't mind waiting.' Anita was quite content to hang around in the reception area. A grand staircase with wide stone steps led directly up from the entrance hall and branched to right and left to reach the next floor. From a high, ornately decorated ceiling above the stairs hung a low lamp which illuminated a bust of Dun Karm Psaila, the Bard of Malta, who peered studiously down at her from his marble pedestal. She attempted some small talk with the receptionist and explained that she was from Sweden; hence her interest in Björnstahl, who was also Swedish and may have come to Malta. It sounded so vague, and she could tell the receptionist was only feigning interest out of politeness. It was with some relief on his part when the phone rang and he answered it. 'If you would like to go upstairs, they have found a book for you. Turn right at the top there,' he said pointing to the stone staircase, 'and make yourself known to the librarian.'

She walked into a vast space on two levels, the second accessible by stairs leading onto a balustraded balcony. Every vertical space was lined with books, and at one end of the room was a recess supported by Doric pillars, above which was a coat of arms in plaster relief. There were only three other visitors in the room, two poring over books whilst the third was idly flicking through a newspaper. She was greeted by a cheery librarian, who showed her the book he had found; but before she could read it, she had to register as a researcher. She filled in a form and showed her passport. With the registration complete, Anita retreated to a desk and gingerly opened the old book: *Briefe auf Reisen durch Frankreich, Italien, die Schweiz, Deutschland, Holland, England und einen Theil der Morgenländer – Jacob Jonas Björnstahl*. The first disappointment was that it wasn't in Swedish. The second, that it wasn't in English. It was in German.

She racked her brain for the vestiges of her school German. As she quietly turned the pages, she realized it was a journal of journeys in France, Italy and other European countries during the early 1770s, the book originally being published in 1777. There was a handwritten note to the Malta reference at the front of the book, written in English. She found it on page 172. Though she wasn't entirely sure what it was about, it seemed to be referring to a voyage Björnstahl had taken from Toulon to Civitavecchia, the port of Rome. He'd left Toulon on 4th December, 1770, and appeared to describe the ship as being like Noah's Ark and the Tower of Babel in terms of the languages spoken on board, which included French, Spanish, Swedish, Provencal, Arabic and Malti. Her German didn't stretch to fully comprehending the reference to Malta, other than that it had something to do with the Punic language. That didn't sound very interesting. She spent another twenty minutes going through the book, but at no point could she find any evidence of Björnstahl having actually landed on Malta, let alone spending some time there.

Anita closed the book and took in her surroundings. This was exactly the sort of place Björn would love to study in and wander around, like the Carolina Rediviva library at Uppsala University where he now worked. That is until he was distracted by the next attractive woman who passed his way. The combined knowledge these heaving shelves supported brought back to mind another of her life's regrets – that she hadn't gone to university. But she knew in her heart of hearts that it was really a fanciful idea, as she hadn't the powers of concentration or the patience to apply herself to serious learning. Her job as a cop was similar to that of an academic in terms of research, asking questions and drawing conclusions. But her line of work demanded faster results!

She took off her glasses and gave them a thorough wiping with the hem of her skirt. Was this just a dead end? She could look Björnstahl up when she got back to Sweden, but then what? If Ivar's Björnstahl find had any significance, it was because of Malta. And it wasn't as though she could go and ask Ivar, as Zetterberg would ensure she wasn't allowed near him. It wasn't her case. Yet without any answers, it was nagging at her. She popped her glasses back on. There was only one thing for it – she would have to go back and see Linus.

The pain in Danny's shoulder was excruciating. He knew they had taken the bullet out last night, though it might just as well have still been in there. But he must be grateful that he was still alive. How had McNaught found him? He couldn't shake him off. His throat was dry, and it wasn't through a lack of fluid intake; it was fear. McNaught was still out there. To make matters worse, he couldn't make a break for it, as his ankle was strapped up. He had sprained it in the final jump down the concrete steps at the station. He was stuck here. Would McNaught be able to get into the hospital? At least there was a policeman on guard outside the door. They were taking precautions.

He leant over and gingerly picked up a glass of water and drank thirstily. It didn't make any difference. What was he to do? He hadn't been interviewed properly since he'd had the operation. The doctors had wanted him to rest. To the hospital he had given his name as Grant Mitchell. The name of the character from the British soap opera *Eastenders* was the only one that had popped into his head. He hoped that they wouldn't connect him to the photo of the man wanted for Leif's killing. He still wasn't sure how he was going to explain McNaught's attack. Mistaken identity? Innocent tourist in the wrong place at the wrong time? It wouldn't wear for long. And it showed what a serious situation he was in – he was implicated in a murder he hadn't committed on the one hand and on the other, McNaught was so desperate to keep him quiet that he was willing to risk killing him in a public place. What was his best option? There wasn't one.

CHAPTER 28

When Anita buzzed Linus's apartment, he wasn't best pleased that she'd returned. He reluctantly let her in, and when she entered, he went into the gallery window, which had a small table and two rickety wooden chairs squeezed into the space. He sat down in front of a cool beer, which had only recently been opened. Anita thought it looked tempting.

'Lost your partner?' he enquired.

'No.' Anita sat down on the other chair, uninvited. Below, she could see the street, and the workmen who were noisily renovating the building opposite. There was a steady procession of cars making their way down the steep, narrow road, edging past the phalanx of parked vehicles. Where the traffic was heading to along such a claustrophobic thoroughfare was difficult to ascertain.

Linus took a swig. 'Get the impression that your colleague doesn't like you much.'

'Then she's got something in common with you.' He managed a hollow laugh. 'I'm not here about you. I want to know about Björnstahl.'

He shot her a quizzical glance. 'Really?'

'Yeah.'

'In that case, can I offer you a beer?'

'Thank you.' He got up and wandered into the next room and returned with an opened bottle of Cisk. It was cool to her touch and tasted refreshing after the unrelenting heat of the pavements outside.

'If you want to know about Björnstahl, you should really talk to Ivar. He knows more than me.'

She couldn't admit that there was absolutely no chance of that happening. 'It's simpler talking to you while I'm here. Saves a trip to Uppsala.' He seemed to accept the explanation. 'I've just been to the Bibliotheca,' she hurried on, 'and found the book of his travels to France and Italy and other places. The mention of Malta is restricted to a couple of pages which cover the time he seemed to be sailing from Toulon to Rome. My German is pretty hopeless these days, but he appeared to be comparing the ship he was on to Noah's ark and was on about the number of different languages being spoken on board. Do you know the significance of the reference?'

'Are you sure you're interested?' He suppressed a smile.

'Of course.'

'Very well. I was amazed you'd even heard of him. He's not exactly a Carl Linnaeus or Anders Celsius. But he is significant. I was curious about Björnstahl because he was the first Swede to really be interested in the Muslim world, and I've spent a lot of my working life in the Arab countries that fascinated him but, ironically, he never visited. His only connection with Malta was an observation on the Malti language, which was being hotly debated at the time. Maltese scholars such as Agius de Soldanis argued that the origin of the native language here was Punic.'

'Punic?'

'It's a Semitic language spoken by the Carthaginians. You know, Hannibal and his elephants fighting the Romans and all that. Modern Tunisia.'

'Fine.'

'The language goes back to the Phoenicians. All very complicated. To cut a long story short, when Björnstahl was on his round-Europe trip, he got on the boat you mentioned and found people from all nationalities, hence the Noah's ark reference, and the Tower of Babel alluded to the numerous languages being spoken. Being a philologist – a linguistics expert,' he added on seeing Anita's puzzled expression, 'what really fascinated him was that among his fellow passengers there were Arab and Maltese merchants. He noticed that they could understand each other really well, which led to his conclusion that Malti had nothing to do with any Punic origins. He rubbished the theory put forward by the Maltese scholars. He said something along the lines that the Punic theory was nothing more than a dream.'

'It doesn't seem such a big deal.'

Linus didn't reply until he had taken a further swig of his beer. 'It appeared that Björnstahl didn't think so either at the time, because the only reference he seemed to have made to it was the few sentences in the book you've just seen, which came out a few years after his original observation.'

'So what did Ivar find?'

'A much-expanded argument by Björnstahl on the origins of Malti. Quite detailed.'

'And it was definitely genuine?'

'Ivar had no doubts. It was definitely Björnstahl's signature at the end of the letter. Besides, who else was going to write about demolishing the Malti/Punic language argument? Rather an obscure subject to bother faking.'

Anita still wore a doubtful expression. 'I don't really understand why Ivar saw it as such a coup.'

'It's not so much the subject matter, though that would be of great historical interest to some scholars. It's that it was an undiscovered piece of writing by Björnstahl. It's like finding an unknown play by Strindberg or undiscovered observations on some obscure plant by Linnaeus. This guy was seriously famous in his time. Royal patronage, the lot. It's more about the person than the content. But this discovery was not made by an academic, but a student. Imagine the impact that would make. And probably did. As I lost touch with Ivar after the... you know what, it's probably how he forged his reputation.'

'OK, I get that, but how did it turn up here if Björnstahl never reached the island?'

'We can only speculate on that. Ivar reckoned that Björnstahl must have written these observations on board the ship going to Italy. Maybe the letter had been written to one of the Maltese scholars and perhaps a Maltese merchant was asked to deliver it. Or perhaps Björnstahl accidentally left it on board when he arrived at Civitavecchia. If he'd lost the letter, maybe that explains why he wrote so little about the subject in his later travelogue. Basically, no one will ever know how it turned up in that Brydone book. And I've never seen a happier man than Ivar when it dawned on him what he'd found. A dog with two tails. It couldn't have been better with Björnstahl being a scholar of the Muslim world; it fitted perfectly into Ivar's field of study. After that, he got into all things Björnstahl, according to Larissa.'

'So, she knew about it?'

'Well, I assume so. They were living together at the time.'

Anita's bottle had warmed up in her grip as she listened to Linus. She took a drink. She put the beer down. 'Do you think Göran found out?'

'He never said anything to me. Doesn't mean he didn't suspect. He may have worked it out that Ivar had found something to do with Björnstahl. It certainly hadn't become public by the time we were at Knäbäckshusen. I think that Ivar was going to unveil it when he gave his doctorate presentation. Amaze the academic world. But that was a year or so off when I last saw him.'

Linus got up and sauntered over to the table in the living room and fetched his cigarettes. He lit up and came back and hovered at the entrance to the gallery. He stared at Anita.

'And what is life like on Malta?'

'You mean the one you condemned me to?' There wasn't the anger of before. Anita didn't rise to the bait. Linus took a quick puff. 'The climate's good. I couldn't go back to Sweden now. Too damned cold. But like anywhere, however nice, it's not easy when you've got no money. And I can't live on Carina's charity forever.'

'Who do you mix with?'

'I don't mix much. There's quite a Swedish set here now; and not just the Gollcher family – you may know of them; they've dominated the shipping business round here for about a hundred and fifty years. I hear Swedish voices all over the place. There are retired people who've come for the sun, or younger ones seeking a better life. I think a lot have moved here in recent years to work in the online gaming industry. I believe there's even a Swedish club which meets somewhere in Sliema. Not my thing.'

'Is it because you're worried about someone recognizing your name from the past?'

He flinched. 'Maybe I'll mix more when you and Inspector Zetterberg clear my name and catch the real killer.'

Anita picked at her rabbit. She had decided to go for Malta's traditional dish on her second visit to D'Office on Archbishop Street. She hadn't set eyes on Zetterberg since they parted in front of Linus's apartment that morning. The jazz music and the Mediterranean-style surroundings didn't distract her thoughts. She was weighing up whether she should tell her about meeting up with Linus again. Of course, Zetterberg would go ballistic; talking to a witness behind her back on a case that she wasn't even working on. But tell her what? That Jacob Jonas Björnstahl left some observations on the Malti language on a boat in the winter of 1770 to be found over two hundred years later? What bearing did it have on the case? As long as Ivar had an alibi, as a course to be followed it was dead in the water. There was obviously serious friction between Ivar and Göran over their work – and then the strange sexual episode thrown in. But was it enough to lead to murder? She couldn't believe that it would. A blind alley, then. Yet it was still swirling around in her head when she tucked into her beautifully sickly pudding.

Klara Wallen passed Chief Inspector Moberg's office and was surprised that he was working so late. She knocked on his door and popped her head round.

'I'm just off. Is there anything else I can do before I go?' This wasn't the Wallen of old, who wouldn't have had the nerve to approach Moberg. But she was more self-assured these days and, though she really wanted to head home and see to Rolf's needs, she appreciated that this was an opportunity to impress the chief inspector, as it was a case that was clearly important to him. And Anita was conveniently out of the way, so she could place herself at the heart of the investigation.

'You were down at Hyllie shortly after the shooting yesterday?'

'Yes. The local boys down there assumed it was gang related.'

Moberg grinned. 'Well, they were wrong. You know I've had a Detective Blentarps from Kristianstad over here checking on the car that was found at Mobilia?'

'Yeah, I heard.'

'And the prints they found matched those of the killer up at the farmhouse near Höör.'

'So, he's probably around Malmö somewhere.'

'Oh, yes. He certainly is. Daniel Foster is right in the heart of Malmö as we speak.'

Wallen looked taken aback. 'Where?'

'In the Skåne University Hospital.'

The penny dropped. 'You mean the young man who was

shot yesterday afternoon at Hyllie station is Daniel Foster?'

'The very same. He was calling himself Grant Mitchell, but one of the officers who was sent to guard him recognized him from the photo that was put through by Kristianstad.'

'So, that's that solved. Though it'll cause quite a stir when the press find out we've got another British killer in our midst.' She remembered only too well the trial of Ewan Strachan for the murder of film star, Malin Lovgren – and the unfortunate connection with Anita Sundström.

'Quite. But I don't think it's as simple as Detective Blentarps thinks it is. That's the trouble with these provincial cops. Too busy looking at the bloody obvious.'

'I don't understand. As you say, they've got this Foster's prints all over the murder scene – and on the car he stole from the farm. Besides, it's not really our case, is it?'

'The shooting in Hyllie is our case, even if the murder isn't. So, we're involved. What puzzles me is that the young man who was shot yesterday didn't have the murder weapon on him.'

'Won't he have chucked it? His ticket was one way to Copenhagen, so he wasn't intending to come back.'

'Possibly. But what intrigues me is that, if the murder of the farmer was a robbery gone wrong as the Kristianstad police believe, who on earth is trying to kill this guy? And from the descriptions from eye-witnesses you've helped to coordinate down there,' Moberg glanced at the notes on his desk, 'the bald gunman sounds similar to the man working with Egon Fuentes on the paving scam. That's why I want you to accompany Detective Blentarps when he interviews Foster at the hospital tomorrow.'

That served her right for calling into the chief inspector's office – her Saturday off would be ruined, and Rolf wouldn't be happy.

Anita didn't know how long she'd been asleep when she

was awoken abruptly by Zetterberg stumbling into the hotel bedroom they shared. Anita turned over and pretended to be still sleeping as Zetterberg groped around for the switch. A minute later, the room was ablaze with light. Even at the distance of a bed's width, Anita could smell the alcohol. Zetterberg had been on the booze.

Zetterberg disappeared into the en suite bathroom and left the door open. Anita could hear her peeing loudly. The snoring was going to be terrible tonight. Thank goodness they were flying back tomorrow morning.

Zetterberg swayed out of the bathroom and sank onto her bed. She sat there for a few minutes and then burst out laughing. 'Are you awake?' she demanded.

There was no point in pretending any longer. 'Yes,' Anita said wearily.

'I can't stand you, Anita Sundström,' she slurred. 'Never could, even before you slept with Arne.'

'I never did.' This was met with a contemptuous sigh.

'But do you know what? I found out a very funny thing the other day.' Anita just wished she'd finish and then she could try and get some sleep. She wasn't in the mood for a row. 'When I was interviewing that stuck-up tart Carina Lindvall, she told me something very, very interesting.' She paused, and Anita thought that she must have forgotten her train of thought in her drunken state. 'While she was a student, she was shagging your husband.' Another rasping peel of laughter. 'Just think of that. That's what I call poetic... poetic... what's the fucking word? Ah, yes, *justice*.' She shook her head. 'I should know that word. But you don't.' And then she flopped onto the duvet, still fully clothed. Moments later, Zetterberg was snoring.

Anita turned away. She couldn't sleep now. Zetterberg had planted a nasty seed. She'd divorced Björn because he couldn't help jumping into bed with his most attractive students. That had started later in their marriage, after she had gone back to work and Lasse was a few years old. Or that's what he had admitted to. She'd learned to cope with that over the years, even if she couldn't entirely forgive. She'd often been too tired for sex, sometimes preoccupied with police cases she was working on, and wanted to spend as much quality time as possible with young Lasse. Now her brain was working overtime to try and do the maths. She had known that Carina Lindvall was one of Björn's students, but at the time of the Göran Gösta killing, she had been left university two years. If she had been sleeping with Björn, it must have been at least during the academic year before that, if not before. God damn it! The bastard must have been screwing her while Lasse was just a little tot, long before she thought he had started to stray. Despite the sad and unedifying way the marriage had ended, those early years had been the happiest times, and the memories she still clung to when looking back. They had made the marriage worthwhile. Now Zetterberg had destroyed that once and for all.

CHAPTER 29

The constable guarding the room stood up as Wallen and Inspector Blentarps approached. Wallen could see Daniel Foster through the door's glass pane before the officer let them into the small, private ward. The young man was drowsily sitting up in bed, his shoulder heavily strapped. The doctor on the floor had already filled them in on the state of the injury – the bullet had been removed but because the wound had occurred to the articulation of the shoulder joint, they had had to rule out the presence of bullet fragments in the area. The patient had suffered severe blood loss and was on antibiotics. He had also badly sprained his right ankle when he'd jumped down the station steps. He wouldn't be running anywhere soon, the doctor had commented wryly. And he had also noted that Foster had received some physical blows fairly recently, one of which had cracked a rib, which were now beginning to heal. He warned them not to stay too long as the patient was weak after his experience.

Inspector Blentarps was a tall, angular man with a receding hairline and melancholy eyes. Wallen thought he must be around sixty. He spoke with a soft voice, which made her wonder if he always took the part of the 'good cop'. So, would she have to play the bad one? That wasn't really her style. And now that they were in the same room as the murder suspect, was her English good enough to get through an interview – or understand fully what was being said so she could report back accurately to the chief inspector? How she wished Anita was with her.

Once Blentarps and Wallen had taken a seat each side of the bed, the Kristianstad inspector asked if the suspect spoke any Swedish. He shook his head. Then he winced. She could see Foster was in a great deal of pain, and when he spoke, it was an effort. His first words were to confirm that his name was Daniel Willis Foster, and he was aged twenty-two. His last known address was in Hereford, England. Wallen had looked it up and seen that it was near Wales. She hadn't really been particularly aware of Wales, or its geographical location, until the recent Euro football championships in which the Welsh team had reached the semi-finals. Rolf had been glued to the competition. Blentarps continued in reasonably confident English:

'What do you know about the murder of Leif Andersson?'

'Who?'

Blentarps didn't bother hiding his surprise.

'He was a farmer who lived near Höör.'

'I don't know him,' Danny said, virtually under his breath.

'Can you speak louder, please?' said Blentarps in his own quiet voice.

'I don't know him.' This time it was audible.

'That is most odd. I will tell you why. Can I call you Daniel?'

'Danny,' the young man mumbled back.

'Danny. We have found your fingerprints all over this man's house, and in a sort of camp in the nearby woods, and on the car belonging to herr Andersson that was found at a car park here in Malmö on Wednesday.'

Danny realized things weren't looking good. 'You don't think I murdered him, do you?'

'To us, it is looking clear that you killed this man.'

Danny let out a deep breath. 'No, I didn't.' Then he

whispered: 'Leif was kind to me.' Wallen had to strain to hear. She was also having difficulty understanding his accent. Why didn't they all speak like the posh people on *Downton Abbey*?

'How? How was Leif kind to you?'

'He helped me. He gave me food.'

Blentarps nodded. 'He was good to you. I understand. So let me ask you, why did you stole... I mean steal his car? And, so his daughter is saying, nearly four thousand kronor her father had in the farmhouse. You still had some money in your pockets when you were brought here to the hospital.'

Danny tried to shift his position, as his backside was sore. He flinched at the pain in his shoulder, which seemed to pass through the whole of his back. At least he was alive. Had they caught McNaught? No one had said anything about him.

'Leif was dead.'

'I ask again: did you kill him?'

'No!' The physical forcefulness of his denial sent another shaft of pain zipping through his body. 'He was already dead.'

'Leif Andersson was badly beaten. We have information from the UK that you were sent to prison for attacking another man.'

That was a bit of a shock. They already knew about his past.

'That was the scrumpy talking.'

Blentarps and Wallen exchanged blank expressions.

'Who is scrummy?'

'Scrumpy. It's a drink. Cider. Made with apples. It's very strong.'

Blentarps had no idea what Danny was talking about and thought better of pursuing the subject. 'What did you do with the gun after you shot Leif?'

Tears were welling up in Danny's eyes. 'I didn't have a gun. I've never had a gun.'

Just then the doctor sidled into the room. He could see

that Danny was upset and assumed that the detectives had been pushing him too hard, too early.

'I think the patient needs to rest.'

Walking back along the corridor, Blentarps gave Wallen a sidelong look. 'What do you think, Inspector?'

Wallen, who hadn't contributed to the interview, was surprised at being asked. 'I got the impression that you're sure he did it.'

'All the evidence points in that direction.'

'He seemed frightened to me. I wouldn't have thought that someone capable of cold-bloodedly beating up an old man and then shooting him would be the type to be so obviously scared of something.'

'I think you misjudge this type of criminal. He befriends an old man, susses out the place and, when he discovers where his money is, kills him. I suspect that's why he beat him up first... to find out where the money was.'

It was plain to see that Blentarps thought it was a straightforward case of robbery and murder.

'So, who do you think tried to kill Danny?'

'An accomplice. They fell out over the money. What we need to find out next is who this other person is.'

Wallen was far from convinced. She knew that people could easily quarrel over amounts of money as small as four thousand kronor, but it was hardly a sum you'd kill for. And she was sure Chief Inspector Moberg would agree.

It was hardly the homecoming Anita was expecting. After two nights without much sleep thanks to Zetterberg, and another flight, she just wanted to put her feet up for a few hours. After entering her Roskildevägen apartment, the last person she wanted to see was her ex-husband. With the events of the last few days, she'd forgotten that Björn was staying over the weekend on a visit to see their granddaughter, Leyla. Bitterly, she remembered she should have been enjoying the delights of the Lake District instead of running into Björn wandering out of the shower with a towel wrapped round his waist. Once upon a time, she would have been pleased at such a sight. Now, with his middle-aged paunch spilling over the top of the towel in an unflattering way, his chest also turning to flab and his thinning wet hair slicked back, accentuating the lines around his eyes, Anita could see how much he'd aged since their last meeting a couple of years before. And now she knew that he'd been unfaithful to her far earlier than she had suspected, if Zetterberg was to be believed, this wasn't a good moment to run into him. His greeting didn't help.

'Oh,' he said in surprise, 'I thought you'd buggered off with your Brit boyfriend.'

Anita left him to dress without saying a word.

'Is it something I said?' Björn ventured when he entered the kitchen, where Anita had made a fresh pot of coffee.

She stared at him fiercely. He was now dressed in his familiar black T-shirt, jacket and trousers. Didn't he ever wear anything else?

'No. I should be on holiday, but it's been cancelled.'

'Hardly my fault. Or is everything still my fault?' he said with a supercilious smile.

She wanted to yell at him. Demand to know whether he had slept with Carina Lindvall while she was caring for his young child. But there was no point; he would deny it, and that would only make it worse.

'Do you want some coffee before you go?'

'Go?'

'You are down here to see our granddaughter.' She was trying to control her temper.

'Yeah. Of course. I'm due to meet them in Folkets Park at three and then we're going back to their place afterwards. I'm buying them a Chinese. I had offered to take them out for a meal, but they thought it might be difficult with Leyla.'

'You could have offered to babysit and given them the money to go out on their own. They could do with a break.'

'Oh.' He frowned. 'Hadn't thought of that.'

'But you never think, Björn.' Anita couldn't keep the disapprobation out of her voice.

'Hey, hold on. What have I done?' He looked genuinely taken aback.

'Nothing.' She was too tired to spark a full-blown row. Björn would never change; he was too self-centred.

His face brightened. 'Why don't you come with me?'

'No. You go. You rarely see Leyla, or Lasse. Go and enjoy their company. I can see them anytime.'

Half an hour after Björn had left, Anita got a call from Moberg.

'How was Malta?'

'Sunny.'

'Nail your guy?'

'Not exactly.'

'Never mind.' It didn't sound as though Moberg was the slightest bit interested. 'Look, there have been developments in the Egon Fuentes case.' He went on to tell her about the scam, how it worked, Egon's role in it, the dodgy building supplier and the bald-headed man. Then he told her about the shooting at Hyllie and the man who had attacked Daniel Foster.

'Blentarps thinks it's an open-and-shut case of a burglary gone wrong, or some such. Klara Wallen thinks there's a lot more to it. She said she thought Foster was really frightened of someone or something. I think it may well be connected to our case. He just happens to be English. And the bald man who attacked him sounds similar to the man described by both the building supplier and the customers we found.'

'What's your next move?'

'We've agreed to keep Foster under guard for the time being. Blentarps has shoved off back to Kristianstad. He's back over on Monday with a colleague. I think they're going to charge Foster. So, I want you to go down to the hospital tomorrow and have a go at the lad before they get to him.'

'Won't that upset Kristianstad?'

'Fuck Kristianstad! This is still technically our case because he was shot on our patch.'

It wasn't going to be the Sunday Anita had planned.

CHAPTER 30

Björn returned at about ten. Anita heard him come in as she was finishing a glass of red wine, the first from a new bottle that perched on the coffee table. Instead of unwinding after her trip, she had phoned Klara Wallen to get the lowdown on Danny Foster and her colleague's impressions of him from the interview at the hospital. Anita wanted to be abreast of all the facts before she talked to him the following morning. She had also been doing a little digging of her own on the Göran Gösta case, which she now knew she couldn't let go of. If Linus Svärd wasn't responsible for Göran's death – and it was beginning to dawn on her that her long-held conviction about his guilt was gradually eroding – then she was duty-bound to help find out who the real killer was. This would be difficult without causing ructions with Zetterberg and antagonizing those in authority. She would have to be subtle; not her strongest attribute. Anyhow, she had managed to track down the original prosecutor on the case and had arranged to meet him the following afternoon. She had a busy day ahead.

'Isn't she beautiful?' said a beaming Björn. 'I love that smile when she wrinkles up her nose.'

However resentful Anita might be towards her ex-husband, she couldn't help smiling herself as she thought about their granddaughter. Leyla had added a joyous new dimension to her life. In a strange way, it had even made her redouble her professional efforts, feeling somehow that she could help make the world a safer place for Leyla to live in. She knew that was a ridiculous conceit. Nevertheless, it was a maxim she happily clung to. And following that principle meant helping to solve a twenty-one-year-old mystery. So, instead of giving Björn a hard time – her natural instinct – she offered him a glass of wine.

Björn took his jacket off and settled down on the daybed. She let him prattle on about his evening with Lasse, and he asked if she would like to come out to lunch with them tomorrow. Apparently, Jazmin's brother and girlfriend were turning up, too. He insisted that Lasse also wanted his mother there. She didn't relish playing happy families and was about to reject the offer – but then agreed, as it might be useful to speak to Hakim after she'd seen Danny Foster.

'Do you come across Ivar Hagblom at all up in Uppsala?'

'Occasionally.'

'What's he like?'

Björn scoffed: 'Bit flash for my taste.' Anita managed to stop herself laughing. Pot, kettle, and black sprang to mind. 'Always on the TV, spouting off about some Middle East disaster or the latest on Syrian immigrants; or seen at some film première with his decorative wife. Why?'

'He was involved in my first murder case. Don't you remember? The one at Knäbäckshusen. 1995.'

'Of course. Never solved, was it?'

'It's been reopened.'

'Heavens! After all this time. You working on it?'

'No.'

He grinned. 'Are you sure?' Even after all these years he still knew her.

'Not officially. It took place near Ivar Hagblom's parents' place. It was a group of ex-Lund students. There was one of yours there,' she couldn't help blurting out.

'Oh?'

'Carina Lindvall.'

'Goodness! I'd forgotten she was in one of my classes.' Anita bet that he hadn't. 'Hasn't she done well for herself?'

Despite the fact that she was desperate to know when Björn had been sleeping with Carina Lindvall, she managed to avoid going down that potentially acrimonious alley.

'Hagblom was into Jacob Björnstahl at the time of the murder.'

Björn swirled the deep red wine round in his glass. 'Doesn't surprise me. Björnstahl was into the Middle East, though he never got beyond Constantinople.'

'I know.'

'We've still got a Björnstahl scholarship at Uppsala.'

'Apparently, Ivar found some writing by Björnstahl on Malta while he was doing his doctorate. A letter. Something no one had ever seen before.'

'That would have helped his career.'

Anita leant over and topped up Björn's glass. 'Can you do me a favour? Can you find out if Ivar used the Björnstahl letter as the basis of his thesis? It was done at Lund. Presumably you still have contacts?'

'Anything for you, madam,' he said in a gentle, mocking tone.

She let that one go. 'I don't know much about Björnstahl. There's nothing much on the internet.'

Björn liked nothing more than an attentive audience: 'Such a pity. He was so famous in his time, yet he's nothing more than a dusty footnote in history.' Björn warmed to his theme. 'He was a brilliant linguist, allowing him to converse with the likes of Rousseau, Voltaire and the Pope. Of course, he started as a student in Uppsala. Apparently, on his first day at university, he was asked to act as an opponent in another student's dissertation discussion, and did so in fluent Hebrew and Greek. He must have been quite something,' he said gleefully, his eyes lighting up. This was the enthusiastic Björn she had fallen for – intelligent, articulate and handsome. How could he have drifted so far? 'He went to Carl Linnaeus's lessons in Uppsala and that opened up the door to Rousseau, whom Björnstahl hailed as his god. But, obviously, he's best known for his travels.'

'I found a book describing some of them in the National Library in Valletta. Unfortunately, it was in German.'

'I think it was translated into various languages, such was his fame. He acted as a private tutor to supplement his income, and this gave him the chance to travel. I think he spent three years in Paris. He went all over Europe... and England, too.'

She poured herself another glass of wine. 'Do we know what he was like as a person?'

'He was much admired by foreign scholars and, I believe, he was very religious. But that wasn't out of the ordinary at the time. I think he was a generous person, full of energy, yet restless. I suppose he had an endlessly enquiring mind. I suspect he wasn't easily distracted.'

'Unlike you?'

Björn pulled a pained expression. 'Harsh.'

'Family?'

'His father was a soldier. So, too, was his grandfather who was killed in some cavalry action. His brother was in the navy and ended up in Holland. So he didn't come from an academic background, yet became a professor in Uppsala and was appointed Professor of Oriental and Greek languages in Lund, though he never lived to take up the position. King Gustav the Third had asked him to go to Turkey. Never made it back.'

'Died in Salonika.'

'Yes. Part of the Ottoman Empire in those days. He left Arabic, Turkish and Persian manuscripts to Uppsala, and his outstanding salary was used to finance his titular scholarship!'

He sank back into the cushions. 'What intrigues me is how Björnstahl can have any real connection with your murder.'

She wondered that herself. Yet her gut feeling was that Zetterberg was wrong to be so dismissive of the Björnstahl letter. Opposite her sat an academic who, when he wasn't contemplating sex, could be excited and stimulated by his subject and be fiercely protective of his work. Had the same thing happened to Ivar Hagblom all those years ago?

Anita arrived at the Skåne University Hospital at around ten o'clock the next morning – another bright day. She'd already been to the polishus and, much to her amazement, had found Chief Inspector Moberg at his desk. There had been a development which might prove useful to Anita when talking to Danny Foster. CCTV at Hyllie station had revealed some slightly blurred images of the constantly moving assailant. But they were clear enough to show the figure wielding a gun was bald-headed and of stocky build, and could well be the man described visiting the builders' merchant's and the Gradin family home. 'See if Foster can tell you who he is. I'm sure there's a connection.' were Moberg's final words on her departure.

As she'd walked down through the quiet Sunday streets of Malmö on the way to the hospital, she had decided on a charm offensive, and Danny was astonished when she presented him with a box of Aladdin chocolates, the Swedish cliché gift of choice. This had thrown him, as had her assertion that the Malmö police were not convinced, unlike Inspector Blentarps, that he was the killer of Leif Andersson. The third card she produced was being able to talk to him in fluent English, so well that he actually asked if she was British. Though he was still in pain, she could see him almost relaxing, despite his eyes occasionally flitting towards the door as though he were expecting someone to burst in at any moment. She eased her way into her questioning:

'I've never been to Hereford. But I was in Worcester a few years ago.'

Danny brightened. 'I used to go to Worcester sometimes on the train. Good pubs.'

'I only went into one.' It had been with Kevin Ash on the Graeme Todd murder. At that stage, she hadn't been sure what to make of the British policeman. Now he was probably moping around Penrith with a week's wasted holiday on his hands. She would ring him later. 'Shall I open the chocolates for you?' Anita could see that it was impractical for Danny to open them with one hand. He nodded. She undid the cellophane and presented the box to him. He took one gingerly. He wasn't sure what to make of Inspector Anita Sundström. 'Mind if I help myself to one, too?' Again, he nodded.

She still had the half-eaten chocolate in her mouth when she asked casually: 'So what brought you to Sweden?'

This took him by surprise. The other detective had been so keen on pinning the murder on him that he hadn't asked the most obvious question.

'Work.'

'What sort of work?'

'Labouring. Laying paving. Drives and patios. That sort of thing.' Straightaway, Anita realized that Moberg's instincts had been on the nose and that this young man was possibly the key to the Egon Fuentes case.

'Hard work, I should imagine,' she commented chattily. Though undoubtedly strong, she had a shrewd idea that he hadn't been as thin as this when he left England.

'Very. Long hours.'

'Good pay, too.'

He gave a dismissive grunt. 'Didn't see any.'

'That sounds strange. Working for nothing?'

'We were promised plenty of money when we'd finished

over here. But we were never going to see any.'

'So why did you stay? Why not just go back to England?'

At first Danny didn't say anything, as though he had conflicting thoughts. Other than Leif, this was the first really friendly Swede he'd come across. Or the first he was allowed to talk to, anyway. But he was still frightened.

'Can I ask you something first?'

'Of course you can.'

'The man who attacked me. Did this.' He glanced at his shoulder and grimaced. 'Has he been caught?'

It was earlier than she had planned, but she produced the images from Hyllie station. 'This man?'

Danny flinched when he saw the familiar face; the one that had wreaked havoc with his waking and sleeping hours these last months. 'Yes. Him.'

'Not yet. We're looking for him.' She could see this wasn't the reassurance he was desperately seeking. 'I'm sure we'll pick him up soon. Unless he's got away to Denmark already.'

Danny stared towards the window for several seconds before turning his fearful gaze towards Anita. 'He won't be in Denmark. He won't leave until I'm dead.'

CHAPTER 31

And then it all came pouring out...

Danny Foster had been brought up in a small village outside Hereford in the West Midlands of England. His mother had died when he was young and he'd been brought up by his father. Their relationship hadn't been good and he hadn't done well at school. His older sister had tried to steer him clear of the wrong crowd, but she had a family of her own to bring up so he was left to his own devices most of the time. Boredom was the biggest problem in a rural area with few amenities. He started with petty thieving, and then moved on to stealing roof slates and reselling them. The gang was caught, but his young age – and the fact it was his first offence – saved him from a custodial sentence. After leaving school, he was unable to keep a job (which were few and far between for someone with no decent qualifications in an economically deprived area). With little money and copious amounts of cheap cider fuelling his frustration, he got into a brutal fight which saw him badly beating an innocent man out on his stag do.

His nine months in prison had been a sobering experience and when he left, he was determined to turn his life around. He wasn't welcome in his father's house, so he stayed with his sister until it became obvious he would never get a job where his prison record was known. So he headed for London in the hope of a change of luck.

That came about when he was leaving the local job centre

and a smart silver Range Rover drew up beside him. It was driven by a stony-faced man with short-cropped hair, who was a complete contrast to the bulky, cheery Irishman who got out and asked him if he was looking for work. The Irishman's name was Tyrone Cassidy. At the time, Danny was staying at a bed and breakfast that was little more than a doss house, paid for by his social security benefits. Cassidy took Danny to a nearby café and treated him to a coffee and a piece of chocolate cake. In the process, Danny gave him a potted history of his life, including his time in prison. Cassidy said that was all water under the bridge and everybody deserved a fresh start. The offer of work was almost too good to be true, and Cassidy asked if he would be happy with £40 a day. Cassidy even pressed a £20 note into Danny's hand, along with a packet of cigarettes, as a gesture of goodwill.

Danny had joined other young men like himself, and for the next month had done paving and tarmacking jobs in and around London. He did get paid, but not the £40 a day that Mr Cassidy had promised. Sometimes not at all, though he was told the shortfall would be made up when money had been received from the clients. Danny was conscious that he had no experience of the work, but neither did most of the others he worked with. He had a feeling that not all the jobs were done to a satisfactory standard, though he was quick to jettison such thoughts when he did see some money.

After the first month, Cassidy turned up at the domestic driveway Danny was working on. Again, the hard-faced driver sat silently in the Range Rover. Cassidy was very friendly and said that there was even more money to be made abroad. Danny said that he didn't have a passport. Cassidy reassured him that that would be taken care of and two weeks later, Danny found himself in the back of a transit van heading towards the Channel Tunnel. There were five other workers, none of whom Danny had met before. All seemed to have been signed up by

Cassidy in similar ways. The driver of the van was an Irishman, answering to the name of Paddy, who communicated in grunts. He kept all the documentation, which he handed through the van window when going through French customs. Danny never did see his passport. On the long trip, Danny befriended a man younger than himself called Jack Harmer. It turned out that Harmer came from a middle-class background before losing his way through drugs. Cassidy's offer had helped him get back to a more normal life, even though he wasn't obviously cut out for the physical work involved.

Their excitement at reaching Sweden was soon tempered by the sight of their accommodation. It was more like a travellers' camp, with dirty caravans as their new homes. Danny shared his with Jack. They were based in a forest and had no idea whereabouts they were. The camp was run by a Scotsman named Mark McNaught. He and three other Irishmen were in charge of organizing the gangs of two or three workers and taking them to the sites. All these men were rough, and the treatment of the ten or so young men at the camp was harsh. They weren't fed well, and no money was forthcoming. If anybody complained, they were met with both verbal and physical abuse. They soon learned to fear McNaught. Their mobile phones had been confiscated on arrival at the camp, and the sense of isolation became more intense as the intimidation increased. They worked fifteen-hour days and were "discouraged" from talking to the customers, most of whom seemed elderly. If they were caught doing so, a beating was often the punishment. The camp became a place of terror.

After it became clear that they were nothing more than modern-day slaves, there was still enough spark left in the new arrivals to plot escapes. But each time they thought they had an opportunity, their resolve failed. After a month, a Cockney lad they only knew as Trigger did a runner into the woods. Three hours later, McNaught brought him back, his face almost unrecognizable. He didn't work for a fortnight. This was the consequence of failure. It got to the point where they no longer knew whether they had been there days or weeks or months, as any self-confidence had been shredded and their sense of hopeless despair deepened into fearful acceptance.

Only Jack Harmer, despite being the youngest of the workers, held out any hope. He was brighter than the rest of them and, initially, he had tried to reason with McNaught and the others to better the slum conditions they were living in. A few well-aimed blows put an end to that. Yet, despite everything, he believed that if they could speak to Mr Cassidy, they would get things sorted out. He had been kind and approachable, and he was obviously oblivious to what McNaught and his cronies were up to.

Occasionally, when they were working on a job, a Swedish man turned up to talk to the customers. He never appeared at the camp, except that last day. A week previously, at one of the sites they were working at, Jack and Danny were left alone while McNaught, Paddy and one of the young lads went off to pick up some more paving. Jack had taken the opportunity to speak to this Swedish man, who was visiting the customer to pick up some money. The man had sounded sympathetic and said he would do something. He had said that he had no idea that the working conditions were so awful.

Then a week later, McNaught stopped Danny and Jack from getting into one of the vans for work and told them they weren't going anywhere that day. He said that they were to wait. An hour later, the Boss turned up with the Swede. They had been in their caravan when Jack saw Mr Cassidy through the window. He'd turned to Danny and said that this was their chance for Mr Cassidy to sort everything out. Danny wasn't as confident, as McNaught hadn't left the camp and was talking animatedly to the new arrivals. In fact, McNaught was pointing to their caravan. Before Danny knew it, Jack was outside and walking over to Cassidy. Danny watched from the *caravan window. As Jack approached, Danny saw the Swede nodding in Jack's direction and saying something to Cassidy. Danny couldn't hear what was being said, but he could see Jack talking to Cassidy. There was nothing cheerful about the Boss's countenance, and McNaught was scowling beside him. Suddenly, Cassidy started yelling at Jack and began to lay into him, punches raining down on the defenceless youngster. It was as though an explosion had been detonated. Danny stared in horror as Cassidy continued to beat Jack in a frenzy of anger. McNaught stood and watched, his gaze impassive, though Danny could see a look of shock and alarm on the face of the Swede. Jack was now on the ground, and Cassidy was kicking him with his heavy brogues. Eventually, the Swede tried to pull Cassidy back. But it was too late. Even from that distance, Danny knew that Jack would never get up again, his body limp and still on the rough ground. Danny hadn't waited... he'd burst through the caravan door and run as fast as he could into the surrounding forest.*

'So, that's when you set up your camp in the forest near Leif Andersson's farm?' Anita questioned rhetorically when the main part of Danny's story was complete. 'What about Leif? How did you meet him?'

Danny didn't want to admit he'd stolen from the old farmer before he'd met him. 'He found me in my camp. He took pity on me. He was kind. He fed me.' Anita could see Danny was getting quite emotional. 'It was my fault that he died. My fault,' he repeated quietly.

'You just found him? Dead, tied to a chair?'

Danny's eyes were moistening. 'Yes.'

'Do you know who killed him?'

'McNaught.'

Anita helped herself to another chocolate. She might buy another box on the way home. 'So, why didn't you report the death to the police?'

Danny looked at her helplessly. 'Why do you think? I'm in a strange country; I have no idea where the police are; I've got no passport. And my fingerprints must have been all over the house: I was in the kitchen, used the shower...'

'But you stole money and Leif's car.'

'I didn't have much choice. It was either that or hang around for McNaught to butcher me. He knew I'd been there. He must have beaten that information out of Leif before he shot him.' Then he paused. He almost choked out the next words. 'God, maybe be didn't tell him! Tried to protect me.'

'We'll never know.'

Danny was still battling with the possibility that the old man might have died because he hadn't given him away. 'I didn't like pinching his stuff. I was desperate.'

It all made perfect sense to Anita, though she had to ask the obvious questions.

'And when did you get to Malmö?'

'Monday.'

'And was Hyllie station the first time you'd seen McNaught since Jack's murder?'

'No. I saw him at the main railway station the day after I arrived. So I kept a low profile. I found out from an American at the hostel that I didn't need a passport to get out of Sweden. I was trying to make a break for it. But he found me somehow.' The fear had returned to his eyes, which again were drawn to the door. 'He's a hunter.'

'You obviously believe that he'll make another attempt.'

'Of course he will. Other than McNaught and the Swede, I'm the only witness to Jack's murder.'

Anita didn't want to tell him yet, but, besides McNaught, Danny Foster was the only witness left alive who could put Tyrone Cassidy behind bars.

CHAPTER 32

Anita phoned Chief Inspector Moberg as soon as she was outside the hospital. It was still warm, and she stood happily in the sunshine away from the shadow of the large, circular building. She gave him a précised account of Danny Foster's story. After listening, he said that he would put out an all-points alert on Mark McNaught. He said he'd want the whole team in by seven the next morning. He was expecting the ballistics report first thing on whether the bullet used to kill Leif Andersson matched the one that was taken out of Foster's shoulder. He was confident now that that would be the case. And he wanted Anita to be in charge of looking into the backgrounds of Mark McNaught and Tyrone Cassidy.

After a pause: 'Well done, Anita.' That was high, if unexpected, praise indeed.

'By the way, it might be an idea to put a couple of constables on Danny Foster's door tonight. McNaught doesn't seem fazed about where he attacks. Hyllie was very public.'

'Do you really think he'll try again? He must be aware that we're looking for him.'

'Danny thinks he'll stop at nothing.'

'Very well.' Moberg sounded doubtful. 'But it'll take time to drum up an extra officer on a summer Sunday. Half the polishus are still on holiday.'

'Lucky them!' She should have been sitting in a Lakeland pub with Kevin at this very moment. 'I'll tell you what. I've got a couple of things on today, but I'll call back later to make sure there are two officers on the door. If not, I'll hang around until someone turns up. I'd feel better.'

'That's up to you, Anita.'

Anita squinted at the sun. 'It might be useful, too. I'll see if Danny knows where Cassidy is based, or anything else about McNaught. It might narrow the field.'

The gathering was in full swing. They were in the communal garden of Lasse and Jazmin's apartment block. The quadrilateral area was surrounded by the backs of other blocks of differing heights and colours, each with their own outside space. Lasse and Jazmin's was the most sizeable and had its own permanent brick barbecue in the corner. Lasse was doing the cooking, Jazmin was putting salads out on a table and Björn was dispensing the drinks in a strange assortment of glasses. Hakim and Liv were playing with Leyla. She was finding the grass more difficult to totter on and kept collapsing on her bottom. But she was a determined little thing, and would be up again in no time.

Anita hugged each of them in turn before scooping Leyla up, babbling baby talk at her. Leyla wrinkled up her nose in that now familiar grin. Anita took her round the garden as the others chatted away. She felt a sudden surge of happiness. Apart from Björn, these were the most important people in her life right now. There was Kevin, of course, and she wished he could be here too. But he wasn't family.

She returned to the throng and released Leyla, who was now impatient to be back on the ground. Anita noticed a couple of bottles of champagne on the table. 'That's generous of you, Björn.'

He had a large tumbler in his hand, full of white wine. 'Not mine. Hakim brought it.'

Anita turned to Hakim with a puzzled expression. 'Champagne, Hakim? But you don't drink.'

'No,' he smiled, and he shared a conspiratorial wink with Liv, who was wearing a pretty blue summer dress with large white spots. 'Can you open it please, Björn?'

'I never need to be asked twice.'

A couple of minutes later, everybody except Hakim had a tumbler of frothing champagne. Hakim's contained Coke. He took centre stage.

'I'd like to make an announcement.' Liv blushed joyfully. 'The beautiful Liv Fogelström, the best constable in the Skåne County Police Force, so arrested my attention...' he waited for appropriate groans. '...that I decided to ask her to be handcuffed to me for the rest of her life. And she said "yes", as long as she got time off occasionally for good behaviour.'

Jazmin gave a delighted scream and rushed over and hugged Liv, nearly knocking her champagne out of her hand. Then everybody raised their glasses and toasted the couple. Anita knew that Hakim must have spent ages working on his mini-speech – it wasn't typical Hakim humour. But she was so pleased for him; for them both, though she couldn't help but harbour worries for Liv. It was noticeable that Uday and Amira were not there. She suspected that their reaction to the news would not be quite as enthusiastic.

'Where's the ring?' asked Jazmin.

Liv held up her ring finger, round which was wrapped a blue rubber band. 'He didn't buy one in case I said "no".'

'He always was mean.'

'Don't worry, I'll make him pay. We're going out to choose one this coming week.'

The general congratulations were interrupted by Björn saying: 'I think something's burning.'

'Oh, shit!' shouted Lasse, who had deserted his cooking station to join in the toast.

Later on, Anita managed to catch Liv on her own. 'So, you've taken the plunge.'

Liv's rounded cheeks were flushed with girlish excitement. 'I know it's not going to be plain sailing. We'll have to tell Hakim's parents soon. But not today. We're enjoying our moment.'

'Good for you. You take care of Hakim.'

'Oh, I will. I know how much he respects you. And I can see that you're fond of him. I'll make him a good wife.'

'Just don't let him get away with anything. Remember, he's been pampered by his mamma for years.'

Liv pulled a serious face. 'No. He'll have to pull his weight or he's out!'

'Out of what?' asked Hakim, who had come over with a plate of food for Liv.

'Women's talk,' replied Anita. Liv giggled.

'Are you not having any more to drink?' Hakim asked Anita.

'No. I've got to see someone this afternoon. I'll need my wits about me. By the way, you'd better have an early night. Moberg wants us in at seven tomorrow.'

'Seven?'

'There have been developments with Danny Foster. I'll tell you tomorrow. This is your special day.'

Anita reluctantly left an hour later, but she had an appointment to keep. She said farewell to all, leaving Björn till last: 'Don't get too drunk.'

'Or I might try and...'

'Don't even think about it. That's never going to happen. Oh, by the way, you haven't by any chance been onto your contact at Lund about Ivar Hagblom's dissertation, have you?'

Björn smacked his forehead. 'Went clean out of my head. I'll follow it up. I promise.'

Nothing new then. Björn was still letting her down.

Ex-Prosecutor Renmarker's most distinguishing feature was his teeth. He seemed to have too many for his mouth, giving him a permanently pained smile which Anita found as disconcerting now as she had twenty-one years before. Of course he was older now, and his hair was a pleasing silvery grey. He was immaculately dressed in a crisp casual shirt and trousers. He was courteous to a fault, but his eyes were as sharp as ever. He was a man who missed nothing. He was now retired, and Anita had tracked him down to his modest home in the countryside outside Lund.

The afternoon was pleasantly warm, and Renmarker suggested they sit in his garden. As Anita waited for him to produce a cup of coffee, she watched a dog (some kind of terrier) ferreting among the shrubs and bushes bordering the large, neatly trimmed lawn. A line of trees at the bottom of the garden obscured the road that she'd driven along minutes before. Anita was sure that Renmarker had been married, but there had been no sign of any wife when he had greeted her at his front door.

Renmarker came out and placed a tray on a black metal table, the centrepiece of a matching set of four chairs. Anita wondered how often they were all filled. She took her cup, but ignored the biscuits.

He took the seat opposite and grinned. Well, she thought it was a grin. 'I remember you now, Inspector. A pretty little thing back then.' His stare was disconcerting, and she pretended to be distracted by the dog that was now running around with a toy bone in its mouth. 'Caused quite a stir among your male colleagues.' It came back to her. Renmarker had a roving eye. Or at least that's what she'd heard from a friend who'd worked in the prosecutor's office at the time.

'You know that the Göran Gösta case has been reopened?'

'Well, I wondered if it might be about that after you phoned me. You must be the only officer from that case who's still serving, I should imagine. Funny that you're working on it again after all this time.'

Anita avoided eye contact, this time by concentrating on sipping from her cup. She knew he wouldn't talk to her if he thought that she wasn't officially involved.

'Fresh evidence has appeared. Of course, we're keeping quiet about it at this stage.'

'Oh, I understand. Sure you won't have a biscuit? I made them myself. I've learned to bake since my wife passed away.' He gave a winsome sigh.

'I'm sorry to hear that. But I still won't have a biscuit.' She patted her tummy, and then immediately regretted the gesture as it reminded her that it was chubbier than she liked. 'Just eaten with the family not long ago.'

'So, how can I help?'

Until now she hadn't been entirely sure what she was going to talk to him about. It was really on an impulse that she had contacted him. Yet he was the only person that she could talk to who was fully conversant with all the facts of the original investigation. And, yes, there was one nagging question that she did want to pose, though she had no idea how to phrase it without causing offence. She would have to lead up to it.

'The murder weapon has been found.'

'Ah, the skewer from the barbecue.' It was clear that he remembered the case.

'And the young witness, Kurt Jeppsson, has changed his story.'

'Has he?' Renmarker sounded intrigued. 'Does it make a difference?'

'Might do,' she said guardedly. 'Enough to question the guilt of our original chief suspect.'

'Yes. Henrik Nordlund was very keen on that homosexual partner of the deceased. I was horrified to hear about Nordlund's death, by the way'

'I miss him. But you're right. We were convinced that it was Linus Svärd who was the perpetrator.'

'If I remember correctly, it was *you* that leaked your suspicions to the press.' The sudden ferocity of the accusatory, gimlet stare wasn't lessened any by the toothiness of the features.

'A misjudgement.' Anita wasn't going to offer more of an explanation to the man whom she felt had forced her to take such a course by his own inaction. In fact, his comment riled her. 'At the time, you wouldn't let us arrest him.' It came out more vehemently than she'd expected.

Renmarker steepled his fingers thoughtfully, which temporarily blotted out his teeth. Eventually he spoke: 'I felt you didn't have enough evidence. It was all circumstantial. I needed more solid facts, which Nordlund failed to produce.'

'We had enough to arrest him. The whole team agreed on that.'

'I didn't,' he stated firmly.

'Why didn't you?' she demanded. 'It made no sense. Even if we hadn't found him guilty, at least we could have had a go at him to find out the truth. You stopped that.'

'Inspector, if you're going to take this high-handed tone with me, you are no longer welcome in my home.'

Anita stood up. The dog disappeared into the trees. 'I don't know what prevented you from helping us back then, but I'm here because the most decent detective I ever worked with is probably going to get his reputation trashed by the scheming woman running this case. Henrik Nordlund spent the last years of his life tortured by the thought that we had failed to bring a killer to justice. And *you* were responsible. That's something for your conscience to deal with. I hope you can sleep at night.'

Anita had run out of steam, but even in her fury she realized the last bit sounded as though it had come straight out of some melodrama. She shook her head and walked towards the house.

'Inspector Sundström!' she heard Renmarker call. She halted at the back door and swung round to face him. He was now standing up. 'I deliberately blocked the investigation.'

CHAPTER 33

They were in the middle of the lawn. The sun was beating down, and a few wisps of cloud hung lazily in the blue sky. For a moment, the leaves on the trees twitched as a flurry of wind passed through them then sank away. The dog's games were at an end and it lay snoozing in the shade under the table. In contrast, Anita's mind was in a whirl. Whatever she had said had had a startling effect on Renmarker. His confidence had melted away as though it had been exposed to the sun for too long.

'There was pressure put on me.'

'Pressure?' she heard herself repeat, yet she was still struggling with his initial admission of deliberately blocking the investigation.

'Yes.' His eyes were moist and he flicked at them with his finger. 'I've always felt guilty about what I did.'

'I don't understand. Who put pressure on you? The commissioner? Or was it political for some reason?' Her mind was racing through the list of those with a vested interest in burying the case. She couldn't match any with a logical motive.

Renmarker scuffed away a rogue blade of grass that had had the presumption to poke its head up above its severely cut neighbours. 'It was a woman, of course. It was always a woman.'

'A woman put pressure on you? What woman?'

Still he avoided Anita's questioning gaze. 'You don't

understand. I can talk about it now that Anna-Greta has gone. She never knew, and that was the price I had to pay. For keeping it quiet.'

Anita was becoming exasperated at Remarker's riddles. 'Just tell me!'

He swallowed hard, and she could see his Adam's apple shimmy up and down his throat. 'In that summer of 1995, I was having an affair. With someone in my department. I'm embarrassed to admit it wasn't the first time, but it was definitely the last. I kept it from Anna-Greta, who was a trusting and devoted wife. I took advantage of that. It was easy. Too easy. But it hadn't gone unnoticed.' Once more, he dabbed at the corner of his eye with a finger. 'When the Knäbäckshusen murder came across my desk, I was as keen as anyone to solve it. Then one night, I was working late at the office. That's not true. I had stayed behind with...' The name of the woman nearly emerged but was immediately suppressed. 'I had a call. It was from a journalist from one of the rags. He informed me that he knew all about my affair with one of my staff. If I didn't put a lid on the case, then the whole world would hear about it, including Anna-Greta. He suggested that I might lose my job as well. That didn't matter, but I couldn't bear the thought of Anna-Greta finding out. The betrayal would have been too much for her. I loved her. I miss her so much.'

His silence gave her time to think. Why would a newspaper put pressure on a public prosecutor to make sure a case never went to court? Then the fog began to clear.

'Was the journalist from a Hagblom paper?'

'Yes. I worked that out pretty quickly. The family wanted it brushed under the carpet.'

Anita was as puzzled as she was shocked. 'I can't understand why. It's not as though the Hagblom family needed to protect Ivar; he had an alibi. Two actually. His girlfriend and Carina Lindvall.'

'In my darker moments I've pondered that one. The only conclusion I can come to is that the Hagblom holiday home was a focal point of the entire investigation. They didn't want the family name dragged through the mud by rival newspapers. And I suppose they were protecting Ivar in a way. By keeping him out of it, his future wouldn't be tainted by scandal. He's done well for himself since. I've taken a morbid fascination in his career ever since we met.'

It didn't sink in at first. 'Pardon? When did you meet him?'

'At the time of the case.'

'Did Nordlund know?'

'No one knew. We didn't meet officially. But I let Ivar Hagblom know that the case wouldn't proceed due to lack of evidence.'

'I don't believe I'm hearing this. Why tell him?'

'I wanted to make sure that word got back to his father so he would call off his hounds and my secret would stay just that. And it did. I finished the affair and remained faithful to Anna-Greta to the end.'

He wasn't going to get any compassion from Anita. 'How did Ivar react? I mean, when you told him.'

'Seemed relieved. But also uncomfortable. I got the impression he didn't want to be there, and was troubled that I'd been put in an uncompromising position. Someone was pushing him. I assume it was his father. From what I've read subsequently, Hagblom senior was an unscrupulous and unpleasant man. I can vouch for the former,' he said bitterly. The self-pity that had overcome him when talking about his duplicity was gone. 'I won't repeat a word of this, Inspector.' There was steely resolve in his voice. 'Even under oath.'

Anita felt nothing but contempt for this man who had let them down so badly two decades before. She left without another word being spoken.

As she manoeuvred her Skoda onto the main road, she

reflected that she hadn't been sure what she would achieve by visiting the ex-prosecutor. Now she'd discovered why the case had disintegrated. Henrik Nordlund would have been horrified if he'd known the truth. The only problem was that the visit had thrown up more questions than answers.

The hospital was busier than it had been earlier that morning. Visitors, many dragging reluctant children with them, were making their way to the wards, clutching grapes, chocolates and flowers. Anita hadn't gone straight to the hospital from Renmarker's place, but had called into her apartment for a refreshing shower after a sticky day, and a contemplative coffee. The old prosecutor had got under her skin, and now she was even more determined to find out who had killed Göran Gösta. Yet she had no idea how to proceed, as Zetterberg was hardly going to willingly let her get involved. She also didn't know what to do with the information that she had got out of Renmarker. He'd made it clear that he wouldn't repeat what he'd told her to anyone else, so it was only hearsay and therefore dubious to say the least. Should she tell Zetterberg? That wasn't a viable option. How could she explain that she just happened to visit the prosecutor on the original case? Zetterberg would probably land her in trouble for interfering and find the information useless anyway if Renmarker was unwilling to corroborate it. So, for the time being, she put it on the backburner as she walked up the stairs to Danny Foster's room.

The constable on the door greeted her with a weary smile.

'Shouldn't there be an extra guard here?'

'Yes. Two officers are supposedly coming down in half an hour to relieve me. Typical that I've been stuck in here on such a sunny day,' he moaned cheerfully.

'There's still the evening. I'm sure a cold beer will do the trick.'

'Too right.'

Before Anita pushed the door open: 'Nothing suspicious?'

He took out of his breast pocket a folded piece of paper with Mark McNaught's CCTV image on it. 'You mean him? No, thankfully.'

Danny glanced up nervously when Anita entered. He was relieved to see it was her.

'How are you feeling?' she asked.

'Have they got him yet? McNaught?'

'It's being sorted.' She wanted to keep him calm.

She took a chair and placed it beside his bed.

'What's going to happen to me?' She could tell that he thought he was in serious trouble.

'I don't know yet. You're not a murderer. I'm convinced of that. You've stolen things, but there were mitigating circumstances. I'm sure if you help us as much as you can, everything can be worked out.'

The reassurance appeared to dampen his agitation. 'Of course I'll help.'

'We need to know as much as we can about McNaught and Cassidy. For example, do you know where they come from in the UK?'

'I don't really. McNaught's Scottish. I know that from his accent. But I don't know anything about Scots accents, so I've no idea where he comes from up there. Not a nice place if it produced him.' She could hear the fear in his voice every time he mentioned McNaught.

'But you thought he was ex-Army?'

'We all assumed he was. Seemed like a military type. Always barking orders and threats and that. Could be SAS or the Paras. He certainly acted like one.'

'Paras?'

'Paratroopers.'

'That gives us a start.' Anita noticed that the box of

Aladdin chocolates was still open and there were a few left. Having turned down Renmarker's home-made biscuits, she was now feeling peckish. She resisted the urge to take one. 'Tyrone Cassidy. What about him?'

'Irish.'

'And?'

'He was very friendly when he picked me up. Like a jovial dad, I suppose. I liked him then.'

'But he picked you up outside a job centre in London?'

'That's right.'

'Where, exactly?'

'Enfield. I was dossing down in Enfield. The job centre was on Windmill Road. I got familiar with that. Next to a station. It was on that road that Cassidy found me; the job centre road.'

Anita was reasonably familiar with London after her year's secondment with the Met. 'OK, north London. Do you know where the others were picked up?'

A thoughtful frown furrowed the young man's brow. 'Sorry, could you pour me some water?'

Anita leant over and poured water from a clear plastic jug into an empty blue plastic cup and handed it to Danny. He took a greedy gulp. 'Thanks,' he said, coming up for air. 'I know Jack was also outside a job centre. I think that was somewhere like Romford. One of the others – Irish lad called Shaun – was living around Essex, too.'

Anita pondered this. If these young men were typical of the areas that Cassidy did his recruiting, they were all north of the Thames. Maybe that's where Cassidy was based.

'By the way, do you know where the camp is that you were working from?'

Danny shook his head hopelessly. 'All I know is that I ran through a big forest and eventually reached the farm. The camp was in there somewhere.'

Anita knew they would have to mount a search, though she was pretty confident that they wouldn't find anybody there now. She was just about to ask Danny another question about Cassidy when she saw him drop the cup and spill what was left of the water over the sheets. 'Oh, Jesus!' he gasped.

Anita's gaze flipped round to the door and a head vanished from view. 'What is it?'

'Him!' Danny screamed. 'It's him!'

Anita rushed to the door and yanked it open. The constable was standing a little way down the corridor talking to a pretty nurse. A bald-headed figure in a flash of blue clothing disappeared through the double doors at the end.

'Who was that?' Anita yelled at the startled constable.

'Just a doctor,' he stammered.

'It's McNaught!' she shouted angrily. 'Alert security! Lock the hospital down!'

A moment later, she was running after McNaught. As she chased the phantom figure, she was disorientated by the circular building's curving corridors. Her bursts of breath seemed to be synchronized with the sound of her sandals flapping along the shiny linoleum. She glanced off an unmanned trolley and heard the contents rattle and someone shout at her from behind. Two alarmed visitors pressed back against the wall as she hared towards them. She managed to pant: 'Bald-headed doctor?' to which one of the visitors pointed in the direction she was heading. She reached some stairs and thought she heard someone running downwards.

She scudded down the stairwell, just managing to keep her balance. At the bottom, corridors curved in both directions. No one was around to ask if they'd seen her prey. She went to her left and a few strides later, she came across a male nurse standing in the doorway of a room. 'Seen a bald-headed doctor coming along here?' she gasped.

'No.'

'She swore and turned and ran back to the bottom of the stairs. The other corridor was empty. Her only hope was that the constable had got security to lock down the hospital, which she knew, when activated, would stop anyone getting into the main building and make it difficult to leave. Colleagues had been called down from the polishus often enough when aggressive patients, many on drugs, got violent. She made her way to the front entrance, where two security guards were standing by the closed glass doors.

'Sorry, you can't go out,' said one holding up a burly hand.

'I'm police.'

'Yeah?' came the sceptical reply. As it hadn't been an official working day, she'd left her warrant card at home.

'Just trust me, I am. I started the alarm off.'

'And why?' the guard demanded. He was obviously incensed that his leisurely Sunday shift had been disturbed.

'There's a gunman loose in the building, that's why!' She was seething now. Both guards at least had the grace to look worried. 'Has anybody left the building since the lock down?'

'No,' said the belligerent one.

'Well, except the doctor,' put in his colleague. 'But he had an emergency on at another part of the site.'

'You're joking! Bald?' He nodded mutely. 'And did he speak Swedish?'

'English. I assumed he was one of the foreign doctors.'

'Fantastic!'

CHAPTER 34

They had watched as the "doctor", in regulation loose blue top and trousers, scurried out of the main entrance of Malmö University Hospital. Anita could even see in her mind's eye the smaller of the guards holding the door open for him and then stopping someone else from entering the building. The door had closed, and McNaught had disappeared from view.

Anita yawned. She hadn't had any sleep that night after McNaught had escaped her clutches. If she hadn't been in the room with Danny Foster, the young man would probably have had a bullet in his head. The officer on Danny's door was in for an almighty dressing down by someone today.

Anita sipped her umpteenth coffee. It didn't do much to sharpen her brain. She'd managed to raise a general alert which, on top of Moberg's instructions of the previous day, meant that every available officer was dragged out onto the streets in search of McNaught. As she expected, there had been no sign of him. He was a master at melting away. She herself had spent the night at the polishus on the end of a phone, ensuring there were enough officers at the hospital to protect Danny Foster and trying to co-ordinate the search on the ground. At just after one in the morning, she had been called out by a squad car that had seen a bald man acting suspiciously near the Central Station. By the time she got there, the officers had discovered it was a drunk who'd missed his last train. It was that sort of frustrating night.

'Right,' called out Moberg as though bringing a room full of noisy teenagers to heel. There was only Anita, Hakim, Brodd, and a very disgruntled Wallen, who'd been called in so early she hadn't had time to make Rolf's breakfast. Moberg had already filled them in on the details of what had happened the day before. He was fuming that a case that was his own personal crusade was now coming under the scrutiny of the commissioner, local politicians and the press. 'We can't have this gunman menacing Malmö. It's making people high up nervous; so the shit heads our way.'

'But we know he's only targeting one person,' Brodd pointed out helpfully.

'But innocent citizens might get caught in the cross-fire,' Moberg said brusquely. 'This guy is single-minded. It seems he'll stop at nothing to kill Danny Foster. Obviously, our priority is to apprehend McNaught. I'll be in charge of that. I'm liaising with Larsson and his team. They can do the running around. We also have to move Foster. Any word from the hospital on that possibility?'

Anita was stifling a yawn as the chief inspector turned to her. 'His doctor isn't very keen from a medical point of view, but I spoke to the hospital's administrator, who doesn't really want Danny around as it might put other patients in jeopardy. So, yes, that's OK.'

'We need to move him today. We've got a safe house down towards Skanör we can put him in.'

Anita remembered that was where they'd stored Mick Roslyn before...

'It's pretty open down there,' observed Wallen, who was calming down now. 'The house can be easily seen from the road.'

'Granted, there's not much in the way of cover. But, imagine what havoc he might cause in a city apartment block. The point is, we haven't got anywhere else immediately available; unless one of you lot want to put him up...? Thought not.' He paused, his meat-plate hands resting on the table in the meeting room. 'What is important here is that we mustn't lose sight of the overall case. If Danny Foster is telling the truth, and Anita believes he is,' he said with a sideways glance at Anita, who was blinking with tiredness, 'then McNaught killed Leif Andersson. We now know exactly what Egon Fuentes was up to. Our job is to bring to justice the murderer of the young man in the van, who we believe is called Jack Harmer. According to Danny Foster, that person is Tyrone Cassidy, who is probably the man behind the paving operation. I presume he's safely back in England...' Moberg thought for a moment, '...or Ireland. Foster thinks he was Irish. We also believe the driver of the van was also Irish, though he was only known as "Paddy", so he might be difficult to identify. Firstly, we need to find out where this Cassidy is. Secondly, we need to discover how he came over to Sweden. That's your job, Mirza. Check flights, trains... all the usual things. We need to prove he was here, in Sweden, at the time that Foster claims he saw Harmer's murder. From what Foster told Anita, she reckons the murder probably took place on the seventh or eighth of August.' Hakim nodded.

'That brings us to the crime scene. Brodd, I want you to get up to Höör and meet Inspector Blentarps at Leif Andersson's farm. He'll have men with him, and you're to comb the woods for the camp. I don't expect it'll still be there, but there may be evidence we can gather.'

'That's a lot of woodland.' Brodd grimaced. It sounded like a lot of walking.

'Well, you'd better leave straight after we're done here – and put on a stout pair of boots. And be nice to Blentarps! I gather he's pissed off that we've now taken over the investigation. Apparently, this was going to be his first big murder case. He's taking early retirement soon, and he wanted to go out with a bang, so to speak. Use your famous charm.' Even Moberg couldn't resist a smirk.

'Anita, if you can keep awake long enough, I want you to get onto your friends in the UK and see what you can dig up on Cassidy, McNaught and Jack Harmer.' At least she could rest at her desk while she was doing it. 'Finally, Wallen, I want you to organize the moving of Danny Foster from the hospital to the safe house and get him settled in. Make sure that all his medical requirements are covered. Take some officers with you, but out of uniform so you don't draw attention to yourselves. Take every precaution,' he said holding up a warning hand. 'McNaught is still out there.'

Szabo and Erlandsson had been through a similar meeting with Zetterberg, though at the more civilized time of nine thirty. Zetterberg had debriefed her team on her Malta visit, during which she had come to the conclusion that Inspector Sundström had been wrong all along about Linus Svärd. 'He may have had a potential motive, but I think the timings are too tight for him to get off the beach, confront Göran, kill him and dispose of the murder weapon. And why on earth would he go back to the chapel to cradle his dead lover? Besides, having talked to him at length, I don't think he has it in him to kill someone. The sap still loves Göran after all these years.' The obvious satisfaction that that had given her was tempered by the fact that they were virtually back to square one with their suspects. After much thought, she said she was coming round to Lars-Gunnar. He was the only one without any sort of alibi; he couldn't account for his movements. He might not even know he'd done it. The drugs connection gave him a motive, and he might not have been as smashed as was claimed by Carina. He had easy access from the garden to the chapel. He could have slipped away while Carina was working – she wasn't keeping a constant eye on him.

With this in mind, she herself would visit Lars-Gunnar while they could talk to the returning Larissa. She told them that they were to ask her about the Björnstahl letter. Neither of them had heard of him so Zetterberg enjoyed being able to give them some background on the traveller and linguist in a manner that sounded as though she was familiar with the great man, and that they were stupid for being ignorant.

Szabo and Erlandsson were waiting for Larissa Bjerstedt when she arrived at the Malmö University Library. She was late in after a delayed flight back from Oslo last night. Instead of entering the building, they shepherded her towards the Inner Harbour. The day wasn't quite as warm as Sunday, and the sky was woolly with white cumulus clouds. There was a stiff breeze that teased the water in front of them. Across from where they were standing, people were streaming in and out of the Central Station. Larissa appeared quite relaxed at the detectives' reappearance and seemed more than happy to delay starting work.

'We thought you might want to know that Linus Svärd has been traced and interviewed,' began Szabo.

'Is he OK?' she said with a hint of concern.

'I believe so. He lives on Malta.'

'Malta?' Erlandsson registered the surprise in Larissa's eyes.

'Yes. He's living in an apartment owned by Carina Lindvall.'

'Carina's got an apartment on Malta?' She sounded incredulous. 'Why has she got an apartment there?'

'She goes there to write. It seems one of those quirks of fate that Linus should end up where the breakdown of his relationship with Göran began; well, according to most of your group.'

'It is strange,' she said ruminatively.

'Actually, it's that week you all had on Malta that we're here about.'

'Oh,' Larissa said cautiously as though Szabo was about to spring a surprise question.

Szabo flicked away the hair that was forever falling over his face. 'It's been mentioned that while on Malta, Ivar found something that he was very excited about. Research material. Do you know anything about that?'

'Not really... oh, wait a minute. Do you mean the Jacob Björnstahl letter?'

'Yes.'

'He got very excited about it. Don't know why. Pretty turgid stuff from what I remember. I wasn't interested, but it turned Ivar on.'

'Is it true that Ivar didn't want Göran to find out what he'd discovered?'

Larissa raised her eyes. 'Boys' stuff. Like a couple of warring kids. You're right, though. Ivar didn't want Göran to find out, though it was pretty obvious that he'd found something. I'm sure Göran must have been suspicious, and that probably drove him mad. But at the end of the day, it wasn't a big deal.'

'Who else knew about the letter?' This was Erlandsson.

'I did. Linus, obviously, because he was there when Ivar made his discovery. I don't know about the others. Carina, possibly.' There was an edge to her voice that Erlandsson noted.

'And Göran?' pressed Szabo. 'If he'd found out, that could have heightened the tension between them.'

Larissa gave a non-committal shrug. 'No idea.'

'But Göran threatened to do something that would "affect Ivar the most". Carina had had an argument with him about supplying drugs to Lars-Gunnar. According to Linus's interview, everyone except Lars-Gunnar heard the argument. Do you know what Göran was referring to?'

'No, it would just be Göran venting his frustration on us.'

'But he must have upset someone enough for them to kill

him,' observed Szabo. Larissa didn't answer. 'Our boss thinks that Linus is innocent, so it's down to four suspects now.' He left it there.

'Is that it?' Larissa asked. 'I'd better get to work.'

'That's fine,' said Szabo.

'Why don't you like Carina?'

Szabo was vexed at Erlandsson. 'I think we're finished.'

'Why don't you like Carina?' persisted Erlandsson. 'Because of her success? Or is it something more personal?'

Larissa appeared momentarily disconcerted. 'I've nothing against her.'

'She told our boss some interesting things about you and Ivar.'

'What? What did she say?' She sounded defensive.

'She questioned your version of your break-up with Ivar. Said he "dumped" you. Moved on to someone better, someone more useful. The way she put it was that you couldn't cling on to him any longer.'

'She's a cow, if you must know. And not a very talented one.'

'Our boss got the impression that Carina had probably slept with Ivar. They're still good friends.'

'I don't care about either of them. I've just got on with my own life.'

Erlandsson could see that she had rattled the woman, and she wanted to press home her advantage. 'Ivar said some very harsh things about you, too. He reckoned that you followed him up to Uppsala because you wanted to start up the relationship again despite the fact he was married.'

'Ivar said that?' She said it as though it was a betrayal.

'Oh, yes. And more besides.' Erlandsson took out her notebook. 'I've written down some of the things he said to our boss when she visited him in Uppsala. He admitted that he had discarded you because, as he put it, "he had moved on." Larissa simply stared hard at Erlandsson without saying a word. Szabo was watching carefully; he was amazed that his new colleague had the bottle for this line of questioning.

Erlandsson deliberately took her time glancing through her notes. 'He described you as just a "student fling". Erlandsson looked up from her notebook. 'Not very nice.'

'It's true,' Larissa said at last, with a hint of moisture round her eyes.

'Yet you followed him up to Uppsala.'

'I told you that it was for a job.'

'That's not how he saw it. He admitted that your break-up hadn't been as amicable as you suggested. He thought you turning up in Uppsala was "bizarre". His word, not mine. He said you couldn't accept the split.'

'I'm not going to listen to this,' retorted Larissa with a gulp. She spun away.

'Ivar said that your relationship was never serious on his part,' Erlandsson called after her.

Larissa stopped, her head slumped.

'Thank you for your cooperation,' said Szabo as he nodded to Erlandsson that it was time to go. There was nothing to be gained from tormenting the woman any further.

Larissa turned round, almost in slow motion. She muttered something. Neither Szabo nor Erlandsson could catch what she said.

'Sorry?' Szabo prompted.

Larissa had real tears in her eyes. 'He wasn't there.'

Szabo and Erlandsson exchanged mystified glances.

'I don't understand,' said Szabo. 'Who wasn't where?'

'Ivar. Ivar wasn't there.'

Szabo took a step forward so he could hear her more clearly.

'Ivar wasn't where?'

'He wasn't with me when Göran was killed.'

CHAPTER 35

Anita put the phone down just as Hakim came in brandishing a sandwich and coffee.

'Thanks a lot,' she said in English. Then she giggled. She continued in Swedish. 'I've spent the last two hours speaking to various people over in the UK; I was still thinking in English.'

'I thought you'd need these.' Hakim placed his offerings on her desk.

'How much do I owe you?'

'Forget it. I'm in a generous mood these days. I think Liv's got her eye on an expensive ring.'

Anita eased off the plastic top on her coffee, and a burst of steam misted her glasses. 'I'm genuinely pleased for you two. I'm sure you'll be really happy together.' She managed to filter out any bitterness she felt about the institution of marriage. It reminded her – would Björn still be around when she got home? She was unsure of his plans. Just after midnight she'd received a text from him: *Coming back tonight? Or are you out shagging?* Needless to say, she was too busy to bother replying.

'I think it'll work, whatever other people think.' Anita could guess who he was referring to. 'Anyway,' he said, cocking his head in the direction of her phone, 'Any luck?'

'Not with McNaught. If he were in the Special Air Service, it might be difficult to get hold of his records. But I've got someone looking at general British Army records. That's if he was in the army at all. Danny and the others only assumed he was in the military. More luck with Jack Harmer, though. He's officially down as a missing person. His family live in Brighton. Haven't had details, but the local police there are going to speak to them. We'll need to get some DNA to verify it's actually Jack who's lying in our morgue. It'll be dreadful for them to learn their son's not only dead, but murdered.'

Anita unwrapped the sandwich and bit greedily into it. She was too tired to register exactly what else was in it among the lettuce leaves. She still had the residue of bread in her mouth when she started speaking again. 'But I've found Tyrone Cassidy. It was quite easy. Lives in London. Highgate. There are various articles about him on the internet.' She swivelled her computer screen for Hakim to look at. 'Aged fifty-seven. Married with five kids. Seems to be a legitimate businessman. Owns two stone quarries and runs a large building firm. Also has another company that does paving in the south east of England. No mention of any foreign connections other than interests in a couple of hotels and a chain of restaurants back in Ireland run by his brother, Donal. Does lots of good works in the community. That's his local Roman Catholic church, where he donated the money for a new hall. That's him opening it.' Hakim stared at the hefty man in the tweed jacket, smart corduroys and shiny brown brogues, looking like some country squire straight out of an episode of *Midsomer Murders*. He was beaming at the admiring priest and parishioners. An affable face. Bushy eyebrows, a strong nose and slightly crinkled, faded ginger hair. A jovial giant to all appearances. But it was the hands that caught Hakim's attention. They were spread out in front of him like those of a saint forgiving sinners. They were powerful hands. Hands that had beaten Jack Harmer to death.

'I'm expecting a call from someone I worked with at the Metropolitan Police to find out if he's on their radar. According to a brief bio I found, he hails from Limerick in the

Republic of Ireland. Went over to England as a young man. Done very well for himself. Very rich, it seems.'

Hakim's eyes wandered from the screen. 'We've got to get him. But I've had no luck. He didn't travel by air. I've checked flights into Kastrup, Sturup and even Arlanda around those dates from all British and Irish destinations. And he doesn't seem to have come by train across from Denmark. I'm running a check on all British and Irish cars that have come across the Öresund Bridge, and hire cars, but that'll take time to follow through. His passport certainly hasn't shown up.'

'Could have been using a false name.'

Hakim sighed heavily. 'Oh, I know. Not much we can do about that. At least if I can take some pictures of him from the internet, it'll help with the search.'

'Trouble is,' said Anita thoughtfully, 'unless we can prove he was in Sweden at the time of the murder, we've got no chance of getting his extradition.'

Larissa shifted uneasily under Zetterberg's intense gaze. She was in an interview room and didn't seem too happy to be there with three police officers. Zetterberg and Erlandsson sat opposite her while Szabo lolled against the wall behind them. As soon as she'd made her confession to Szabo and Erlandsson, they had taken her straight to the polishus. Szabo had phoned Zetterberg, who had failed to find Lars-Gunnar. The post office depot in Ystad had told her that he hadn't turned up for work that day. She was about to head off to his family home when she got Szabo's call. She couldn't believe it – 'So now none of them has got an alibi!' Her mind had raced as fast as she had driven back to Malmö. The implications of what Larissa had confessed blew the case wide open. This was the breakthrough they needed. Sundström was going to look pretty stupid after this.

'So, let me get this straight,' started Zetterberg, finding

it difficult to contain her eagerness, 'You are saying that Ivar Hagblom was not with you in your room at the time of Göran Gösta's murder.'

Larissa had the look of someone startled by the headlights of a car. At first, she said nothing. Zetterberg waited. She had time. Eventually, Larissa nodded.

'I need you to speak up, for the tape,' she said, indicating the small microphone on the table.

'Yes.' It wasn't much more than a whisper.

'Where was he?'

Larissa took a sip of water from a bottle Erlandsson had provided while they were awaiting Zetterberg's return from Ystad. 'He said he was out, looking for Linus. He was worried about him.'

'So, wandering around by himself?'

'As I said, he was worried. Linus was his best friend. He'd been upset by Göran's treatment of him.'

'Why did you lie? You claimed that you two were making love.'

'He asked me to.'

'He asked you to?' Zetterberg's contempt was clear. 'Why did he ask you to give him an alibi?'

Larissa fiddled with the water bottle's blue plastic cap. 'He didn't want to have to explain to the police that he was... you know, out there. They might have jumped to the wrong conclusion.'

'They might have jumped to the right conclusion if you'd told the truth.'

For the first time, Larissa became animated. 'Just that. Your reaction. He didn't kill Göran. He was trying to find Linus.'

'Do you believe him?'

'Well, of course...' Larissa hesitated. It was as though, for the first time, she was contemplating what she had always thought to be impossible; or at least never dared to think. 'No, he can't have.' The protest was far from fervent.

'You're guilty of obstructing the course of justice.'

'Don't you think I know that?'

'Basically, you lied for Ivar because you were in love with him. Isn't that true?'

'I was fond of him.' She drained the last of her water.

'Obsessed more like. Isn't that why you've come out with this now?' Zetterberg was in her stride. She had her quarry cornered. 'He chucked you, and yet you still chased after him to Uppsala. I think you can't take rejection.'

Perversely, this attack seemed to give Larissa more confidence. 'I haven't done this to get back at Ivar. It's been on my conscience for the last twenty-one years. I've had to live with the fact that I lied to the police to protect my boyfriend. And I'm not stupid; I also realize that by telling you this, I've stripped myself of an alibi.'

'True.' Zetterberg leant across the table. 'So what exactly were you doing that night if you weren't being amorous with Ivar Hagblom?'

Larissa cleared her throat. 'I cleaned up in the kitchen for a while. I always felt responsible for keeping the place tidy because it belonged to Ivar's parents. The others were a lot messier. I was always clearing up after them. I didn't want Ivar to be given a hard time by his parents because we'd trashed their beautiful holiday home.'

'And then?'

'I went to our bedroom to try and relax. It had been a fraught day with the Göran/Linus fight on the beach.'

'Did you hear Carina next door? That's where she said she was working.'

'No. But I was tired. I dozed off. Next thing I knew, there was a commotion. Carina came in and said that something had happened to Göran at the chapel.'

'It was Carina who told you?'

'Yeah.'

'And when did you first see Ivar after that?'

'When Carina and I went down to the chapel. He appeared from somewhere. I can't remember from where.'

'OK. During the hour before Carina came into your room, did you either see or hear her, or Lars-Gunnar?'

Larissa nodded. 'Lars-Gunnar was in the garden. I noticed him from the kitchen. Zonked out as far as I could see. Obviously, I didn't see him after I went to the bedroom. I didn't see Carina at all. I assumed she was in her room.'

'That's interesting,' said Zetterberg allowing herself to sit back in her chair. 'Yet Carina claimed that she heard you and Ivar having loud sex through the wall. Called you a "screamer". Now, why did she do that?'

Larissa screwed the cap back onto the empty water bottle. 'Ivar must have persuaded her to say that. It backed up the alibi that we were in the room next door together.'

'A double alibi. Extra insurance.'

'I suppose.'

'And why do you think Carina supplied you two with an alibi?'

Larissa's eyes lit up. 'I would have thought that was obvious. It gave *her* one!'

CHAPTER 36

'Any sign of McNaught?'

Moberg just grunted. Anita took that as a no.

'Hakim's found no trace of Tyrone Cassidy coming into or going out of the country. And that's not all the bad news either.' She glanced up at the street map of Malmö behind the chief inspector's back. There were five red pins stuck on various locations. They represented possible sightings of McNaught. Judging by Moberg's mood, they were false trails. 'I've been onto a contact at the Met – Nick Sherington, a detective I worked with while I was over there.'

'And what's the bad news?'

'We know all about Cassidy; the public Cassidy that is. He's not only wealthy, he's well connected, particularly in the police. Basically, Nick warned me off, in the politest way possible, of course. He hinted that they knew that some of Cassidy's enterprises weren't all kosher. Problem is that he's untouchable. Reading between the lines, he's got senior policemen in his pocket.'

'Bloody hell!'

'I'm afraid they haven't got the best reputation over in Britain. A lot of bad stories have come out of there over the last few years.'

'I heard about Stephen Lawrence.'

'Tip of the iceberg, I'm afraid.'

'How trustworthy is your Nick Sherington?'

'He's a good detective. Well, he was when I knew him. But he's probably right about Cassidy.'

Moberg raised his great bulk with an exaggerated groan, stepped over to the window and gazed out. 'Being a cop is hard enough without your colleagues being corrupt.' Anita knew he was thinking of Karl Westermark. He lumbered round like a ferry about to dock. 'Anything on McNaught's background?'

'Yes,' said Anita, flicking open a notebook. 'I've managed to gather a bit of information. He was born in Dumbarton in 1974. That's near Glasgow in Scotland. Joined the army at sixteen – The Gordon Highlanders. In 1994, the regiment was amalgamated with the Queen's Own Highlanders to form—'

'Just cut to the chase.' Moberg was at his most irritable when things were out of his control; and McNaught roaming around Malmö was definitely one of those things.

'He transferred to what is called "special operations" in 2001. Probably means the Special Air Service. We haven't much chance of getting any information out of the military without a government request at a high level. If he was in the SAS, he may well have fought in the Second Gulf War. He was back in civilian life four years ago. Then he disappeared from sight.'

'He's good at that,' Moberg muttered bitterly. 'And Jack Harmer?'

'The local Brighton police have informed the family. His dad is flying over tomorrow. At least we can get a DNA match – I'm afraid the body's not really in a fit state to identify.'

'Poor man.' Moberg was capable of genuine sympathy on the odd occasion. 'Wallen phoned in half an hour ago to say that Danny Foster is now in the safe house. We just have to make sure he stays bloody safe.'

Anita flipped her notebook shut. Moberg returned to his seat and eased himself down. The chair sighed.

'So, what are we going to do about Cassidy?' grunted Moberg. 'If we can't touch him, we're stuffed. He's unlikely to oblige us by returning to Sweden and the scene of the crime. By the way, Brodd and the Kristianstad bunch haven't located the camp yet. Still searching. The exercise will do Brodd good.' It was the sort of physical exertion that the chief inspector himself should be undertaking, thought Anita.

'As for Cassidy,' she said slowly, 'I've got an idea.'

Zetterberg was like a cat on hot bricks. She paced round the Cold Case Group room, ignoring her two junior colleagues who were waiting for her to come to some conclusion after the interview with Larissa Bjerstedt. Larissa had been allowed to go, with the proviso that she didn't take any sudden trips abroad.

At last, Zetterberg came to a halt in front of the suspect board. 'We start afresh,' she announced. 'Except now we're down to four. And now I've broken all their alibis, the real investigating begins.' Erlandsson and Szabo rolled their eyes. They realized that they were working with a boss who was quite happy to take all the credit for their efforts.

'Is Linus Svärd no longer a suspect?' Szabo asked.

'I'm confident we'd be wasting precious time and resources on him. As I've said before, I'm convinced the timings are too tight to fit the scenario. And my gut instinct says he's not capable of doing the deed. Besides, we now have people with equal opportunity, which didn't have before. And none of them liked Göran. Linus loved him. What we need is to find the trigger that set it all off.'

'Are we including Larissa?' Szabo asked.

'Of course. She hasn't got an alibi.'

'But she admitted that.'

'Hell hath no fury like a woman scorned. I think it's her way of getting back at Ivar. I'm convinced she's done it purely out of spite. And maybe he did kill Göran, but Larissa still stays in the frame, though it's difficult to look past Ivar and, particularly, Carina.' The last name was spoken with some relish.

'And Lars-Gunnar?'

'I'm not sure about him. Larissa and Carina both confirmed he was in the garden, somewhat the worse for wear. But he wasn't far from the chapel. He could have been there and back in the garden in a matter of minutes. As I didn't get to speak to Lars-Gunnar, I want you, Erlandsson, to go and see him. Threaten him if necessary. I think he knows more than he's letting on. And you can also go into the four suspects' phone records. I want to know who's been talking to whom since the beginning of this investigation. They all put up a united front, but now it's starting to unravel.'

'Do you want me to go with Bea to see Lars-Gunnar?'

'No. We,' she said looking directly at Szabo, 'are going up to Stockholm and Uppsala as soon as possible. We need to have some serious conversations with Ivar and Carina. They've both lied in this and the original investigation. It's time to get heavy with them – they've a helluva lot of explaining to do.'

'You want me to do *what*?' The disbelief in Kevin's voice was heard in every syllable.

'It shouldn't be a problem. You're a brilliant detective.'

'Now you're going over the top, Anita. I don't mind being soft-soaped, but I know my limitations.'

Anita had taken her time to work up to her request. He'd been delighted that she'd called, and she kept the small talk going for a few minutes. Then she'd asked him how he was filling in his days on holiday. 'I'm watching a thing called *Vikings* on Amazon. It was the only Scandinavian thing I could find, as I wasn't actually going to be spending the week with you. I'm already half way through the second series because I've nothing else to do.'

'So you're bored?'

Kevin sighed. 'Sort of. And I haven't even got someone to be bored with,' he said pointedly.

'Well, I've got a cure for that.'

Then she filled him in on the background to the Jack Harmer murder before asking him if he would like to go down to London and discover the movements of Tyrone Cassidy around the seventh and eighth of August. When he quite reasonably suggested that she go through the Met, she had to admit that that wasn't a viable option.

'So, you're asking me, on my holiday, to snoop around some major villain who has just beaten someone to death; and this said-same *violent* villain the Metropolitan Police have warned you off because he's got senior officers in his pocket?' expostulated Kevin incredulously.

After a short pause, Anita said: 'And your problem is?'

'Oh, nothing really. You're bloody mad, woman. No. Correction. I'm the bloody mad one. So instead of looking forward to season three of *Vikings* in the comfort of my own, albeit dull, home, I'm going to be risking life and limb playing Philip bloody Marlowe with some seriously dangerous people. If either Cassidy or the Met get wind of what I'm up to, I'll be up the flaming creek without a paddle,' he spluttered. 'They'll probably snap my paddle. My career will go down the pan. And that's looking on the bright side.'

'Are you always this negative?'

'Don't play that game with me, you Swedish sorceress. And when do you want me to do this insane thing?'

'Tomorrow.'

She could hear him gulp at the other end of the line. 'A last-minute train will cost a fortune.'

'There you go again: being negative.' She knew she had a nerve asking him to do her this favour, yet she never doubted that he would do it – after a bit of coaxing. But they had to play the game. 'Look, I'll refund the train fare.'

'And what else do I get out of this? That's if I live long enough.'

'I'll come over as soon as the case is solved.' Then she uttered a little sexy moan. 'And then I'll make sure that your new bed witnesses some really hot action. I promise I'll do things to you that'll make you forget that you ever went to London.'

'Why am I so easily bought?' he huffed theatrically. 'That's the trouble with being so shallow.'

'That makes two of us,' she laughed, relieved that he was on board.

'One of these days, Sundström, you're going to be the death of me.'

Now that she was starting to appreciate how ruthless these people were, Anita fervently hoped that that wasn't going to be prophetic.

To Danny, the safe house was disturbingly similar to Leif Andersson's single-storey farmhouse, which wasn't reassuring. It was in better condition than Leif's but appeared not to have been used for some time. Earlier in the day, he had been bustled out of a back entrance of the hospital by the female detective who had been there when the police first spoke to him. She called herself Klara something. He didn't catch her surname. There had been four of them. They all wore casual gear, but it was obvious that they were police. He'd been bundled into a car, which hadn't done his aching shoulder or his swollen ankle any favours. He'd sensed their nervousness; that wasn't a positive sign either. McNaught was still out there, still gunning for him.

He was ushered into the living room. It hadn't much furniture other than a simple sofa and matching armchair, a wooden table with four chairs round it, and a small TV in the corner. There was a bookcase, but all the books seemed to be in Swedish. As he was trying to get his bearings, he was beginning to wonder if he should have been so candid with Inspector Sundström. It hadn't stopped McNaught. Could they really protect him? Even if the Swedish police did intercept the madman, what then? Return to Britain? Cassidy or one of his mob would probably seek him out because as long as he was alive, he was still a danger. Even if he stayed in Sweden, Cassidy might send another assassin. Klara Wallen offered to make him a coffee, which he distractedly accepted.

'By the way,' she said, 'we've found the camp.'

Danny didn't answer; he couldn't see how that would help. Maybe, just maybe, if he could get word to Cassidy and promise never to be a witness against him, he would lay off him, leave him in peace. As he stared out of the window at the fields beyond, he knew that that was a hopeless thought brought on by desperation. And fear. Gut-wrenching fear.

'You'll be safe here,' said Wallen, handing him a mug of steaming coffee. It was black. He hadn't the energy to ask for milk. He took it blankly. His shoulder hurt. For a brief moment when he'd talked to Sundström, he had felt a weight lift from him. He had shared his horror with an empathetic listener. A listener who had assured him that McNaught would be caught. Then his nemesis had turned up – and escaped again. He was still out there. Danny anxiously scanned the fields outside. But where?

CHAPTER 37

Anita slept incredibly well and didn't wake until after nine. By the time she'd crawled into bed, she had been awake for thirty-six hours. She'd been so exhausted that she hadn't even woken up in the middle of the night to worry about asking Kevin to investigate Tyrone Cassidy. When requesting the favour, she hadn't really appreciated the possible danger he might face, but he was a big boy and could look after himself. However, now that she was brewing her first coffee of the morning, she was starting to have doubts. Maybe she'd put him under unfair pressure. She went back into her bedroom to phone him and tell him not to go. Too late: on her phone she found an SMS saying that he was on the London-bound train and would reach Euston Station just after eleven.

Anita returned to the kitchen and noticed a scribbled note sitting on the top of the microwave. It was from Björn. He must have put it there on Monday morning.

Sorry to have missed you last night. Are you avoiding me? Thanks for the bed for the weekend. Great catching up with Lasse and Jazmin; and isn't Leyla a star? I think she's going to be as stubborn as you.

Hope you get away on holiday sometime, even if it is with your Brit boyfriend.

See you sometime.
Hugs and kisses,
Björn

PS By the way, my Lund contact confirmed that Ivar Hagblom didn't use Björnstahl in his PhD. Any use?

Anita held the note in her hand as the percolator hissed and bubbled ferociously behind her back. Typical of Björn in the middle of his thanks to have a dig at her private life at the same time. But that PS: *Any use?* She didn't know. She couldn't see the significance of it other than that it was strange that Ivar hadn't used the Björnstahl letter after all. It would have been quite a coup within his academic circle. Was he the type to pass up such an opportunity? Not the Ivar that Linus Svärd had described. Maybe his heart wasn't in it after the murder; his triumph over Göran no longer of any importance. Still...

The drizzle streaked Bea Erlandsson's windscreen. The weather had turned, though there was still no hint of an early autumn chill. She'd seen the forecast before she left home, and heavier rain was due this afternoon. The weather matched her mood. Zetterberg and Szabo were off to Stockholm, and she had drawn what she considered to be the short straw – Lars-Gunnar. After Larissa Bjerstedt's revelations, Erlandsson was convinced that their murderer was either Carina Lindvall (though she hoped it wasn't) or Ivar Hagblom. Lars-Gunnar was a sideshow. Nothing that Larissa had said had changed the evidence concerning him. Yet now she was sitting in her car watching the windscreen steam up, and having second thoughts.

Erlandsson had turned up at the post office depot in Ystad at half past nine only to be told that Lars-Gunnar had failed to turn up for work the second day running. He hadn't phoned in sick, which the supervisor said was unusual; he was a reliable employee. She had driven the twenty minutes to Veberöd, only to find that Lars-Gunnar was not at home. No one was. Her peering through the windows of the Lerstorp house had aroused a neighbour's suspicions, and he demanded to know who she was. After producing her warrant card, she explained she needed to speak to herr Lerstorp. Just routine enquiries. The neighbour told her that he'd seen the family leave a couple of days ago in their car. He had assumed that they were going on holiday, as they had suitcases with them. Erlandsson tapped the steering wheel with her notebook. Why had Lars-Gunnar done a disappearing act? Were they getting too close to the truth?

She took out her phone and called Zetterberg.

Zetterberg took the call while in a taxi on the way from Stockholm's Arlanda Airport to Carina Lindvall's home in Norra Lagnö. There had been no messing about on trains to Stockholm – she and Szabo had flown up on the first flight from Sturup, Malmö's airport. She didn't want to waste any time. The accounts department would have to handle the bill. In Zetterberg's mind the expense was justified. And it was worth it just to see Carina's face when she opened the door. The welcome wasn't warm.

'I thought we'd said all that was needed on your last visit.' Carina made it clear that she wasn't going to let Zetterberg over the threshold.

'That's when we thought you had an alibi. Now we know you don't.'

Carina returned the hostile scrutiny. Then her eye caught sight of Szabo. Her gaze drifted up and down the young detective.

'You'd better come in. And bring your toy boy, too.'

They took seats in the same living room that Zetterberg had been in before. However, this time the novelist was more suitably dressed in a flouncy, blue top and short, white skirt. Judging by where Szabo's eyes were glued, Carina still had the legs to carry off the hemline. Before she even sat down, Carina had lit up a cigarette.

'I hope this won't take long. I'm due in Nacka for a lunch appointment.'

'That depends on you,' said Zetterberg, making herself comfortable and looking forward to making Carina as uncomfortable as possible.

Carina swatted away the first plume of smoke to emerge from her mouth. 'Well?'

'We've discovered that you lied about hearing Ivar and Larissa having sex at the time of Göran Gösta's murder.'

'Ivar didn't tell you that, did he?' Zetterberg's grin gave her the answer. 'Of course not. So it must have been the lame Larissa.'

'This raises two very interesting questions. Firstly, why did you lie about Ivar and Larissa? And, secondly, where were you during that time? The fact is you no longer have an alibi. And you've got a good motive: protecting your boyfriend from his unscrupulous dealer.' Szabo shifted uneasily; he wasn't sure that his boss should be taking such delight in putting a suspect under the spotlight, especially one with such nice legs. Carina crossed them, and he caught a momentary hint of her white knickers. 'How would one of your fictional characters get out of that one?'

Carina gave a smoker's cackle. 'I'd conjure up a better alibi, and I'd employ a brighter, better-looking detective. Oh, I was forgetting; I already have. In twelve best-selling books.'

Zetterberg spat out: 'Just answer the questions.'

'The answer to your first one is simple. Ivar asked me to give him an alibi. He'd been out looking for Linus. And as he couldn't account for his movements, he realized that the police would immediately suspect him. I knew it couldn't have been him, so I was happy to tell a little white lie.'

'That little white lie could have stalled this investigation for twenty-one years, for God's sake!'

'I was young, naive. We all were. I was just protecting a friend. An innocent friend.'

'Oh, I think he was more than a friend.'

'What do you mean by that?' Carina bridled, aggressively flicking ash into her cut-glass ashtray.

'Come on. Larissa's antipathy towards you can't just be about your writing success. There's something deeper. Are you trying to tell me that you and Ivar weren't lovers?' Zetterberg knew that she was guessing, though she was fairly confident she was on the right track. She'd observed from the way that Carina talked about Ivar in their previous conversations that there was some spark there.

Carina held her cigarette elegantly in her fingers as she considered what to say. The smoke coiled hypnotically upwards.

'We were lovers.'

'When did it start?'

Carina still made no attempt to smoke her cigarette. 'Malta. It was just a one-off. We were all drunk. Lars-Gunnar was too far gone to get an erection. Larissa had flaked out, and there were just the two of us left. I was in the mood, so was he. It just happened.'

'But that wasn't the only time.'

'No. It resumed that summer in Knäbäckshusen. Life was getting increasingly difficult with Lars-Gunnar. He was so into his drugs, I couldn't see a way out. And I think Ivar was starting to get bored with Larissa. She was getting very clingy. He wanted a bit of freedom.'

'Which you provided,' Zetterberg said scornfully.

'Occasionally. It wasn't easy with Larissa around. Ivar was her ticket to a better life. She wasn't going to give that up easily. But sometimes when she was sunning herself on the beach and Ivar said he had work to do, we'd sneak in a quickie.'

'Did Larissa discover you two were carrying on behind her back?'

'No, of course not. We were bloody careful. I didn't want to upset Lars-Gunnar either.'

'That was very considerate of you.'

'You may mock, Inspector, but I did care for Lars-Gunnar. He's a decent human being, and there aren't many of those around these days.' Her stare was firmly aimed at Zetterberg.

'Did anyone else get wind of what you and Ivar were up to?'

Carina shook her head. Then she half started to say something and stopped.

Zetterberg seized on the hesitation. 'Someone did, didn't they?'

'Well, not exactly. After one of our quickies, I did bump into Göran as I was coming out of Ivar's room. I made some excuse for being in there. Returning a book or something. He couldn't have heard anything. We always made sure we grunted quietly.'

'And how long after that did you have that argument with Göran about the drugs?'

'I can't remember. A couple of days, possibly.'

Zetterberg noted that Szabo was scribbling down Carina's answers. 'That explains why you vouched for Ivar, but we still don't know where you were at the time of the murder.'

Carina gave up on her cigarette and plonked it onto the ashtray to smoke on its own. 'I was exactly where I said I was. In my bedroom. I'd seen Lars-Gunnar through the window lolling around the garden when I first started work then I got engrossed in what I was doing. The next thing I know, there's all this activity in the street. I went out and was told that something had happened to Göran at the chapel. I got Larissa from her room and we went down.'

'That fits in with what Larissa said. So, you didn't see Lars-Gunnar for most of that time.' She paused: 'We've been trying to talk to him. He's disappeared.'

'Has he?' For a moment Zetterberg caught a flicker of concern on Carina's face. 'You lot have probably frightened the poor guy off. He was never the most robust of people. The drugs were his way of hiding from life.'

'What about Larissa? Where was she?'

'As I said, she was in her bedroom. Earlier, I heard someone in the kitchen at some stage. I assume it was her, as she was always Little Miss Tidy. Tediously so. Always clearing up. Always badgering us to keep the blessed place shipshape. Trying to make a good impression for what she thought would be her future in-laws. Deluded bimbo.' With a wave of her now-free hand: 'Obviously, I didn't mention that; it wouldn't have fitted in with Ivar's story that they were together.'

Carina spoke as though she were having a normal conversation and not being interviewed about a murder.

'What can you tell us about Jacob Björnstahl?'

'Who's he when he's at home?' Carina screwed up her eyes to emphasize that she had no idea what Zetterberg was talking about. 'I can't be expected to remember the names of all my young admirers,' she added flippantly with a sidelong glance at Szabo.

'Jacob Björnstahl. He was a famous orientalist. Ivar found some of his writings from the 1770s on Malta. He got very excited about them apparently.'

'Ah,' Carina said in recognition. 'I've never heard of this Björnstahl, but it explains why Ivar was so energized at the time. He got more turned on by those daft things from the past than he did by sleeping with the likes of me, which is not exactly flattering. None of us knew what it was about, and that got on Göran's tits. I do remember that.'

Carina adjusted her expensive gold wristwatch. 'Look, are we going to be much longer? My luncheon date won't wait.' She recrossed her legs and smiled at Szabo. 'Unless I get a better offer, of course. I like silent, blond types.'

'We're finished,' said Zetterberg. 'But don't think about taking any trips any time soon.'

'I'm due to go to a crime book festival in Dublin at the weekend.'

'I suggest you cancel it. I don't want you leaving the country.'

'And why not?' Carina was indignant.

'I don't think you appreciate the seriousness of your situation. You've lied to the police, which is obstructing the course of justice, in a murder investigation where you have no alibi and a strong motive. You've just gone to the top of our list of suspects.'

CHAPTER 38

Bea Erlandsson drew into the polishus car park and switched off the ignition. At this time of year it was easier to find a space. The rain was heavier now. She was about to get ready for a dash to the front of the building when the passenger-side door opened and Anita swiftly took the seat next to her. Before speaking to the surprised Erlandsson, Anita shook the rain away from her hair.

'Sorry about that,' she said, as she could see that she'd partially sprayed the dashboard. 'Anyhow, how's the case going?'

'Big developments since we last spoke.'

'Oh, yeah?' Anita was immediately intrigued.

Erlandsson outlined the two interviews with Larissa, and the confession which resulted in the fact that no one had an alibi after all. Zetterberg and Szabo were now up in Stockholm on the trail of Carina Lindvall and Ivar Hagblom. And in the meantime, Lars-Gunnar appears to have done a runner.

When she'd finished, Anita gave a soft whistle. 'That's incredible! So, the story they all stuck to has unravelled after all this time. We should have been able to break them down. Not that we had much chance of that.'

'Why's that?'

'I can't really tell Zetterberg this as it's not my case. The last thing she'll accept is me interfering.'

'But?'

'I went to see Renmarker on Sunday. He was the prosecutor back in 1995. At the time, he wouldn't let us proceed with the case against Linus Svärd because of lack of evidence. It was frustrating in the extreme. It turns out that the Hagblom family put him under pressure through a journalist on one of their papers. Basically, they blackmailed him to stop the investigation getting any further. In fact, Renmarker actually met Ivar. Not that *we* knew any of this at the time, of course. I'd like to ask Ivar why the family put the squeeze on Renmarker, but I can't. Maybe you can.'

Erlandsson didn't take long to understand the implications. 'Even with an alibi, albeit a false one, he was making sure that you wouldn't get anywhere near the truth?' Erlandsson stared at the windscreen and wiped it with her hand, as it was starting to steam up. 'I know what! They won't have had a chance to speak to Ivar yet; they were going to Carina's first. I could ring Szabo and let him bring it up. He could just say I'd found out, but not go into detail.'

'It might be enough to spook Ivar. Unfortunately, Renmarker won't go public with the information, so it can't be used officially.' Anita put her hand on the door and was about to open it. 'Oh, you could also get Szabo to ask Ivar why he didn't use the Björnstahl letter in his PhD. It was a God-given gift, yet he didn't use it. I'd be interested in hearing his answer.'

'So would I,' Erlandsson said thoughtfully. 'So would I.'

'Danny Foster is safe for the time being,' said Wallen, opening a resumé of where they were with the Egon Fuentes case. 'We've set up a rota of officers to be down there. We're trying three at a time, but numbers are short at the moment, so it may end up being only two.'

'I want one of the team here to be with him most of the time,' said Moberg. 'He'll probably need reassuring as long as McNaught is out there.' He thumped the table. 'For fuck's sake! It can't be beyond the resources of the Skåne County Police to find some bald Brit in the city!'

'I take it there's no news,' said Anita, who was catching up after her Moberg-sanctioned lie-in.

'No.' Moberg jerked his stubby thumb over his shoulder at the map of Malmö and an increasing number of red pins. 'Loads of false leads. The problem is trying to do it without alarming the public too much.'

'They're pretty used to shootings and grenade attacks these days,' said Brodd brightly.

'That's hardly the point, Brodd. A foreign gunman is more likely to get international attention. And you know that sort of thing puts upstairs and the mayor's office into a spin.'

'I haven't found out much more about McNaught. A bit of juvenile crime in and around Dumbarton,' said Anita consulting her notebook. 'Sounds as though the army was the making of him. I spoke to his ex-commanding officer at the Queen's Own Highlanders who said he was a "highly efficient soldier". You can read into that what you will. He couldn't say what he did after he left the regiment, as that was classified. We're trying to track down his mother, who's still alive. There's also a brother somewhere. We're working on that.'

Moberg's temper wasn't much improved when he moved onto the next murderer on the agenda. 'And Tyrone Cassidy... have we any good news on that front?'

'I'm stumped as to how he got in and out of the country,' shrugged Hakim. 'I've drawn a complete blank, both over here and in Britain.'

'That's a great start. We can't even prove he was here. What about the camp you found late on yesterday?'

Brodd spread his arms. 'Bit early to say. Latest update is that forensics have found traces of blood at the site. It's being analyzed as we speak. I suspect it'll only confirm that that's where the victim, Jack Harmer, was killed. They couldn't get any footprints – they'd be deliberately obliterated before the camp moved on. There were tyre marks from the caravans and other vehicles, one of which was a Land Rover. We do know that a convoy of caravans and trucks crossed the border into Norway on Wednesday the tenth; two days after the murder.'

'Maybe Cassidy came in through Norway,' suggested Wallen.

'It's a hell of a long way from the border to Höör,' countered Moberg. 'But I suppose we'd better check it out. Hakim?'

'OK,' Hakim said resignedly.

'Anything else?'

'I've got a friend of mine, Detective Sergeant Ash, looking into the matter privately.'

'This your boyfriend?'

Anita coughed. '*Friend.* Anyway, he's with the Cumbria Constabulary and has nothing to do with the Met, so should get in under their radar. He's already heading to London to make discreet enquiries. Hopefully he can turn up something.'

'I hope so.' Moberg didn't sound convinced. 'He's our best bet.'

'Who was that?' Zetterberg asked as Szabo took his seat opposite her on the train to Uppsala. Szabo had taken the call on his mobile near the wagon door, as he was expecting to hear from his relatively new girlfriend and didn't want to answer it in front of an over-inquisitive boss. It had been Erlandsson. She'd passed on Anita's information. She said it was up to him how he brought it up. He decided to keep it to himself for the moment. He'd felt like a spare part during the Carina Lindvall interview. Zetterberg wasn't remotely interested in him contributing, and he was there simply as a back-up and extra intimidation – outnumber the suspect. He wanted to prove himself, and now he had something up his sleeve.

'It was Bea. She's trying to track down Lars-Gunnar. No success yet, though she's found out that his wife's parents have a summer place on Öland. That might be a possible bolthole.'

'The sooner he's found, the better,' Zetterberg huffed. 'I've got a funny feeling about Lars-Gunnar. Being out of it at the time of the murder is just a trifle too convenient for me. It meant that all the people who saw him just assumed he was too far gone to do anything. It's a great cover.'

Szabo stretched his leg in the aisle. He felt the muscles strain. It was a relief. He'd done a lot of sitting today. 'So you don't think it's Carina?'

Zetterberg's lips fluttered at she let out a gasp of air. 'Far from it! She's not the sort of woman you can trust. We already know she's a liar. She lives in a world of silly stories. Her account of her movements could be complete fiction. Working in her room is hardly an alibi.'

'But if she is telling the truth, she's given Larissa one.'

'Only partly. Thumping about in the kitchen is hardly concrete. And remember, it would only have taken minutes for either of the women to leave the cottage, cross to the chapel, commit the murder, hide the skewer in the field and get back to her room.'

'Except Larissa doesn't appear to have a motive. Disliking someone is hardly a reason for murdering them. On the face of it, Ivar doesn't seem to have an obvious motive either, other than he and Göran being highly competitive.'

'Don't forget, Göran hit on him on Malta, showing that he didn't care as much for Linus as everybody thought. Ivar didn't like the way Göran was treating his best friend, and the advance just exacerbated that dislike.'

Szabo moved his leg to let a mother and young child past as they headed for the toilet. 'What do we hope to get out of Ivar?'

'Why he got two women to lie for him. And still lie for him twenty-one years on.'

Szabo now knew that Ivar Hagblom had a lot more questions than that to answer.

CHAPTER 39

Kevin Ash got out his mobile phone. The coffee was steaming in front of him in what looked like a soup bowl: there was no handle. He was still trying to work out how to pick it up. The coffee shop was near the top end of Highgate High Street before its dramatic descent towards Archway. Outside, the street was busy. Every street in London seemed busy to Kevin; bees buzzing, frenetically focussed on their own purpose. In genteel Highgate, the locals weren't exactly rushing, but they were still moving with determination. After the initial thrill of being back in a big city, he found that it had only taken a matter of hours for the feeling to dissipate, and he found himself thinking fondly about the fells of the Lake District.

Mind you, the prices hadn't helped: this coffee was so expensive, he'd reneged on buying the chocolate brownie he'd had his eye on, and before entering the café, he'd spent a couple of minutes staring in an estate agent's window and had nearly fainted at the money being asked for very modest dwellings. The world was going mad. Well, London was. In a trendy bric-a-brac shop, he'd seen a renovated garden chair for £250. It was exactly the same type as his ex-wife had thrown out for being too old-fashioned. It had ended up in a skip in the Byker tip, Newcastle's finest recycling dump. Recycling down here was money for old rope; no doubt old rope went for an arm and a leg as well.

These had been incidental distractions from his main

purpose of locating Tyrone Cassidy's residence and doing Anita's bidding. He'd found Cassidy's home in a leafy street that reeked wealth. It was gated, and it was difficult to see the house beyond the high walls and umbrageous trees. But he could tell it was a big Victorian pile. Too late, he'd spied a CCTV camera. He'd be on there. Hopefully, they'd just think he was an inquisitive passer-by. Then he'd done the rounds of local shops to try and glean some information about Mr Cassidy, who turned out to be well known and well respected. What he'd found out wasn't helpful.

'Hello,' he said cheerily when Anita answered the phone.

'Any luck?' she immediately asked.

'What about, how are you? How was your journey? How's your holiday?'

'I didn't bother because I assume you're having fun. But what about Cassidy?'

'You're single-minded, you. Nothing much to report so far. I found Cassidy's gaff. Must be worth millions. The prices round here are eye-watering. Everybody I've spoken to thinks he's the bee's knees. Haven't heard anyone say a bad word about him. Are you sure you've got the right man?'

'He's a brutal businessman who exploits vulnerable young men. He's also a killer.'

'Is that all? The people I've spoken to are a bit vague about what they think he actually does, other than being a successful businessman. One shopkeeper said that he thought Cassidy was in the building trade. He also said that a couple of years ago, he had a big extension built on his house, and he now runs his business from there. Which is a pity, as that means he hasn't got an office I can visit. That's the sort of place you can get information about his movements. So, that's a dead end.'

Anita was quiet at the other end. 'No chance of breaking in?'

He realized he'd just said 'Fuck off!' loudly, and he got

some stern and disapproving looks from the other clientele as they tore their gazes away from their phones. He responded with a quickly mouthed 'Sorry.'

'Who are you saying "sorry" to?'

He lowered his voice: 'The nice people frequenting this coffee shop. It's so posh that they serve coffee in cups without handles so you can't pick them up until your drink has gone cold. And you pay a fortune for the privilege.' He heard her chortle at the other end of the line. 'Look, there's no way I can get into Cassidy's home. It's like Fort Knox. Besides, it would be inadmissible in court.'

'I know,' she said gloomily. 'It's just that we're getting nowhere here. We can't work out how he got in and out of the country. We can't even prove he was in Sweden at all. We've only got Danny Foster's word for it.'

'And you believe him?'

'Yes, I do. So, what's your next move?'

'To drink this coffee when the cup becomes touchable.'

'Stop mucking about, Kevin. Remember my promise if you succeed,' she said seductively. 'Though I might not be allowed into the UK after Brexit.'

'That's a thought. There are plans to deport EU undesirables. Lucky for you, you're very desirable.'

'Flattery will only get you so far. Results will ensure you can go all the way.'

'Well, I'd better see what I can do.'

Zetterberg and Szabo eventually tracked down Ivar Hagblom having a late- afternoon cup of tea outside the cathedral. They had been directed there by his wife, and he was already expecting them. The weather in Uppsala was far pleasanter than it had been when they had set off from Malmö at the crack of dawn. Ivar was sitting at one of the outside tables; an empty plate with lingering crumbs of cake, a pot of tea and a half-filled cup in front of him. The beautiful, tall twin spires of the cathedral pierced the blue of the firmament in their never-ending quest to reach God. Ivar greeted them with a smile. 'I often come here for afternoon tea. I can pretend to be British. And it's an inspiring view of a truly great ecclesiastical building. It's my favourite. Just look at the sun on the brick – it makes it look as though it's on fire. A good place to escape from the library and my more earnest students.'

Zetterberg was in no mood for small talk. 'I think we'll need somewhere more private.'

'Oh, dear, is it that bad?' The accompanying smile was self-mocking.

They wandered up from the cathedral through the trees towards the back of the adjacent castle without anyone saying a word. All were gathering their thoughts, though the climb was starting to tell on Zetterberg.

'That's far enough,' she ordered, slightly out of breath. 'No one can hear us.'

They had rounded the corner of the salmon-pink-stuccoed, rectangular building and were standing with their backs to the multi-fenestrated heights which comprised the rear wall. A detached wooden bell tower presided over a stand of cannon to their right; Szabo was struck by the similarity to the more modest one at Knäbäckshusen. From this vantage point, they had a splendid view of the Botanical Gardens with their symmetrical lines and geometrical topiary, and, further along the skyline, the cathedral and university town. Szabo had never been to Uppsala before. Maybe he'd bring his girlfriend for a romantic weekend when this was all over.

'Obviously, I know why you're here,' Ivar said, opening the conversation. He was resting casually, arms folded, against the metal railing that cordoned off the bell tower. 'Carina phoned me after you left her this morning. Larissa spilled the beans.'

'Serious beans.'

'I appreciate that. It's been on my conscience all these years, Alice.'

The friendly use of her name cut no ice with Zetterberg any more. 'If it was on your conscience, why were you still lying about it to me last week? You all were.'

'Protecting ourselves, I suppose. In case you mistakenly started thinking it was one of us.'

'Yes, it was interesting that when we last spoke, you indicated that you thought it was Linus.'

'That was the unfortunate conclusion I came to. To be perfectly honest, though I can't condone what he did, I don't blame him entirely. Göran was good at pushing people to their limits. I assume you've talked to Linus?'

'Oh, I have, Ivar.' She fluttered her eyelashes at the professor. 'I can call you, Ivar?'

He flashed a deprecating smile. 'Of course, Alice.'

'Well, Ivar, you might be surprised to know that we don't think it was Linus. In fact, I'm almost certain.' This conclusion produced a fleeting look of puzzlement from Ivar.

'That's good,' he said uncertainly. Zetterberg knew she had got him on the back foot.

'For him, yes. For the rest of you, no. Not one of you has an alibi.'

'Then it's serious.' Ivar had quickly regained his composure. 'Time for the truth. After the barbecue, I went off to try and find Linus. I was afraid he might do something stupid. I thought he might be suicidal. As it happens, I didn't find him. When I came back, all hell was let loose down at the chapel.'

'So, when did you decide to get the girls to alibi you?'

He thought for a minute. 'I suppose fairly quickly. We were all interviewed briefly that first night. Can't remember who came up with the sex idea. Anyway, it fitted. And then I thought it was a good idea to get Carina to corroborate it, as she hadn't an alibi either. She was working in her room, but no one had seen her. She was happy to cooperate.'

'I bet she was. Presumably, she was easily persuaded, as you were screwing her behind your girlfriend's back.' Zetterberg wanted to build up the pressure.

Ivar cringed. 'So, you know about that? Not my finest hour.'

'And did Larissa know?'

'Heavens, no! I made sure that didn't happen. She was bad enough when we did break up. If she had known then, we'd have finished long before we did.'

The wind began to pick up, and the trees down the embankment swayed gently. Splashes of blue fought for space in a clouding sky. Zetterberg seemed distracted, as though she was sensing this wasn't playing out as she'd hoped. Ivar was too confident. He wasn't back-peddling as she'd expected. She tried Björnstahl.

'My little chats with your old friend Linus revealed what you'd discovered on Malta; the thing you were being so vague about when we last talked. It was a letter written by Jacob Björnstahl.'

'Yes.'

'I gather in your sort of academic circles it was quite a find. Yet you didn't want Göran to know anything about it. Is that correct?'

'You could say so. It wasn't something I would want to share with a rival.'

'So he was definitely a rival?'

'We were doing the same thing, in the same field, with the likelihood that we'd end up going for the same jobs.'

'So, why didn't you use it in your PhD?' Zetterberg swung round to face Szabo. Where had this come from?

It was Ivar's turn to be distracted. A group of tourists were walking up the flight of steps leading up from the Gardens to the castle. 'I couldn't use it.'

'Why?' Szabo pressed.

'Why?' There was a doleful tone to his voice. 'Because it disappeared. I lost it.'

'Lost it?' Zetterberg said, seizing back the initiative from Szabo. 'When did you lose it?'

'It was... erm... it was around the time of Göran's...'

'You had it at the cottage at Knäbäckshusen?'

'Yes. I didn't want to leave it at the university. While we were at the cottage, I did some work on my thesis.'

'When was the last time you saw it?'

'That has driven me mad over the years. A few days before, I think. It was in our bedroom. I kept it in the bottom drawer of an old chest.'

'And when did you realize it had gone missing?'

'The day before the... But I just thought I must have misplaced it. There was a lot of drink consumed at that time.'

'And drugs.'

'And drugs,' he conceded. 'Then with the whole Göran business, the last thing I thought about was the Björnstahl letter. It was a few days later that I searched for it. Gone! It's tortured me ever since. Was I so intoxicated or high that I'd done something with it? It's the greatest regret of my career. And now that I'm at the same university where Björnstahl made his name, I'm constantly reminded of what I missed out on. I let a golden opportunity slip through my fingers.'

'Could it have been stolen?'

Ivar's eyes widened in surprise. 'Stolen? Who would want to steal it?'

'We know Larissa and Linus knew about it. Either of them could have.'

Ivar shook his head vehemently. 'No. No way. Larissa wasn't interested. And Linus had no cause to. It wouldn't have been of any use to him.'

'Göran then?'

'He didn't know anything about it. I know he suspected I had something, but not that.'

'What about his threat to Carina that you would suffer the most? If he had stolen the letter, that would have been a brilliant way of getting back at you.'

'But he couldn't have known about it. Only two other people knew of its existence.'

'So, what about Linus?' ventured Szabo, who was fed up being sidelined. 'You've admitted that his relationship with Göran was at a low ebb. Could Linus have been desperate enough to win back his lover by giving away your secret?'

'Look, Linus may have been many things, but he was always loyal to his friends. More than I have been, shamefully.'

Zetterberg eyed Ivar, who was no longer the self-assured man of a few minutes ago. He had given them much to ponder. She was about to conclude the chat when Szabo weighed in again.

'Why did your family put pressure on Prosecutor Renmarker to stall the case?'

Both Zetterberg and Ivar were left open-mouthed.

'What's this?' demanded Zetterberg.

'Apparently, to ensure that the investigation went no further and that Inspector Nordlund and his team couldn't interrogate Linus, Prosecutor Renmarker was, shall we say, "leant on" by a journalist from one of the Hagblom newspapers.'

Zetterberg only just managed to hide her fury that Szabo was coming out with information that she wasn't privy to. 'Is this true?'

The colour had drained from Ivar's face.

CHAPTER 40

It was a pint that Kevin reckoned he deserved for all the tramping around he'd done on Anita's behalf. One thing he did still like about London was the pubs, and this was a satisfying example. It was an old building on Highgate High Street with a dark, wood-panelled interior that gave it a Dickensian feel and an intimate atmosphere. There were cricket photos on the wall, so it must be the watering hole of some local team. Kevin had taken his pint and packet of peanuts, a winning combination in his mind, out through the back door to an extremely compact beer garden with wooden tables and benches. The drinking area overlooked Pond Square. The Square was ill-defined; the grit-covered expanse was more triangular in shape. Huge plane trees added interest, and the hotchpotch of well-kept Georgian houses on the periphery gave it an ambience of refinement. At one end, there was a public convenience, opposite which was the imposing white facade of the Highgate Literary and Scientific Institution. Kevin was starting to feel vaguely uncomfortable in this high-brow, high-maintenance world. And the only thing that would quell his disquiet was another pint of the excellent beer he'd just finished.

He was about to rise when a suited figure slipped onto the bench on the other side of the table. He was greeted by a half smile. The man was immaculately dressed with a sharp blue tie and crisp white shirt. He was tanned, with thinning hair that had gone grey at the temples. His nose was a prominent feature. It seemed to be pointing accusingly at Kevin, who was now firmly seated again. The grey eyes weren't smiling. To anyone else, this could have been a well-heeled, middle-aged businessman who had popped into the pub on his way home from work. But to Kevin, he was nothing of the sort. He could smell a cop a mile off. A Met cop.

'If you think I'm buying you a pint, you're going to be disappointed,' Kevin said as he examined the new arrival.

'That's not very friendly. But I'll pass on that. Just here for a little chat.'

'OK. I like football, cricket, pubs, history... now I do like history. Do you want to start with that?'

'No,' said the man, fishing a piece of paper from his inside pocket. He laid it out on the table and used the palm of his hand to iron out the creases. 'This.' He swizzled round the A4 piece of paper so that Kevin could see it. Kevin recognized his own face. A CCTV image. It was a close-up of him standing outside Tyrone Cassidy's house.

'Nice house,' said Kevin. 'I was thinking about buying it.'

'It's not for sale.' Then the man gave Kevin a disparaging glance. 'You couldn't afford that house, even in your dreams.'

'A man's entitled to dream.'

'You've not only been hanging around Mr Cassidy's house—'

'Oh, is that the owner's name?'

'You've been asking questions about him.'

'I like to know who I'm buying off. Why are you so interested? Are you his estate agent?'

The man wasn't appreciating the humour. His hand went back into his inside suit pocket, and out came his warrant card. Kevin read: Detective Inspector Nicholas Sherington. He recognized the name. Anita had mentioned it over the phone – this was her Met contact and ex-colleague. That was a bit of a shock.

'And what has my chatting to a few pleasant Highgate folk got to do with the Met?'

'Because we like to protect our important citizens. They're entitled to their privacy. And since we got this,' he said, tapping Kevin's photo with a finger sporting a bulging gold ring, 'we've done a bit of checking on you. Turns out you're one of our own.'

'I'm not one of yours. I come from a proper force.'

'Don't make me laugh. A load of sheep-shaggers.'

'We care as much about our sheep as you do about your important citizens.'

'No need for the lip. I can't understand why someone with your accent ended up in some northern hole with a bunch of hillbillies. But that's your problem. Let's get down to business. My guess is that you've got some connection with Anita Sundström.' Kevin didn't reply. 'She's sent you down here to snoop around. She's not only beautiful, but determined. Bet she's still a great shag,' he said winking suggestively. 'The whole squad were trying to get into her knickers when she was with us.' He left the implication hanging that he might have succeeded. Kevin resisted the urge to punch him in the face. 'I tried to warn her politely that Cassidy is off limits. She's wrong to pursue him.'

'That's not the only thing she got wrong.'

'What do you mean?'

'She told me you were a straight cop.'

Sherington was suddenly all controlled fury, and he stabbed the same ringed finger towards Kevin's chest. 'Look here, Ash. I'll spell it out so even someone as stupid as you can understand. You're to leave Tyrone Cassidy well alone. He's out of your reach – and Anita's. If you carry on, you can say goodbye to your career. When we've finished with you, you'll have nothing left except your fucking sheep. And if you hang around these parts for much longer, Mr Cassidy's friends might take exception, and you'll end up joining Karl Marx in the cemetery down the road there. Get my drift? Go home.'

Kevin rose to his feet and picked up his empty pint glass. 'I hope you're not still here when I come back.' He untangled his legs from the bench. 'And I'll send Anita your love.'

Zetterberg, too, was on the beer. She put her empty glass down. 'I'll have another.' Szabo was only half way through his first drink. However, he felt unable to refuse the boss given that he had seriously upset her earlier on.

They were in the bar of Sherlock's in Klostergatan. It was a boozy shrine to Conan Doyle's great detective and an appropriate setting to discuss a police investigation. Zetterberg had soon become bored with the pleasant barman who was trying to explain in enthusiastic detail the huge number of beers available. She'd just pointed at one and said she'd have that. She'd actually paid for the first drinks while Szabo escaped to the toilet, which was an experience in itself. The room was adorned with Sherlock Holmes paraphernalia and through an antiquated speaker, the sound track from one of the Basil Rathbone Hollywood films in which he'd played the world's most famous sleuth in the '30s and '40s came crackling out. Szabo, peeing in such incongruous surroundings, found the whole episode delightfully disconcerting.

After they'd finished with a shaken Ivar Hagblom, Zetterberg said that it was too late to head south to Malmö and they'd have to stay the night in Uppsala. She'd found a cheap hotel, and then they'd headed straight to the pub; not, however, before giving Szabo a blast as to how he knew about the PhD and Prosecutor Renmarker. He'd tried to brush it off by saying that it had come from Erlandsson, which was true. Zetterberg had been furious that Erlandsson hadn't reported directly to her. She would have words when they got back on Wednesday. In the meantime, she was still cross that he hadn't passed on the information. He'd apologized profusely and said that it was a misjudgement on his part. He hadn't been sure how reliable the information was. It was a feeble excuse, and one that didn't wash with Zetterberg, whom he knew would hold it against him in the future. He had sussed out that she was that kind of person. Nevertheless, she did concede that it had stunned Ivar, and his rather rambling explanation had satisfied neither of them.

Ivar admitted that it was he, not his father, who had approached the editor of one of the Hagblom newspapers. The man was an old family friend – and his godfather. He wanted to see if there was any way to stop the potentially bad press coverage that would inevitably surround the case once someone was charged. They would all have to appear in court, and their lives would be scrutinized in great detail. And he realized that if he got embroiled in a murderous scandal, it could seriously affect his future chances. Also, he claimed that he had wanted to save his friend Linus, as it was becoming clear that the police were closing in on him. The editor had put Ivar onto his leading investigative reporter, who had looked into the private lives of the main members of the investigation team and the prosecutor. He'd found nothing incriminating on the team members, but had been able to firm up on rumours about Renmarker, who had a bit of a reputation concerning female colleagues. It was simple then to apply the appropriate pressure. The prosecutor was easily persuaded. Renmarker had met Ivar and explained that if he would call off the press snooping into his private life, the investigation would go nowhere.

Zetterberg plunged into her second pint before speaking. 'Is Ivar our man?'

'It's not looking good for him.'

'How have the mighty fallen.' She took another long gulp. She'd have downed her second before he'd finished his first at this rate. It might be a long evening. Szabo had a sudden, horrible thought: would she try it on with him?

'Ivar and Göran have become great academic rivals,' Zetterberg carried on. 'So there's tension already when they meet up in Knäbäckshusen. Malta is where it all started to go wrong. Göran is beginning to fall out of love with Linus; that's if he really cared for him in the first place. This in itself upsets his friend Ivar, and Göran trying to snog him won't have helped. Then Ivar discovers this Björnstahl material and is cock-a-hoop. This upsets Göran because he doesn't know what it is. It's probably eating away at Göran, especially if Linus won't tell him. Or did Linus tell him? In that position, wouldn't you?'

'If I was desperate to keep my lover. Probably.'

'I think when things were going from bad to worse at Knäbäckshusen, Göran wanted to get back at the rest of the group, who were starting to reject him. I believe his threat to Carina about Ivar suffering wasn't just him venting his frustration, as Larissa claimed. I think he'd found out about the Björnstahl letter from Linus. That's it! Linus spilled the beans, and Göran pinched the letter. Ivar admitted he'd been looking for it just before the murder. So, what did Göran do with it?'

Szabo was becoming excited. He clicked his fingers. 'He burnt it! He bloody burnt it!'

Zetterberg's eyes were ablaze. 'Of course! His last words. That's it, isn't it? So, that night, Ivar comes back from looking for Linus, whom he doesn't find.' She put her glass down with a thump. 'Or maybe he did, and Linus confesses that he's told Göran about Björnstahl. Whatever. Ivar comes back, finds the skewer on the beach, sees Göran go into the chapel and follows him. He confronts Göran with the awful thing his rival has done – or, if he didn't already know, a gloating Göran tells him that he's burnt his precious letter. It tips him over the edge.'

'And then he starts covering up,' said Szabo, who was getting caught up in Zetterberg's enthusiasm. 'He gets the two girls to alibi him and then gets the investigation derailed. He was seriously taken aback when that was mentioned. He must have presumed that would always remain a secret.'

'We've got to get back to Malmö as soon as possible tomorrow. I've got to see Prosecutor Blom straightaway and present our findings. I think she'll agree we've got enough to officially bring Ivar down to Malmö for questioning. Then we can squeeze the truth out of him.'

Anita watched Danny Foster as he sat fidgeting near the living room window. The blind was down. She had come back in after seeing the doctor out. The medic had said that Danny was all right, though he'd be happier if he were back in hospital. Anita had promised him that as soon as the matter was cleared up, she would personally return the patient to his care. She saw Danny lean forward to peek round the blind.

'No!' Anita ordered firmly. Danny sprang back, startled. He groaned, as he'd hurt both his ankle and his wounded shoulder in the process. 'Sorry, but when it's dark, we don't want you looking out.'

'In case I make myself a target.' There was nothing Anita could say to deny it. She was annoyed with herself for betraying the tension that she and all her colleagues on duty were feeling after Kevin had called to tell her about his "accidental" meeting in a Highgate pub with DI Nick Sherington. The implication was clear – Cassidy would now know they were after him. She'd immediately spoken to Moberg about heightening security at the safe house. And to ensure that she was on top of things, she had decided to spend that night with Danny and the three officers scheduled for the overnight shift.

'Why can't you catch McNaught?' Danny said accusingly as he sat down again.

'It's under control.' Anita wished it were. 'And you're safe here.' She could tell Danny was dubious.

'What about Mr Cassidy? How are you going to deal with him?'

'We've got a team working on in it London.' That was a horrible lie, and she felt awful for deluding the young man, but what else could she do? Tell him that their only hope had been scuppered by a dodgy cop at the Met?

A tall, blond policeman brought in a couple of mugs of tea. Danny took one without a glance in the officer's direction. Anita took hers with a nod of thanks. The officer left the room.

'How did I get into this mess?' Danny gazed at the steam slowly rising from his mug.

'Life's difficult. Things happen.' It seemed an inadequate response. 'I've a son about your age.'

Danny craned his neck up to look at Anita. 'You don't think of policewomen having kids. Don't know why.'

'We've had our ups and downs. Like you and your dad.'

He smirked. 'If he could see me now, I'd get "I told you so, you no-good..." That sort of thing.'

'I'm sure he'd be worried.'

'No. He'd say I've got what I deserved.'

'All parents worry, even if they don't let on.'

Danny picked up his mug and blew on it. It rippled the surface of the milky tea. 'I bet your son has never got into a bloody nightmare like this.'

'He did once.' Anita's mind flitted back to the pier at Ribersborgsstranden. She still shivered every time she thought about it. 'Like you, it wasn't his fault. You can't blame yourself.'

He sipped his tea thoughtfully.

'Jack Harmer's dad flew in today. It's a nightmare for him and Jack's family.'

Danny put his mug down. His eyes were tearing up.

'Poor Jack. I don't think I can take any more of this. I'm so frightened.' Anita resisted her natural instinct to give the young man a supportive hug.

'It'll come to an end soon.'

'Will it? Even if you catch McNaught, I'll never be safe. Cassidy has people. There'll be other McNaughts.'

'We'll protect you. I promise.' She didn't have time for more reassurances. The tall officer who'd brought the tea returned. Without speaking, he gave Anita an anxious glance. She was needed.

Anita closed the living room door behind her and followed the officer quickly down the corridor to the kitchen where another colleague, whom she recognized as Mikael Palm, was standing nervously near the window.

'There may be someone outside. Nina Kovac thought she heard something.'

'Where is she?'

'She's gone out there.'

A headstrong, impulsive policewoman wasn't what was needed just now. 'Right,' Anita turned to the tall young man, 'you go back in there and keep an eye on Danny. Turn the lights off, and for God's sake keep him away from the windows.' The officer swiftly left.

Anita pulled out her service pistol. 'OK, Mikael, you go round the front and check all is clear. I'll go out the back and try not to shoot bloody Nina.' She flipped off the kitchen light and stepped through the back door. All was quiet. The grass was damp from the day's rain. The dark clouds were now dispersing, and a waxing gibbous moon had broken through and was gleaming on the countryside around. The garden at the back of the house stretched towards a field beyond, which had recently been ploughed. It wouldn't be ideal for McNaught to approach from that direction. The front wasn't an easy option either, as here there was a long, straight drive down to the main road: no cover. But at the side of the house, there was a small copse of trees and some thick bushes at the boundary edge. She hunched down, her pistol held firmly in both hands in front of her. She listened intently. There was a faint sound coming from the direction of the copse. The crack of a twig. Anita tensed. As her eyes got used to the semi-dark, she could see a figure moving carefully among the bushes. She slowly unwound and stood up, her pistol pointing in the direction of the shape, her finger hovering over the trigger.

The figure stepped out from the shadow of the trees. A splash of moonlight lit up the unmistakable outline of a handgun in its hand.

'Don't move!' Anita shouted out in English. 'Drop the gun or I'll shoot!'

'It's only me, Inspector,' came back the reply in Swedish. 'It's Nina. It's OK. Nothing out here.'

Anita exploded.

CHAPTER 41

St. Jerome's & St. Jude's was an uninspiring 1960s red-brick building with a tower that resembled a chimney stack. Originally, Kevin had assumed that someone with the money and influence of Tyrone Cassidy would have worshipped at the magnificent, domed St. Joseph's on Highgate Hill. Maybe the well-established, wealthy worshippers there thought a newcomer flashing his cash was a bit vulgar for them. Instead, the more down-at-heel St. Jerome's & St. Jude's had benefitted from his munificence – the giveaway was the spanking new hall next door. Kevin realized this was his last chance.

After his meeting with DI Nick Sherington, he'd phoned Anita. She'd been deeply shocked that the detective she once knew had been bought by backhanders and had joined the ranks of the corrupt. It had also set alarm bells ringing. If Cassidy was aware of someone sniffing around, it was even more imperative from his point of view that McNaught deal with Danny.

'We'll have to be extra vigilant.' Then her voice softened. 'So will you, my darling.' He couldn't remember her calling him 'darling' before. He was thrilled. 'I shouldn't have got you involved. It's too dangerous. Go back to Penrith tomorrow and forget about it.'

'Does that make your *promise* null and void?'

She sniggered. 'No. You did your best.'

'You know Sherington hinted that you and he...' He'd

306

sworn to himself he wouldn't raise the subject, but it just slipped out.

'Give me a break! I liked Nick, but I wouldn't have gone to bed with him. Kevin Ash, my first rule has always been: never sleep with a cop. But I made an exception for you.'

Kevin felt foolish yet relieved, but Sherington had rattled him.

'Sorry, it's just...'

'Look.' Anita sounded concerned again. 'Please. Please go home tomorrow. No more investigating. It was a bad idea in the first place. I don't want you ending up in Highgate Cemetery.'

'That's because you'd have to pay an entrance fee every time you wanted to visit me.'

But in the end, he had promised. All the same, he was still standing outside St. Jerome's and St. Jude's. He knew it was partly because he still wanted to help Anita. But mainly it was because he wasn't going to be warned off by a shit like Sherington.

The door creaked as he opened it. Inside, it was quiet. Unlike some of the Catholic churches he'd visited over the years, with their chapels and statues and over-the-top paintings and ornamentation, this was quite simple. And none of the claustrophobic darkness of the older churches; light flooded in through the clear-glass windows. Rows of plain wooden seats serried up to the altar, which was dwarfed by a gaudy mosaic of Christ on the Cross behind it. Now that the building was fifty years old, it was beginning to show its age and could have done with a lick of paint. Beside the altar was a woman in her seventies, who was gathering up the wilting flowers from last Sunday's service.

'Hello,' Kevin ventured as an opening. 'What a lovely church!'

The woman had tightly-curled, grey hair and bright eyes

beaming out from a lined, careworn face. She may have ended up in Highgate, but this was someone who'd seen life. She wore an old-fashioned, brightly patterned, nylon full-length apron like the one Kevin's gran used to wear for doing the housework.

'It is, it is. Welcome to St. Jerome's & St. Jude's.' The accent was unmistakeably Irish. 'Have you come to pray, young man? If so, I will leave you in peace.'

'Well, actually,' he began, switching on his most winning smile, 'I was wondering if you could help me.'

'Father Goodwin is the man you should be speaking to.'

'I'm sure you're just as good. Is Tyrone Cassidy one of your fellow worshippers?'

She slowly put the bedraggled flowers in a plastic trug and eyed him suspiciously. 'And who are you to ask?'

Kevin automatically reached inside his jacket for his warrant card and then stopped himself. It would get back to Sherington if he used his police authority. All the same, he took it out and flashed it so quickly she had no chance to read it. 'I'm a journalist. The name's Peter.' Where that came from, he had no idea. 'Erm... Peter O'Toole.'

'Gracious me! Fancy having the same name as that actor fellow. Any relation?'

'Yes, actually,' he found himself saying. 'Er, yes. On my mother's side.'

'Your mother's side?' she queried.

Christ, he was useless at this improvising. Anita was much quicker thinking on her feet. 'Yes, yes. She was an O'Toole as well. Both my parents were called O'Toole. Their ancestors came over after the famine.'

'It's common enough,' she conceded, though he could tell she wasn't entirely satisfied.

He pressed on swiftly before she had time to work out he was talking drivel. 'You see I work for... for the *Northern Catholic*.'

'I have to confess I haven't heard of it.'

'It's only a small monthly publication covering the Catholic parishes of my part of the north of England.'

'You don't sound as if you come from the north.'

'No, I was brought up in Essex. But it was God's wish that I head north and do his work up there among the heathens.' She remained stony-faced. 'Sorry, do you mind if I ask you what your name is?'

'Why?' she said defensively.

Kevin whipped out his notebook. 'So I can use it in my article. That's why I'm here. We're doing a series of features on great modern Catholic benefactors, and Tyrone Cassidy was an obvious choice.'

'Well, why didn't you say, young man?' The beam returned. 'I'm Mrs Dillon. Kathleen Dillon,' she added shyly.

Kevin pretended to write her name down. 'Kathleen, if I'm going to be perfectly honest with you, I'm doing this article on Mr Cassidy because my editor wants to put a little pressure on some of our richer parishioners up north. From what we've heard about Mr Cassidy, he's exceedingly generous.'

'Oh my, yes.' Her pride was clear. 'Do you know he paid for the entire cost of our new church hall?'

'That's staggering.'

'He's got a heart of gold, that man. Truly sent here by God.'

'And I assume he attends Mass regularly every Sunday?'

'Of course he does. Brings all the family, too. So nice. And then afterwards he always comes to our coffee and tea in the hall and mixes with the other members of the congregation.'

'Except when he's away on business, I suppose.' Kevin was trying to get round to Sunday, the 7th of August, which was when Cassidy might well have gone to Sweden – the murder was committed the next day, according to Anita.

'I don't think that happens. Holidays obviously.' Then

she frowned and patted down her apron. 'Funny you should mention that; he did leave straight after the service the other week. Off somewhere, as he'd didn't come to the hall afterwards.'

'Can you remember which Sunday? It's just that I can follow this up and explain to my readers that even when he has important business, he still finds time to attend church.'

She nodded in agreement. 'You're right, Peter. Well, let me think on it. It was just over two weeks ago.'

'Would that be the seventh? Just for accuracy. I pride myself on getting all my facts right.'

'Yes. You're right, there. That was the very day.'

For the next fifteen minutes Kathleen Dillon filled Kevin in on all the wonderful things that Cassidy did for the church; the St. Patrick's Day parties, funding Sunday-school outings, and providing hampers at Christmas for the elderly members of the congregation who were no longer fit or able enough to make the pilgrimage to the church and enjoy the pensioners' festive lunch in the hall. Kevin was now getting bored and was in the process of extricating himself from the now-garrulous Irishwoman. He had confirmed that Cassidy had headed off somewhere on that particular Sunday, but that by itself was of little use. He hadn't got anywhere. He would head for Euston and get the first train back to Penrith.

He was saying goodbye and thank you to Mrs Dillon while stepping slowly backwards in the direction of the church entrance, with his new friend in equally slow pursuit. Then she clapped her hands together. 'Jesus, Mary and Joseph, what is my memory like? I'm getting that... what is it?... dyslexia?'

Kevin's heart sank. She'd thought of another thing that Saint Tyrone had done.

'My sister. My dear, departed sister, Maureen.'

Kevin tried to unglaze his eyes.

'She died of cancer last year.' The relevance was lost on

Kevin. 'Before she died, Tyrone Cassidy fulfilled her last wish to visit Lourdes.'

'Very considerate,' Kevin mumbled appropriately.

'He flew her there. And me. With Father Goodwin, too, and three other elderly members of the church.'

'That must have cost him a bit in air fares.'

'Oh, no. We went in his private plane.'

Kevin stood rigidly in front of her, the hairs on the back of his neck tingling. 'Tyrone Cassidy has a private plane?'

There was a big red circle drawn round the photo of Ivar Hagblom. As soon as Zetterberg and Szabo had arrived back after their early-morning flight from Arlanda, they had made straight for the polishus and were gathering the evidence for Zetterberg to present to Prosecutor Blom. Szabo was feeling hungover after far too many drinks at Sherlock's the night before. Zetterberg seemed totally unaffected. Szabo had been grateful that she hadn't propositioned him, though she had patted him on the head like a dog as he made for his hotel room. Erlandsson was feeling tremulous, as she was expecting Zetterberg to ask her where she had got her information from about Ivar's PhD dissertation (that could be explained simply enough by saying she had contacted someone at Lund University) and the blackmailing of Prosecutor Renmarker (not so easy to give details without bringing Anita Sundström's name into the frame). In fact, much to her relief, Zetterberg didn't broach either subject.

The case they were forming against Ivar Hagblom was compelling, but hardly watertight. Though the incidents in the escalation of his fractious relationship with Göran over the months leading up to the latter's death were not in themselves enough to commit murder, the revelation of Göran's probable discovery and subsequent burning of the Björnstahl letter was certainly enough to push Ivar over the edge. A real motive.

Though Ivar had denied that Göran knew of the existence of the letter, surely he *must* have known. All the friends had heard Göran's threat to Carina about Ivar. Surely Ivar must have put two and two together when he couldn't find the letter just before the murder? But it was his subsequent actions that pointed to his guilt. He had no alibi and had coerced the two women in his life to provide one. Then his putting Prosecutor Renmarker under pressure to stall the case, in itself an illegal action as it was tantamount to blackmail, was the clincher as far as Zetterberg was concerned.

'Won't Blom want us to eliminate the other suspects before she allows us to go ahead with the official questioning of Ivar?' asked Erlandsson.

'Of course she will,' said Zetterberg in some annoyance, implying she was about to move onto that anyway. Referring to the photos on the board: 'I've discounted Linus for reasons I've set out before. The timing from when he was seen on the beach to when Kurt Jeppsson heard the murderer leave the chapel was very tight. The original investigation thought the motive was to do with their broken-down relationship. I have to disagree. I think he loved Göran too much to murder him. Of course, he may have unwittingly caused his lover's death by admitting to Ivar that he had told Göran about the Björnstahl letter. He denies doing so, however.'

'We've tracked Lars-Gunnar down,' said Erlandsson. 'He stupidly used his mobile, which was traced to his in-laws' holiday home on Öland. Taken refuge there. According to the local police who picked him up, he said he'd been freaked out by all the memories brought back by the reopening of the investigation. It rings true in light of his recent behaviour.' Szabo nodded in agreement.

'I'll go with that,' said Zetterberg briskly. 'And all the others did say that they thought he was out of it on the night of the murder. That was one thing they've been consistent about.

Which brings us to the girls. Larissa appears to have been in the kitchen, as heard by Carina. She was also in her room later, as she claimed, when Carina came in and told her that something had happened at the chapel. And Larissa doesn't appear to have a motive. Though she was the only other person to know about the Björnstahl letter, there's nothing to suggest that she would have told Göran about its existence. The opposite, in fact. From everything we hear, she was protective of Ivar. Over-protective. She was obviously smothering him, which is why he turned to the charms of Carina Lindvall. No, the only niggling doubt I have is about Carina.' She aggressively tapped the photo of the writer. 'I'd love it to be her. She lied about Ivar and Larissa. It conveniently gave her an alibi. No one can vouch for her movements until she went to Larissa's room. She had a motive: protecting Lars-Gunnar, who she seemed to have been genuinely fond of, even if she was being unfaithful behind his back. If the evidence growing against Ivar wasn't so strong, I'd be after her. Right, anything else?'

'You asked me to look into the phone records,' said Erlandsson. 'Lars-Gunnar wasn't in touch with any of the others according to the calls made in the last couple of weeks.' Erlandsson consulted her list. 'A number between Ivar and Carina.'

'We know they were in touch,' said Zetterberg dismissively. Unperturbed, Erlandsson carried on. 'Carina rang Malta a few times, and Larissa spoke to Ivar once.'

'Obviously, Carina spoke to Linus. She warned him that it was likely that I'd turn up on his doorstep. I don't think calls have much bearing on the case now.' Erlandsson shoved her list back into a folder.

'I suppose it boils down to who could have been on the beach to pick up the skewer,' said Szabo, who was trying to untangle his booze-befuddled brain. How could Zetterberg drink so much? He'd never try and keep up with her again.

'Linus was out and about; so too, Ivar. The others would have had to make a special effort to go down to the beach to find the skewer and pick it up. It's not as though they would know it was down there in the first place.'

'Good point. Another reason why we need to pull in Ivar.'

Zetterberg's mobile phone began to play the theme from *Star Wars*. She answered it. She listened carefully. 'No, that's fine. I'll be along in ten minutes.' She put her phone down. 'That was Blom. Let's get the show on the road!'

CHAPTER 42

'Are you ringing from Penrith?' Though Anita was glad that Kevin had rung, because she wanted to apologize again for putting him in danger, she was too preoccupied for unnecessary chit-chat. The incident in the safe house garden had just indicated how edgy everyone was becoming. There was a clever, resourceful and ruthless killer out there who would stop at nothing to shoot their one and only witness to Jack Harmer's murder.

'No. Essex.'

'Essex? Are you visiting your sister?' Anita didn't quite catch his reply over the noise of an aircraft taking off nearby. 'Sorry, what did you say? Sounds as though you're at an airport.'

'Kind of. It's a private aerodrome.'

'What are you doing there?'

'Helping the most gorgeous policewoman in Sweden.'

Anita was totally nonplussed. Then she began to get exasperated. She had specifically asked him not to do any more. He wasn't to put himself in peril. 'What have you been up to?' she demanded.

'I know how Tyrone Cassidy got in and out of Sweden.'

'What?' Anita gasped.

'Our murdering wealthy benefactor owns a private plane. It's a Cessna Citation CJ2. 2003 model. He bought it second hand in 2010 from an American. He keeps it here in Essex at the Hockley Heath Aerodrome. It used to be an RAF airfield during the last war.'

Anita couldn't contain her amazement. 'How did you find this out?'

'Thanks to Kathleen Dillon, a little old Irish lady of my acquaintance.'

'And she gave you all that detail about his plane?' Now she was incredulous.

'No. She put me on the trail. I posed as someone from the Civil Aviation Authority doing a survey of flights in and out of the United Kingdom to EU countries over the last two months from small or private airfields.'

'And they believed you?'

'I said it was a consequence of the Brexit vote. Luckily, the guy I spoke to was only too happy to provide information, as he was obviously one of those deluded souls who thinks we're going to put the Great back into Britain. I think that boat sailed in 1914. You know, I'm quite enjoying this pretending-to-be-other-people lark.'

'But Cassidy?' she said impatiently.

'Yes. He flew out of here on Sunday, the seventh of August at 14:00 hours bound for southern Sweden. Somewhere called Tommy Lilly or something.'

'Tomelilla.'

'That's it. Flew back in late Monday afternoon, August eighth. There was only Cassidy and his pilot on board on both flights. It wasn't the first time he'd flown there either. And he's also made recent trips to Norway and Holland.'

'You are a fantastic man.'

'Why, thank you, madam.'

'I think you should go to the nearest pub and reward yourself with a pint.'

'You can read my mind.'

'And if you can read my mind at this moment, you'll

realize that you're going to get some X-rated action when I come over.'

Kevin nearly dropped his phone.

Moberg was pleased to receive some good news at last. Anita didn't enlighten him as to exactly how Kevin had found out. He wanted action. Hakim was immediately dispatched to Tomelilla. A quick check had shown up an old airfield in the area which was thought to have been abandoned.

As soon as they could confirm that Cassidy's Cessna plane had landed in Sweden on the 7th of August, they could prove he was in the country at the time of Jack Harmer's murder. Then they could start extradition proceedings to impel him to face justice in Sweden. But it would be fruitless if McNaught got to their only witness first.

Moberg, Anita and Wallen debated whether they should move Danny to another location. The alternatives were apartments in the city. Having got to know the rural safe house, Wallen now argued that any apartment could be easier for McNaught to infiltrate, and if shooting broke out, innocent people might get caught in the crossfire. Anita was also uneasy about transporting Danny from one location to another. Whatever precautions they took, there would be some spot on the route which would be vulnerable to an attack. The trouble was that they still had no idea where McNaught was. They had no new leads. Finally, Moberg decided that Danny should stay put.

'One other thing,' Wallen said. 'Jack Harmer's father. We've got a DNA sample off him. I persuaded him not to view the body. Too upsetting given there isn't anything really recognizable. But he's asked if he can speak to Danny. I think he wants to know about his son's last weeks. It's understandable.'

The request left Moberg thoughtful. 'OK. I'm not entirely happy about it. Get Brodd to take him down to the house this afternoon. He's only got an hour, mind.'

'I think he'll appreciate it.'

As Anita was leaving Moberg's office, she saw Liv Fogelström coming in the opposite direction.

'How are you?' Anita asked.

Liv's face lit up as she held up her left hand. The sparkle coming from her ring finger was the reason for her happiness.

'That must have cost Hakim.' Anita held Liv's hand and examined it. It wasn't to her taste – too glitzy. But Liv clearly loved it. 'It's beautiful. Are you setting a date?'

'Oh, no. Maybe next year. We're not rushing things. We've got certain things to iron out first.' Anita knew she meant Hakim's parents.

'Well, I'm pleased for you both. By the way, there's something I want to ask you...'

CHAPTER 43

Ivar Hagblom was relieved to reach the reassuring surroundings of the Carolina Rediviva that Thursday morning. He'd hardly slept the last two nights since being interviewed by that seriously unpleasant policewoman. But it had been the younger detective who had really thrown him with the revelation about Prosecutor Renmarker. He had safely assumed that that piece of information would never see the light of day. Why had Renmarker blabbed now? If he had kept quiet, everything would have blown over. But now it was out, there was no way he could convincingly deny it.

And the damned Björnstahl letter! He had been so thrilled at its discovery at the time – he'd seen those few handwritten pages as a passport to speedy academic fame – and now he fervently wished that he had never unearthed them. He didn't need a sharp-suited, expensive lawyer in a fancy office in Stockholm to tell him that he was in deep trouble.

Yet the library was a sanctuary. The familiar faces of the staff, the accumulation of knowledge in the bulging shelves, the quiet serenity of the reading room; even the small museum with the magical remains of the 6th-century *Codex Argenteus* in the Gothic language. The *Codex* had always appealed to his love of linguistics, which unfortunately brought him back to bloody Björnstahl. He'd been up early and left the apartment before his wife had even stirred. He'd come in to prepare for a meeting with a talented PhD student. It hadn't gone well, as he had been too preoccupied, and he eventually called it a day after apologizing for not giving the student's work the proper attention it deserved. They rearranged a time in the following week. Ivar needed a break. He would go to the cathedral café and try and get his head round the paper on the present state of Syria, which he was scheduled to deliver at the beginning of September at a conference at Yale University.

Ivar headed out of the main library doors and had reached the top step beneath the colonnades when he noticed a couple of camera crews poised behind the bollards that separated the library forecourt from the street. Behind them was a police squad car. Were they filming a new cop show? There were so many these days. Maybe it was the one Carina had been talking about the last time they met. He knew she was desperate to get her books on TV.

Then it dawned on him that the cameras were trained on him. Suddenly a woman stepped forward. It was Detective Alice Zetterberg.

'That's brilliant! Good work!' Moberg put his phone down with a flourish.

'The airfield?' Anita asked eagerly.

'Yep. That was Hakim. A Cessna Citation did land on the seventh of August. And it flew out the next day; the day of the murder. Also, he's found a witness who has identified the photo of Cassidy that you got off the internet. They said he was picked up by a Land Rover. We know that a Land Rover was at the campsite. And the driver sounds as though it could well be McNaught. I'll get straight onto Blom and the commissioner and get them to start diplomatic proceedings to haul him over here.'

'Hope we have more success than we've had with Julian Assange.'

'I don't think the Ecuadorian embassy will have room

for yet another asylum seeker,' he commented wryly. 'At the moment, Cassidy probably thinks he's safe behind the protection of the Metropolitan Police.'

'He'll remain that way if we can't keep our witness alive. Presumably, there've been no more sightings of McNaught?'

'One more. One more blank. I suppose his background is all about blending in. How's Danny holding up?'

Anita decided to be truthful. 'Not very well. He's feeling the pressure. We all are.'

'Is Wallen with him today?'

'Yeah. I'm taking over tonight, and Hakim will relieve me in the morning.'

Moberg pushed his chair away from his desk. 'Do you think he's up to testifying?'

Anita was pensive. 'As long as McNaught is roaming free and Cassidy is safely in his millionaire home, then no.'

'My client has already explained in great detail the events of the day and the evening of Thursday, the twenty-seventh of July, 1995.' Zetterberg had taken an instant dislike to the lawyer who had been waiting at the polishus when she'd arrived back with Ivar Hagblom just after lunchtime. For starters, she seemed far too young, far too elegant and far too attractive to be a proper lawyer. Zetterberg thought that she would be given an easy ride by this piece of legal fluff. She'd been wrong, and Malin Axrud was earning her inflated fee by proving to be a tough obstacle to overcome. The immaculately dressed lawyer was sitting next to an anxious Ivar Hagblom. Opposite them sat Zetterberg and Bea Erlandsson. Zetterberg had surprised the other two members of her team by choosing Erlandsson. It was partly as a slap on the wrist for Szabo for not revealing information to her before they talked to Ivar in Uppsala – and partly because she wouldn't countenance any interruptions while she was officially interviewing their chief suspect. She didn't trust Szabo to keep quiet – she was confident that Erlandsson wouldn't interfere.

'As I'm sure your client would agree, if you actually let him speak, he is in a very difficult position. He has no alibi for the time of the murder, and he then coerced two other people to lie on his behalf. Not the actions of an innocent man.'

'I think, Inspector, that my client has given a perfectly adequate account of his movements and his reasons for asking the young women for their help. Naturally, he is deeply sorry for this and the difficulties it has caused them and the police. It was a mistake.'

'And his dealings with Prosecutor Renmarker?'

'Again, a misjudgement. He was only trying to protect a friend he believed, at the time, to be utterly innocent. And he is willing to face the consequences of his actions. There will be consequences?'

Zetterberg gave Axrud a waspish grin. 'You can be certain of that.' Ivar stared despondently at the table.

'Let me turn to the motive,' continued Zetterberg. 'That's if it's OK with your client, fru Axrud?'

'He believes that there is no motive.' The reply was tight-lipped. 'But carry on.'

'I've already discussed with herr Hagblom the little things that were starting to undermine his friendship with the deceased. Göran Gösta's treatment of Linus Svärd for one; Göran generally falling out with the group another.' Looking at Ivar fully in the face: 'Then there was your academic rivalry with Göran Gösta, which really picked up steam on Malta when you discovered a book inside which was part of an original letter written by Jacob Björnstahl. Why didn't you want Göran to know about that?'

Ivar looked up. Zetterberg noticed the dabs of sweat on his forehead. She could feel his anxiety.

'It was a big find. I wanted to make the most of it. Make a

splash when I brought out my thesis. If I shared the knowledge with someone working in the same field, I couldn't be sure it wouldn't get out into the public domain prematurely.'

'So you didn't trust Göran?'

Ivar wavered before answering. 'I suppose not.'

'And only Linus and your girlfriend of the time, Larissa Bjerstedt, knew?'

'Yes.'

'Yet you never used the Björnstahl letter?'

Ivar shook his head.

'Can you speak up? For the recording.'

'No.'

'And why not?'

'It disappeared.'

'But you had it with you at the cottage in Knäbäckshusen?'

'Yes.'

'And when did you notice it had gone missing?'

'I didn't think it *had* gone missing. I'd just misplaced it.'

Zetterberg's voice exuded scepticism. 'Are you trying to tell me that this dramatic academic find that was going to change your life had disappeared and you just thought you might have misplaced it? Surely you'd have guarded it with your life.'

'I knew... I thought it was around somewhere. I kept it in the bottom drawer of a chest in our bedroom. I hadn't looked at it for a few days. And there was a lot of drink and some drugs going on. We were all pretty laid back at the time.'

'It hardly sounded *laid back*,' Zetterberg weighed in dismissively. 'Everybody seemed to be at each other's throats. Relationships being put under pressure. Arguments.'

'It didn't seem like that at the time. It's easier in hindsight...' Axrud appeared to be on the verge of jumping in to save her client, but couldn't find the pretext to do so.

'Shall I tell you what I think happened? I think Linus,

desperate not to lose his lover, Göran, told him about the Björnstahl letter. It had been an area of conflict between you and Göran since Malta, and between them as well. Göran then finds the letter, which he steals. He even makes it clear in his overheard argument with Carina about Lars-Gunnar. The threat that you would suffer the most and—'

'That was nothing,' burst in Ivar. 'Just hot air.'

'It was even hotter than that. I believe that Göran actually carried out his threat and burnt the letter so you could never use it.'

Horror was etched across Ivar's face. 'Burnt it?'

'Göran's last words in fact. He'd destroyed your precious discovery. With all the other things that had happened between you two, this was the straw that broke the camel's back. He probably boasted about it to you in the chapel. I can imagine your fury. Your dreams shattered. You snapped. And you killed him. Yet afterwards, in a totally calculated way, you went about covering your tracks, and you've done that successfully for over twenty years.'

'But I didn't know that he'd burnt the letter. I didn't know what had happened to it.'

'What did you think had happened to it?' Zetterberg asked sarcastically. 'It had blown away in a Baltic breeze?'

'No. I just didn't know. I was frantic, but I couldn't find it anywhere after the murder.'

'Of course you couldn't. It was ash.'

There wasn't a shred left of the composed and confident man that Zetterberg had first come across in Uppsala. Or that of the public figure on his numerous television appearances. This was a broken man before her, and Axrud was quick to intervene.

'I think my client needs a break, and I need to consult with him further.'

'I think you do. Interview suspended at 16:36.' Zetterberg's jaunty agreement showed how close she was getting to a result.

The Chinese restaurant on Möllevångstorget was far enough away from the polishus not to be frequented by any colleagues. It was on the way home for Anita, who wanted to return to her apartment for a shower and change before she took over at the safe house. God knows how Klara Wallen was explaining to her demanding Rolf why his supper wasn't on the table these days.

Anita sipped a glass of water as she waited for Bea Erlandsson. In front of her was an open file of Erlandsson's case notes on the Göran Gösta murder that she had surreptitiously passed on. It contained her own work and everything that had been reported back by Zetterberg and Szabo. Anita was pleased to see that Erlandsson was very thorough. The Chinese restaurant was nearly empty at that early time in the evening; only a father and son waiting for a carry-out order and having a quick beer while they hung around. Outside in the square, most of the market stalls had packed up for the day, though a number of men were still sitting on the benches on the far side idly discussing life and the universe. All were of Arab origin. So were most of the stallholders.

Erlandsson had come to her office after Zetterberg's interview with Ivar Hagblom. She told Anita all that had gone on and filled her in on information that had been gleaned from Zetterberg's last trip to Stockholm and Uppsala. Anita had been grateful, and wasn't totally surprised that Ivar was on the point of being charged with Göran Gösta's murder. After her visit to Renmarker and his revelation about deliberately undermining the case, she had started to see the original investigation in a fresh light. Yet she still had doubts, and she could see that Bea Erlandsson did too, despite the evidence stacking up against Ivar. They'd decided to pool their ideas away from the polishus. Erlandsson had left her notes with

Anita and, in return, Anita had asked Erlandsson to look something up for her while she herself promised to make a phone call. This she had done. Now she was eager to see Bea Erlandsson.

The young detective came in and immediately apologized for being late. She said that by the time she left the office, Zetterberg was closeted with Prosecutor Blom. Zetterberg was confident that the arrest of Ivar Hagblom would be made official tomorrow. She was talking about organizing a press conference for midday.

'Alice Zetterberg likes her publicity,' Anita commented dryly. 'Her turning up in Uppsala and picking up Hagblom was very public.'

'Oh, yes. She'd tipped off the TV stations.'

'Made him look guilty. However much you say he's only helping police with their enquiries, everybody assumes he must be the one.'

They waited while a smiley waitress came and took their order in broken Swedish. Erlandsson had a beer. Anita would have loved to have joined her but knew it would just make her drowsy later on.

'So, how did you get on?' Anita asked after the waitress had left a bowl of prawn crackers. She snapped one in her mouth as Erlandsson fished for a file in her bag. It was an old file – twenty-one years old. Erlandsson opened it.

'You were right; it was worth looking at again. The forensics report mentions that the ash left at the barbecue did contain faint paper residue. Old paper, though it wasn't radiocarbon-dated at the time.'

'I thought I'd remembered something of the sort because there was a discussion with Henrik Nordlund about any possible significance. Of course, we couldn't find any because the Björnstahl letter was never in the equation. We thought it had just been put on to help the fire.'

Erlandsson shut the file. 'So, it appears that Göran burnt the letter after the barbecue broke up. Sweet justice. He must have gone down there, set it on fire and then gone into the chapel. Presumably we'll never know why he was in there.'

'Someone saw him go in – or someone found him there, anyway. But you don't seem convinced that it was Ivar?'

Again Erlandsson shook her head. 'There was something about Ivar today that made me believe him. I know he did everything to distance himself from the murder, which doesn't look good. But I watched him carefully in that interview room today, and I think he genuinely didn't know what had happened to that letter.'

Anita tucked into another prawn cracker. She realized she was really hungry. 'Maybe he didn't. I rang Linus Svärd an hour ago and told him what was happening. He swears blind that he didn't tell Göran about the Björnstahl letter.'

Erlandsson downed some beer and then coughed because she had drunk it too quickly. When she'd stopped spluttering, she said: 'I know Larissa was supposedly the only other person who knew about the letter, yet Ivar was sleeping with Carina at the time. He might have let it slip. Pillow talk. But even if she did know about it, that's no reason to kill Göran. But you can't escape the fact that she's got a different motive, and she hasn't got an alibi. I know I don't want it to be her because I love her books. Maybe it's appropriate that the crime writer is the murderer.'

'It could be her,' agreed Anita. And she would have been quite happy for Carina to be the perpetrator now that she knew that she had seduced – or been seduced by – Björn; the information that Zetterberg had drunkenly implanted still rankled. 'There's one thing that struck me when I was looking through your case notes. You'd better have them back, by the way. Don't want the lovely Alice finding out I've seen them.' Anita closed the file and passed it across the table and

Erlandsson returned it to her bag.

'If you ask any of my family and friends, Bea, they will tell you that I'm not the most organized of people. Or particularly house-proud.' Erlandsson beamed at her. 'I can see from your notes that you are very organized. What I always had trouble getting my head round in the original case was the murder weapon. We couldn't find it. However, our theory was that it had accidently been left on the beach, and that Linus had picked it up while down there. And now, according to Zetterberg, that's what Ivar must have done. And the timings work. I can't argue with that. But there was someone in that household twenty-one years ago who was incredibly organized. Someone who wanted to keep the cottage looking nice. It may have been for mercenary reasons – she clearly wanted to keep on the right side of Ivar's parents. Larissa herself said that she was in the kitchen, and Carina, in her last interview, admitted she heard someone, and it could only have been Larissa. So, if Larissa was in the kitchen cleaning up after the barbecue, she'd notice that the skewer was missing. She doesn't seem the type of person who'd just let it go. What if she left the kitchen and went down to the beach to find it? What if she recognized what had been burnt and wondered if Göran had destroyed the Björnstahl letter?'

'That implies that she knew Göran knew about the letter.'

Anita could only shrug. They didn't continue with their discussion until their dishes of steaming hot food arrived. Erlandsson picked up a pair of chopsticks. Anita opted for the safety of a spoon and fork.

'There's another thing that I can't explain,' ventured Erlandsson after her first mouthful of noodles. 'I was asked to check the mobile phone records of the suspects. They all seemed to fit with who is in touch with whom these days. Except one. Just after Anders Szabo and I talked to Larissa the first time, she made a call to Ivar.'

'To warn him presumably,' replied Anita with a half-eaten sweet and sour pork ball still in her mouth.

'But they claimed not to be in touch. And other than that call, there's no evidence to suggest that they were in any sort of regular contact. She only came out with the story about the false alibis when I goaded her with the derogatory things that Ivar had said about her.'

Anita suddenly pointed a fork, brandishing another pierced pork ball, at Erlandsson. 'There's something else in your notes that got me thinking. When Ivar confessed that it hadn't been his father that had sought ways of halting the investigation, but he himself, it made me think back to my little chat with Renmarker. He got the impression that someone was pushing Ivar to stall the case. Like Renmarker, I assumed it was Old Man Hagblom, who had a fearsome reputation for being utterly ruthless. But, what if that person was Larissa? Could she have been the one to suggest the alibi and not Ivar?'

'So, the phone call?'

'It was to warn him. But also to make sure he towed the party line.'

'Makes sense. What doesn't though is why kill Göran?'

That halted the conversation, and both women reflectively returned to their meals.

'OK,' said Anita, putting down her fork. 'This is pure conjecture. If Larissa was on the beach and realized that the Björnstahl letter had been burnt, the first thing you'd expect her to do was tell Ivar, wouldn't you?'

'Yeah,' Erlandsson acceded.

'She didn't. Why? Because she already knew that Göran knew about the letter.'

'Because she was the one who'd told him and was feeling guilty!' Erlandsson said with mounting excitement.

'Exactly. She saw him go into the chapel from the beach and, in her fury, rushed up to confront him. You can imagine the rest. Then she hides the skewer, and then cleverly starts to manipulate Ivar. The alibi. Prosecutor Renmarker. Ivar thinks he's helping Linus when in fact he's shielding Larissa. The trouble is that it all goes horribly wrong for her personally. She may have seen Ivar as her ticket to a glittering future, but she seems to have genuinely loved him. Obsessively so. Otherwise, she wouldn't have followed him up to Uppsala years after he cynically discarded her.' Anita paused. 'Just think about it: she must have gone mad over the years thinking that she'd killed Göran because she loved Ivar and not being able to tell him as she would have had to admit that she was a murderer. Almost worse, she would have had to admit that it was her fault that the letter disappeared and was burnt. She sacrificed everything for him and got nothing in return.'

Erlandsson's eyes were gleaming. 'It all fits.' Then her lips twitched. 'Except for one thing.'

'Why did she tell Göran about Björnstahl? I don't know. I suggest you ask her very soon before Alice Zetterberg hangs Ivar Hagblom out to dry.'

CHAPTER 44

Anita drove south of the city. Her mind was a jumble of thoughts and emotions. Her Chinese meal with Bea Erlandsson had lifted her spirits. She had left convinced that they had uncovered the real murderer – just a pity it was twenty-one years too late. Now a couple of hours and a shower and change of clothes later, the doubts were reappearing. After spending the last two decades convinced that Linus Svärd was the killer, it was difficult to readjust her sights. It didn't help that she wasn't close to the case anymore and had to learn things second-hand from Erlandsson. So much had been revealed that hadn't been apparent back in 1995. The sneaking feeling that they could have done more continued to gnaw away at her. The fact that they hadn't been able to unravel the alibis was a stumbling block they should have been able to overcome. In retrospect, they might have done so if Prosecutor Renmarker hadn't had a seedy past and had given them more time to investigate. Or maybe that was impossible then, as all the characters involved had changed over the years and only now had the fault lines emerged. What was worrying her big time was that after getting it all wrong in 1995, the police were getting it all wrong again.

Anita turned her car off the main road and onto a flat, straight track. She could see the safe house in the distance. There wasn't much light from the building, as all the blinds and shutters were in place. They didn't want to attract attention from passing traffic – and they didn't want McNaught getting a free shot at their witness. The wind was stirring, and she could see the dark shapes of the trees swaying in the copse off to the left. The air smelt autumnal. Soon the leaves would be plucked off the branches, and this pleasant, rural summer retreat would turn into a bleak prison. The older she got, the more her heart sank at the first signs of nature shutting down for the winter. The gap was too long until the late Swedish spring began to spread its fingers lightly over Skåne.

The headlights picked out Klara Wallen waiting for her by her car. Anita could see she wanted to make a quick getaway. The breeze tugged at Anita's hair as she greeted her.

'Everything OK, Klara?'

'Yeah. Yeah, everything's fine. Three officers are inside, including Hakim's girlfriend.' Wallen was already opening the door of her car.

'How's Danny?'

'Bit upset I think. Brodd brought Jack Harmer's father earlier on. They were left to have a chat. Don't know if it did either of them any good.'

'I just hope Brodd was vigilant when he drove down and made sure he wasn't followed. You know how careless he is.'

'You don't have to tell me. Anyhow, the sooner this gunman gets caught, the sooner Danny and the rest of us can relax.'

Wallen was sitting in the driver's seat about to shut the door when they heard the unmistakable crack of a shot. Then another. Anita swung round to face the house and instinctively whipped out her pistol. The gunfire had come from inside the building. Wallen, also with weapon in hand, was quickly by her side.

'McNaught must be in the house,' Anita whispered hoarsely. 'Where's Danny?'

'In his bedroom. Shall I call for back up?'

'There'll never get here in time. Look, you go round the

back, and I'll head to his room.'

Wallen nodded and slipped away. Another shot hurried Anita along the low front wall of the old, single-storey farmhouse and round the corner. The first window was Danny's bedroom. The blind was down, but there was a thin beam of light at the edge. The last shot hadn't come from there. The sound seemed to have come from the far end of the building, the one nearest the copse. She hoped Klara was all right. Anita tried to open the window, but it wouldn't budge. She had to make a quick decision. There might be dead people in there now. All she could think of doing was to tap loudly on the window. Nothing. Was Danny still in there? She'd have to break the glass and climb in and just hope McNaught hadn't found the bedroom yet.

All of a sudden, Anita found herself in a blaze of light. The blind had been pulled up, and there was Liv Fogelström cautiously peering out with her pistol pointing directly at Anita.

'It's me!' Anita shouted, holding up her pistol to show she wasn't going to use it.

Liv opened the window. Anita immediately asked: 'Where's Danny?'

'In there,' Liv said breathlessly, indicating the solid, old-fashioned wardrobe by the bed.

'Quick, let's get him out of here!'

Liv's hand was on the handle of the wardrobe door when another shot exploded in the room. And then another. Anita's brain could hardly take in what she saw next: Liv seemed to spin round in slow motion, her mouth open in horror and her eyes staring in disbelief, before collapsing in a bleeding heap on the bed. Anita was helpless. She couldn't see the intruder, who must have fired from the doorway. She resisted the frantic impulse to clamber through the window as she was collected enough to realize that she would only make herself an easy target. She just hoped to God that McNaught didn't realize she was there.

'Come out, Oh Danny Boy.' The last words were sung to the tune of the famous Irish song. 'Marky McNaught is here.' Despite the thick Scottish brogue, Anità understood every menacing word.

She could see the wardrobe door from her vantage point and was praying that McNaught wouldn't spray it with bullets before he came into her line of fire.

'Come on, boy. Don't be shy. I've got a present from Mr Cassidy.'

Ever so slowly, the door opened, and out hobbled a petrified Danny Foster. Anita could see him shaking.

'I won't tell, I promise. Please Mr McNaught, I'll never say a thing.'

'No, laddie, you won't.'

Anita heard the click of McNaught's gun. She had to do something; anything. She shot randomly upwards. Anything to distract the bastard. Danny jumped in fright, and she heard McNaught swear as flakes of plaster showered from the ceiling. A bullet zinged through the window past Anita's head as McNaught fired blindly in her direction. In that millisecond, McNaught flitted into her line of vision. Panic and anger surged through her, and she squeezed her trigger as hard as she could. Danny screamed.

The whole of the front of the farm house was lit up. The wind was stronger now, and the arc lights flickered. Two squad cars were parked on the verge. Moberg and Anita were watching the last of the whining ambulances rush down the drive.

'God, what a night!' Anita said as she watched the flashing blue lights turn onto the main road and tear off towards Malmö.

Moberg put a gorilla's hand on her shoulder. Such a gesture

didn't come easily to a man who found it difficult to be tactile.

'You've done a good job, Anita. You saved our witness.'

Anita sighed heavily. 'But at what a cost! Mikael Palm is badly injured, Nina Kovac got hit...'

'She'll be fine.'

'And Liv. She may not survive. Shit! Has anybody told Hakim?'

'Yes. Klara phoned him. He'll be waiting at the hospital.'

'They've only just got engaged.' Anita wiped away a tear.

Moberg swung her round so she was facing him. 'Fogelström was doing her duty. So were you all. Kovac said that McNaught just appeared and took them totally by surprise; and then just started shooting. Liv ran off to protect Danny. McNaught could have taken you all out. You stopped him.'

Moberg took out a packet of cigarettes and offered Anita one. She refused. 'Go on, you need it.'

He cupped his large hands, yet still had difficulty lighting the two cigarettes in the wind. He handed her one. She drew on the first cigarette she'd had for a few years. Moberg was right; she needed it.

A van turned up the drive and headed towards them.

'That'll be forensics.' Moberg took another long drag on his cigarette and let the smoke billow into the night air. 'Unofficially, I'm glad you killed McNaught. There'll be a tedious enquiry, and questions will be asked. Always are. We may not come out of it very well, as per usual. The commissioner likes his scapegoats. But if McNaught had gone to trial, I don't think our justice system would have given him the sentence he deserved.'

The forensics van drew up, and out jumped Eva Thulin and two assistants. She greeted Anita with a grim smile.

'Come on then, Anita, better show me the latest mess you've left.'

Anita dropped her cigarette and stubbed it out with her shoe. 'Follow me, Eva.'

Anita led the forensic technician through the front door of the safe house. She hoped that once all this mess had been cleared up, the mess that she had created as a young and over-enthusiastic detective twenty-one years earlier could also be untangled. Linus Svärd deserved to be exculpated and Göran Gösta's real murderer finally caught.

CHAPTER 45

The hospital was busy with staff scurrying about and patients wandering around the corridors. Anita was dog tired. She had spent half the night with Eva Thulin. They had to be thorough, as the whole business would be scrutinized to see if they had acted within official guidelines. It was odd how official guidelines didn't seem to take into account single-minded, ex-SAS gunmen on a mission. One thing was for sure – that safe house wasn't safe anymore.

After making enquires at the desk, Anita managed to find a doctor to report on the three officers who were being cared for. It had been quite a lively night for the A&E and theatre staff. Nina Kovac was fine and would be sent home later that day. Mikael Palm was out of danger, but would not be back at work for a very long time. As for Liv, the news was both good and bad. The good news was that she would live; the bad was that she might never walk again. Anita's heart sank. She was told that her boyfriend was with her.

First, Anita sought out Danny Foster. Heaven knows what his mental state was after last night. She found him with a male nurse plumping up his pillows.

'No chocolates?' he asked with a grin.

'Sorry. I'll get some.'

'Only joking.' The nurse left.

'How's the shoulder?'

'Hurts to buggery. But I'm alive.' He stared at Anita, who

wasn't sure whether to pull up a chair or not. 'Thanks to you.'

'We all tried to help.'

'I know. I'm grateful. How is that nice girl who came into my room? She was so calm.'

'She'll live.' Anita didn't want to go into any details. She was having enough trouble processing the doctor's prognosis as it was.

'I'll testify, you know.'

Anita was surprised and relieved. 'We're already working on Tyrone Cassidy's extradition. We can prove he was over here when the murder took place. Even his friends in the Met won't be able to save him.'

'I'm not doing it because of that. My chat with Mr Harmer. It was hard. He was crying. I realize I owe it to Jack and his family. And to the people here who helped me. Leif at the farm. He died because he was kind to me. And the police officers last night who were putting their lives on the line.'

'They're professionals.'

'But they've got family. Friends. No one really cared a shit about me before I came here.'

Anita hoped this young man could achieve some peace of mind after all he'd been through over the last few months.

'Maybe we're turning you into a Swede,' she said flippantly.

'Do you know, I might just do that. I've nothing to go home to.'

'I'm not happy about being here. She'll kill us if she finds out.'

'Oh, shut up, Anders! We've nothing to lose.' It had taken a long phone call the night before to win Szabo round. Now he was having second thoughts. They were standing outside the door of Larissa Bjerstedt's apartment in one of the new buildings overlooking the Outer Harbour. Larissa was expecting them, as Erlandsson had rung ahead and said that they needed to clear up a couple of things. She said she wasn't due to go to work until lunchtime and they would find her at home.

When she opened the door, Larissa seemed nervous and distracted. They followed her into the living room and before she even offered them a seat, she said: 'What are you doing to Ivar? I saw him on television yesterday. Is he under arrest?'

'Yes. And the world will know it at a twelve o'clock press conference our boss is giving.' It was Erlandsson speaking. She had told Szabo to let her do the talking. As he wasn't comfortable with the whole venture, he didn't object. 'Do you mind if we sit down?'

Larissa waved at them to do so. They both sat together on a lime green IKEA sofa. The rest of the room looked as though it had been furnished on the same shopping trip, but there was some interesting artwork on the walls.

'You've got the wrong person.' Larissa was ringing her hands. 'It's not him.'

Erlandsson knew it wasn't. Was this going to be a straightforward confession? 'Who was it then?'

'I gave you enough clues. It was Carina, of course.'

Anita stared through the glass in the door for several minutes, unsure whether she should go in. Liv was surrounded by a barrage of machinery, with wires and tubes everywhere. She was lying motionless. The only clue to her actually breathing was the squiggly lines on a medical monitor. Hakim was hunched over her, his body seemingly shrunk by the tragedy.

Tentatively, Anita opened the door. She could now see that Hakim was caressing Liv's ring finger. He turned. He'd been weeping. She knew that nothing she could say would really help, but she tried anyway.

'Liv's a fine officer. Her first thought was to protect our witness. She's a brave girl.'

'I know.' Tears once again were brimming in his dark,

expressive eyes. 'I can't understand what she was doing there. She had a couple of days off.'

Anita swallowed. 'I had to call her in.'

'Call her in?'

Anita didn't know where to look. 'We were short-handed.'

The hurt and disbelief on his face said it all. He turned away from Anita to gaze at the prone body of his new fiancée, his back an admonishment. Anita left quietly.

'Carina?' Erlandsson repeated the name. 'Are you sure?'

'Yes. Why do think she was so keen to give Ivar and myself an alibi?'

'And why did she kill Göran?'

'Because of the argument. We all heard it. She did it because she was protecting Lars-Gunnar against that snivelling creep.'

'And the proof? She may have had a motive. And she may have had the means, but what about opportunity?'

Larissa was pacing the floor in front of them, blocking the view across to the Finnlines ship docked on the other side of the harbour.

'I saw her.'

'You saw Carina?'

'That evening. She sneaked out of the house that evening.'

'Where did you see her from?'

'The kitchen.'

'Are you sure she wasn't just seeing how Lars-Gunnar was?'

'She went straight past him.'

'Why didn't you mention this before? You could have said something twenty years ago.'

Larissa pressed her hands to her mouth and spoke though her fingers. 'I don't know.'

Erlandsson watched Larissa carefully before she spoke. 'Tell you what puzzles me. Why did Göran say "burnt it" before he died? He was referring to the letter written by Björnstahl that Ivar had found on Malta and which was going to be the basis of his thesis, wasn't he? Someone had told Göran about it, and he had burnt it in revenge for the way he thought Ivar and the rest of the group were treating him.'

'Carina must have known about it. She must have told him.'

'She didn't know anything about it. But Linus did. And you did. Why did you tell Göran?'

'I didn't! I didn't.' She tugged at her hair as though she wanted to pull out an unruly clump.

'We think you did. You *were* in the kitchen as you claimed. Cleaning up. Then you noticed one of the skewers was missing. It would only take you a couple of minutes to get down to the beach. You found it next to the embers of the barbecue fire. That wasn't all though, was it? The letter. You saw the remains of some burnt leaves of paper, and you knew exactly what they were – and who had put them on the fire. Then you must have seen Göran going into the chapel. You marched up to confront him, with the skewer in your hand. We don't know what was said between you. We know the outcome, though. You got rid of the murder weapon and went back to the cottage. After that, you helped concoct your alibi, and you persuaded Ivar to interfere with the case by nobbling the prosecutor; the fact there was something he could be blackmailed over was a stroke of luck. You had to stop the case because if Linus had been grilled, the whole Björnstahl business would have emerged, and the investigating team would have got round to you eventually.'

Larissa looked as though she was about to swoon. She slumped into an easy chair, her face ashen.

'The remarkable thing,' Erlandsson went on, 'is that, despite everything, you still love Ivar. You still want to protect him by blaming Carina. What is so sad about all this is that you made the ultimate sacrifice for the man you love, and you've never been able to tell him. Even when Ivar treated you badly, you still had to keep the one secret you couldn't, you daren't, share. It must have been eating you up all these years. But it's not too late, you know; he might look at you differently if he knew what you'd done. This is your chance to save him.'

CHAPTER 46

It took Anita some time to drive the relatively short distance from the hospital to the polishus. The roads were frustratingly jam-packed. She needed a break. She needed that holiday that this case had denied her. She needed to spend time with Kevin. He was good at taking her mind off her worries. Mind you, he'd have his work cut out obliterating the image of Liv Fogelström being shot twice in front of her and the awful consequences of that moment.

She parked her car at the polishus. There were a few things to do before she could go home and have a long sleep. On the way home, she would call in and see her beautiful granddaughter; that would cheer her up. And she needed to tell Jazmin and Lasse about Liv. That wouldn't be an easy conversation.

She locked the car and glanced at her watch. It was six minutes to midday. She noticed the vans from a couple of local TV stations. Of course, Zetterberg was holding her much-heralded press conference. Her mind immediately turned to Bea Erlandsson. Had she gone and seen Larissa Bjerstedt? Anita thought she might pop in and see what had transpired. Anyhow, she should be there at the conclusion of a case she failed to help solve.

Her mobile phone sprang into life. She didn't recognize the number.

'Anita here.'

'It's Bea. Look, I've been trying to get hold of Inspector Zetterberg, but she's not answering her phone.'

'She'll be in the press conference. It's about to start. Why?'

'Blast! We're bringing in Larissa Bjerstedt. She's confessed.'

'Confessed?' Anita was gobsmacked.

'You were right about her. She just broke down and admitted it. She can't bear the thought of Ivar going down for the murder. She still loves him. It all started with Göran taunting her about Ivar and Carina carrying on behind her back. Said he'd heard them at it. She didn't believe him. Anyway, she was so upset that she retaliated by blurting out about Ivar's Björnstahl discovery. Of course, once the letter disappeared, she knew exactly who had taken it. The rest is what we thought. When she went to the beach to find the skewer, she noticed the burnt paper. She knew what had happened. She confronted Göran in the chapel. He was totally unrepentant – "Ivar got what he deserved" – and she just couldn't help herself. Lost it. Next thing, he was dead. Or she thought he was dead.'

'Well done, Bea! Look, I'd better go in and try and catch Zetterberg before it starts.'

'Right, we'll be there in a few minutes.'

By the time Anita reached the press room, the conference was under way. She slipped in at the back. There were two TV cameras busy filming proceedings, and half a dozen photographers snapping away. And at least twenty press and radio journalists were gathered in the seats below the dais, behind a phalanx of microphones. Zetterberg had wheeled out the big guns – not only was Prosecutor Blom there, but also Commissioner Dahlbeck. He'd obviously bought some new hair dye for the occasion. He was in the process of introducing Zetterberg.

'...and now I'd like to hand over to the head of our new

Cold Case Group, Inspector Alice Zetterberg.'

Alice Zetterberg leant forward confidently. She spoke clearly into the microphone, and couldn't quite hide the self-congratulatory tone.

'Thank you, Commissioner Dahlbeck. The Skåne County Police set up the Cold Case Group to look at cases that have never been solved. We wanted to show the people of Skåne that no case is ever dead; that we are always prepared to go back in and tackle old crimes by uncovering new evidence. Our role is to provide a fresh perspective on investigations that failed, be it due simply to circumstances at the time, or the fact that perhaps the original investigation, for whatever reason, wasn't carried out rigorously enough.' Zetterberg surveyed her audience. She spotted Anita hovering at the back of the room. 'The murder of Göran Gösta may well fall into the latter category.'

Zetterberg paused and pretended to consult some notes. In fact, she'd spent the previous evening rehearsing exactly what she was going to say. She wanted to make a good impression on the public as well as on her superiors. She now switched on her serious, yet emphatic voice.

'My team was also very conscious that we had a debt to pay to Göran Gösta's family – to give them the opportunity to achieve closure at long last. The details are straightforward enough. On the evening of Thursday, the twenty-seventh of July, 1995, Göran Gösta was murdered in the St. Nicolai Chapel in the village of Knäbäckshusen. During the original investigation, there were five suspects, all Gösta's fellow ex-students of Lund University, sharing a holiday cottage. Though the police at the time singularly failed to produce a result, the team was convinced that one particular student was guilty and, though no legal action was taken against him, his name was unfortunately leaked to the press.' Again, Zetterberg's gaze strayed towards Anita.

'I am here today to tell you that after new evidence became available, there was a thorough reinvestigation of the facts, and following exhaustive interviews of the original suspects, I can reveal that I have made an arrest. Ivar Valborg Hagblom, professor of Middle Eastern Studies at the University of Uppsala has been charged with the wilful murder of Göran Gösta.' There was an excited stir from the audience.

The door opened and in glided Bea Erlandsson. 'They'd already started,' Anita mouthed to her. Erlandsson raised her eyebrows and then made her way behind a television camera towards the dais.

Zetterberg continued, with half an eye on the advancing Erlandsson. 'This has not been an easy case, and I'm proud of the way that I... and my team, of course, have approached it. We've left no stone unturned.' She noticed Erlandsson indicating that she wanted to say something to her privately. The potential interruption was greeted with exasperation. 'In fact, this is one of my team,' she couldn't help saying petulantly. Swiftly, she regained her composure: 'Excuse me; I will answer all your questions shortly.'

Erlandsson nervously leaned over Zetterberg's shoulder to whisper in her ear. Both Commissioner Dahlbeck and Prosecutor Blom showed their disapproval. Anita saw growing consternation cover Zetterberg's features. Her eyes opened wide – she was panic-stricken. She looked around helplessly, and inadvertently, her gaze fixed on Anita – who was grinning broadly.

NOTES

Jacob Jonas Björnstahl (1731-1779)

I came across a reference to the linguist, traveller, chronicler, encyclopaedist and orientalist, Jacob Jonas Björnstahl when I was doing my initial research for *Menace in Malmö*. It turned out I'd stumbled across a fascinating character who was incredibly well known in his day, but who is not familiar to many modern Swedes. Though he was an Uppsala contemporary of the illustrious Swedish botanist, Carl Linnaeus, and conversed on equal terms with Voltaire and Rousseau, his fame has been lost in the mists of time.

He was born and raised in Näshulta parish just outside Eskilstuna. A memorial plaque was unveiled there on January 23rd, 1961 in the presence of Prince Wilhelm of Sweden, himself an author. It was appropriate, as Björnstahl had gained the royal patronage of King Gustav III, who sent him to Constantinople, the centre of the Ottoman Empire. He was never to return, dying in Salonika. His writings covered academic and scientific subjects, and, of course, his journeys. It was in his description of his travels to France, Italy, Switzerland, Holland, England, Turkey and Greece that I found my Malta connection and his views on the origins of the Maltese language. His unequivocal opinion on the ongoing debate was that "The Punic theory is nothing but a dream.".

Björnstahl was a forerunner of the evolution of a more systematic study of the Muslim world in the 18th century. Ironically, when he died at only 48, having ignored warnings not to drink the local water, he had never had the chance to visit the Arabic-speaking lands that occupied so much of his working life.

British men trafficked to Sweden

I was amazed to read in a British Sunday newspaper a few years ago about young British men being forced to work in Sweden. In this day and age, it seemed incredible that this slave labour could be happening in such a civilized country. As I read on, I discovered what a lucrative business it actually is for British and Irish gangs such as the fictional one run by Tyrone Cassidy.

A BBC investigation in 2012 uncovered a number of victims; vulnerable young men who had been picked up off the streets in the UK. One young man the BBC spoke to described arriving in Malmö with two other Britons who had been homeless. They worked 14-hour days for little or no pay and lived in appalling, cramped conditions. They were too frightened to escape. He said: "I've seen people threatened with pickaxes. I've seen people kicked, punched. I've nearly been pushed off a moving vehicle. It's very tense. You're waiting for the next thing to happen." Like others, he had been tempted by the promise of a good wage and accommodation. Another such victim was a young man from Bournemouth who ended up working in Falkenberg, just north of Skåne. He was luckier because one day, three police cars pulled up and the officers said they wanted to help as they knew about their working conditions. This was his chance to escape. The bosses were arrested and stood trial but were acquitted, as under Swedish law in 2009, you had to be under lock and key to be considered to be in forced labour.

A report in Sweden published in 2010 found 26 instances of human trafficking for non-sexual purposes. "In particular, these concern British and Irish tarmac and paving layers in Sweden." The gangs have made good money. A confidential Swedish police report, obtained by the BBC at the time, estimated (a "conservative calculation") that the gangs were making about £3m a year. In 2007, Norwegian police estimated traveller gangs were making more than £11m a year. Evidence suggests these gangs have also been operating in Germany, Holland and Denmark. The European Commissioner for Home Affairs, Cecilia Malmström, said at the time that she feared it was only the tip of the iceberg.

One positive end to this depressing story is that the young man from Bournemouth decided to stay in Sweden and begin a new life.